FIND
THEM

JULIA ASH

DEDICATION

To my amazing sisters:

Dina Butterfield
Karen McClave
Paula Witherow

ಐ ೞ ಐ ೞ

ALSO BY JULIA ASH

Mystified

a standalone, ghost fiction mystery

Writer's Digest HONORABLE MENTION
(Self-Published E-Book Awards, 2022)

"This story is absorbing, with a complex plot
and characters whose lives are all interwoven.
High drama that keeps the reader wondering who's responsible,
what exactly happened, and how all the pieces fit together."
— *Judge, 10th Annual Writer's Digest
Self-Publishing E-Book Awards, 2022*

THE ELI CHRONICLES

a dark fantasy series

The One and Only *(Book #1)*

The Tether *(Book #2)*

The Turning Point *(Book #3)*

Writer's Digest HONORABLE MENTION
(Self-Published E-Book Awards, 2020)

BookLife by Publishers Weekly SEMI-FINALIST
(The BookLife Prize, 2020)

"Ultimately, Ash's ability to weave together multiple genres
into a well-paced synthesis of science fiction, fantasy, and horror
(with appealing dialogue and welcome moments of humor)
makes this futuristic series a genuinely one-of-a-kind experience."
— *BookLife Reviews*

*"You can run,
but you can't hide."*

~ Joe Louis

FIND THEM

JULIA ASH

1

THE TRAIN WHISTLE was a false promise, teasing me that the impending disaster might be averted.

Wearing new red pumps and holding the handle of my design portfolio, I stood on the platform and clenched my teeth. My jaw muscles stiffened.

The time: already 9:00 a.m.

Trains in general, but especially from the Northeast Regional line, were becoming habitually late.

An advancing roar raced along the arched, geometric ceiling.

If only hearing my ride to Baltimore's Penn Station could magically turn back time.

I glanced at my smartwatch. Again.

Shit de la shit.

My train would *never* recover twenty minutes.

Ordinarily, being behind schedule could be explained. Not today. One hour from now, I had to help pitch a marketing campaign to a fickle client who had requested to work with me for the first time. My boss, Cecelia, had voiced a concise directive: Do. Not. Be. Late.

Tardiness was one of Cecelia's pet peeves on a normal day. All excuses were suspect, even from me, a valued employee perched a few rungs below the top tier at Dunham & Berkey.

I pictured the soured faces of our client's launch team, impatiently waiting for the doors of our conference room to open. *"Finally,"*

Cecelia would snark as I made my entrance. *"This is Nora Bliss, everybody. She's our creative director who refuses to drive to work. Apparently, commuting by train to reduce her carbon footprint and arriving on time are mutually exclusive."*

Stress was affecting my self-talk.

In truth, Cecelia would never admonish me in front of clients. *That,* she'd reserve for our private meetings out of earshot from Human Resources.

The grind and rattle of metal on metal grew louder to my left, and I saw my ride's headlights appear in the distance—two yellow, quivering eyes.

Hurry. Please.

At least my boss couldn't complain about my work ethic. Even though I was never the early bird, I consistently clocked the longest hours. My productivity was off the charts.

Two pesky flies buzzed around me, adding to my agitation.

Without warning, I lurched forward on the platform, slightly rolling my ankle.

What the hell!

Someone had bumped into me from behind.

Glaring over my shoulder, I looked to see who.

The culprit was a disheveled man. He wore a torn, trench-styled raincoat stained with grimy soot. His personal cloud of pungent body odor wafted around him. Age wise, he looked to be about 40, an entire decade older than me.

"So sorry," I said, even though he had done the bumping.

Slightly hunched forward, the man stopped and scowled at me. I mean, *scowled.* His eyes narrowed. His lips trembled with anger. And as he resumed walking, he snarled.

The guy had probably misjudged where I had been standing in relation to where he was going. Everything had an explanation. Still, if looks could kill.

Hopefully, he wouldn't be around when I returned to the station that night at a time when passengers had already thinned. I didn't savor the idea of trekking alone to the parking lot to retrieve my Tesla. Especially with "Mr. Hostile" lurking around.

D.C.? Not the safest city after sundown.

That's why I kept pepper spray inside my purse which was strapped over my shoulder. Just in case.

Dex wasn't thrilled about me getting home in the dark, but he understood the "opportunity cost" at play. When something was gained (like success in the workplace), something else was lost (such as arriving home at a safe, decent hour).

The train's brakes screeched, releasing a shrill.

Goosebumps erupted as a chill swept across my skin.

An unfamiliar vibe permeated the platform atmosphere. *Unsettled* was the only word which flashed into my brain.

In my peripheral vision, I noticed a woman to my right take hurried, awkward steps back on the concrete.

Weird. Most commuters moved forward as their train approached. A natural tendency for those in a hurry. Which was almost everybody when their train was late.

Maybe the variable catching my attention was *how* the woman moved. She slightly arched her spine and raised her chin as if avoiding a thrown object. And she wobbled on high heeled sandals like her body was shouting to back up before her legs could adjust.

As the woman stumbled from my line of sight, I saw the source of her clumsy retreat.

The man in the raincoat. The one who had bumped into me.

He barreled toward me like a crazed animal.

Instinctively, I knew I needed to get out of his way.

But my legs felt cemented in place.

Why wasn't I widening my stance to counter the imminent collision? Or swinging the oversized portfolio clutched in my hand to knock him off balance? Or even *attempting* to reach into my purse for the pepper spray?

Instead, I stood there. A deer in headlights.

Immobilized. Speechless.

Consumed by confusion.

Processing. Always processing.

Why was he stretching his arms in my direction? What did he want?

The man grabbed my right arm, squeezing my bicep like his fingers sought to puncture through my muscle to reach bone.

I shrieked in pain.

A frosty mist marked my exhale.

He pulled me close to him so our bodies touched.

I became a statue, rigid from shock, standing inches from the edge of the platform.

Brushing his lips against my right ear, he whispered with a raspy voice, "Out of my way. Ghosts are after me."

Ghosts?

I was processing his words when the unthinkable happened.

The man launched me. Pushed me off the platform.

My fingers released the portfolio.

Primal terror pulsed through my veins.

Was I going to die here? Today? At Union Station?

As I fell toward the tracks below, I flailed my arms in hopes of grabbing something. *Anything* but air.

A person on the platform released a high pitched guttural scream. The sound was raw and visceral, bouncing off the tunnel walls.

The train's brakes hissed and squealed.

My heart jackhammered in my chest. Pounded in my ears.

I didn't want to leave this life! Leave my husband. My sister.

When the right side of my face slammed against the tracks, a flash of blinding white light exploded in my head.

Right before darkness swallowed me whole.

2

Friday, May 24, 2024
MedStar Washington Hospital Center: Washington, D.C.

PESTERING DEX HAD worked. He handed me the mirror from the toiletries collection in my hospital room.

Resting in bed with the mattress propped upright as far as it could go, I gazed at my face for the first time since my accident at Union Station two days ago.

My husband's reluctance made sense.

Although certainly not my worst injury, my right eye would likely garner the most attention. The white of my eyeball had transformed into a solid red billiard ball. Okay, *slight* exaggeration. Still, instead of blue, my iris looked purple—visually intensified by an eggplant-colored bruise encircling the whole freaky spectacle.

Other injuries weren't as obvious. My right temple for starters. To complement my pixie cut, I had long bangs on my right side, forming a curtain of black hair. There was a hint of what might be found underneath, however, mostly because the natural streak of silver in my bangs was stained with blood.

I gently moved my hair aside. Talk about a canvas of color—purple, blue, red, vomit green. More like colors of a nightmare.

"You're lucky to be alive, Nora." Dex sat on the edge of the bed. "Jesus. I almost lost you. Thank God for the person who pulled you from the tracks."

"I hope we can get his name," I said, putting down the handheld mirror. "I want to thank him for his heroism."

5

Dr. Reselda walked into the room holding a clipboard. "Good morning. How's my patient?" he purred, curling his lips into a lopsided half smile. Definitely the type of guy who knew he was good looking and relished the effect he had on others.

"I'm ready to go home, Doctor."

"Let's review your progress," he said. "Then I'll have my nurse go over the discharge papers with you."

Good looking *and* possessive. He didn't say, *the* nurse. He said, *my* nurse. *My* patient.

In advertising, every word spoke volumes.

Dr. Reselda explained that the internal bleeding near my temple had stopped and pressure on my brain subsided. My concussion was also improving. The multiple broken blood vessels in my right eye would simply take time to heal. As would my bruised ribs. But across the board, no permanent issues were expected.

All great news.

"I would be remiss," Dr. Reselda cautioned, "if I didn't mention the emotional component to the trauma you've had. You might experience some post-traumatic stress, and I always recommend getting ahead of the curve." He reached into his lab coat pocket and retrieved a business card. "Give Dr. Simon a call. Drop my name. Estelle will fit you into her schedule right away." He winked.

I expressed my gratitude.

Nodding, the doctor sauntered out of the room. On second thought, more of a swagger.

My husband reached over and caressed my hand.

Something was on his mind.

"What?" I asked.

"This can't happen again," he said. "You were nearly killed."

"I have to be more mindful of my surroundings, that's all. Plus, I need to react. To *do* something." I locked eyes with him. "My God, Dex. I saw the guy lunging for me. And I froze. I did nothing."

"Please tell me you're not blaming yourself."

"I'm just disappointed. I allowed myself to become a victim."

"You didn't know he was going to push you onto the tracks." He shook his head again. "It's happening more and more, but who thinks it'll ever happen to *them?* Which segues to a suggestion."

"You're going to hire a bodyguard for me?" I smiled.

"Let's leave the city," he said. "Move someplace rural."

My pulse raced. "The man who attacked me. He was taken into custody. Right?"

"Yes, but how long will he be off the streets? And do we really think he's the only mentally unwell person in D.C.? Or in Baltimore? He thought *ghosts* were chasing him." Dex lightly squeezed my hand. "Anymore, Nora, city streets and subways aren't safe."

"But our jobs…"

"Loads of people telecommute." He shifted his eyes to the left, ever so slightly. He was about to tell me something I wouldn't like. "I sort of floated the idea to Cecelia when she called to check on you. About moving and working remotely. She agreed to consider it."

What the *what?*

I longed to take a deep breath to calm myself, but my ribs would've retaliated. Dex had never inserted himself into my lane. And although circumventing me proved how adamant he was about leaving the city, it didn't make his interference acceptable. Yet, I had no energy to engage in a disagreement.

Besides, the idea wasn't completely new.

Our retirement dream, after our would-be kids had flown the coop for college, was to move to the country, far from the hustle and bustle of a city.

"Are you suggesting we build our forever home *now?*" I asked.

He answered affirmatively by showcasing his pearly whites.

When Dex gave me his best smile, any agitation I harbored tended to drift away. Shallow as it sounded, my husband's cosmopolitan looks helped calm rough waters. His great grandparents had immigrated from Norway, and he possessed the stereotypical Nordic features—blond hair, green eyes, straight nose, tall stature. (My tastes for handsome.) He wasn't offended when people said he looked Swedish or Norwegian. He was proud of his heritage.

Although clean cut, Dex had the conviction and strength of a Viking warrior. Quite the opposite of me. I fancied myself as a peacemaker, albeit with a flamboyant flair.

In that spirit, my right side displayed a large dove tattoo: the tip of its head reached the base of my neck, its body was inked onto my

7

shoulder and arm, and its tail ended at my elbow. The dove's right wing fanned out onto my chest and its left wing, onto my back. An olive branch was in its beak, tattooed halfway around my neck.

My tattoo was a bold statement, but not all that surprising. After all, I was in marketing and design.

Since my husband was the actual fighter between us, I wondered why he'd suggest running away to the country. Had my accident affected *him* that much?

"I was thinking," Dex continued. "Maybe your sister could find some available land in rural Pennsylvania. We'd be closer to her then. Would you consider it?"

By using my sister as the enticing hook for relocation, he proved how crafty he was, though I wasn't sure craftiness was a required skill for a national director of Wakeford Global, an international property valuations conglomerate. Nevertheless, my older sister Madeline was my best friend. I missed not living near her, especially after our parents were killed in a car accident. And Dex knew it.

Not to mention, my big sis was a realtor in the Scranton area.

"I suppose looking into properties couldn't hurt," I said.

There was that smile again.

The nurse walked into the room carrying a hefty stack of discharge papers.

Here I thought being released from the hospital would be the most significant development of my day. I never would've guessed we'd be contemplating relocation.

Death pounding on my door had changed everything.

3

Saturday, May 25, 2024
The Palisades: Washington, D.C.

I WOKE UP the next morning, thrilled to be out of the hospital.

Walking from our main bedroom to the stairs, I passed our home office; the door was halfway open. Dex was already making business calls on a Saturday. Something about delaying a commercial appraisal in Georgia. Made sense. Until my recovery had a few days to marinate, my husband would be telecommuting from our waterfront townhouse in the Palisades, as Dr. Reselda had ordered.

On the staircase, I clutched the railing as I took one step at a time.

Rays of sunlight warmed the wooden planks on the first floor. I padded my way to the kitchen, loving the feel of gliding my bare feet across the smooth wood. Another perk from my near death experience: appreciating the simple pleasures again.

After filling my mug with coffee, I shuffled over to our kitchen island and gingerly lowered myself onto a stool. Dex had placed the morning paper and my charged cellphone on the countertop.

Beyond our three sets of sliding glass doors, the Potomac River glistened as if diamonds had been sprinkled on its surface. I'd miss the river the most if Dex and I were to move.

When my cellphone rang, I flinched, causing a tearing sensation in my ribcage.

Madeline was calling.

I closed my eyes to manage the pain.

On the fourth ring, I picked up.

9

"Hey, Mad." I swallowed. Slowly. "I was going to call you."

"You sound…*off*. Are you having a setback, little sis?"

I gave Madeline the latest rundown on my injuries.

"New subject," she said, now that she was convinced I wasn't dying. "It's been driving me nuts. What unbelievable thing did you want to tell me? Are you…*pregnant?*"

The mere thought of having a baby in my womb, pressing on my ribcage, took my breath away.

"I was too tired to get into it last night," I said. "I didn't mean to leave you hanging."

"Spill the beans, already. Am I going to be an aunt?"

"Not yet. My announcement is still a shocker, though." I paused for dramatic effect. "Dex wants to move to the country."

"Really? Are we talking somewhere far out or closer to the city? You know, rural country versus suburb country."

"Rural."

"Wow. Unexpected. What part of western Maryland? I might know a realtor for you."

"Try Pennsylvania."

"Pennsylvania?"

"Between Scranton and the Poconos," I said, enjoying my playfulness.

There was silence as the news soaked in.

"Damnity Damn!" Madeline cheered.

"Fuckity fuck! Right?"

"Are you going to do it, Nora? Move…*near me?"*

"Depends. Are *you,* madam realtor, going to find Dex and me some awesome, amazing land to build our forever home on?"

Madeline's excitement made all my physical ailments fade into the background. I even managed to chuckle without wincing in pain.

I described what Dex and I had agreed on. We wanted around 20 acres, with some of the parcel already cleared and not too rocky. If there was a lake, pond, or stream nearby, even better.

"Freaky coincidence," Madeline said. "A property is about to come on the market. Second week of June. It's a 30-acre parcel in Boulder. And I'll have the exclusive listing."

"How far is that from you?"

"About forty-five minutes."

I smiled. "Go on."

"About half the property is cleared, flat, and sits on top of a hill. It was once farmland, so way fewer rocks. We're talking fertile topsoil. And get this, the parcel overlooks a lake and wildlife sanctuary, Boulder Lake State Park to be exact. It'll sell quickly."

"How many people live in Boulder?"

"Twelve hundred," Madeline said.

"Compared to a whopping seven-hundred-*thousand* in D.C."

"You said rural."

"Rural *and* safe," I clarified.

"You can't buy that, Nora." She sounded big sister serious. "Take it from me: Safety requires skills—in the city and the country. I'd recommend learning how to use a firearm."

"A gun? *Me?*" I shook my head even though she couldn't see my negative reaction. "That's Dex's territory."

"Should be yours, too. In these parts, law enforcement can't respond in a couple of minutes. Not with country roads. So we learn to defend ourselves."

"I have pepper spray."

"Will that work better in the country than the subway?"

Ouch. The kid gloves were off. Madeline hit me hard.

Not that I blamed her. I had a habit of seeing what my heart wanted to see. Sure, my life motto was *everything had an explanation*. But the gap between explanations of the heart and those of fact was vast. Probably why I was good at creating advertising campaigns; designs were powered by emotions way more than logic and facts.

"Rural living is like insulation," I countered, hoping to sound like an expert. "The cold still exists, but the added layers make it harder to get to you."

"I desperately want you to move here, so whatever you say."

I needed to change the subject before I snarked back.

"If we fall in love with the property," I said, "could we make an offer before it's listed?"

"Ordinarily. But the lot's not at that stage yet. Some minor legal issues are being ironed out. Estate stuff."

"When *can* we look at the property? Before everybody else?"

"How about June eighth? Two weeks from today. The property should be green-lighted by then. And hopefully you'll feel better."

"Perfect." I paused. "Speaking of which, the land sounds almost too good to be true."

"There's one downside that might turn off some buyers."

"A family graveyard in the middle of the lot?" I asked, dreading her answer.

"Nothing *that* bad," Madeline said. "More like thirteen miles up the road is the largest federal penitentiary in Pennsylvania. For the worst of the worst. Including the criminally insane. But think of it this way: If Dex ever loses his marbles and gets caught breaking the law, you'll only have a short drive to visit him."

"Not funny."

"Seriously. If you purchase the land, the prison will be the last thing on your mind. You'll never give it another thought. Promise."

4

PARADISE. THE WORD which popped into my head as Dex and I stood, alongside my sister, at the farthest end of lot 16—a flat field situated on top of a hill. We stood near the edge at exactly the spot where we had the best view overlooking the lake and valley below.

My ears were tuned into the simple and subtle, the kinds of sounds typically drowned out by the harshness of city noise.

No sirens blared in the background. No honking. Not even road hum, as we called it.

Instead, I heard late morning wind rustling through leaves on mature trees, those beyond the northwest quadrant of the lot, to my left. Birds and cicadas were chirping. And flitting from one wildflower to the next, butterflies and buzzing bees performed their pollen polka.

I took a deep breath through my nose, my ribcage allowing it now, and savored the sweet fragrance of freshly mowed grass. The owner must have recently bushhogged the field ahead of showing the property to potential buyers.

"Why aren't people fishing or swimming in the lake?" I asked my sister. "Especially on a sunny day."

"Not allowed," Madeline said. "The park exists for wildlife conservation. The state doesn't even publicize its location. It'll be like having your own private lake. And no one's around to notice if you and Dex were to run down your hill and sneak a dip."

13

I heard what she did. She said, *your* hill. Clever sales speak.

"How deep is Boulder Lake?" Dex asked.

Funny how tall people were usually interested in ceiling heights and water depths.

"Fifteen to twenty feet at its deepest."

There was an island in the middle of the cobalt-blue water, maybe five acres in total. Its shores were dotted with rocks and boulders of varying sizes. And the water's edge was laced with blooming lilies and spiky cattails. Dense, tall pines blocked my view of the other side.

"Let me guess." I pointed. "The island is called Boulder Island."

"Wow," Madeline replied. "Did the name of the lake and those huge rocks give it away?"

My bloodshot eye, no longer vampire red, could eyeroll once again, so I let it rip.

"Come on!" she countered. "Teasing is fun. It's a big sister thing."

Dex was doing a three-sixty. No doubt, assessing the 15 acres of buildable land.

"I think we'd situate the house this way, Nora," he said, staying on task. He pointed toward the ridge of mountains on the horizon. "The front of our house could face east. Imagine watching the sunrise." He turned toward the lake. "And our back patio could face west. Picture the sunset over the water. How does that sound?"

A train whistled in the distance.

My heart instantly accelerated, making me short of breath. An invisible force squeezed my chest. Inhaling was impossible. Moisture beaded on my skin from thousands of pore-sized volcanoes—all erupting simultaneously.

I heard the train's brakes screeching, the shrill reverberating throughout my body. The rattle of metal on metal. And a man. *The* man in the raincoat. I could see him inside my mind. Feel him on my arm. He grabbed me so tightly I thought he might crush my bones. I could smell him, his body odor, like sweaty feet, curdled milk, and raw onions mixed together.

The confusion in his eyes. I saw his distorted desperation, exacerbated by anger.

A wave of nausea crashed over me.

"Nora." I heard my name spoken, as if the male voice was coming from the faraway end of a dark tunnel, followed by a louder, more determined, "NORA!"

I reached out my hand in the direction of Dex's voice, even though I lingered in the depths of my mental rewind. He grabbed my fingers, which were trembling by now, and he pulled my body against his. Burying my head in his chest, I started to register where I was. I stood on grass. Safe. My husband had wrapped his arms around me as I pressed against his body.

My sister's hand rubbed my back.

"What's wrong?" Madeline asked, her voice registering concern.

"The train whistle," he answered, squeezing me a little tighter. "Is that it, babe? Did the sound trigger a flashback?"

I nodded, still trying to regain my footing. At least the nausea was starting to pass.

Dex and I held our embrace. His heartbeat grounded me.

The breeze evaporated moisture from my skin, cooling me off. My panic subsided.

"Sorry," I said, stepping back from Dex and supporting my own weight again.

"Don't apologize," Dex scolded. "Dr. Reselda said you might experience some PTSD."

I briefly locked eyes with Madeline's. I knew what it meant when her long lashes and hazel eyes stilled and glazed over, when they were distant and present at the same time. When the kindest, most natural face I knew (freckles were her only makeup) was seemingly frozen. That was when my sister was searching for a solution.

"Try reminding yourself," Madeline said, tucking the sides of her brown hair behind her ears. "The train running through Boulder only carries grain. There's no station with commuters. No strangers. That difference might help."

Yes, the next time I heard a train whistle, I could tell myself that.

After my mental trip to what I called *The Nightmare at Union Station,* we returned to our discussion about where our modern farmhouse could be situated on the property.

Dex took a dozen steps. "Our bedroom would be around here."

Near where he stood, I noticed a swath of ground, perhaps four feet in diameter, which had fallen or sunken below the natural surface. Dirt edges, jagged and two inches deep, outlined the dropped ground. The "hole" was shaped like an imperfect circle.

"Wonder what happened?" I asked.

Madeline moved closer.

My husband lowered to his knees and pressed down on the sunken ground as if it might give way.

"Oh that," my sister said. "A sinkhole. Didn't you know? Potholes and sinkholes, Pennsylvania is cursed with them."

"Are sinkholes a...*problem?*"

The moment the words left my mouth, I realized my question wasn't the wisest. I had seen news videos of houses and cars being swallowed by sinkholes. Gobbled up like the earth had been hungry.

"Not this one," Dex said. "It's small." He stood and brushed off his knees. "Over time and with moisture, soft rock can give way underground. When we excavate, the land will be leveled out. No more sinkhole."

"Did you say *when?*" my sister pressed.

Dex looked at me and smiled. "I'm game if you are."

Before I could answer, I became distracted again, turning my head toward the lake.

A roar rushed across the lake's surface, instantly leaving white caps in its wake. Rising off the water, the strong gust rushed up and over the hill in our direction.

The wind howled as it approached. Or was it more of a wail?

Yes. It sounded like someone was crying. Weeping.

My blouse flapped. Bangs, twirled.

"Did you hear that?" I asked, feeling a chill tickle my arms.

"Sounds like approval to me," Dex said, his eyebrows raised. "What do you say, little sis?"

Paradise was difficult to turn down.

"I say, make an offer! One the seller can't refuse."

5

SETTLEMENT ON THE lot was tomorrow. A lawyer from Honesdale had agreed to meet Dex and me at his office on Church Street. On a Saturday afternoon, no less. I was already impressed with the locals, a classification Dex and I would be joining soon.

Today, I was in the process of driving up to Boulder a day ahead of Dex who had a business obligation in New Jersey. We'd meet at settlement and then planned on doing something outside of the box for both of us (since we had become fully indoctrinated with city life). We had purchased camping equipment—a tent, sleeping bag, citronella torches, lanterns, cooler, and a portable grill—so we could spend our first night on our land as official property owners.

I couldn't think of a better way to embrace rural living than to sleep under its stars.

My goals for today started with a visit to the town of Boulder to see what it offered. Then I'd pop by the lot to develop ideas on where my greenhouse and chicken coop could go. After dinner, I'd retire to a Bed and Breakfast in Honesdale where I had booked an overnight stay.

I was eager to learn about the area we'd be calling home.

Slight snag in my plans because actually *seeing* my surroundings might be challenging. When I exited Interstate 84, I drove into dense fog which hadn't eased up. It had gotten thicker the farther north I went. Hopefully, the sun would break through and clear things up.

At least the fog hadn't dampened my spirits. I felt like a teenager before a first date.

Including the fact that I had to pee.

The drive from the Palisades to Boulder was over five hours, one half-hour of it spent on recharging my Tesla at an EV (electric vehicle) charging station. I used the restroom then, but because of my excitement, I needed to go again. I hadn't considered that the final leg of my trip would be on country roads. Roads which didn't have fast food places or gas stations at every intersection.

A newbie miscalculation for sure.

A road sign reported Boulder as one mile ahead. My car's GPS confirmed it.

I entered the town. A general store was on my right. The building looked like it had been converted from a house. A diner was on the left, more like a trailer sided in polished aluminum. A hand-painted sign read: Rita's Home Cooking. Three trucks were parked in front.

Residential houses followed on both sides of the road. Most of them were painted white.

A four-way stop was next. No other cars were at the intersection, so I kept my foot on the brake and looked around. A gas station with two pumps was to the right. The main building was the size of a shed. Definitely no bathroom there. To my left was a pharmacy—the back half looked like it doubled as a post office. And a small bank was across the street.

My car wipers swiped the windshield, removing beads of moisture. The landscape around me was wet and dark gray, especially for early afternoon, causing my headlights and fog lights to remain on. In fact, the fog had become so thick that I couldn't see the town peripherally. Maybe there were shops, restaurants, and business offices down the side streets.

I drove through the intersection. After passing the bank, trees and pines immediately crowded both sides of the road again. I was back in the forest.

Madeline described Boulder as eye-blink small. Guess I had anticipated a D.C. blink.

Unbelievable. The town was already in my rearview mirror.

Since I was the lone car, I stopped in my lane, turned around, and headed back. At the general store, I pulled into the graveled parking lot. This was my best hope for a public bathroom.

When I opened the store's front door, a bell jingled. A woman with curly gray hair, maybe in her sixties, sat behind the counter. She was playing cards by herself.

"What can I do you for, hon?" she asked, eyeing me up and down and then placing a card on a pile. "Looks like you need something."

"I'm from out of town and didn't plan wisely on my restroom stops." I cleared my throat, sounding nervous. More like, embarrassed. "Do you have a bathroom I could use? Please?"

"Sure. There's a bucket out back. And a fresh pile of leaves for wiping."

"Excuse me?"

She broke out into a raspy laugh. "I got you on that one!" She pointed. "Down the hall. Bathroom is on your left."

"Thank you so much."

Afterwards, I bought a sports drink and some mints, mostly to support her business since I appreciated her hospitality. After all, the sign on the restroom door had read: Employees Only. As far as I could tell, that meant her. Singular.

"What fancy city you from, hon?" she asked at checkout. The woman looked beyond me—out the window and at my car.

My newbie-ness was *that* obvious. Maybe my vibe contributed. My nose piercing—a small diamond stud in my nostril, along with the silver streak in my bangs, were city artsy. Not to mention the olive branch in the beak of my dove tattoo which was inked on my neck. In contrast, Dex looked way more conservative. He seemed to fit in everywhere. Me? My looks could spark a reaction.

More like judgment.

"D.C.," I answered. "But my husband and I are buying some land beside Boulder Lake."

"That right? Is the land part of the old Williams Farm?"

"Actually, it is. Lot sixteen."

"*Sixteen?* The one at the end of the field? Closest to the lake?"

I smiled. This woman knew her local geography. "That's the one!"

"Strange."

"Oh?"

"Rumor's always been that Virgil Williams—he was the owner of the original farm—had written in his last will and testament that lot sixteen could never be sold. Never. And here you are buying it."

"Curiosity has me," I confessed. "Do you know *why* the lot was never to be sold?"

Her eyes shifted ever so slightly. And she ran her upper teeth over her bottom lip. Both cued me into thinking that the next words out of her mouth might be light on the truth.

"Haven't you heard, hon? Curiosity killed the cat."

She had opted for deflection instead. With a hint of morbid.

"Good thing cats have nine lives," I countered, winking.

"Got me on that one!" The woman chuckled, making her whole body jiggle. "Reckon a seller's market swayed the grandchildren to override the will and collect on a lucrative price. Simple economics is my guess. And now lucky for us, we get to claim you as our own."

Kind. And at the same time, interesting. I mean, the woman had answered a totally different question. I didn't ask why the lot was put on the market. I asked why the owner had never wanted the land to be sold in the first place.

After repeating my gratitude for being allowed to use the restroom, I got back into my car and entered the lot's address onto my dash's control panel screen.

Eight miles to paradise.

6

THE FOG WAS thick, but with my GPS and white knuckle grip on the steering wheel, I arrived at our lot without incident.

Putting my car in low gear, I crawled up the steep dirt drive and parked at the top.

Tiny beads of moisture greeted me as I traipsed across the field, heading west toward the farthest end of our land where our property overlooked Boulder Lake (on a clear day).

I was thankful for my good sense of direction.

Footwear was another story. I needed waterproof hiking boots.

Standing near the edge of our lot, I could see nothing but mist, like a dense cloud had dropped from the sky onto the hilltop and valley below. The fog weighed heavy on everything. Nothing moved. Nothing made a sound. Visualizing where to place our greenhouse and chicken coop wasn't happening. Not today.

I couldn't see a bloody thing.

Anyway, all would not be lost. I'd check on the sinkhole. Something about it bugged me. Unsettled me. I'd feel better if I knew it hadn't grown or deepened.

The sunken patch of ground was difficult to locate in the fog, but I eventually found it.

I knelt and leaned over, touching the sinkhole's exposed dirt edge with my fingers.

Shit de la shit.

During our first visit, I had made a mental note that the circular sinkhole was a two inch drop below the surface.

The increase from then was discernible.

A *five* inch drop now.

Why did the sinkhole make me feel so uneasy? Maybe because the reason for it was unknown. Like *why* the man at Union Station had wanted to kill me. *Ghosts* were clearly an excuse. A delusion.

Everything had an explanation. I just didn't know them all.

Which made me feel vulnerable.

I ran my fingers over my right temple. The lingering soreness reminded me. Being thrown onto the tracks had really happened.

In the stillness, I heard something behind me.

Footsteps?

Yes. Running, if I had to guess. Running toward the lake. At least I thought the steps were heading in that direction.

Springing to my feet and turning, I glimpsed a shadowy figure getting swallowed by the mist.

Something or *someone* had disappeared into the fog.

My heart thundered in my chest.

"Hello?"

Nothing.

"Is anybody there?"

In the distance, a windy howl answered me. The sound grew louder and louder until it became a roar.

Was I about to have another flashback?

I swatted at the fog. I could barely see my shoes or my hand held out in front of me. But at least I was still in our field. My mind hadn't been hijacked to Union Station.

A hint of claustrophobia tightened around my neck. My chest.

Uneasiness concentrated in my veins. Raced to every muscle.

Was someone else…*here?*

Did I need to run? Would I even be able to find my car in the fog?

My bangs rustled.

A gust slammed into me, nearly pushing me off-balance. I leaned into it and fortified my stance by placing one leg in front of the other while slightly bending my knees. The wind burst felt like thirty to forty miles per hour, but I was guessing.

I heard something else. A shrill. A desperate high pitched scream piercing through the wind.

Was a person wailing? Or maybe a wounded animal?

Something similar had happened our first time at the lot. Only this time, the weeping was more distinctive, more anguished.

Goosebumps erupted on my arms.

The fog dissipated enough to see the edge of the woods to my left. The treetops violently bent with the gust's assault. Branches pounded and scratched against each other.

As quickly as it came, the wind raced away, carrying the cries eastward.

Stillness returned, but my anxiety remained.

I speed dialed my sister's cellphone number and she picked up on the first ring.

"Do you know why Virgil Williams's estate held on to this parcel?" I asked her, short of breath. "Why his will prevented it from being sold off when the farm was subdivided?"

"All I know is his grandson, Duncan Williams, was able to convince the court that retaining the lot was a hardship. Something about his father's senior care expenses."

"Doesn't help. What I really want to know is why Virgil Williams would prohibit, in his will, the lot from being sold. Seems like there'd be a story behind that."

"Does it really matter, Nora? The past is the past."

"It *feels* like it matters."

"Focus on what we know. The family's financial hardship is your reward. It's business."

"Sounds heartless."

"These things happen. And if you don't buy the land tomorrow, little sis, someone else will."

7

Saturday, July 13, 2024
Lot 16: Boulder, Pennsylvania

OVERHEAD, LOOKING OUT through our tent's circular vent, the heavens appeared to have lowered for Dex and me. Flickering stars were as close as fireflies.

Zipped together within our two-person sleeping bag, I was draped over Dex's naked chest, soothed by his heartbeat, my thighs still warm from lovemaking.

Crickets and tree frogs serenaded us. Maybe even an owl.

Flames from our campfire cast an orangish glow, illuminating our shelter. Every now and then, our tent's fabric fluttered and flapped, reminding me of a flag in the wind.

July 13th ranked as the second best day of my life. The first being our wedding day.

Our lot's settlement had taken place this afternoon at a law office. Afterwards, Dex and I had set up camp on our property, near the western edge where we'd have the best view of the lake. Consistent with a game we played whenever we vacationed, each of us got to pick one rule for the weekend. I opted for no cellphones. Our devices had to be off and kept in our cars for the entire camping excursion. Dex's rule was less tangible. He wanted no thoughts or mention of the sinkhole. Guess I had given him an earful about it.

Spaced citronella torches, their stakes driven into the ground, marked the boundaries of our campsite. After grilling our meal, we sat in beach chairs beside the crackling campfire and ate our dinner.

And when the sun dipped below the horizon and the skies transitioned to a tapestry of pink and orange, we toasted our new purchase with dry champagne, admiring our incredible view.

The bottle had emptied quickly.

We retired inside our tent for passionate lovemaking. Maybe the champagne had contributed, but I truly felt Dex and my electricity had flowed as one.

"Penny for your thoughts," he said, his voice easing me back into the present.

"I was re-living this evening. Thinking how much I love you."

"Same." He squeezed me tighter. "I orbit around you, Nora Jean Bliss. You're my world."

I kissed his chest.

Perfect marriages eluded most of our friends, so I tried not to counter their whispered frustrations by mentioning the ease of my three year marriage with Dex. It wouldn't help their situations knowing I couldn't think of anything significant in mine that needed improvement. Truth was, if our marriage wasn't the quintessential partnership, I had no clue what one might look and feel like.

How could perfect be made perfect-*er?*

Then again, champagne was liquid putty; when consumed, it smoothed over another person's flaws until they were forgotten.

"I've been meaning to ask you," he said. "In ten months, you'll be working remotely. From here. Are you worried about being isolated? Because I'll still have to travel a lot."

I pushed myself up with my forearm. The campfire's glow glinted in his eyes. "I've acclimated to the idea. I think some alone time will work out fine."

"How often will you report to the office? Did Cecelia mention?"

"Twice a month is the plan." I lowered my head back onto his chest. "I'm so grateful we have the means to do this. Sadly, not everyone who wants to leave the city can afford it."

"Your social compassion always impresses me."

A coyote howled in the distance.

I flinched. Tree creatures were one thing. Coyotes quite another—they traveled and hunted in packs…on the ground. The *same* ground shared by our tent.

"Relax," Dex whispered. "Coyotes want nothing to do with us. Besides, I brought my pistol in the duffel bag. No worries, okay?"

I don't think I ever answered him because when my eyes opened, time had clearly elapsed. A fainter, reddish glow brightened the side panel of our tent, this time from campfire embers instead of flames.

Dex's breathing was slow and even. He had fallen asleep, too.

A shadow darted by.

My heart went ballistic.

Another shadowy figure? Seriously?

I had seen one yesterday. In the fog.

Dex rolled onto his side.

The rustle from his movement, and the fact that I wasn't alone, instantly reassured me, replacing my fear with a sense of security.

My imagination had to be playing tricks on me.

No! There was the shadow again—heading back in the direction from which it came. Heading toward the lake.

Given the earlier howling, I might've expected a coyote's shadow. Except, the darkened shape was upright, not short and long.

And I heard something. Spoken softly. A female's voice perhaps?

Holding my breath, I froze in hopes of deciphering any sounds.

There it was again. The elongated whisper.

The voice thrummed, *"Them…"*

Them? As in, Dex and me?

I prickled with anger at the intrusion and glanced at my smartwatch. Midnight.

Dex and I would be building and eventually moving to rural America…to avoid unwanted encounters. To separate ourselves from the unpredictability of crowded places.

Yet here we were on our very first night: Vulnerable in our sleep, with some unknown, unwelcomed stranger already invading *our* space. *Our* rural insulation.

Irritation fueled my new commitment to *do* something in the face of danger.

No more deer in headlights.

Slowly and quietly, I unzipped my side of the sleeping bag and wiggled out. Thank goodness I had put on an oversized T-shirt and undies after we had made love.

Tiptoeing to the tent's opening, I began to unzip the flap.

"What's going on?" Dex asked, looking back at me and sounding beyond groggy.

I felt like I had swallowed a baseball.

"Go back to sleep." I managed to swallow. "I'll be right back."

He lowered his head, seemingly satisfied that all was well.

Anyway, if the intruder turned out to be a legitimate threat, I'd scream. Then Dex could morph into my protector.

Outside, the full moon and low ceiling of stars brightened the landscape. No flashlight needed. Long, stretched out shadows from a few nearby tree branches danced on the grass.

Could I have mistaken a swaying branch for a running figure?

And the word I heard, could the wind have created it?

I looked around for something out of place. For something that didn't belong.

Nothing was unusual.

Except in a *good* way because the landscape was spectacular.

My eyes scanned the lake.

Moonlight glistened off its rippled surface.

Inhaling, I filled my lungs with fresh, mountain air.

Wait.

I blinked. Blinked hard.

Movement caught my attention on Boulder Island.

I squinted to see through the lacey mist rising where lake water met the island's rocky shoreline. Squinted, in hopes of discerning what my eyes perceived.

Yes. I saw a figure.

A girl.

At least, she looked to have long hair, light in color. And she wore a white dress which fluttered in the breeze. A belt or sash was tied around her waist.

And now she was pointing. Pointing at *me*.

The timing didn't add up.

If the girl had been responsible for casting the shadow near our campfire, no way could she have run down our hill and swam to the lake's island. In a dress, no less. And certainly not in that short amount of time. Impossible.

Instead, maybe she was pointing at a friend.

I turned to look behind me.

Nothing. No one.

A wisp of wind tickled the skin on my neck, sending chills racing down my spine.

In the moonlight, a silhouette of a bat twisted away from me.

I glanced back at the island. At the shoreline. Looking for the girl.

Whoever had been there was gone.

However, my lingering annoyance remained.

I made a pact with myself then and there. If I saw her again, I'd get to the bottom of her intrusion. Find out why she was trespassing in the middle of the night. A *teenager,* no less.

Also, she needed to be told.

Things had changed.

This was Dex and my land now.

8

Sunday, July 14, 2024
The Palisades: Washington, D.C.

HOME AN HOUR ago from our camping trip on our lot in Pennsylvania, I stood at the kitchen island making late afternoon sandwiches while chewing on my lingering annoyance from this morning's conversation with Dex.

At the crack of dawn at our campsite, I had described my encounters from the middle of the night. Dex hadn't expressed the least bit of worry. As he poked at the campfire to see if any embers remained, I chronicled all that had happened to me after waking up. He never raised an eyebrow about the unexplained shadow or the eerie voice. Or gave a curious look when I described the mysterious girl on Boulder Island.

Instead, he had wanted to place a bet on how long it would take to reignite the campfire and boil water for morning coffees. Really?

I had countered with a tart expression—going for facial creases galore. And when I mentioned I didn't appreciate him acting cavalier, Dex resorted to emotional avoidance in the form of logic, accompanied by a smattering of condescension. Either I had imagined the events—which wouldn't be far-fetched, he had said, given I hadn't camped since childhood, or else I had been hovering in that consciousness where wakefulness and sleep intersected, blurring the lines between reality and dreams.

For Dex, stress was always a potential root cause. Perhaps I was more anxious about moving than I had realized or admitted. Another

29

possibility, he had calmly pontificated, was that local teens made a habit of partying on Boulder Island (he would if he was that age), and I had simply spotted one of them. Nothing sinister had happened. Nothing threatening. No need for the Viking to brandish his shield and sword.

The trip home had been a bit icy. I hardly said a word.

In my opinion, all Dex needed to do was believe me and agree to be on the lookout when we visited the property again in August. *That* and maybe he shouldn't have banned a topic, even for one weekend, which I felt compelled to discuss. Like that fuckity fuck sinkhole.

Ugh. I was in a mood.

While I prepared lunch, Dex was making phone calls upstairs from our home office. At four o'clock, he'd be leaving for an overnight road trip, so he wouldn't have time for round two with me.

Perhaps my sister would provide the affirmation I desperately sought. Then I could move on. Un-grump.

I left my tomatoes on the counter and headed toward the dining room table where my purse was perched on a stack of mail. Retrieving my cellphone, I was surprised to find my screen was black. After I rebooted my device, I speed dialed Madeline.

"Do you know how many times I tried calling you this morning?" she asked before saying hello. "I even tried Dex. Neither one of you answered. I started to get worried. Seriously worried."

My sister could turn *mama bear* on me, especially after our parents had died. Forget that I was 30 years old and married. But being her cub wasn't so bad, so I'd let her over protectiveness slide.

I admitted that Dex and I had instituted a "no cellphone rule" while camping. I had forgotten to turn my phone back on.

With barely a breath in between, I launched into describing the strangeness which had occurred in the middle of the night. Including my unresolved irritation with Dex.

"When did you see the shadow?" she asked. "What time?"

I really didn't get why the time was important, but I answered her anyway—that the shadow had passed our campfire two times around midnight.

My sister slowly exhaled.

"Your take on Dex's reaction?" I pressed. "Annoying, right?"

"Did you actually tell Dex what you wanted from him?" she asked. "Specifically, I mean. That you needed him to believe you?"

"The implication was obvious."

"Not between Mars and Venus, little sis. You need to spell out your needs. Otherwise, don't expect the emotional support you're hoping for. Remember, Mars is desert dry."

"Come on, Mad. The gender theory of Mars and Venus is embarrassingly ancient."

"It holds up for you and Dex, doesn't it?"

Her comment seemed like an insult on several levels. Not to mention, she was 32 and single. Should she really purport to be a relationship specialist?

And since Madeline had pinpointed where *I* went wrong, in the whole galaxy I might add, I felt compelled to test her on the antiquated theory, especially the *spelling out your needs* part.

"Okay. I need *you* to believe me that something strange and illogical happened," I said. "Do you?"

"Given what you saw and heard, it was definitely not ordinary."

"Thank you."

"If I were you," she continued, "I'd swim out to the island. Better still, buy a paddle board. Bet you'll find empty beer bottles and cigarette butts left behind by teenagers."

My temperature rose. "Now you sound like Dex."

"You're the one who always says *everything has an explanation.*" She paused. "Hey, I want to change subjects. To tell you the reason I tried calling you a dozen times this morning."

"What's going on?"

"Since your cellphones were off, you probably haven't heard national news. There was a prison break at the Fairview Federal Penitentiary. The one I told you was thirteen miles from your property. I called your cellphones to warn you."

"Oh my gosh. No, we didn't hear." My mind began to race. "What time was the prison break? How many inmates? Do you think the shadow or the girl I saw could've been one of them?"

"The girl couldn't have been an inmate. All three escapees were males since that's who the penitentiary serves. They broke out around three a.m., so the shadow at midnight couldn't have been from any of the prisoners either. Besides, they're probably long gone from the area. Still, you needed to know."

"Excavation on our lot is right around the corner. In August."

"They'll be caught by then," my sister stated with authority.

"You said we'd never even know the prison was nearby."

"In fairness, the facility has never had a prison break. We're talking maximum security, so it's unexpected. To say the least."

Dex walked into the kitchen, staring down at his cellphone.

"I'm catching up on my text messages," he said, clearly not noticing I was on my cellphone. "Did you hear? There's been a jailbreak close to our property. An alert was sent, like, ten hours ago."

He looked up at me. "And your sister called me twice."

9

Monday, August 26, 2024
Lot 16: Boulder, Pennsylvania

BY LATE AUGUST, one of the escapees from the federal penitentiary had been captured. Two were still at large.

Not surprising that I imagined hawklike eyes staring at Dex and me from the dense woods across from our property after we arrived at our lot to speak with Bart Lancaster (the construction manager we had hired). Forget *imagined*. Goosebumps on my arms suggested the possibility was real.

I needed to refocus on the good news. Our breathtaking property was transforming before our eyes.

Dex and I stood beside our hybrid SUV as Bart approached, driving an enclosed side-by-side utility vehicle. After getting out of the UTV, he immediately took off his hardhat and placed the underside flat against his chest. Bart was originally from Wyoming, and I could easily picture him with a cowboy hat and spurred boots.

"Dexter. Ma'am." Bart nodded and returned the hat to his head, leaving the strap unsnapped. "Sure glad you could meet me here. Why don't you hop in?" He tilted his head toward the direction of his utility vehicle. "I'll drive us to the western side of your property. That's where we're finishing up excavation. It'll give us a chance to talk about our progress and the construction timetable."

Before Dex climbed into the front passenger seat, he opened the rear door for me.

"Those hardhats are for you all," Bart said, pointing to the seat behind him on the driver's side.

I handed Dex one and placed the other on my head.

As the UTV rolled forward, I scanned the hilltop. This half of our acreage had been cleared and tilled. Leveled out, too. Looking massive and completely private.

Sweet.

As we traversed our land in the utility vehicle, I noticed a large mound of rocks and boulders piled high to my left. Bart must have noticed me gawking at them.

"I call them petrified dinosaur dung, Ma'am. Mostly because they're a stinking pain in the ass. These parts are littered with them." He chuckled. "Sorry for my foul language."

Ass hardly compared to fuckity fuck or shit de la shit, but okay.

Maybe city dwellers like me were verbally vulgar despite being pathetically reliant on modern conveniences while locals were naively polite, yet fiercely self-sufficient.

Too bad cursing didn't qualify as a survival skill.

"Have you run into any challenging issues?" Dex asked our construction manager.

"None. Including the sinkhole. We've been moving dirt over the depression all morning. Haven't encountered a problem. Wasn't very deep, so we're good."

My chest tightened at the mention of the sinkhole. Which was, in and of itself, ridiculous. I mean, who else claimed sunken earth as their nemesis?

At least Dex had made Bart aware of it. More importantly, my worry seemed for naught.

By the edge of the property, Bart shut off his UTV and pointed to the lake. "That's a mighty fine view. Mighty fine." He emphasized his compliment by adding a drawn out *mmm*. "In fact, I would've purchased this lot, had I known it was going on the market. You've probably been told that a trust forbade descendants of Virgil and Vivian Williams to sell this parcel. Of course, that didn't stop folks from drooling over its potential for decades." He opened his door. "I'm jealous. Y'all must've had the inside scoop."

"My sister's in real estate."

"*Aah.* Lucky you." He closed his door. "Your gain is my loss."

Madeline was right. Did it really matter why Virgil Williams didn't want this parcel to be sold? If Dex and I hadn't bought the land, someone like Bart Lancaster would've snatched it up.

As we faced eastward, standing behind the back of Bart's UTV, I inventoried the work taking place. Toward the woods to my right, a machine was drilling holes in a large roped off area. Two construction workers in hardhats and orange vests were shouting instructions to the woman operating the industrial auger. Straight ahead, a lone operator of an excavator was manipulating its bucket to spread and even out dirt from a nearby mound. The tractor-like machine was near where the sinkhole used to be.

Used to be sounded glorious.

Around the middle of our property, in the distance, a rocklift used its tongs to grab boulders from the rock pile we had passed, picking up each dinosaur dropping and lowering it into an idling dump truck. To my left was a significant stack of flat pewter-colored stone (flagstone if I had to guess). The stones were probably being saved for our landscaping.

Workers shouting orders against an irregular backdrop of diesel engines, those moaning and sputtering, reminded me of city noise. Puffs of exhaust wafted in the air, creating small gray clouds which hovered above the ground before being whisked away by the wind.

Bart pointed to our right. "The geothermal loop field will be located within the roped off area. Should be done installing the collectors next week."

"We'll have a vertical tube field, right?" Dex asked him.

"Have to. The tubes need to be installed deep enough to collect warmth from the ground to heat your home. You're aware we have harsh winters in these parts. Right?"

Dex proceeded to school Bart about his line of work. That he traveled throughout the country, including far north, to valuate commercial properties. So yes, he was well aware. But he politely thanked Bart for his concern, albeit with a frosty tone.

"Meant no disrespect," Bart countered. "It's just we've seen city folks run back home after their first winter, tails between their legs. Locals like to say Boulder requires leather skin."

"Actually, my ancestors immigrated to this area. From *northern*

Norway. Ever heard of Norwegian leather?"

This was turning into a male pissing contest. You know, testing whose stream could reach the farthest and all the while smiling as if the competition wasn't really happening.

Despite being an entertaining exchange, higher stakes were vying for my attention.

As I watched the excavator out in front of me, I noticed every time the machine passed over a certain spot on the ground, the equipment looked slightly off-kilter—like the left track pad was sinking into the ground, tilting the cab where the operator sat.

The machine was close enough that I could see the person behind the controls. A twenty-something guy whose long blond hair peeked out from under his hardhat. He wore aviator sunglasses and a red sleeveless T-shirt. Large earmuffs covered his ears, and his head bobbed in a rhythm consistent with listening to music.

My gut and brain were wrestling.

While my intuition sensed alarm, I worried about overreacting. Let's face it: Dex believed the shadow, voice, and girl were all products of my irrational imagination.

A new development, however, tipped the scales in favor of me saying something.

Beyond the machine, I noticed a dust devil had formed—a miniature vortex of whirling dirt. Its spinning column, 10-feet high, was heading toward the excavator.

Accidents usually occurred when two or more missteps collided.

Was no one else seeing this?

I pointed toward the operator backing up the machine, encroaching on the deepening depression in the ground, just as the mini tornado took aim. "Excuse me, but…"

Too little, too late.

As the dust devil hit the machine on its right side, the excavator's left track pad sunk into the dirt. The equipment teetered for a moment before crashing over on its side. When the machine slammed into the dirt, the ground shook. Toppled over on its side, the excavator's engine whined, piercing through the air.

The entire worksite appeared to freeze.

Except for Dex and Bart.

They took off running toward the fallen excavator, so I followed on their heels.

"Tell me what you need me to do," Dex hollered to Bart.

"Call 911."

"Let me do that," I said, grabbing my cellphone from my back pocket. "You help him."

Three hours later, the firetruck, recovery vehicle, and police cruiser drove off our property. The ambulance had left for Honesdale's Wayne Memorial Hospital two hours ago. Gary, the excavator's operator, had broken his left arm on impact and suffered a two-inch gouge on his leg. Thankfully, his hard hat had prevented a concussion. He would be okay.

Now, an industrial tow truck loaded the damaged excavator onto its flatbed as Bart, Dex, and I huddled near the western edge of our land, our backs to the lake.

"Spoke too soon," Bart admitted, sounding solemn. "We're going to need an engineer to evaluate this. Let's hope an unmarked grave isn't the cause of the sinkhole."

"Who should I contact?" Dex asked.

"I have a friend whose company specializes in analyzing and repairing sinkholes. He owes me a favor. Let me call." He speed dialed someone and walked away, holding his cellphone to his ear.

"You don't think this lot is cursed or haunted. Do you?" I asked Dex, knowing my conjecture sounded a bit crazy.

"Seriously?"

"I mean, every time we're here, strange things happen."

He frowned. "And everything has an explanation. Remember?"

Why did he have to use my expression to prove *his* point?

Bart returned. "Evan will pop over tomorrow and call me with an estimate. I'll reach out to you then, to get a green light."

"When do think repairs might be completed?" Dex asked.

"Like I said, Evan owes me a favor. He agreed to make any reinforcements to the ground during the week. Can you meet us back here on Friday? We can summarize how repairs went. Better in person. And the three of us can talk foundation then."

Dex looked at me and I nodded. "Sure," he answered. "Friday."

10

Friday, August 30, 2024
Lot 16: Boulder, Pennsylvania

NO BURIED BONES or coffins. Talk about extreme relief.

As scheduled, Dex and I were meeting at the lot with Bart and his engineering friend, Evan. The sinkhole repairs had already been completed.

Midday was overcast, stagnant, and thick with high humidity. Clearly, summer was making its last ditch effort to hold on, but some trees in the woods were already yellowing.

As the four of us spoke near the spot where the sinkhole had tried to swallow the excavator and its operator, Evan's black Lab zig zagged around the property in a trot, nose to the ground, tail stiff.

"How do you know for certain there wasn't an unmarked grave underneath the sinkhole?" I pressed Evan.

"We used ground penetrating radar or GPR to look for anomalies beneath the surface," he answered. "Nothing significant was found. The technology is pretty failproof. Has to be when you need to rule out possible burial grounds."

"Any ideas on why the sinkhole formed?" Dex followed up.

"Environments are constantly changing. Shifting. That includes the ground. We found nothing extraordinary, though. Other than minor weathering below the surface, accelerated by groundwater flow. Over time, softened materials can collapse."

Sounded to me like his standard spiel.

"How did you repair the ground?" I asked.

38

"Dug out the hole first, before pouring a concrete plug—one that includes light rebar for reinforcement. Covered the affected area with clay sand and finished off the repair with topsoil. Simple, really."

Bart piggybacked into a discussion about the foundation which actually wouldn't impact the repaired sinkhole. In terms of positioning, the reinforced ground would be outside of where our main bedroom would be located. None of our house would be sitting on top of it.

That discussion transitioned to the geothermal field.

"Off subject," I said, when the updates had finished. "You guys are locals. Any inside scoop on the escapees from Fairview?"

"We don't worry about folks with ill intent," Evan said, as he pulled up his right pantleg to show us his ankle holster, pistol, and calf strap. He raised his eyebrows and smiled.

"Takes a while to get," Bart chimed in, pulling up his own pantleg to model a similar setup. "But I'd apply for a concealed carry permit. I never leave home without my Glock. Helps me focus on work instead of thugs."

Dex yanked up his pantleg to affirm he was already a member of the pistol posse. "I have a permit in almost every state in the lower forty-eight," he bragged. "Alaska, too."

Okay, maybe Madeline was right. Some males still had a Mars mentality: *I'll show you mine if you show me yours.* Testosterone could be so annoying. And predictable.

Next, they'd be ripping off their shirts, oiling their chests, and flexing their muscles.

"All right, so everyone's packing but me," I said. "How does that answer my question?"

"Your question again, Ma'am?" Bart asked.

Maybe these men needed to shore up their cognitive skills instead of diving headfirst into Wild, Wild West mode.

"The escaped inmates," I reminded him. "Any local chatter on their suspected whereabouts?"

"None that I've heard, but I predict they're far away from here," Bart answered. "You don't shake the beehive and stick around to see if you're gonna get stung."

The men from Mars all chuckled.

Evan's dog began barking at the pile of flagstone stacked to the left of us. He sounded agitated.

"I better get Duke," the engineer said, after he stopped laughing. "Don't want him getting mixed up with a porcupine. He won't win."

As he walked toward his dog, we followed like sheep.

"The flagstone is going to be used for our patio, right?" I asked.

"We figured why waste what God has provided," Bart confirmed. "We're already over budget, given the sinkhole repair, so anywhere we can save money helps."

The dog's hair along his spine stood straight up. Exposing his gums, he growled and barked. Drool dripped from his teeth.

A chipmunk darted along the rock pile and disappeared into a dark inlet between slabs of flagstone.

"Stand down, boy," his owner said, grabbing his dog's collar and pulling him back from the rock pile. "No sense losing your mind over a chipmunk. Not much meat there anyway."

When Evan walked backwards with his dog, I noticed scratches on the top flagstone. Was I seeing...*words?*

Curious, I walked closer to the pile.

Yes. The words *FIND THEM* had been carved into the stone, written in rudimentary form. About two dozen flies were clustered on the surface, walking in jittery circles around the letters.

Goosebumps erupted on my arms and the nape of my neck.

"Who wrote this? What does it mean?" I asked, more rhetorically than actually thinking someone might know the answers.

Bart came over and ran his fingers over the chalky, engraved words. The flies scattered.

"Not sure," he said. "But we'll buff the words out." He wiped his palms together, dispelling the white dust. "No worries."

The dog was still carrying on.

Echoes of his barking assaulted the hilltop.

All things *unexplained* were accumulating.

11

Thursday, May 22, 2025
Windy Hill Farm: Boulder, Pennsylvania

MOVING-IN DAY at Windy Hill Farm had started at six o'clock in the morning. And now, as evening approached, the moving crew was close to wrapping up their work.

The name we had given our property was a no-brainer. I mean, with the sudden waves of wind that swelled off the lake, growing stronger and higher until they crashed up and over our hill and raced across our land toward the east, the name was truly a perfect fit.

Unloading our belongings had proceeded without a hitch. The only sour note to the day was the date itself: May 22nd. The one-year anniversary of the day "Mr. Hostile" whispered into my ear something nonsensical about ghosts before pushing me onto the tracks. If we could've picked any other day to move, we would've; but the next available date was in late-June, and we were ready to start the next chapter of our lives.

At least moving was a positive distraction.

My accident wasn't the only event gnawing at my memory banks. Nine months and nine days ago, three prisoners had escaped from Fairview. Two were still on the loose. And eight months and three weeks ago, I had found the words *FIND THEM* carved into a flagstone after the sinkhole on our property had been repaired.

The unexplained caused me the most anxiety.

Thankfully, the sinkhole was a distant thought since it had been controlled.

I could thank therapist Dr. Estelle Simon for helping me adopt a new coping strategy. After the sinkhole accident, I started seeing her in D.C., as Dr. Reselda had recommended.

Dr. Simon wanted me to identify what I could control and what I couldn't. The differentiation grounded me when I spiraled, when I figuratively felt as though whitewater currents were thrashing me around, slamming me against obstacles and stealing my breath.

During one of my "drowning" episodes (that's what I called them), I started focusing on how I could save myself. I visualized a log in the rapids. Something tangible I could grab onto.

Sometimes my "log" was locating an exit in a building. Or talking on my cellphone to Dex or Madeline when feeling anxious. Sometimes it was clutching my pepper spray.

One thing was certain, I had become keenly aware of time because crises happened in a snapshot. One second, life was normal, safe, and *click,* the next it wasn't. Even though I couldn't control time, I could be acutely aware of what was happening within each snapshot, within each frame. Eventually, I got better at finding my rescue log *before* being submerged and battered.

Today and every day, Windy Hill Farm would be my life raft. Three-thousand square feet of a modern farmhouse rancher with light-colored wood planks throughout, high ceilings with timbered beams in the kitchen and great room, and a wood-burning fireplace. Not to mention, a full basement. All this, insulated on 30 acres bordering a wildlife sanctuary and lake.

At our kitchen island, I ran my fingers over the smooth granite. It would take time to sink in that I was safer than I'd ever been.

"Excuse me, Mrs. Bliss." The moving supervisor approached me with her clipboard. "Everything has been placed according to your map and the van is empty. We're cleaning up. Can I get your signature on some paperwork?"

After signing the papers and watching the tractor trailer pull away down our drive, Dex and I were finally alone in our forever home. Ordering pizza for delivery would've been our first choice, but Boulder was pie-less. And taco-less. And sushi-less.

Farm to table would be our new reality. But since my greenhouse wasn't currently green, I was thankful for the homemade soup and crusty bread I had packed. And the red wine.

After dinner, Dex and I called it an early night. We were beyond exhausted.

A normal sized window was on Dex's side of the bed, facing the front of the house. A massive window was on my side, overlooking the backyard.

Dex had cranked two of my window panels open, allowing crisp spring air to funnel into our bedroom. A waxing moon shined a spotlight across our bed.

I rested my head on Dex's chest as his hand rubbed my back.

"Shouldn't we close the windows?" I asked.

"Are you cold?"

"No. It's just that two prisoners are still on the run."

"They're long gone. Everybody says so. Remember?"

"We can't be sure. The escapees could survive in the woods. Even after a year. Didn't that bomber guy—Eric Rudolph, I think his name was—survive in the mountains for five years before getting caught?"

"That was in North Carolina, Nora. We're not as remote here. Besides, it was a long time ago." He squeezed me for reassurance. "Sounds like you're in need of a rescue log."

He was privy to my coping strategy when I felt vulnerable.

"Have one in mind?" I asked.

"Me for starters." He chuckled. "And my pistol's a solid backup."

I stretched my neck until my lips found his. I kissed him so he understood how much he meant to me. How much my life was complete with him in it.

Why did I pick fear over confidence when I was blessed with my own personal guardian?

Anxiety was exasperating.

I wasn't sure how long it took me to transition from our goodnights to my dreamland. Regardless, I knew I had arrived when I was in the lake, lying on a paddle board, stomach down, paddling with my arms toward Boulder Island. The wind caused ripples on the water's surface, making slapping and gurgling sounds against my board. The sun felt warm on my back.

I heard a voice. Calling my name.

Straining, I looked behind me to see who it was.

Dex. He stood on top of our hill, waving for me to come home.

I wanted to return. I did.

Yet, something compelled me to stay the course.

So instead, I looked ahead at the island.

Only now, the skies were dark, nearly pitch black. A wispy fog rose from the shoreline.

My pulse quickened.

The girl.

She stood in the water up to her knees. Her full white skirt floated around her like a jellyfish with tentacles. Her long blonde hair was wet. Her sash was no longer tied around her waist like the night Dex and I had gone camping. Instead, it was wrapped around her neck. Her skin was deathly pale.

And she pointed at me.

The water became rougher and my board thumped on the surface.

Thump, thump, thump.

I clutched my board so I wouldn't roll off.

Thump, thump...

THUMP.

The last thump was so violent, my eyes flew open.

Like the fog in my dream, mist streamed from my mouth with each exhale.

Thump.

Did that just happen?

Had my nightmare chased me into reality? Because my side of the bed had lifted and dropped. Literally. While I was *awake*.

Dex was still asleep. The man could sleep through anything.

I scanned our bedroom.

Nothing seemed strange except for the mist billowing from my nose and lips. From Dex's, too. The temperature outside had probably plummeted during the night. If I was brave, I would've gotten out of bed and closed the open windows.

Instead, I shut my eyes and spooned against Dex, wrapping my arms around him. Waiting for sunrise to save me from my terrifying imagination.

12

TWO WEEKS AFTER the bed thumping incident, I barely thought about my nightmare which had featured the pale, wet girl pointing at me as she stood in the lake near the rocky shoreline of Boulder Island. I had even agreed with Dex on the fundamental causes for my surreal experience: exhaustion and stress.

Instead of lightening my workload, though, I became even busier, throwing myself into physical chores at Windy Hill Farm by unpacking boxes, hanging pictures, and planting flowers. I also maintained a frenetic pace virtually, impressing Cecelia and my D&B colleagues with my work output.

The remedy for worry is staying busy, Mom used to preach.

I validated her words because I didn't have time for worry. And stress had difficulty fermenting without it.

Today would be more of the same.

Busy started with the imminent arrival of our hens and rooster.

Our coop was ready. Similar to our house, the large hutch was paneled in wide, vertical white siding and topped with a black metal roof. I even included a flower box on the structure's eye-level window which doubled as a hatch to collect eggs. The chicken enclosure included a long fenced-in run. I planned to leave the gate open during the day so the flock could roam freely on our property. Before sunset, when stomachs started growling in the predator world, I'd tuck the chickens inside their coop to keep them safe.

Roxanne was my chicken liaison. Located on the other side of Honesdale, she raised a variety of egg laying breeds—Cinnamon Queen, Plymouth Rock, Brahma, Lavender Pekin, and Rhode Island Red. Most importantly, she served as a consultant for every stage of egg production. Since my recent bird encounters had mostly been with low flying seagulls on the Potomac, I was a sponge around Roxy, absorbing every tidbit of knowledge on all things *poultry*.

For me, having chickens would be a test of my maternal instincts. While most people chose dogs to practice their parental dispositions, chickens presented a similar exercise. Affection, feeding, hygiene, and protection: every living thing needed them.

Only, chickens offered a part of themselves every morning at breakfast, sunny side up.

Roxy had texted me from the bottom of our driveway, giving Dex and me enough time to position ourselves beside the coop.

"A welcoming party for...*chickens?*" Dex asked.

"Don't diss the flock." I playfully elbowed him. "Roxy says chickens can outperform dogs in intelligence challenges. I'm serious. There's data."

"Of course there is." Dex rolled his eyes while looking at me. "You're not going to begin laying factoids on me like your new bestie—the chicken whisperer. Are you?"

The van crested the incline of our driveway, continuing toward us.

"*Laying,*" I mused. "I heard what you did there. And what if I do?"

"I'll cry fowl."

And here I thought chicken jokes were limited to when they crossed the street.

My husband swallowed his laughter as the van labeled *Breed, Brood, and Biddy* parked and the vehicle's door opened. Roxy, with her wild auburn hair, stepped out in skinny jeans, boots, and a tight yellow T-shirt that read *Eggsellent.*

"I've been so stoked for this day," she cheered, rhythmically jutting her chin in and out with each step. "Remember. They've already socialized with one another, including with your cock, who's gotten impressively big."

Dex's eyes widened.

Big and cock were undoubtedly popular words on Mars.

Once Roxy opened the back of the van, she proceeded to release our eleven hens onto the grass, one at a time, followed by my Brahma rooster whom I had named Omelet. Because I had sprinkled feed and fresh apple slices on the grassy pathway leading into their chicken run, the flock meandered in and out through the open gate.

Except for one.

My Lavender Pekin hen whom I had affectionately named Biddy. She remained, pecking at the ground around my feet. Topped with a red fleshy crown, Biddy was beautiful. She had light gray feathers that reflected shades of lavender in the sunshine.

"I think she imprinted on you during your visits," Roxy said. "Go ahead. Pick her up."

Biddy didn't even try to run away when I bent down and scooped her into my arms. She remained there, content, as Roxy refreshed me on acclimating my feathered friends to their new home. While listening, I ran my hand over Biddy's silky feathers until her eyes closed. All the while, Dex patiently stood by my side, seeming focused on Roxy's auburn frizz which grew wilder and fuller with every bluster of wind.

After Roxy left, Dex and I went our separate ways for the remainder of the day. He headed to the barn to retrieve the riding mower. And I spent the day toggling between keeping a watchful eye on the flock and gardening in the greenhouse.

We each had plenty of work until dinnertime.

Supper was on the back patio, watching the sunset over the lake, which I was certain would never get old.

Dishes were the only chore left since our chickens were already enclosed in their coop and Dex had locked all our outbuildings. Even though we had an eco-friendly dishwasher, we enjoyed doing the dishes together. I washed. He dried.

Before retiring for the night, we had agreed to watch television in the great room.

Our day had been close to perfect until Dex turned on our new television, the one mounted over the fireplace. Instead of a high definition picture, the television projected grainy snow and emitted a garbled roar—a loud, ear piercing *herrrrrr*.

"I've got it," Dex said, as he got up from the couch and grabbed a

47

small flashlight from the end table. "It's probably a loose cable wire on the back of the TV."

I crisscrossed my arms, running my hands over my biceps.

"Did you lower the thermostat?" I asked.

"Jesus, Nora. One issue at a time."

I wanted to protest about his snarky-ness but an escalating rumble distracted me. I stayed completely still and listened.

An actual tremor followed.

The house shook. Not violently, but enough to tilt picture frames hanging on our walls. A crystal globe paperweight chattered on top of our coffee table. The water and ice in my glass vibrated.

In a seamless movement, I jumped up from the couch and made my way to Dex's extended hand. My "log" in the room.

"An earthquake?" I asked, clasping his fingers. "Should we head outside to be safe?"

Holding hands, we walked toward one of the sliding glass doors leading out to the patio.

The light pendants hanging from the timbered beams above us began to sway. A door slammed somewhere in the house. The lights flickered as the television blipped off.

I held my breath, hoping the shaking would pass quickly.

"This area can have mild tremors," Dex said, still sounding calm. "Nothing significant, thankfully. Let's stand here until it's over."

A booming crack assaulted our ears, like when a lightning bolt connects with the ground too close for comfort. Whether the sound came from outside or inside, I had no clue.

At the same time, a few of our lightbulbs burst. Some sort of power surge, no doubt.

Dex thrust a slider open and pulled me outside onto the patio.

The night sky was clear, dappled in stars. No storms were on the horizon.

"I think the sound came from back here," he said, turning on the flashlight. "Behind our bedroom." He continued to clutch my hand as we walked over.

Behind our bedroom.

The location sparked a memory in my lockbox of things I wished to forget…*but couldn't.*

48

The chickens clucked frantically from their coop on the other side of the house.

As Dex shined the flashlight on the ground behind our bedroom, my brain made the connection to my dreaded memory.

The sinkhole.

In the dark, with the flashlight beam illuminating the backyard, my eyes couldn't deny what I saw.

The sinkhole had returned.

Only, it was twice the size and the ground had dropped a full foot below the surface.

13

Sunday, June 8, 2025
Windy Hill Farm: Boulder, Pennsylvania

OMELET CROWED AT the crack of dawn. Waking up to his *call to rise* was wonderful and I couldn't wait to check on the flock, especially on Biddy.

Thunder rumbled in the distance. The weather forecast called for mid-morning rain.

My excitement dampened when I remembered the night before.

The earthquake. The sinkhole.

How I had slept so soundly was beyond me, except I had stayed pressed against Dex. His warmth and heartbeat grounded me in the dark. Crisp mountain air and hard work had probably contributed.

As we made the bed together, we discussed our plans for the day.

We'd start by flipping through the local television channels to learn the extent of the damage inflicted in the area by the quake.

When we had a better idea of what had taken place, I'd access the website for the United States Geological Survey (USGS). In Dex's line of work, he was familiar with this science bureau, a part of the Department of the Interior. Apparently, people who felt an earthquake could report it online. USGS displayed maps and information about all sorts of geological events, especially quakes.

While I submitted information to USGS, Dex would contact three people: our construction manager, the engineer who repaired our sinkhole (rather, who *attempted* to repair it), and our insurance company to initiate a claim.

As we sipped coffees at our kitchen island and navigated from one morning news report to the next, my confusion grew. Station hopping proved to be a dead end.

"Absolutely no one is reporting a strong tremor or quake," I said.

"Weird." He paused as if an idea was percolating. "Hey, don't most stations have a hotline where you can report news?"

"Great idea."

On my cellphone, I asked Siri to get the telephone number for the closest news station to Boulder. Siri found a station in Scranton, and I called the hotline.

"WSET's news hotline," someone said. "You inform, we report."

The broadcaster was named Jim Stevens and I answered all his contact questions, including where the news event had occurred, the date, and at what time.

"The tremor was strong enough to burst lightbulbs in our home," I said. "And to leave behind a sinkhole that's about eight feet around. Has anyone reported something similar?"

I avoided the weeds with Jim, never mentioning the sinkhole had formed once before and that an engineer had tried to repair it with concrete and rebar.

"Let me put you on hold," he said. "I'll find out."

Country music replaced his voice.

Minutes later, I heard a click on the line. The song abruptly ended.

"My station manager recognized your last name from a national news story," Jim said. "Are you the same Nora Bliss from D.C.? The one who was thrown onto the tracks and survived? With help from a good Samaritan? Happened about a year ago."

The Nightmare at Union Station just kept giving.

I inhaled through my nose. "That's me," I said with my exhale.

"Listen." His voice had turned kind and empathetic, less businesslike. "We've had no reports of any seismic activity in Wayne County last night. And we'd know. We've got two reporters who live out in that area. One's in Honesdale. The other's in Waymart—that's close to you. Anyway, my manager happens to have a relative who works for IRIS…"

"IRIS?" I interrupted, not sure if IRIS was a woman or an organization.

"Oh. IRIS is the Incorporated Research Institutions for Seismology. They work closely with FEMA and the USGS. Damn it. I did it again. Sorry. They stand for…"

"No problem. I know those acronyms."

"Okay. Good. IRIS has a station that records seismic activity in the area. It's located in nearby Promised Land State Park. In Greentown. My boss wouldn't mind giving a call to his cousin. Should he reach out?"

I told Jim how grateful I'd be if his boss inquired. He joked that he hoped I'd remember the station's extra efforts in case the sinkhole swallowed our house and WSET requested an exclusive. When I didn't laugh, he apologized, acknowledging that I had already been through enough, given I had been thrown onto the tracks and all.

Regrettably, the *"and all"* were multiplying.

Since we were still in the early hours of morning, Dex left the house to get a head start on his chores before the rain hit. He agreed to make his calls about the sinkhole when he returned. As for me, I went out to the coop to feed the flock and open the gate. I even collected an egg!

An hour later, Jim called me as I returned to the house.

"You were right," he said. "My boss's cousin confirmed there was seismic activity last night, but it was isolated to your precise location. Unusual, right? No worries, though. He's heard of this happening when a water table dries up and the void collapses on itself. He recommended calling a geophysical engineer. And seriously, if your sinkhole gets bigger, maybe we can do a story."

Thanks, but no thanks. Dex and I had moved to Boulder to get farther away from the grid, not to garner more attention by being at the center of a news feature. As it was, my reputation as the woman who had gotten pushed onto the tracks at Union Station stuck to me like gum on a shoe. Nevertheless, I remained gracious and thanked Jim for his assistance.

As I disconnected from the call, our large television in the great room blipped on, projecting grainy snow like it had yesterday. The volume was on seek and destroy, blaring that annoying *herrrrr*. The sound was overwhelming. It agitated my nerves. Made my head pulse. Or was it more of a throb? Pulse or throb, my brain felt like it might explode and splatter on the walls. Okay, *slight* exaggeration.

Bottomline, this house pissed me off. We had poured love into every nook and cranny. Everything was new and shiny. Custom. Top of the line. And this was what we got in return? A house that wanted to toy with us? To make us miserable?

I briefly closed my eyes, ignoring the noisy assault.

My self-talk was spiraling.

I was spiraling, drowning in the whitewater.

My "log" in this moment had to be logic. Somehow the television's timer had been programmed to turn on. And somehow, the channel for our cable (channel three) had been accidentally changed; hence, the grainy snow. Fixing both would be easy.

I had to resist panic and irrational fears.

Everyone knew: New houses were *not* haunted.

Taking a deep breath, I slowly released it, feeling like I had regained a smidge of control.

As I walked toward the remote on the coffee table, the room temperature dropped. The goosebumps on my arms confirmed it.

That's right. Dex needed to check the thermostat. I had felt a similar chill last night and had mentioned it to him. Only, the tremor and sinkhole had distracted us.

I reached for the remote, but the television turned off.

Before I even touched the device.

Keeping my emotions in check would be tough in this house.

Taming my imagination? Darn near impossible.

I closed the distance between me and the television. An inanimate device was not going to best me. I'd remove the television from the fireplace if that was the only way to regain control. I could even picture myself stomping on it. Until it was destroyed.

For now, I simply unplugged the device, knowing Dex would fix the problems later and reconnect it.

Light from the window cascaded across the black screen.

That's when I saw them. When my heart stalled.

Two words had been fingered on the dusty screen…

FIND THEM

14

EVERY MORNING, AFTER I fed the flock and opened their gate at the end of the run, Biddy would keep a step or two behind me as I continued with my chores. She'd stay with me while I tended to my plants in the greenhouse and harvested the ripe veggies. She'd accompany me while I watered the apple trees in our small orchard. And she'd cluck behind me, strutting with her head held high, as I entered the house to prep Dex and my dinner for the end of the workday.

We had a routine. A togetherness.

I even kept small bowls with feed and water in a kitchen nook.

As I placed silverware in the drawer, I was glad the engineer and his team had wrapped up their repair work on our persistent sinkhole. No more drilling. No more beeping as concrete trucks reversed to get closer to their target. No more strangers on our land barking orders to one another. Just Dex doing his work and Biddy and I doing ours.

Thankfully, the tremor hadn't caused any structural damage to our home, above or below ground. More positives: Our water table was fine. Our rock sediment, stable. Our ground structure, strong. And in terms of financing, Evan's company, since it had done the original sinkhole repair, was working with our insurance company to cover all new costs.

Take that you fuckity fuck sinkhole.

The final assessment was that a rare seismic occurrence had taken place. No way to predict it. No way to prevent it.

Bottomline, we lived on a spinning planet—one expanding and contracting. And sometimes, shit happened. That was the engineer's conclusion anyway, with a little more science lingo mixed in. But that was the gist of it.

Perhaps recent events were trying to teach me that not *everything* had an explanation.

Our television in the great room, for example.

While Dex had found a loose cable wire and fixed it, there was still no explanation on why the words *FIND THEM* had been written on the screen. If some other message had been fingered in the dust, it wouldn't have been so disconcerting. But these were the same two words, written in all caps, that had been carved into the flagstone nearly a year ago, before our house was built.

I heard our windchimes on the patio, dancing in the breeze to their own music. Despite my unsettled feelings about the unexplained, I smiled. Windy Hill Farm had captured my heart. Mysterious words couldn't change that. Or any other freakish occurrence for that matter. My soul had found the very spot for which it was intended. The place where I could grow and thrive.

From outside, Dex opened a sliding door into the great room and walked inside. After taking off his boots, he placed them on a nearby doormat.

Biddy clucked at him. Loudly.

"I keep telling you," Dex said. "Bonny shouldn't be in here."

"Biddy."

He lowered his chin and raised his eyebrows. "The chicken."

"Hen."

"Jesus, Nora. You're turning into Roxy. At least get her a crate for the house." He tapped his smartwatch. "Did you get the text alert? About the prisoners?"

"No. I'm not wearing my watch. What's happened?"

"Let's catch the news on TV."

Our fickle television was in the same category as the sinkhole. I stayed away from both.

Dex grabbed the remote and pressed the on button.

55

National news was already airing the story. The second prisoner from the Fairview escape had been caught in Arizona during a traffic stop for an expired registration sticker on the license plate. Coverage showed him handcuffed and being guided into a patrol car.

"Told you escapees would be far away from here," Dex boasted.

"I *told you so* is definitely from Mars."

"*Mars?* What does that mean?"

Biddy pecked one of his feet. She got it.

"Don't start following me around," he snarked at her. "I weed whack. As in, regularly."

"Although the third prisoner is still at large," the television reporter said, holding the mic close to her red lips, "a resident of Lake Wallenpaupack, in Pennsylvania's Pocono Mountains, snapped a cellphone picture of someone who resembles Richard Peter, the remaining escapee. The photo you're about to see was distributed via the Associated Press yesterday."

My throat was dry. I could barely swallow.

Lake Wallenpaupack was less than 25 miles from us.

Dex was notably speechless about the nearby locale.

Half of the TV screen displayed a blurry photograph of a guy sporting a long grayish-white beard, along with dark sunglasses and a brimmed hat. The other half of the screen showed Richard Peter's mugshot from his arrest five years ago.

The resemblance gave me chills.

According to the report, Richard Peter's likeness had been spotted on the shoreline of a secluded cove on Lake Wallenpaupack. One of the boaters had the wherewithal to take a photograph before the suspicious man retreated into the woods.

I wondered if I could respond at that level: *To think quickly. And act quickly.*

Dex turned off the television. He walked over and wrapped his arms around me.

"Remember my rumored business trip to LA?" He frowned while looking down at me. "I got a call from my boss a half hour ago. The trip has been scheduled."

"When? For how long?"

"I'm supposed to leave Thursday. For two weeks. I'm canceling."

"You can't do that, Dex. They depend on you."

Releasing me, he covered his eyes with his hands and rubbed. He was clearly tormented.

"I'll be fine," I assured him.

"Your sister," he said, refocusing. "She could stay here with you. That might work."

"Except I don't want to depend on Madeline every time you go out of town."

Biddy cackled.

"You're not thinking Bonny here can protect you," he teased.

"Biddy."

"The hen."

"*Aww,* you said hen instead of chicken. See? You're learning."

A thought shot into my head.

"Are you taking your nine-millimeter to LA?" I asked.

"No." He raised his eyebrows. "Are you thinking what I'm thinking? That I could teach you how to use it? As protection while I'm gone?"

I smiled.

Never in my wildest dreams had I pictured myself brandishing a pistol. But Madeline's words had begun to resonate with me: *Safety requires skills.*

After placing the flock securely in their coop, I spent the rest of the afternoon as Dex's student, learning how to handle a firearm and shoot with accuracy.

Not going to lie. I was way better than pitiful.

15

Friday, June 20, 2025
Windy Hill Farm: Boulder, Pennsylvania

I HEADED TO the barn for heavy duty clippers. A branch in the apple orchard had snapped and was still dangling from the tree's young trunk. I had company. Biddy followed closely behind me.

Dex had flown to LA yesterday. Which meant, last night was the first time I had slept at the farm without his warmth and protection beside me. With his recommendation, I had tucked his loaded pistol under his pillow, with the barrel facing away from me. The direction of a firearm's barrel seemed obvious, but Dex had hammered into me that keeping the pistol pointing away from the body was safety 101. According to him, expert shooters could become foolishly comfortable with their guns, leading to carelessness—an accident waiting to happen.

When Omelet crowed earlier this morning, in concert with the sun peeking over the mountain tops, I was relieved. One night down. Only 13 more to go until Dex came home.

Daylight just felt safer. Even more so since I was accessorized with Dex's weapon. He had adjusted his ankle holster and calf strap to accommodate me as best he could, but I had to wear a hand towel against my skin to make it fit snugly.

At first, I had resisted being armed 24/7. But when Dex asked me why I wanted to be protected at night and vulnerable during the day, I couldn't produce a logical answer, especially since my accident at Union Station had taken place in daylight.

No doubt Dex's Wild, Wild West pistol posse would be extremely proud that I was carrying.

The front of the barn was where my husband's office was located so I headed toward the back where the farm equipment was stored. He hung landscaping tools like branch clippers on the wall to the right of our riding mower, backhoe, and utility vehicle.

I entered the code to activate the garage door and it opened with a jolt and rattle.

To my surprise, one of our canvas tarps was crumpled in a heap to the left of our UTV. An empty candy bar wrapper peeked out from one of the folds. Why hadn't Dex cleaned up his mess?

Refolding the tarp, I placed it back on the shelf.

As I walked to the tool wall after stuffing the wrapper into my back jean pocket, I rehearsed how I'd scold him.

Odd. One of the hooks was empty.

I scanned the other tools to identify which one was missing. I knew our tool inventory; Dex had schooled me on our collection. That's how I knew the missing tool was Dex's machete knife. I wasn't finding it. I'd fuss about that, too, because what if the clippers had been misplaced? Surely, he could put things away where they belonged. Or what was the point of having a tool wall?

Sighing, I grabbed the clippers and headed out. After Biddy cleared the barn, I pressed the button to lower the garage door.

With my hen a few paces behind me, we headed toward the orchard located to the right of my greenhouse.

Three vultures circled in the blue skies. Nature was always busy. Animals were always in search of their next meal.

In the distance, I spotted a reddish brown *something* between two apple trees. Was a fox hunkered down in the grass waiting to pounce on a mole or mouse?

Something lifted with the breeze. Wait. Was that a...*feather?*

I dropped my clippers and took off running.

Biddy shrieked and flapped her wings, briefly getting airborne.

Oh dear God!

The *something* was my hen Cinnamon, lying dead in the orchard.

Kneeling beside her, I lifted her head. Cinnamon's neck had been snapped. A bone protruded from torn skin on the back of her neck.

I didn't understand. Tears streamed from my eyes.

This clearly wasn't the work of a natural predator. No fox, coyote, bobcat, or eagle would've made the kill and then run or flown off without its harvest. And Cinnamon had died at least an hour ago. Flies were already swarming.

A wave of nausea overwhelmed me. As hard as I tried to force my breakfast back down, my eggs and toast erupted all over the grass. Sweat beaded on my forehead. My hands trembled.

It took several minutes before my stomach settled.

Wiping my mouth with the heel of my hand, I looked around. Could someone be on our property? Could Richard Peter have traveled 25 miles from Lake Wallenpaupack to *here?*

If he had, snapping my hen's neck would be nothing to him.

After all, he had murdered a teenager, a female, landing him at Fairview. *That* and he was a bonafide sicko. I had read a news article after he escaped. Richard Peter had strangled his victim and shoved a used condom down her throat. His DNA guaranteed his conviction. In fact, a psychologist at his trial had described him as being afraid of his own evil, as knowing he couldn't stop killing. He planted the condom to ensure he'd get locked up.

Maybe years behind bars had changed his mind. Maybe he had escaped to kill again.

A roar started to build beyond the western edge of our property.

I was familiar with the strange phenomenon by now.

Reaching out my hands while still kneeling, Biddy accepted my invitation. I held her, hunched over as the gust slammed into us.

The wind raced toward the mountains and was gone soon after, taking the embedded cries with it.

Feeling shaky after unloading my breakfast, I began walking back to the house for a granola bar.

Obviously, I'd need to be observant around the property to notice if anything else was suspicious. Like maybe that candy wrapper and missing tool weren't Dex's doing.

I stopped for a minute to roll up my pantleg, exposing my husband's pistol strapped around the hand towel and my calf. Showing I was packing might deter someone if they were watching me. They wouldn't know I had only learned to use a firearm three days ago. Anyway, with my pantleg folded up, I'd have easier access if I needed to *deploy* it—the official term.

Even before I entered the house through our front door, I could hear that blasted television.

Another wave of nausea swelled in my throat.

Squeezing my eyes shut for a second, I hoped to reset myself. From scared (and sick to my stomach) to Rambo.

"Think quickly. Act quickly," I whispered out loud.

I deployed the pistol. I didn't cock the hammer, but I visualized how to do it if needed.

Stepping inside the house, I quietly closed the door behind me.

The first item on my to-do list, once again, was unplugging that bastard of a television in the great room. Reaching and clutching, I yanked the cord that was camouflaged between the stone fireplace and the adjacent built-in bookcase.

The television blipped off.

With Dex's pistol at the ready, I methodically carried out the next items on my mental checklist. I went room to room, checking every nook and cranny in the house, including the basement. I closed and locked all the doors and windows. No one was hiding. All was clear.

Although I preferred fresh mountain air to air conditioning, I turned the AC back on so the windows could stay closed. At least I'd feel insulated from dangers beyond our house.

As Dex suggested, I had purchased a crate for Biddy's house visits and overnights. In our bedroom, I placed her inside it and grabbed the key ring from my dresser.

I locked the front door on my way to finish chores.

Outside, I collected the flock and placed them inside their hutch. I'd feed them at the end of the day, but this way, they'd be safer until I got a handle on what was going on. And I would not lose another member of my flock.

Walking the length of our property to the east, I grabbed a shovel from the greenhouse to bury Cinnamon, which I did on the orchard's edge. Leaving her carcass fair game for vultures didn't feel right. She deserved dignity in death.

After returning the shovel, I locked the greenhouse door and hurried back to the house.

"Don't mess with me asshole," I screamed at the top of my lungs before unlocking the front door. "I'll go Rambo on you!" I brandished the pistol to emphasize my point, not even knowing for sure that a person was responsible for Cinnamon's death.

Once inside, I bolted the door behind me.

I spent the rest of the day on my computer, getting lost in my work by designing a campaign for one of D&B's potato chip clients. Despite the stress of day two, I was happy with my creativity. Cecelia was also pleased when she reviewed my drafts online.

Orange rays of sunlight streamed through the sliding glass doors leading to the patio overlooking the lake. Sunset approached, reigniting my angst. My mouth grew dry. I had to hurry.

I fed my flock faster than ever.

Back inside our house for the night, I turned on every outdoor light we had. The barn, greenhouse, driveway, our home—all illuminated by spotlights and outdoor lighting.

When Dex called, I didn't mention any of it. Instead, I thanked him for teaching me how to use his pistol because I felt safe. I mean, why worry him about something I couldn't prove? Been there, done that. Anyway, his job wasn't optional, and I was an adult with a gun.

After our goodbyes, another wave of nausea reared its ugly head. Again. *Really?*

I remembered. I had forgotten to eat a granola bar earlier. And had, in fact, worked the entire day without sustenance. Still, one throw-up and two additional bouts of nausea? Unusual.

Biddy clucked from her crate as I walked into our bathroom to grab a pregnancy test from my toiletries closet. I kept a few test kits on hand since Dex and I weren't *not* trying.

The nausea made me curious.

Fifteen minutes after peeing on the stick, I checked the results.

Positive.

Were the results accurate?

I reread the directions more closely. Studied the possible illustrated results. Line, no line. Pretty straightforward.

From every perspective, the stick read positive.

Lightning flashed. Thunder rumbled shortly after.

My flood gates opened. In a blink, I was crying hysterically.

Sobbing and gasping for air.

Day two without Dex had been a clusterfuck of the irrational. Of being controlled by my own fears. I understood that now.

If Dex came home this instant, I'd be embarrassed. Every single light was on—inside and out. Our house was locked up tight. Not to mention, I had unplugged our possessed television.

I'd bawl to Dex about finding Cinnamon dead, her neck snapped. I'd mention the tarp and missing tool in the barn. And ramble on about my suspicion that Richard Peter himself was lurking around Windy Hill Farm, playing his deadly game of cat and mouse.

I'd sound one egg short of crazy.

How could I ever be a good mother?

I was a hot mess.

16

Saturday, June 21, 2025
Windy Hill Farm: Boulder, Pennsylvania

LIGHTNING STROBED THROUGH the windows in our bedroom, followed by a crack of thunder. I wasn't sure of the time, but I guessed it was after midnight.

Between lightning flashes, the room became pitch black. No hazy glow seeped in from our outdoor lighting. The red dot on our television had disappeared. And our bathroom, normally lit by a nightlight, was dark. Clearly, the electricity had shut off in the storm.

I rolled onto my back.

Funny how storms affected me differently. When Dex was beside me in bed, they beckoned me to snuggle, to feel my husband's protective arms around me. And while being serenaded by the maracas of rain and the drum rolls of thunder, I could be lulled back to sleep under my cozy blanket of security.

Alone, though, storms were mostly foreboding. Like this one.

Despite the lack of air conditioning, I had goosebumps.

Bottomline, sleep wasn't going to happen.

Biddy must have felt the unsettled atmosphere, too. From her crate, she cackled.

My bed thumped like someone wanted me to wake up. It was reminiscent of my paddle board nightmare to Boulder Island when my dream reality had followed me into wakefulness.

I deeply inhaled to ward off my pesky, unrelenting imagination.

A flare of lightning brightened the room.

My pulse spiked.

By my bedside, I saw a figure. A silhouette. A man by its size.

He leaned over me.

His hands were reaching out. Fingers splayed.

Warm breath violated my skin.

I was in between frames within a snapshot of time—the two seconds when everything would change. The first second, I was safe, and then *click,* the next I'd be fighting for my life.

The figure's hands clasped around my neck, instantly constricting my airflow. Each fingertip pressed deeper and deeper. Clasped tighter and tighter.

I remembered what intent felt like. It felt like the man at Union Station once he grabbed my bicep. There was no mistaking what he wanted. He wanted me out of his way. He wanted me *dead.*

This figure. These hands. They wanted the same.

The pressure on my neck was crushing. Unbearable.

My eyes might pop from their sockets.

If I didn't find a rescue log soon, I would pass out.

I had to do something. The life growing inside me depended on it.

Despite the mental fog that thickened with oxygen deprivation, I thought of something. My husband's pistol was under his pillow.

The figure applied even more force, pressing me down deeper into the mattress.

I reached under Dex's pillow with my left hand, my movement concealed by darkness. My fingers frantically searched.

The man grunted, as if making his final push to the finish line.

I felt the cool metal of the handgun. My log in the rapids.

A burst of adrenaline surged through my bloodstream.

I clutched the gun, more like I was holding a rock than a pistol.

Without thinking, I swung my arm toward the figure until I felt the handgun connect with his skull. I had no idea where I hit him exactly, but I swung again and again, crashing the weapon with blunt force into his head.

I would've done it a thousand times if I had to.

His hands released my neck.

I gasped for air, filling my lungs.

I hit him one more time. As hard as I could.

He slumped off me, falling to the floor. Silent.

The bed sheets felt like tangled vines around my legs. I kicked and kicked until they released me.

I needed to call 911.

My cellphone. It was on my nightstand charging. I fumbled to find it in the dark and when I did, I bolted off the bed on Dex's side, still holding the pistol.

A miracle happened.

The house rumbled as the electricity powered up.

Racing to the door, I flipped on the light switch.

Our lamps lit.

I backed into the corner on Dex's side, away from the intruder. He had dropped onto the floor on my side of the bed so I could no longer see him from where I stood.

My thumb trembled as I tapped 911 on my cellphone's keypad.

Once connected, I told the operator—with my neck throbbing and voice shaking—that someone had broken into our home and tried to strangle me. That I had knocked him out. That I'd shoot him pointblank if I had to.

"You're doing great," the operator calmly said. "Can you tell me, is he conscious?"

Placing my cellphone on "speaker," I laid it down on the mattress. I inched over toward my side of the bed. My arms were extended in front of me. The pistol was cocked, ready to fire.

The intruder was on his back. Blood oozed from various gashes and wounds around his right temple. His eyelids were still closed but quivering. He released a moan.

"He's coming to," I said. "There's something else."

Looking at him, I had no doubt the intruder had cut off his long beard. His facial hair was clipped unevenly. He had probably used Dex's machete knife for the haphazard trim.

I felt a twisted sense of relief. If this monster's weapon of choice had been a knife, I wouldn't be alive. Lucky for me, his was strangulation. So I had been given a fighting chance.

"The intruder," I panted to the operator. "He's Richard Peter."

17

Saturday, June 21, 2025
Windy Hill Farm: Boulder, Pennsylvania

MY ARMS SHUDDERED as I aimed the pistol in Richard Peter's direction, hoping my adrenaline would hold out long enough for officers to arrive and take over.

I had moved by the door leading to the hallway. From this vantage point, I could only see the escapee's legs.

Hopefully, I wouldn't need to fire the gun.

I wasn't sure if it was in me to shoot someone, even when that someone had almost killed me.

Damn it. His legs moved.

Then his bloodied fingers clutched my comforter.

"Stay where you are," I ordered. "Police are on the way."

He ignored me and pulled himself onto his feet, standing about six feet tall. He touched the right side of his face where I had bludgeoned him with the pistol. Blood streamed down his neck, soaking the collar of his soil stained T-shirt. His underarms were wet with perspiration and I smelled his soured ripeness.

If I diverted his attention, stalled him, then maybe he'd stay put. I could buy some time. Time to hear sirens in the background.

"You killed my hen," I blurted out. "Why? For food?"

"I didn't kill your fucking chicken," he snapped. "What did you think I'd do? Pluck its feathers? Build me an open fire and roast it? Mix up fancy dipping sauces? I'm a fugitive for Christ sakes."

The man was a liar. The only truth from his mouth was that he

67

was a fugitive. Who else would've broken Cinnamon's neck?

"If you were hungry enough, you would've," I argued.

"Lady, you're a stupid bitch. But you're right about one thing."

"What?"

"I'm starved," he said. "I'm no do-it-yourselfer, though. I reckoned if I killed you in your sleep, then the stuff in your fridge would be mine for the taking. Easy food. Supplies, too."

He took three steps toward me, ignoring my cellphone on the bed which was still connected to the 911 operator.

"My plan can still work with a few tweaks," he added, in a more ominous tone. "Cops won't get here for fifteen minutes. And I didn't avoid capture all this time to get caught now."

"Stop. I mean it." I straightened my arms and double checked my aim. "Or I'll shoot."

He paused and narrowed his eyes. "You think I didn't watch you learn how to fire a gun? Or hurl and boohoo over that dead chicken? You're an amateur, lady. *Not* Rambo. You won't take me down."

A feeling of violation washed over me. It felt dirty. Perverse.

Richard Peter had been trespassing and staying on our property. He had been watching us. Judging us.

I felt victimized.

He started walking toward me again.

I aimed for his thigh. "Do. Not. Move."

He took another step.

I pulled the trigger.

The blast violently rattled the windows and made my eardrums pop and ring.

Biddy shrieked, frantically flapping her wings. Loosened feathers escaped from her crate.

Richard Peter dropped to the floor, clutching his thigh.

"Motherfucker!" he cried, grimacing.

Blood soaked the denim of his pantleg. His hands turned crimson.

"You've hit a goddamn artery, bitch!"

I cocked the hammer. "If you move again," I warned, "I'll splat your brains all over this bedroom."

Strange. I was acting more like a warrior than a peacemaker.

Sirens sounded in the distance.

"I'll bleed out first," he said solemnly, his skin turning ashen.

Murderers were such hypocrites.

Richard Peter wasn't afraid of killing others—even with his bare hands; it was his *own* dying that terrified him. Which meant, oddly enough, that he was probably telling the truth about his condition.

Keeping the pistol pointed at his head, I backed up to Dex's walk-in closet and reached inside, grabbing a belt. I walked back and tossed it to the pathetic creep.

"If you want to live, make a tourniquet," I said.

I told the 911 operator where we were located in the house. Minutes passed before rotating red lights from police cruisers and a SWAT van flashed around my bedroom walls.

Three officers stood on the other side of my window (the one facing the backyard). Their pistols were deployed and pointed at the escapee who was still pulling one end of the belt to keep pressure on his thigh.

"It's okay, Ma'am," an officer shouted through the glass. "We've got him in our sights. Go to one of the sliding glass doors and unlock it. We'll take it from here."

Grabbing my cellphone from the bed, I jogged to the door while thanking the 911 operator before disconnecting.

Once the police were inside and had the situation under control, I called Dex as I sat in the great room. I shared the basics about the horrific ordeal and vowed to call him back as soon as I could. He wanted to book a flight home, that minute, and I made him promise to wait until we could discuss our next steps. He agreed.

Thankfully, a female officer grabbed the crate from the bedroom before interviewing me. In my presence, Biddy calmed down right away. She helped settle my nerves as well.

Four hours later, as Omelet crowed to welcome the morning sun, law enforcement, forensics, and news media left our house, having gathered all the evidence and information they needed.

Earlier, I had overheard an officer say that Richard Peter had been transported to the hospital in Honesdale where he'd undergo surgery for his gunshot wound. Sometime soon, though, he'd be heading back to Fairview to resume his life sentence.

I called Dex again, explaining the timeline between Richard Peter and our property. He had made his way from Lake Wallenpaupack to our farm and had been sleeping in the barn. Worse, since our house was mostly unlocked, he was able to get inside, both day and night. Not only that, but he confessed to officers that he had initially found our property after the jailbreak. Before our house was built.

"He's been toying with us," I told Dex. "I'm sure of it. Richard Peter was the one who messed with our television. Who wrote *FIND THEM*. Who killed Cinnamon. Who thumped our bed at night. I can't tell you how relieved I am that he's been recaptured. That all these mysteries can be explained."

"What about the girl you saw on Boulder Island?"

"I think you and Madeline are right. Kids must be hanging out on the island at night. I'll buy a paddle board and head out there sometime, to quiet my imagination."

"And the sinkhole?"

"I'll accept the engineer's conclusion: Shit happens."

"I'm proud of you," Dex cooed. "To begin with, you defended yourself tonight. So bravely, Nora. No need to doubt yourself anymore. You may be a peacemaker, but you'll fight if needed. And now all your worries—about our property, the girl on Boulder Island, the Fairview escapees—can be put to rest. Can be behind us."

There were new worries on the horizon, of course. Being parents would be a huge role for us. One with immeasurable responsibilities. But I'd wait to tell Dex the exciting news when he got home. When we could be in each other's arms.

"Please don't cut your trip short," I said. "Madeline is on her way to help me clean up the bedroom. I'll be fine. The danger is over."

"You shouldn't be alone, especially at night," he countered. "What you just went through was significant. Mind blowing. I wouldn't be surprised if it triggers a panic attack."

"If I need Madeline to stay here, I'll ask her. But you've got a job to do there. Impress Wakeford Global like you always do."

I shook my head at my absurd imagination. "Anyway, at least we know Windy Hill Farm isn't cursed. Or haunted."

After pausing, I added, "I'll finally be able to sleep soundly."

18

TWELVE HOURS AFTER my terrifying ordeal, a heavy cloak of exhaustion blanketed me. I was eager to fall into a deep sleep and mentally escape from my harrowing experiences with Richard Peter, the evil madman who had murdered a teen five years ago and managed to escape from Fairview. Who had tried to strangle me to death. In my own bedroom.

Pulling on thin cotton pants and a matching night shirt, my pajamas never felt so good.

I reflected on how my day had gone as I climbed into bed and fluffed my pillows.

Madeline had been a Godsend. She left about an hour ago after a late dinner together. I promised her I'd be fine alone. I was still swimming in pools of relief since the culprit of everything *unexplained* on our farm was back in custody. Anyway, my big sis had her own life. I didn't want to take advantage of her protectiveness.

Even Biddy was spending the night with the brood.

I was alone and more confident than ever.

In terms of cleaning my bedroom, Madeline and I had decided to trash the sheets and bedspread that Richard Peter had defiled with his bloodied hands. We even tossed the throw rug on my side of the bed, given it had also been stained with his blood. To replace them, we drove into Honesdale and went shopping.

The new sheets felt like a calming sea of silky softness.

I reached under Dex's pillow for reassurance that his pistol was accessible. The cool metal bolstered my sense of security. I was safe. In control. Free of raging whitewater.

Smiling, I acknowledged I was changing—responding to dangers before they swallowed me. No more painstakingly slow processing that left me vulnerable to those with ill intent. I was rewiring my brain. Ensuring I no longer became immobilized. Helpless.

I had stopped Richard Peter. Fought for my life and survived.

After turning off the lamp on my nightstand, I lowered my head onto the pillow and remembered nothing else. I must have instantly fallen asleep.

Except sometime later, I heard something…

Scratch.

Scratch.

Scratch.

Was something scraping against glass?

The spine tingling sound crept into my slumber and agitated me into wakefulness.

My eyelids fluttered open, and I turned toward my window.

I gasped.

The girl! The one I'd seen on Boulder Island.

The moonlight illuminated her. Made her glow.

With palms against the glass, she clawed at the surface with her long, pointed fingernails. She was dripping wet. A mist streamed from her lips. Like in my dream, a sash was wrapped snugly around her neck. Blackened circles shadowed her sunken eyes. Her skin was as white as her soaked dress. And her long strands of blonde hair were matted with blades of lake grass.

I started to reach for the pistol.

But she waved for me to come. To join her.

She looked innocent. Desperate. In such need of help.

Her urgency tugged at my heartstrings. Something was wrong. Maybe she was in some sort of trouble. Ill, perhaps. Or maybe one of her partying friends on the island had gotten hurt.

Instead of Dex's gun, I grabbed my slip-on moc shoes, hopping as I tugged them on while making my way to the great room. I opened a sliding glass door and bolted outside and into the night.

I looked beyond our patio, scanning our entire backyard, but the girl wasn't there.

Had she run away again? Or gone down our hill toward the lake?

Racing to the end of our lawn, I peered over the hillside to the valley below. There she was, standing by the lake's shoreline, waving for me to follow.

"You come *here!"* I yelled instead, wanting to know more before I made any commitments.

How quickly I had resorted back to "processing." Bottomline, if she or another teenager were in serious trouble on the island, my slow response could make the difference between life and death.

Turns out, my hesitation didn't affect her.

The girl splashed into the water and began swimming toward Boulder Island.

I needed to act quickly. Navigating around rocks and uneven ground, I worked my way down the hill.

At the water's edge, I made my decision. I'd follow. Anyway, I was a strong swimmer. As in, captain of the varsity teams at high school and college. And it wasn't like I had never swum at night. Alone.

I looked at my feet. I'd keep my mocs on. They were tight fitting, so they'd stay on. Which meant, they could protect my feet from the rocks and jagged branches undoubtedly hiding on the lake bottom.

I looked across the water in front of me. The moon had created a shimmering pathway on the lake's black surface. The golden glimmer was narrow where I stood and widened as it touched the island's shoreline in the distance.

The girl continued to swim away, with the moon's spotlight keeping her visible.

Water lapped over my shoes and ankles as I walked into the lake.

Good. The temperature was nearing 70-degrees. Not too cold. When I was deep enough, I pushed off and began swimming freestyle toward the island.

Halfway out, I stopped to check my position.

Only, I was alone.

No more splashing. No more girl, swimming.

Except for the water around me, the lake's surface was glassy.

Treading water, I did a 360-degree turn, scanning the area for her.

She was gone. Nowhere in sight. She wasn't even on the island.

I felt floating weeds or a twig brush against my ankles, and I kicked them away.

"Where are you?" I shouted. "I want to help!"

Panic prickled my nerves. Maybe she had gone under.

Oh dear God. Not that!

Entering the water (alone and at night) maybe wasn't my smartest move despite my swimming skills. I should've called 911 right from the start. Instead, I put everything at risk: the girl, me, my pregnancy.

I'd swim back to shore and make the call.

As I took my first stroke, something tugged on my left shoe. Or was it more of a snag? Like from a vine wrapping around my moc?

A hard yank and I was pulled under.

Confusion coursed through my veins.

I thrust myself upwards.

When my face broke the surface, I gulped air.

Another strong tug. I was under for a second time.

I opened my eyes below the surface.

The moonlight brightened the water enough so I could see.

There she was amid bubbles and swirling grayness: the girl in her billowing white dress. She pointed toward the darkened water below my knees—where I could see nothing but blackness. Other than that, I couldn't decipher her expression.

Her next move, though, was crystal clear. She swam away from me, underwater. Abandoning me. Never even surfacing for a breath.

Had she tricked me? Hoping I'd get tangled in weeds below me?

I thrashed my arms and kicked.

Raising my head above the water, I gasped for air.

Down I went again.

The grip on my shoe got tighter.

If I didn't break away, I would drown.

I had never wanted to die at Union Station. Or in my bedroom. Or now, at this moment.

Living was something "fighter me" was willing to defend.

I'd do everything I could not to be a victim.

With my right foot, I wedged the front of my moc into the heel of my left shoe, forcing it off when I pushed down. Freed from the mysterious grip, I took off swimming, faster than I had ever swum.

When my feet could touch the bottom, I raced onto the shore, moving the water with each heavy stride. I hardly felt the sharp stones and pointy twigs cutting the bare skin on my left foot. Adrenaline dulled the pain and exhaustion. Or maybe it was fear.

I coughed to clear my lungs of lake water.

Lowering myself onto a large, flat rock beside the shoreline, I focused on catching my breath. I filled my lungs with air, inhaling deeply before each elongated exhale.

When I recovered, I gazed across the water. Without a breeze, the surface was placid. Glassy.

The lake and island were undisturbed.

Nothing moved.

Then and there, I accepted two possibilities for what had just happened. That I was either losing my mind or that something beyond the laws of nature had occurred.

Something paranormal.

Something that wouldn't hesitate to kill me.

Something I couldn't ignore.

19

Sunday, June 22, 2025
Windy Hill Farm: Boulder, Pennsylvania

AFTER FILLING MY mug with the last ounces of decaffeinated coffee, I emptied the used grounds from my French press into the sink. I'd spray them down into the disposal later. Right now, I was eager to conduct research on my laptop. My device sat on the countertop of our kitchen island, already fired up and waiting for my fingers to enter a question or destination.

Last night's near drowning had solidified my understanding of what was happening.

Since I considered myself lucid, except for a few perplexing dreams, I wasn't losing my mind. Instead, my experiences in the lake, with the girl, fell squarely within the supernatural realm. Which meant, learning about hauntings was imperative. In my world, ghosts were what kids dressed up as for Halloween. And what film directors, authors, and advertisers inserted into their entertainment projects to scare audiences. For fun. And most definitely for *sales*.

Beyond those motivations, I had never taken ghosts seriously.

Until now. Until one menacing spirit threatened my life.

I had to resolve the paranormal misfortune plaguing our farm *before* our baby was born in March. Before anyone got hurt.

Walking to my laptop holding my warm mug, I pampered my left foot, shifting my weight to my right side as best I could. When storming from the lake last night, I ended up gashing the bottom of my foot on a sharp rock. I had cleaned and wrapped the injury after

76

returning to the house, but the pain reminded me of the entire ordeal.
I sat on a stool and googled my first question:

Are there different types of hauntings?

A website called "G3" for ghouls, ghosts, & goblins was the first
search result listed on my screen. I clicked on the link and began
reading.

RESIDUAL HAUNTINGS: Ghosts associated with
this type of haunting are comprised of
remnant energy from their former lives.
Think of a battlefield where a soldier's
ghost runs across the same stretch of field
every foggy night. Or a historical home
where the footsteps of a former, deceased
resident can be heard walking the length of
a hallway every time there's a storm.

For those frightened of the paranormal, no
need to worry. Not only is this type of
haunting the most common, but it should
also be the least unsettling. Picture a few
frames of an old film being projected and
looped on a wall. The actor in the film is
repeatedly heard and seen, but he's no
longer interacting with the world he's left
behind. In fact, he's not really present.
All that remains is his lingering energy.
An unintentional whisper of his past life.

That type of haunting didn't fit. The girl appearing on our farm
had no limits to where she manifested—near the house, in the lake,
on the island. Plus, she seemed very intentional.
I read on...

INTERACTIVE HAUNTINGS: Ghosts associated
with this type of haunting have a purpose.
They are spirits of deceased humans who
have unresolved business preventing them
from resting in peace. Maybe they had an

important message they never got to deliver
in life. Maybe they were privy to a crime
and seek justice. Or perhaps they were
violently murdered and want their killer
exposed. Whatever the reason, they have
intentionally gathered energy to manifest
themselves as ghosts. Moreover, they need
the living to help them fulfill their
mission.

For those frightened of the paranormal,
there is mostly good news. Interactive
ghosts have the same personalities they had
alive! Happy people (compelled to return
after death) become pleasant ghosts. Ornery
people return as crotchety spirits. It's
only menacing people who emerge in their
afterlife as dangerous entities.

The telltale sign of this type of haunting
is the ghost's obsession to interact, to
share with the living what it is they need.
They will use any means to get their
message across. These ghosts are present in
real time and are hauntingly intentional.

An interactive haunting sounded like a match.

I had the distinct impression the girl was trying to tell me something and if I didn't help her, she'd hurt me. Kill me, even. That seemed clear after last night. Talk about motivating me to get involved. Did I really have a choice?

I continued reading the website page in case there was another type of haunting which might apply. Shadow people were observed as dark masses, so that type was out. The girl I kept seeing looked real. Not to mention, *detailed*—like the lake grass tangled in her hair.

Demonic hauntings terrified me to my core but, to my relief, they didn't seem to apply either. Demons were non-humans with evil energy aimed at wreaking havoc on a person. Havoc could be extreme, such as *possessing* them.

I was certain the girl at Windy Hill Farm had been human once.

The only uncertainties fell into the category of unanswered questions: *Who was this girl? How was she connected to our property? And what did she want from me?*

A possible association popped into my mind. Maybe the girl had something to do with Richard Peter. Could she have been his victim? After all, he was in prison for strangling a local teenager. And he had come onto our property *twice.*

Back when he escaped, I had googled him. Perhaps I hadn't dug deep enough to find a photo of his victim. At this point, I'd be able to tell if she was the same girl haunting our farm.

I started an electronic search. Five minutes later, the answer was displayed on my screen.

Richard Peter's victim was *not* our ghost.

The young woman he murdered was Lisa Marley Stanford (17 years old) of Lake Ariel, about 12 miles from our farm. Lisa had a brown bob and a mole above her right upper lip.

Our ghostly teen had neither.

"Who *are* you?" I asked out loud, frustrated by my lack of clues.

I looked at my smartwatch. Biddy and the flock would be wondering where their morning meal was. Time to start my chores. At least with Richard Peter behind bars, I didn't need to accessorize my leg with Dex's pistol. Bullets would be useless on a ghost.

Walking to the sink, I felt a chill. Goosebumps were becoming annoyingly familiar.

Lowering my mug into the basin, I could hardly believe my eyes.

Written in the coffee grounds coating the bottom of the sink were the words *FIND THEM.*

A lump formed in my throat.

All this time, I had attributed those words to Richard Peter, thinking he had carved them into the flagstone and fingered them onto our television screen. Written them to keep us unsettled. On edge. His way of boasting he had access to our property. Our home.

Here, the ghostly girl was responsible for the words all along. Clearly, her message was an attempt to interact.

"Find... *WHAT?*" I yelled.

Deeply inhaling, I tried to regain my composure. "Please. Stop bugging me unless you can give me more. Your name for starters.

And then specify what you need me to find."

I held my breath, staring at the coffee grounds. Waiting to see if she'd write out her answers.

Nothing happened. Nothing moved.

Only the ticking wall clock made a sound.

"Bitch," I whispered, just as an idea materialized.

Grabbing my cellphone, I called Madeline. I'd delay the purpose for my call for a few minutes. First, I'd share good news. Make it hard for her to say no to my ultimate request.

"Hey, Mad. I need you to keep two secrets," I said, skipping my typical niceties.

"Oooh. I'm intrigued. Do tell."

I disclosed I was pregnant and holding off telling Dex until he returned from his business trip in LA. I wanted to share the exciting news face to face with my husband. Something much more intimate than over the phone.

Madeline cheered so loudly that my eardrum hurt.

Once she regained her sanity, she bombarded me with inquiries: *When was I due? How was I feeling? Which room would be the nursery? Would Dex and I want to find out the baby's gender?*

I answered each question: March; fine, but occasionally nauseous; the cream guest room; and yes.

Dex and I had already discussed all things *baby*. Just in case.

"Your second secret can't top being pregnant," she said. "But spill the beans. What is it?"

"The girl I've been seeing isn't human."

"What do you mean?"

"I mean, she's a *ghost.*"

My chatty, cheerleader of a big sis was speechless.

I didn't let the silence linger, explaining what had happened in the lake. Only, I avoided details about the danger I'd been in. I wanted to bypass a well deserved lecture on being reckless even though she knew I was an expert swimmer. Still, she'd point out I was pregnant now and she'd be right. I needed to start thinking differently.

"Leaving you alone last night was a mistake," Madeline said.

"Anyway, I'm going to buy a paddle board," I announced, moving the conversation toward my request.

"What's that have to do with your revelation?" she asked.

"The paddle board will make it easier to inspect Boulder Island. It's what you and Dex originally suggested."

"What's the point? You no longer believe the girl hangs out with a group of kids who party there. You just admitted you think she's a, she's a..."

"Say it, Mad. She's a *ghost.*"

"I'm not getting why you'd need to go out to the island now?"

"I think she wants me to find something. She keeps urging me to go there."

"Okay..." She paused. More like, hesitated. "Then what do you need from me?"

"Come with me. Please?"

20

Monday, June 23, 2025
Boulder Lake State Park: Boulder, Pennsylvania

WITH CRISSCROSSED LEGS, Madeline sat near the front of my new, white paddle board. I stood on the deck pad a few steps back from the middle, balancing the board.

The water swooshed as I paddled on one side and then the other, propelling us toward Boulder Island.

The mid-morning sun was radiant.

The lake was placid. Humidity, low.

From trees and pines outlining the lake, songbirds filled the air with cheery melodies.

Expanding rings dotted the lake's surface, marking where water skimmers had been (that's what my sister and I had called them when we camped as kids). The spiderlike bugs had been skating across the water until a trout or a largemouth bass swallowed them for breakfast, leaving a circular ripple in their place. Otherwise referred to as "empty plates" in our family.

"Shouldn't I be paddling?" Madeline asked, turning her head to look at me. "I feel guilty sitting here while you're doing all the work. Especially in your condition."

"My foot? No worries. I'm wearing water shoes. The bandage will keep my cut clean."

"Not *that*. You're pregnant."

"Pregnancy isn't an affliction, big sis. I'm fine."

"Your new boldness…I'm impressed. Maybe a little sad, too." She slumped her shoulders. "You won't need a mama bear anymore."

"Quite the opposite." I stopped paddling and let the board drift. "Maybe I can defend myself against a human now. But a...*ghost?* Not something I can tackle alone."

The timing was right to tell Madeline the entire story about my near drowning incident.

She massaged her eyes as I spoke, similar to what Dex did when he was anxious. She wanted to prevent stress from concentrating into a migraine. And when I mentioned getting pulled under several times, she doubled her efforts by vigorously rubbing her temples.

"You never should've gone into the lake at night. Not without a life vest," she griped. "I don't care how good of a swimmer you are."

"See? I need your wisdom."

"When will you tell Dex...*everything?*"

"After I discover tangible evidence that a ghost haunts this land." I resumed paddling. "He'll need proof."

Madeline studied me.

I could see her doubt. *"You* believe me, Mad. Don't you?"

"Give me time to ease into the idea, Nora. Right now, I'm focused on supporting you. You've been through so much."

Did my sister think I had conjured all this up? As a response to emotional trauma?

"I don't *want* to deal with a ghost," I countered. "This situation found *me,* not the other way around."

I'd rather focus on my pregnancy and new home, but sometimes people didn't get what they wanted. Trouble sought them out. At no fault of their own.

I knew that reality better than anybody.

As we approached the island's shoreline, lilies and cattails grew thick. I lowered the paddle vertically into the water until the blade's tip touched rocks and sand. Pushing off from the bottom, the board glided forward. When the water was calf-deep, Madeline and I hopped off and lifted the board onto the narrow beach.

"The plan is to start walking the shoreline," I said. "You travel right. I'll head left. Every time we pass one another, we'll inch inward, moving closer to the center with each rotation."

"And if I find something?" she asked. "Like empty beer bottles?"

"Holler and I'll make my way to you."

I didn't yell out when I found a deflated silver birthday balloon snagged on a large fallen branch. Not what we were looking for. I stuffed the shell and ribbon into the back pocket of my shorts and continued circling, passing Madeline with more frequency until we stopped at a massive boulder crowned with bright green moss, marking the middle of the island.

The pine trees were thickest around the boulder, except for a flat swath of ground in front of it which was covered in a flat blanket of browned pine needles.

"Thought so," I said. "I didn't think we'd find evidence of *real* kids hanging out here."

A fly landed on my arm, and another circled my head.

"There's no evidence of a *real* ghost either," Madeline added, tucking the sides of her hair behind her ears.

Point well taken, but at least we knew the truth. There was no evidence indicating the girl, or any teens for that matter, were making the island their party getaway. No campfire structure was present. No trash or disturbed ground either.

I swatted a couple more flies. Madeline did the same.

"We should've sprayed down with bug repellant," I said.

"Listen. Do you hear that?"

I stood perfectly still and then nodded.

If I had to guess, the buzz sounded like a significant swarm of insects. Flies were the most likely culprits, given the pesky visitors flying above our heads, but I wouldn't rule out mosquitos or bees either. One thing was certain, we weren't talking a few airborne bugs.

"Let's head back," I said, pointing in the direction of my board.

As we walked, maneuvering around trees and fallen branches, the shrill grew louder.

"Strange," Madeline said.

"No arguments from me."

One more tree cluster before we'd see the shoreline…

The buzzing stopped. Abruptly.

We froze in place.

Only the breeze whispered through the pines. Even the songbirds had gone silent.

"What is it with this place?" Madeline whispered.

"Right?" I raised my eyebrows as she looked at me. I was dying to say *I told you so,* but since I knew how those words felt, I pressed my lips together until I swallowed the urge.

We inched our way around the trees, careful not to snap a twig or make crunching sounds with our feet. *Quiet as mice on carpet,* Mom used to say.

The shoreline was visible, but I didn't register the anomaly. Until I did. My white paddle board was black, completely covered in a vibrating blanket of...

Flies.

What compelled them to behave so oddly? Had the board's manufacturer coated the surface with a sweet smelling shellac?

"Gross," I said near my sister's ear, as I pictured the flies secreting saliva all over my board.

"What are we going to do?"

I picked up a baseball sized rock. "When the flies scatter," I whispered, "run to the right side of the board. I'll go left. We'll lift it and race into the water, keeping the board flat so the paddle doesn't fall off. Swim below the surface until the coast is clear or we need a breath." I paused. "What do you think? Good plan? Bad plan?"

"Good plan."

Dad was a fan of the MLB, so he insisted on Madeline and I learning how to throw and catch a baseball. My well developed hand/eye coordination had paid off many times.

I threw the rock. It landed near the board's handle, scattering the flies which instantly transformed into a swirling, shifting black cloud. Accompanied by a deafening buzz.

Equally paced with my sister, I arrived on my side of the board as she arrived at hers. The flies were everywhere, bombarding our skin and clothes. I kept my mouth clamped shut to prevent the unthinkable, hoping Madeline was doing the same. Not that I'd know. I could barely see her. That's how thick the swarm was.

Lifting the board, we bolted into the water and continued running until the water depth reached our midriffs.

I took a deep breath through my nose and submerged, continuing to hold onto the board while kicking.

All I wanted was to add distance between us and the island. Between us and *them*.

I could feel flies in my hair—those which had gotten tangled in my strands and were now drowning. Not to mention, the few which had gotten themselves trapped between my T-shirt and skin and were squirming to find a way out.

Madeline and I kept kicking as we swam underwater for what felt like an entire minute.

Holding my breath was no longer an option. I raised my head above water, covering my mouth and nose with my cupped hand. I gasped for air.

My sister was doing the same.

As we replenished our lungs, the black cloud of flies retreated, twisting and turning its way back to Boulder Island.

21

Friday, July 4, 2025
Windy Hill Farm: Boulder, Pennsylvania

THERE'D BE PLENTY of time to tell Dex about the freakish swarm of flies on Boulder Island, a topic I intentionally avoided while he was away on business. Now wouldn't be the right time either. He'd been unpacking since he got home, and I was about to unveil my special dinner. One aimed at keeping the evening celebratory.

Dimming the lights, I called Dex to the dining room table located in the kitchen nook. A vase of fresh flowers decorated the center of the table, flanked by candelabrums. The lit candles reflected off the wall of windows, causing flickering shadows to dance on the ceiling. Beside my chair on a pedestal, an ice bucket chilled our bottled beverage. And for the first time since we moved, our wedding china was making its debut, along with the crystal glassware.

Fancy schmancy my sister and I used to say as kids.

I was even using Mom's domed plate covers to keep our entrée a surprise. Maybe that was wishful thinking. The aroma of grilled whole trout was hard to mask. Still, the cover added excitement, an emotion on par with my pregnancy news.

Dex strolled into the kitchen, paused for a second as if absorbing the ambiance, and then approached me. Placing his hands on my hips, he pulled my body to his.

"You missed me, didn't you?" He winked.

"I did…in between farm chores and shooting a prisoner on the most wanted list."

He kissed my neck. "You've been a busy badass." He raised his head and touched his lips to mine, adding, "That's a turn-on."

I pushed him back. "Sit. We're not starting with dessert tonight."

"Bossy, too." He rubbed his hands together while smiling. "My good fortune runneth over."

After he sat, I lifted his plate cover. Aromatic steam (infused with lemon, rosemary, and basil) wafted up from his serving.

Dex locked eyes with me. "Wow. This is five star cuisine."

Pulling the bottle from the ice bucket, I carefully popped the cork.

"Champagne, too?" he added. "You've got my attention."

I poured until his flute was half full. Legions of bubbles chaotically launched from the golden liquid, bursting near the rim like infinitesimal water balloons.

At my place setting, I filled my own flute halfway.

"Happy Independence Day." I sat and raised my flute. "I'd like to make a toast, if you'll indulge me."

He raised his glass. "I'm all ears."

"Til små føtter."

"If only I spoke Norwegian."

I winked. "Drink and you might figure it out, Einstein."

Sipping, he struggled to swallow. "Yikes! Ridiculously sweet." He pursed his lips and grimaced. "Is this…sparkling *apple juice?* As in, non-alcoholic?"

"Ja." I smiled, enjoying my theatrics. "Let me translate my toast." I raised my flute again. "To little feet."

Dex tilted his head and everything in our world seemed to momentarily pause as he processed the news.

Pushing back from the table, he stood and closed the distance between us as I rose from my chair. He gently placed his palms on each of my cheeks, bringing my face to his.

"I'm going to be a dad!" He kissed me. "I'm the happiest man alive, Nora! I'll work every single day to be the best father ever." He glanced around the kitchen and great room as if he was admiring them for the first time. His eyes glistened in the candlelight. "Windy Hill Farm is the perfect place to raise kids. To raise generations for that matter."

A door slammed in the house, probably the door to our bedroom.

I flinched.

"No worries," he said. "The wind and pressure outside can create a vacuum inside."

Thunder rumbled in the distance.

"Before the storm hits," Dex added, "I've got a surprise for you, too. In the backyard."

I wouldn't say we wolfed down the meal, but I wouldn't deny our attempt either. Dex had something up his sleeve that couldn't wait for tomorrow. Anyway, I was famished, and the fish was moist and flaky, so I gladly complied and ate like a five-minute timer was ticking.

"Mind if we delay eating pie until after my surprise?" he asked.

I stood. "Lead the way."

Holding hands, Dex led me to the backyard, to the edge overlooking the valley below. Two canister tubes were secured in the ground, tilted toward the lake. A fuse peeked out from each tube.

Here, I thought he'd been unpacking the whole time.

"Fireworks?" I asked.

"Wait until you see them." He was beaming. "Both are custom made. I picked them up before I left for LA. Hope they don't disappoint."

I squeezed his fingers in approval. "I'll love them. But no matter what, the thought always counts more."

He released my hand and grabbed the handheld lighter he had staged beside the tubes.

Tonight, with thick cloud cover, the valley was pitch black except when a flash of lightning strobed in the distance, briefly illuminating the lake and hillside.

He lit the first fuse. The firework launched, squealing and whirling as it skyrocketed upwards before exploding into shimmering glitter that was briefly suspended in the air, forming a heart and my name within it, glistening in red and gold.

I jumped in place several times, clapping my hands. But as the sparkles fell from the sky, destined to extinguish, I glimpsed the silhouette of a figure standing on our hill, halfway between where we stood and the lake's shoreline. In the dim flash of light, I had no clue whether I was seeing the girl or the dark shadow of a real person.

Dex had clearly been watching me for my facial reaction. "Was it *that* bad?"

Reaching up, I clasped my hands behind his neck and buried my face in his chest. "Oh my gosh. It was unbelievably wonderful. I'm stunned. That's the expression you saw."

No way was I going to ruin our romantic vibe by admitting I saw something...

A breeze crested the hill and rustled our hair. I could hear faint crying in the distance.

"The temperature's dropping," Dex said, sticking to all things *tangible*. "The stormfront must be close." He lifted my chin so we could lock eyes. "Hey. Your heart's racing."

"Wasn't that your intention?"

He gave me his full-on smile. "Guilty."

One benefit of sparkling apple juice was that the non-alcoholic beverage didn't dull reaction times. My comeback was sober quick, so he didn't probe any further.

Dex lit the second fuse and the tube's payload blasted off.

When the firework reached its altitude, it burst into a circular shape with the words *I Love You* forming in the middle.

I quickly glanced down the hill.

No one stood there now.

"Was that a Viking shield?" I asked.

"You got it! I worried you'd think it was just a circle."

I hugged him again. "I love you. So much. Thank you."

We stood, embracing, until the wailing wind urged us to find shelter inside the house.

As Dex reached down to make sure the tubes were still planted firmly in the ground so they wouldn't blow away, another flash of lightning lit the valley.

In that brief strobe of light, I could see the hillside again.

The silhouette of the figure was back.

22

Saturday, July 12, 2025
Oliver's Grocery Store: Carbondale, Pennsylvania

KETCHUP. AS I paused beside the condiment shelf at Oliver's, gripping the shopping cart handle, I realized ketchup epitomized one of the differences between city and rural living.

Regardless of which D.C. grocery store I had popped into when Dex and I lived in the Palisades, my ketchup options seemed endless. I could select from a variety: regular, organic, vegan, reduced sugar, no salt, spicy, veggie, jalapeno, or the gross sounding hotdog blend (a combo of ketchup, mustard, and relish). Not to mention, the myriad of brands and bottle sizes which were available.

City life was not for those who were easily overwhelmed.

Here in Pennsylvania's Lackawanna and Wayne counties, *keep it simple* was the overarching rule. I had two options: buy a 20-ounce bottle of regular ketchup (there were only four on the shelf) or make my own variety from scratch, using tomatoes from my greenhouse.

I sighed before grabbing one of the ketchup bottles, not quite ready to tackle homemade.

Giving up modern conveniences continued to be hard.

The cart's right-front wheel whined and clattered as I entered one of the three checkout lines. I began placing my items on the small conveyor belt.

"Did you find everything, Ma'am?"

I looked up and saw a young woman with freckles on her cheeks and a pleasant smile. Her long brown hair was pulled into a ponytail, finished off with a red bow. And the nametag on her Oliver's green T-shirt read *Amelia.*

"Yes, thank you," I said, handing her my reusable bags.

In reference to her *did you find everything* question, I avoided mentioning that the word "everything" had been ruralized to mean the one and only option Oliver's offered of a product. Like ketchup. Or all-purpose flour, almond milk, and laundry detergent. Butter and brownie mix, too.

The list could go on and on.

"You're new to the area, right?" Amelia asked.

"Pretty much." On the conveyor belt, I placed a four pack of the one brand of paper towels sold at Oliver's. "My husband and I moved six miles up the road in May. To Boulder."

"Where abouts? I grew up there."

"Windy Hill Farm."

Amelia scanned the American cheese. "Never heard of that farm."

I chuckled. "That's just what we named our property. The land is better known as part of the old Williams Farm. We built a house on the parcel next to Boulder Lake."

Her forehead creased. "That acreage wasn't supposed to be sold."

Weird how everybody in the area knew that.

Maybe Amelia could fill in some blanks. Couldn't hurt to ask her a few questions while I was in line.

"Did you and your friends ever hang out on Boulder Island? When you were teenagers? I mean, I probably would've. Had I grown up near there."

"Once. As a dare," she said, scanning my grapes. "But only then."

Amelia's tone had gone from bouncy friendly to flat and serious.

"I don't want to sound nosy or rude," I said, "but do you mind me asking why you didn't congregate there? *If* there was a reason."

"Has something else…*happened?*" Her voice shifted again, from serious to mildly panicked. "Besides the prisoner being caught on your property?"

"No, no," I assured her, pushing the cart further down the lane so I could start loading my bags into its basket. "It's just that I paddled out to the island recently. And there were no signs of anyone else venturing out there. Not for years, anyway. Guess I found that odd."

She leaned toward me. "The land is haunted," she whispered. "Every local knows it."

Life had a twisted sense of humor.

The truth could be revealed anywhere: in the highest court, after months of deliberations, or at a checkout line in Oliver's, as quickly as it took to scan grapes.

Not only that, but Amelia's revelation was my first validation. I clearly wasn't the only one who knew a ghost was haunting the property. The locals were also aware.

"Wouldn't a ghost serve as a lure?" I pressed. "Make kids want to sneak out there and tell spooky stories under the moonlight? Hold a séance? That sort of thing?"

"Kids around here know the difference between being scared for fun..." She handed me my receipt. "And being scared to death."

A chill raced down my spine.

Amelia glanced beyond me to the next customer in line. "Did you find everything, Mrs. Martin?"

23

Saturday, July 12, 2025
Windy Hill Farm: Boulder, Pennsylvania

THE THUNDERSTORM KNOCKED out our electricity at the exact moment Dex and I were about to climb into bed. I rolled my eyes. Never had I lived in a place where the electrical grid was this stinking unreliable.

I walked to my window and cranked open one of the panels enough to keep air circulating, before returning to bed. While I poked and fluffed my pillows, I recalled what I had learned about our less than stellar grid.

Apparently, an unstable atmosphere was common in mountainous areas due to updrafts: When warm, moist air (like in a valley) rose and clashed with colder air at higher elevations. A soup bowl of instability was created.

In summer, that meant thunderstorms. In winter, blizzards.

With electrical lines above ground, they were vulnerable. Trees fell on them all the time. Hence, glitches to the grid.

Electricity or not, at least Biddy and the flock were staying dry and safe in their hutch tonight.

I spooned against Dex as the rain pelted our metal roof.

With all my thoughts about moisture and instability, my brain took a cognitive leap to the sinkhole. Which instantly pissed me off. I did *not* want to think about that blasted thing. Not at bedtime when I was winding down. Trying to relax. All I needed to remember about the sinkhole was that it was dead and buried. Gone for good.

In its place, my mind drifted to Oliver's and the next time I planned to shop there. I'd make sure Amelia was working. I'd pick her checkout line so I could ask her more questions.

Bottomline, time was flying by. I was already five weeks pregnant and all I had learned was that other locals believed, as I did, that our land and the lake were haunted.

But had anyone else ever *seen* the girl ghost before? Did they know who she was? Why she was instigating havoc instead of resting in peace? And most importantly, could anyone guess what the girl wanted someone (namely, *me*) to find?

My eyelids felt heavy...

Sometime in the middle of the night, Dex nudged me.

"Hey," he said near my face. "Mind closing your window?"

I blinked rapidly to wake myself up.

"Why?" I asked. "Has the AC come back on?"

"No, but don't you think it's chilly? Besides, rain could be coming in through the open panels."

Picking to sleep on the side with the massive window facing the backyard might've been a huge mistake. Compared to me, Dex would have to take a measly twenty *extra* steps to get to the window. Had that insignificant differential really necessitated waking me up?

I huffed.

"Sorry. It's just that you're closer," he said.

I slipped out of the bed and walked to the window. The room was dark, but natural light from outside, amplified by occasional lightning, allowed for some visibility. The wood planks felt icy on the soles of my feet. With the stormfront, temperatures must've really dropped. Sure enough, as I cranked the window closed, my breath left a patch of mist on the glass.

Frosty condensation in July. Strange.

In D.C., our skin would've been lacquered in sweat.

Returning to bed, I stepped in a puddle. Water *was* accumulating on the floor from the open window, like Dex had cautioned. To check it out, I padded over to my nightstand and grabbed the flashlight. I shined the light beam on the puddle and beyond.

What the *what?*

Annoying goosebumps erupted on my skin.

The puddle wasn't the only collection of water on the floor. There was a trail of it leading out of our bedroom and down the hall—as if someone wet (*drenched* was more like it) had walked across our floors while dripping profusely.

My mind instantly formulated an obvious suspicion but jumping to "imaginative" conclusions would only irritate Dex's sense of logic. I'd bite my tongue and give him space to figure it out.

"Dex, wake up. We have a problem."

"Did rain soak the floors?"

"There's water in here *and* down the hall," I said, continuing to shine my flashlight.

"What the hell?" He threw off the covers, walked over to me, and asked if he could use my flashlight. "I swear. I'll lose my mind if our brand new roof is leaking."

Dex shined light across the ceiling in our bedroom. Dry as a bone. No signs of moisture on the ceiling in the hallway either.

"What do you think made that trail?" I asked.

"Not sure." He had lowered his voice to a whisper and placed his index finger on his lips to signal I should project the same volume.

Tiptoeing to his nightstand, he opened the drawer, took out his pistol, checked that it was loaded, and made his way back to me.

"Stay here while I investigate," he said.

If the girl had left the wet trail, Dex's gun would be ineffectual.

Fear lodged in my throat, making it hard to swallow.

I pictured myself on the night I had nearly drowned in the lake. I didn't want that kind of aloneness for either one of us.

"No," I managed to whisper. "We stick together."

He nodded, albeit reluctantly. With his pistol in his right hand and the flashlight in his left, he started down the hall.

The trail of water led to the kitchen, but it didn't stop there.

The basement door was open.

"Did you forget to close this door?" he whispered.

"No, it was shut when we went to bed."

Dex shined light down the stairway. Water pooled on each step. Some of it was even dripping down to the next step like a trickle flowing over rocks in a stream.

"This isn't good," he said.

24

Saturday, July 12, 2025
Windy Hill Farm: Boulder, Pennsylvania

THE DELUGE OF rain and the electrical blackout persisted as Dex and I stood in the kitchen near a puddle at the doorway leading to the basement. Staring. Without saying a word.

The flashlight's beam shined down the stairwell, making the eerie space resemble a long, wet tunnel leading deep into the ground where the light failed to reach the other end. Weak batteries contributed to the illusion, no doubt.

"I'll check it out," Dex finally said. "My hunch is a wild animal. One seeking shelter from the rain. Probably got inside through one of our ground level windows in the basement."

My anxiety level made my fingers tingle.

"There are more possibilities," I said.

"If someone wanted to hurt us, they would've already. In the bedroom. While we slept. You know that better than anyone."

In my mind, the ghost ranked high on the list of suspects. After all, she wore a dress soaking in lake water. Not only did she haunt our property, but she didn't hesitate to come inside.

Dex started to take the first step and I grabbed his arm.

"What?" he asked, his voice raspy with irritation.

The information I had been withholding started to bunch up in my throat like an unruly crowd pushing toward the entrance at a rock concert. Never mind that verbal purging (to release the pressure) would be happening at the worst possible time.

"The girl from the lake," I blurted out. "I didn't want to tell you, but she's a ghost."

"No, you reconciled your imagination with reality. You said so."

"Then something else happened. And I didn't mention it because I knew you'd blame the whole thing on my *irrational* imagination."

He tilted his head. "Something *else* happened while I was in LA? In addition to Richard Peter?" Concern had returned to his voice.

"The girl lured me into the lake. And after I swam halfway to the island, she tried to drown me."

"Tell me you were wearing a life vest."

I shook my head at the slow speed of embarrassment.

"Every time I see her," I continued, "she's dripping wet. That's why you shouldn't go down there. To the basement. Not while the electricity is off."

"Jesus, Nora. Your imagination is going to get *you* killed, not me. Seriously. You've got to stop this crazy bullshit."

"I was careless: swimming alone without a vest. But I'm right about the ghost. Locals know this place is haunted."

"Says who? Specifically?"

"The checkout girl at Oliver's. She told me when I was shopping."

If only I had rehearsed in front of a mirror. Then I would've realized how unscientific I sounded. Still, I believed Amelia. She had no reason to lie to me.

"This is out of control," Dex countered. "I'm not blaming you. I'm *worried* about you. You're going to be a mother." He sighed. "I think it's time for another visit to Dr. Simon."

Maybe he didn't intend to sound condescending, but if his patronizing were a physical sign, it would be fluorescent and flashing. Mounted on the freaking highest skyscraper.

The temperature dropped.

Streams of mist billowed from our mouths.

"See? A broken window downstairs is letting in cool air," he said. "Everything has an explanation."

"Please don't go. Trust me," I said, knowing full-well that not too long ago, I was a woman who hadn't even trusted her own instincts.

"We'll talk about this later." He took one step and stopped. "Will you be okay in the dark?"

FIND THEM

I nearly killed Richard Peter in the dark, but okay.

Dex's comment proved that relationship dynamics took a long time to change. We should talk about *that* later, too.

"Of course," I answered, feeling sad and misunderstood. "Be careful. The steps are probably slippery with all that water on them."

He started down the stairs, unable to hold the railing since his right hand clutched his handgun. As he descended, darkness filled the space behind him.

A gust of wind violently rattled the window over the kitchen sink.

I turned my head toward the sound.

The instant I looked away, Dex screamed.

I heard his body slamming and tumbling down the stairs.

25

Saturday, July 12, 2025
Windy Hill Farm: Boulder, Pennsylvania

"DON'T MOVE," I screamed from the doorway, looking down the darkened stairwell. As I processed what had just happened, I felt a wave of nausea.

When Dex fell, he must've released the pistol and flashlight on impact. I had no clue where the handgun had ended up, but at least it hadn't accidentally discharged. On the other hand, the flashlight had landed near my husband. The stream of light was shining on him. Which was helpful and horrifying at the same time.

Even with limited light, I could see he was on his stomach, with his head awkwardly turned toward the steps. Something about his position looked unnatural. The same could be said of his right arm; his elbow was bent in the wrong direction.

He looked...*broken.*

I needed to stop processing.

Think quickly. Act quickly.

Grabbing the railing, I started down the stairs, willing myself not to fall. Or throw up.

The steps were dark and wet, but not as slippery as I'd anticipated.

At the base of the stairs, I knelt beside my husband.

Oh dear God! Please let him be all right.

Dex moaned. "My neck."

"Stay completely still. I mean it. Don't move."

"I don't think I can." He grimaced. "I'm scared."

Scared? That wasn't an emotion Dex had ever expressed.

I gently touched his back, not wanting to disturb his position, but hoping to comfort him, if he could even feel my hand. The thought terrified me that he might not be able to.

"Listen," I said. "I'll have to leave you for a minute to get my cellphone. To call 911." I grabbed the flashlight. "You'll be in the dark, but not for long."

Whatever had left the trail of water (ghost, intruder, wild animal), it wasn't advancing on us. Any threat was secondary now. Getting Dex immediate medical help had to be my only focus. It was all I cared about.

I was *not* going to lose my husband.

"Tell them I slipped," he said softly.

"I'll give them the details. Promise."

I saw a tear race down his left cheek, and I touched his back again.

"No," he corrected. "I mean, don't tell them I was pushed."

Was he delirious from shock?

"I'm not following, babe," I said. "I'm sorry."

Another tear.

"I was pushed," he repeated. "I didn't fall."

My heart thumped against my sternum.

"Pushed?" I asked. "Tell me what happened."

"I heard a gust slam against a window. Had to be in the kitchen."

I remembered. I had heard it, too. The gust rattled the window over the sink, and I had looked away from the stairwell, toward the sound, at the same time Dex fell.

"The loudness took me by surprise," he explained. "I slightly turned and looked up at you. I could see your silhouette. You were still standing in the doorway. And that's when I felt hands on me. Hands that pushed me down the steps. With force."

"You're sure?"

"One hundred percent." He winced. "I think you're right. This place is haunted."

The door at the top of the stairway slammed shut.

I hated that damn ghost.

"Bitch!" I yelled at the girl whom I pictured standing on the other side of the door. Upstairs. In our kitchen. In our house. Dripping all over our wooden floors.

"You won't even tell us who you are!" I screamed at her. "Or what you want us to find!" I sounded close to hysterical. "All you do is hurt the ones I love!"

"Sorry I doubted you," Dex whispered, his voice turning groggy.

"Don't pass out," I ordered. "And don't move. Not an inch."

I stood, feeling like a warrior. Nothing was going to stop me.

"I'll be right back."

I meant every word out of my mouth.

26

THE SMELL OF crisping bacon wafted into the bedroom, nudging my senses to engage with the world of the living. Which meant, sometime after I had gotten home from the hospital—which was 4:00 a.m., Madeline had arrived at the farm to provide the support I desperately needed.

I was exhausted, having slept through Omelet's wakeup call and my sister's arrival.

No wonder. Last night was the worst nightmare of my life.

It was worse than getting thrown onto the tracks by "Mr. Hostile." Worse than being strangled by Richard Peter or being lured into the lake and nearly drowned by the ghost.

Worse, because I had failed to protect the love of my life.

If I could rewind time, I would've refused to let Dex go down those blasted basement steps. I mean, how could I give myself a pass? Even though he didn't believe me at the time, I knew there was a ghost. A ghost who had tried to kill me.

What made me think she wouldn't attempt the same with Dex?

I should've been unrelenting. Unyielding.

Instead, I let him go anyway. And now my husband faced an uncertain future.

The unknown constricted my throat. Crushed my heart.

Dex had, indeed, broken his neck and arm in the fall.

Although the doctors said it was too soon to tell if he would suffer any permanent paralysis (they wouldn't know until inflammation affecting his neck and spine had moderated), a long recovery process was absolutely guaranteed. As soon as he was stable from his surgery, he'd be transferred to a rehab facility for at least six to eight weeks.

I couldn't even fathom the possibility that Dex might be paralyzed. Not to mention, the prospect that I might become the sole caregiver of my husband, our baby, and the farm.

All because of a vicious ghost.

Because of *her,* my whole life had changed in a snapshot, and I had no clue what rescue log I'd be able to cling to. Currently, I was drowning in raging white water. Beginning to sink.

I heard dishes clanking in the kitchen, snapping me out of my hopeless reverie.

Madeline. She'd help me sort through the disaster that was Windy Hill Farm. Help me decide what my next steps should be *before* depression immobilized me.

Throwing off the covers, I put on my new mocs and bathrobe and headed to the kitchen.

When my sister saw me, she jogged over and threw her arms around me. We hugged, without saying a word, for at least a minute.

"Sit at your kitchen island," she said, sounding like Mom while wiping her eyes. "I've made breakfast. You've got to eat properly." She smiled. "Bacon doesn't count."

God, how I loved her! She'd help me cope.

"While you eat," she added, "tell me everything. Start to finish."

That's what I did. Recounted every detail. Every emotion.

Sisters required no filters.

After another shared cry about Dex and the severity of his bone fractures, I asked her what I should do next...about the uncertainty of Dex's prognosis. About the ghost. The farm. My job. My pregnancy and life.

"In overwhelming circumstances," she said calmly, "you've got to break down your troubles into manageable chunks. Limit yourself to a few action items on your daily to-do list. For now, stick to those which have easily attainable solutions."

"Like what? Where do I start?"

"Dex is who matters most. Doctors are managing the medical side of his injuries and you can help with the emotional side. Visiting him will lift his spirits and motivate him. So, doing farm chores and getting to the hospital should be today's priority number one."

Her advice made sense. Nevertheless, my mind raced forward.

"And the ghost? How can I resolve *her* problem?"

"You can't. Not without her name. Not without knowing what happened to her. Or what in the hell she wants to make her situation better. As in, to bring her peace."

"Are you suggesting we wait until she tries to kill one of us again?"

"I've heard of buyers," Madeline said, ignoring my snarky comment, "who've gotten a priest or minister to bless their new home. As protection. One of my clients mentioned that a formalized blessing can drive out lingering spirits." She picked up my empty plate and headed to the dishwasher. "Might be something to try to see if it works. But I can think of a more infallible solution for you and Dex. One that bypasses trial and error."

"What?"

"Sell this place."

"*Seriously?*" I could feel myself sinking deeper in the turbulent water. "I'm supposed to walk away and let some other unsuspecting buyer become the ghost's next victim?"

"There are plenty of buyers who crave haunted properties, Nora. We'd disclose it."

"No." I shook my head. "Windy Hill Farm is Dex and my forever home. We built it from the ground up."

"Life requires adjustments," Madeline continued. "If you had a lead about the ghost, something to go on, maybe staying might work. You could get to the bottom of what's happening. Maybe fix it." She sighed. "But you don't. We only know your family is in danger."

I started crying. Again.

My sister rubbed my back, comforting me. She meant well.

"No decisions need to be made right away," she added. "Just think about it. For today, let's focus on finishing chores around the house and farm. Then you can get to the hospital. What can I do?"

I asked Madeline to tackle the house. I'd feed the flock and water greenhouse plants and the apple trees in the orchard.

105

Within a half hour, we were off and working.

I fed the flock, deciding to keep them inside their enclosed run since we'd be leaving for the hospital. With one exception: Biddy was allowed to follow me to the greenhouse.

Halfway there, I heard loud shrieking and cawing. Deafening, to be more accurate.

I glanced at the woods to my right.

Ravens dotted all the branches in the canopy. Birds were as concentrated as ornaments and balls on a Christmas tree. Clearly, my once normal world was turning upside down.

A massive raven approached us, swooping down with talons extended. No doubt hoping to grab Biddy for its meal.

I rushed to her, scooping my hen into my arms.

The raven turned at a sharp angle. I heard the swoosh of its wings as it flapped away toward the woods.

"Hope you're happy," I screamed at the birds. "We may have to sell this place!"

I stroked Biddy's feathers. "I'll always have your back," I whispered, kissing her head.

Inside the greenhouse, I closed the door and put her down. She'd be safe inside. Anyway, Biddy loved to follow me around as I gathered ripened veggies, herbs, and fruits.

After plucking a cracked zucchini off the vine, I tossed it onto the floor. Biddy liked to peck and eat the insides while I fed the plants. Grabbing the watering can, I headed to the sink.

I froze, staring at a name fingered in the thin dusting of dirt on the countertop...

ISABELLE

27

Sunday, July 13, 2025
Windy Hill Farm: Boulder, Pennsylvania

MADELINE AND I were hand washing and drying dinner dishes like Dex and I did most nights. Biddy walked the floors, looking for crumbs that might've escaped from a plate.

"Was this done in the city?" my sister asked, scrubbing the lasagna pan. "Treating a hen like a household dog?"

"Wouldn't surprise me since city dwellers don't project their own expectations onto someone else." I reached up and placed a dried glass on an open shelf. "As a former city dweller, let it be known that individuals can identify however they want on our farm. And Biddy embraces a dog's life."

"Someone forgot to tell the raven your hen thinks she's a dog."

"That's why she has me, Mad. To help others understand. Or, to protect her if they refuse."

We chuckled, enjoying our familiar ribbing.

For as long as we could remember, Madeline and I were consistently opposites. Two different puzzle pieces, each with distinct parts of a scene displayed on our surfaces (mine: modern and edgy; hers: retro and wholesome), but each of us was equally needed to make the picture complete.

Together, we were the epitome of balance. Like Dex and me.

"Did you tell Dex the ghost's first name?" Madeline asked.

I nodded. "But I'm not sure he heard me. They're keeping him heavily sedated for now."

"No mention of selling the farm then?"

How quickly the scales of balance could tip.

My skin prickled with irritation.

"Whatever happened to the importance of knowing her name?" I shoved the dried utensils in the drawer, making sure they clanked. *"You're* the one who said it was paramount to staying here, to solving the mystery so she'll stop haunting us."

"Her *full* name," she countered. "Googling *Isabelle* won't get you anywhere. Right?"

Irritation blossomed to anger. The kind with sharp thorns.

I looked her squarely in the eyes, hoping my words would sting. "If Dex and I decide to sell, you'll be the first to know. In case you're hankering for another real estate commission."

Madeline stopped scouring the pan and closed her eyes. A tear raced down her cheek. She knew my comment had nothing to do with money or a desire for it. Her words had hurt me, and I was verbally lashing back.

"I'm not being fair," my sister admitted. "I'd sell this place in a heartbeat, but I shouldn't pressure you to want the same. I'm sorry. I'm worried, that's all."

"I understand." I folded the dishtowel. "Just give me some credit. I'm following your advice. Taking one step at a time. And knowing her first name *is* progress."

"You're right, Nora. That makes sense."

I turned off the light over the dining room table. "Tomorrow, I'm going to google Virgil Williams. After all, he's the one who established the trust which governed this property for over seventy years, which prevented this lot from being sold. Maybe I'll find the name Isabelle mentioned in his obituary; she might've been a relative. Her first name may turn out to be more beneficial than you think.

"Right now," I continued, "I'm exhausted, so my hen dog and I are heading to bed."

The sliding doors leading to the patio were still open; thankfully, the screens were keeping out the bugs. Madeline agreed to shut and lock them before turning in for the night.

We hugged before I walked to my bedroom with Biddy in toe.

When my hen slept in the house instead of her hutch, I no longer had to place her inside the crate. Now when I opened the gate, she walked in, knowing the routine.

Slumber must've come as soon as my head hit the pillows. However, as was annoyingly common these days, something woke me in the middle of the night and stole my rest.

In the dark, I tried to identify the culprit.

The windchimes hanging in the backyard patio. They were singing louder than usual. In fact, I couldn't recall ever hearing them from Dex and my bedroom. Not when the sliding glass doors were closed. Could Madeline have forgotten to shut them when she went to bed?

Biddy cackled.

"I know," I said to her. "I need to check it out. Be right back."

I padded down the hallway, through the kitchen, and into the great room. Sure enough, one of our three sliding glass doors was still open. No harm done. Except after Richard Peter, I insisted the house be kept locked, especially at night.

The waxing Gibbous moon cast light across the patio and through the slider's screen, brightening Dex's T-shirt which I wore to keep him close. As I glanced at the sky, crickets and cicadas chirped their nighttime chorus. The starry ceiling was always breathtaking from our mountain hilltop.

I remembered being in awe the first time I slept under these stars, back when Dex and I had camped out on the property after settlement. On July 13, 2024.

Standing at the slider, I realized that today had marked the one-year anniversary of when we had purchased the property. Sadly, instead of celebrating with my husband, I had spent most of the day watching him trapped in an induced sleep, remaining perfectly still.

My heart ached.

As I slid the glass door across its track, a thickening concentration of mist caught my attention on the patio.

The ghost appeared.

She was dressed in her standard garb—a white dress with a full skirt, soaked and dripping on the pavers. A sash was wrapped around her neck, the ends fluttered with the wind. Her hair was tangled and matted with lake grass like before. Her eye sockets were darkened. Skin, pale.

An explosion of adrenaline made my hands tremble.

Mist streamed from my mouth with each exhale and a chill crawled down my spine.

Instead of closing the slider, I thrust it open. Moving the screen door out of the way, I stepped onto the patio. Into the night.

"You!" I sneered. "You're Isabelle, aren't you?"

She nodded.

"What do you want from me?"

I had to remember to ask yes or no questions, but in this case, she answered anyway.

Isabelle waved for me to follow.

She turned toward the hillside and lake.

"No way," I snapped. "You pushed my husband. Broke his neck and nearly killed him!"

She looked back at me, shaking her head no and creasing the skin across her forehead.

I didn't understand.

Why would she deny assaulting Dex?

It wasn't like my husband *imagined* being pushed. His mind didn't work that way. He was governed by logic. If he felt hands on him— forcing him to fall, that's what happened. Besides, he would've done anything to avoid admitting that Windy Hill Farm had a ghost.

Wait. Could there be more than one entity? The possibility was doubtful, but not completely out of the question. These days, everything warranted consideration.

"Are you by yourself?" I asked her. "Alone?"

She nodded.

I came back to the most likely reason she denied pushing Dex: Isabelle was a trickster. A villainous spirit. A deceiver. The same in death as she probably had been in life.

How innocent and victimized she had looked when she lured me into the lake to follow her! Yet, she had gotten me tangled in weeds. Pulled me under. And when she was sure I was drowning, she swam away. Left me to die.

In the moonlight, I noticed her ankles looked raw, with a bruised ring around each of them. I hadn't noticed before. Clearly, she had been injured in a horrific way around the time of her death.

Perhaps Isabelle believed her anger in the afterlife was justified.

"Did you die in the lake?" I asked, putting my anger aside.

Isabelle shook her head no.

That surprised me since she always seemed drenched.

Waving her hand again, she summoned me to follow. Only this time, she didn't wait for my response.

She started jogging down our hillside.

My need for answers compelled me to consider her plea.

28

FOLLOWING ISABELLE TO Boulder Island didn't mean I'd be making the same mistakes as the first time I was lured into the lake.

Swimming at night was no longer an option.

This time I'd hop on my paddle board, protected by the life vest I had grabbed from a chair on the patio. And since I was wearing cotton shorts under Dex's T-shirt, I had quickly stuffed our flashlight into one of my pockets, hoping to keep it dry while paddling. My replacement mocs were the only repeat from before. They effectively doubled as water shoes as long as I kept them on my feet.

With my life vest buckled, I ran down our hill, holding my paddle.

Lakeside, the breeze smelled of moss and dark soil enriched by decaying leaves. Ripples sparkled across the water in the moonlight.

I saw and heard splashes from Isabelle as she swam freestyle.

My paddle board leaned against a boulder near the shoreline. Gripping the center handle, I hoisted the board and walked into the water, steadying it before climbing on.

Isabelle was already halfway to the island.

Would she disappear again? Before I got there? Abandon me without providing any new information?

Despite the possibility, I had to take my chances. Anything that could help solve the mystery was worth pursuing.

When Dex was assaulted the night before—pushed down the stairs and nearly killed, ridding the farm of its ghost became urgent.

Our lives depended on it.

Whether I disliked Isabelle or not, mistrusted her or not, I was convinced she wanted me to discover clues about her death. And if I did, then maybe she wouldn't harm us. Maybe she'd accept a one way ticket to her ultimate destination. Then maybe the farm could evolve as the sanctuary we had hoped for. A safe and tranquil place where we could raise our baby.

As I paddled, I kept my eyes fixed on the ghost. To my relief, Isabelle waited for me after she had reached the island.

When I approached the shore, however, she took off running.

I leapt off my board into knee deep water. I placed my paddle on top of the board and grabbed the lanyard. Pulling the board to shore, I left it on the rocks. With my heart beating in workout mode, I ran after the ghost, barely able to glimpse her dress's white skirt as it swayed in between the dense pines.

Beyond the island's shoreline, darkness swallowed the shadows.

Retrieving my flashlight, I shined the beam ahead of me, spotting the hem of Isabelle's dress before she disappeared again.

"Wait!" I shouted.

At least her direction was obvious.

She was heading toward the center of the island.

Dodging trees and fallen branches, I reached the mossy boulder, marking the middle of Boulder Island. I was out of breath and panting. And all alone.

Turning 360-degrees, I shined my flashlight around. I couldn't see anything except trees and vegetation.

As the light illuminated the boulder, I noticed something different. The flattened ground in front of it, blanketed with pine needles, had slightly dropped.

My throat was constricted. I could barely swallow my saliva.

A sinkhole had formed. One that *wasn't* there when Madeline and I had explored the island.

I walked toward the sunken ground, wanting to compare it to the former sinkhole on the lawn behind Dex and my bedroom. I could see that this sinkhole was longer, less round.

Why did I fear the phenomenon was linked to something *supernatural?* Madeline had assured me, more than once, that sinkholes were common in Pennsylvania.

My exhales formed a misty stream. Each tiny droplet glowed with light from my flashlight.

A chill tickled my skin, but not in a good way.

I heard a rumble.

The ground shook.

As I wobbled, my flashlight fell from my hand. When it hit the sinkhole, the bulb went dark.

Damn it.

The moonlight hit the top of the canopy, but light wasn't reaching the ground. I was enveloped in darkness and needed my flashlight to find my way back to the paddle board.

I heard an ominous crunch of footsteps around me.

Lowering on all fours, I patted the ground with my right hand, hoping I'd touch my flashlight. If the bulb hadn't shattered, maybe it could be fixed.

Just as panic began to build, I felt the cool metal of my flashlight and grabbed it.

I almost breathed a sigh of relief. *Almost...*

A hand grabbed my wrist.

Clutched it. Squeezed it. Hard. With a force that reminded me of Richard Peter's fingers clamping down on my neck.

A force that terrified me.

"No! Stop, Isabelle!" I cried, trying to yank my wrist away while not letting go of my flashlight.

Adrenaline exploded within me, coursing through my veins.

I pulled back again, surprised by my newfound fierceness.

The fingers clenching my wrist slipped away.

I raised myself to a kneel and inched back.

Inhaling, I let fresh air fill my lungs, assuring me that I was still alive. Still above ground.

Tree branches rustled.

The wind carried the eerie wailing I had grown familiar with.

I stood, repeatedly pressing the flashlight's button.

Click, click, click.

Nothing happened.

Backing away from the sinkhole, I hit the flashlight against my palm. If striking the ground had loosened its battery connection, perhaps another jolt could restore it.

The flashlight came to life.

I directed the light beam onto the sinkhole. The pine needles and topsoil were disturbed, uplifted, as if the hand had pushed upwards from below ground.

The thought made my stomach squeamish.

Illuminating my wrist, I could see bruises beginning to form in the shape of fingers.

Madeline would view my injury as another reason to sell the farm. And she'd be right.

For the first time, I recognized I was in over my head.

Selling Windy Hill Farm might, in fact, be the only viable solution.

29

Monday, July 14, 2025
Windy Hill Farm: Boulder, Pennsylvania

AT DAWN, I woke up to Omelet's crowing. Biddy joined him by clucking from inside her crate. Sniffing the air for brewing coffee, I detected none. The kitchen was quiet.

Good. I'd use my alone time to google Virgil Williams.

Selling the farm didn't mean I'd stop searching for information that might explain who Isabelle was and why she had chosen to haunt this land instead of departing for her eternal rest.

I glanced at my wrist while reaching for my cellphone on the nightstand. Figures. The finger shaped bruises had deepened from magenta to plum. The only upside to my injury was that it corroborated the events of last night.

Bottomline, a paranormal force—a ghost named Isabelle—wanted me to *FIND THEM*. I still suspected *"them"* were clues. Yet, instead of helping me fulfill her directive, she repeatedly led me and my family into danger. Where we got hurt.

I had to stop following her and start...*leading*.

After entering the name and town (Virgil Williams and Boulder, PA) into my cellphone, I found his obituary:

> (1957): VIRGIL WILLIAMS II died on May 14, one day after sustaining injuries in a single car accident on rural Belmont Bridge. He was 40 and a lifelong resident of Boulder, Pennsylvania (Wayne County).

116

Mr. Williams was a chicken and grain farmer in Boulder on his 2,000 acre farm known as the Williams Farm.

As an active Wayne Library League member, he was a significant donor to the Honesdale Public Library branch. He was also a member of the American Poultry Association.

Surviving Mr. Williams are his wife, Vivian, and their three children: Victoria, Vincent, and Vaughn. Preceding him in death were his parents: Virgil Williams I and Hannah Stockton. (Virgil Williams II was an only child.)

A private ceremony and interment will take place at White Oak UMC in Boulder. In lieu of flowers, donations to the Honesdale Public Library would be appreciated.

My hopefulness took a hit.

There were no children or family members named Isabelle.

The main oddity in Virgil's obituary, other than he and his wife used alliteration by starting their kids' names with a "V," was that he had a private funeral service. That seemed strange for someone who was clearly well known due to his connection with the local county libraries and given that he operated what had to be one of the largest farms in the county. But that was conjecture on my part. People could forgo public services for a myriad of reasons.

Not relevant to my quest, but equally intriguing, was what might've caused Virgil's single car accident. Had he been drunk? Sleeping behind the wheel? Speeding? Avoiding wildlife or a vehicle?

I reminded myself to stay focused on Isabelle.

Maybe googling Virgil's wife, Vivian, might yield the results I hoped to find. For all I knew, Vivian may have remarried—acquired step kids or had more of her own. Maybe Isabelle was one of them.

I found Vivian's obituary.

(1988): VIVIAN HALL WILLIAMS died on October 27 from heart failure. She was 70. Born in Unityville, Pennsylvania (Lycoming County), she moved to Boulder (Wayne County) in 1938.

Mrs. Williams had resided at Five Maples (a retirement home she founded) since 1986, after the farmhouse on the Williams Farm burnt down. According to her eldest daughter, Mrs. Williams has bequeathed Five Maples to the Honesdale Public Library.

She was a member of the Women's National Agricultural and Horticultural Association, a library volunteer, and a devoted mother, grandmother, sister, and aunt.

Surviving Mrs. Williams are her children: Victoria and Vaughn; grandchildren: Rose, Diana, Ross, Ivy, Edwina, Duncan, and Alexander; her sister and brother: Louise and Edgar, and their spouses; as well as her nieces and nephews.

Preceding her in death were her parents: Franklin J. Hall and Sallie Ann Darwin; her husband, Virgil Williams II (who passed in 1957); and her son, Vincent (who passed in 1985).

A memorial service will be held on November 1st at White Oak UMC, with the interment and a church luncheon to follow. The service begins at 11 a.m. All are welcome.

Still no reference to someone named Isabelle. Perhaps she was Vivian's niece, but the odds of her being related were waning. In fact, she might not have *any* association with the Williams family. None at all. Which might make my research close to impossible.

Unless...

Isabelle was a missing person from Boulder or a nearby town.

At least I had an indication of when Isabelle might've been a teenager. Her skirted dress looked 1950s-ish. Since Virgil died in 1957, it was obvious the farm existed in that decade.

Clearly, I needed more information. And both obituaries pointed me to where I should start my search: The Honesdale Public Library on Main Street.

The smell of bread toasting invisibly drifted into my room. I must've been so absorbed in my research that I hadn't heard Madeline making breakfast.

Getting out of bed, I looked for my mocs before remembering they were drying on the patio after last night's excursion to Boulder Island. Throwing on my bathrobe, I hoped the long sleeves would hide the bruises on my wrist, at least until I had a chance to sharpen my senses. Madeline, no doubt, would bombard me with questions once she spotted my injury.

When I opened the crate's gate, Biddy strutted out and I bent down to pat her.

"Good morning, sweetie."

She clucked as she followed me into the kitchen.

"There's my little sis," Madeline said, handing me a mug.

"You're spoiling me." I looked at the yellow liquid in my cup. "Except, this isn't coffee."

"When you're pregnant, ginger tea is better for the baby than decaffeinated coffee."

My sister put a plate filled with eggs, toast, spinach, and fresh fruit at my regular spot at the kitchen island.

"Sit and eat," she said. "You're growing my niece or nephew, you know." She got the orange juice from the fridge and poured me a glass. "Did you have trouble sleeping last night?"

Was I about to get the third degree? I'd lob the question back.

"Why do you ask?"

"Your television was blaring at two in the morning," she said. "I had to turn it off."

"Was the screen grainy?"

Madeline confirmed it had been.

I didn't mention that Isabelle, not Richard Peter, made a habit of turning the television on and off, screwing with our reception, and cranking up the volume.

Come to think of it, Isabelle had probably opened the slider last night, after my sister had gone to bed. But I didn't want to delve into any of that. I wanted to move forward.

"Our television in the great room is faulty. I'll unplug it." I sipped my tea which was rather tasty. "Before we go to the hospital, mind if we stop by the public library in Honesdale?"

Madeline raised her eyebrows, and I understood her question.

I admitted googling Virgil and Vivian Williams and reading their obituaries. I felt certain I could find out more from library archives, especially since the couple had been staunch supporters of that branch. The library had likely retained newspaper clippings on them.

"Well?" I asked. "Will you come with me?"

"Sisters may walk different paths, but they're never farther than a heartstring."

And that was Madeline in 12 words or less.

She might not agree with me, but she'd never be so stubborn as to deny me emotional support or a helping hand.

30

WHILE DRIVING TO the library, Madeline and I had gotten into a heated conversation on Roosevelt Highway near Keen Pond. My sister saw my bruise when my blouse sleeve accidentally lifted. She almost lost her mind until I told her I would be encouraging Dex to sell the farm as soon as he was well enough to engage in the decision.

By the time my sister had turned onto Main Street and parked in front of the library, she acquiesced to my argument that it was harmless to conduct research on a ghost named Isabelle.

To my surprise, the library was a massive brick mansion (Victorian style) with scalloped roof tiles, arched windows trimmed in white, and matching shutters.

At 11:00 a.m., a librarian named Jennifer had agreed to meet my sister and me at the double doors in the front. In response to my request, she'd take us to a private room where we could review newspaper archives and microfilm sheets associated with the Williams family.

After getting out of the car, I strolled up the brick walkway with Madeline beside me.

The door opened. A woman around my age, with beautiful skin in a smooth ebony tone, greeted us dressed in a cheery floral sundress. In kind, I introduced my sister.

"When we spoke on the phone, I forgot to ask you," Jennifer said to me. "Are you relatives of the Williams family?"

121

"No," I answered. "My husband and I purchased the last parcel of ground still belonging to the original Williams Farm. We're here because we'd like to learn more about the land and family history."

"So *you're* the new owner of lot sixteen," she said, nodding. "The whole county was surprised Duncan Williams had been successful in getting his grandparents' wishes overturned by the court. *Surprised* and perhaps a bit disappointed, only because having the parcel idle, untouched, had blossomed into a local legend over the decades. Townsfolk loved to speculate about why Virgil and Vivian had never wanted that corner of their farmland to be developed." She chuckled. "With each passing year, the stories grew larger than life."

Jennifer closed the front doors behind us.

We stood in an elegant foyer, looking more like a home than library. A large, intricate crystal chandelier hung from the 15-foot high ceiling, casting light on an antique hand-loomed rug.

An ornate grandfather clock was chiming...*bong, bong, bong.*

"Any guesses?" I asked, nearly shouting. "About why the lot was never to be sold?"

Jennifer quickly glanced through a pair of open doors forming the mouth of the library, probably concerned my elevated volume had disturbed patrons. When no one appeared to be in earshot, she refocused on me and smiled politely.

"I'm on 'team conservative' compared to some of the fantastical theories I've heard," she told us in a whisper now that the clock had finished chiming. "You know, hauntings and such. But I think Virgil, and later Vivian, simply wanted to preserve their slice of heaven."

She ended her comment with a head bob. A *that's it, final answer.*

Jennifer reminded me of the type of person who always saw the cup half full. And the liquid in the sparkling glass was perfectly brewed sweet tea with a delightful sprig of fresh mint.

In contrast, my cup had been spiked with the bitterness of a ghost named Isabelle, tasting more like soured apple-vinegar than sweet tea.

I missed being naive—when I believed everything had an explanation. A *reasonable* one.

Jennifer walked to the wall on the right side of the foyer, one serving as a shrine to the Williams family. As Madeline and I moved closer, she pointed to a black and white photograph of a woman.

"Vivian donated this building to us in 1988. God rest her soul."

The nameplate under Vivian Williams's photograph was engraved with the year 1955, the same year engraved under her husband Virgil's photograph hanging beside hers.

With high cheek bones, vibrant eyes, and attractive smiles, both Williamses were good looking in any decade.

"How old were they when these photos were taken?" I asked.

"Vivian was thirty-seven. Virgil, thirty-eight. They were in the prime of their lives." She gently caressed the frame of Virgil's picture. "He died two years later. So tragic."

Our guide led us up a flight of maple stairs interrupted by a landing which featured a built-in bench with a red velvet cushion. Above the bench was a stained glass window with light streaming through it, casting primary colors on one of the walls.

"Five maple trees were harvested to construct this three-story staircase," she said, as we reached the second floor.

"You know your history." I hoped to flatter her. "Ever heard of someone named Isabelle? A teenager who might've been associated with the Williams Farm in the 1950s?"

Jennifer stopped in the hallway and placed her index finger under her lower lip, curling it over her chin. Gazing upwards, she was clearly paging through her memory banks.

"Can't say I recall that name," she said. "Then again, the Williamses hired a lot of people to help raise their chickens and cultivate their land." She opened a door to a room with a large table positioned at its center. "Perhaps you'll find that name among the archives."

One plastic, lidded container sat on the tabletop. Next to the container was a clasped manila envelope marked "Williams" with a microfilm reader beside it.

I felt disappointed. "I thought there'd be more to go through."

"Vivian volunteered in our seven county libraries as early as 1940," Jennifer said, as if she had recited this factoid hundreds of times. "That's almost a half century before she donated this building in her will. Goes without saying that she was our longstanding historian for the Wayne Library League, of which Virgil was a leading member. Every record here or in our other county libraries was touched by her. Rumor has it, she was a stickler for details. The collection should be comprehensive."

Jennifer walked to the door and pointed at an antique device mounted on the wall. "This is an intercom. Press the button to talk when you're through. I'll hear you at my desk."

For the next two hours, Madeline tackled the microfilm while I delicately fingered through news clippings, reading every article. Most were associated with awards and recognitions bestowed to either Virgil, Vivian, or the farm.

We also found the property's old deed. Virgil and Vivian had purchased the land in 1946, when Virgil was 29 and Vivian, 28. Their three children were already born (birth announcements for the mini V's were in the archives) before they constructed their homestead and started farming operations.

None of the records, however, included a person named Isabelle.

I was going to call it a day, given our efforts hadn't yielded much. Anyway, missing visiting hours at the hospital wasn't an option. I wanted to spend time with Dex, even though he was still being kept in a drug-induced sleep. (I avoided using the word *coma;* it sounded too life threatening.)

Only two more articles...

I found something: a family photo taken on the steps of the farmhouse in 1955. Chickens were roaming on the lawn in front of the family. Two border collies were in the picture, too.

Excitement made my hands shaky.

Then again, the photograph was pixelated with large dots, which meant details were impossible to decipher. However, I could recognize Virgil and Vivian. But instead of three children, there were four pictured. Two boys and *two* girls. All four were teenagers.

Both girls were the same height. Both wore long braided ponytails. Could one of them be Isabelle?

The lack of clarity made it difficult to tell.

My enthusiasm lessened when I remembered Isabelle wore her hair loose (not braided) in our encounters. But that alone didn't rule out the fact that one of the girls could be her.

"Look at this family photograph," I said to Madeline. "I thought the Williamses only had one girl, Victoria."

"That's right," she said, maintaining her focus on the microfilm sheet displayed on the reader. "What name is listed in the caption for the mystery girl?"

"There isn't one. The caption has been cut away. Maybe you can find the same photo in microfilm. Let's hope the picture is part of a larger article which includes a caption."

My sister's curiosity was piqued. After glancing at the clipping, she feverishly held microfilm sheets up to the light until she found a match. Unfortunately, it didn't have a caption either.

"Let's ask Jennifer," Madeline suggested. "Maybe she'll be able to identify the girl. To ease your mind she isn't your ghost, Isabelle."

My ghost?

Madeline and I were, indeed, on different paths. While I tried to find *the* Isabelle who once lived, my sister hoped to prove the ghost only existed in *my* mind.

I buzzed Jennifer on the intercom.

When she joined us, I showed her the clipping.

"Do you know who the girls are in the picture?" I asked. "I'm assuming one is Victoria. The other must be well known to the family because she was included in their photo."

Jennifer stared at the clipping in silence before pointing at one of the girls. "This is Victoria," she said. "The other girl? I'm not sure who she is. All is not lost, though."

"No?"

"I believe Miss Grace took this photograph. I've been told she took all the professional photos of the Williams family, including the ones of Virgil and Vivian showcased in our lobby."

"Is she still...*alive?*"

Jennifer smiled wide. "She's in her late eighties. Living right here in town. At the assisted living community called Wellspring."

31

WHO KNEW VISITORS had to set an appointment to call on a resident of a "life plan" community which provided tiered housing options for each stage of a senior's golden years? I thought popping in yesterday with a home baked apple pie would be considered neighborly.

Madeline and I were turned away.

Apparently, *neighborly* was limited to Wednesdays and Saturdays, starting at 1:00 p.m. and by appointment only. Minus any food.

After we signed in for Grace Carson and pressed our nametag stickers onto our sleeveless blouses, a nurse named Kelsie led us through multiple hallways until we reached a glass door to the outside. She entered a code on a device and the door automatically opened. We walked onto a long outdoor porch, shaded by a retractable awning. The view overlooked a rolling field that included a thick cluster of trees to the left.

I glanced at my bruised wrist, relieved my stacked bracelets were hiding the wound.

"Miss Grace hasn't had visitors in a couple of years," Kelsie said. "She's been very excited all morning, though she mentioned you've never met before."

"She's right," I said. "Is there anything we should know to help us be sensitive to her needs? Does she struggle with short or long term memories? Is she hard of hearing?"

Kelsie chuckled. "Miss Grace is eighty-eight years old, going on twenty! Sharp as a whip. Excellent hearing." She leaned in toward me and whispered, "She's one of our favorites." Pointing to some chairs, she added, "Make yourselves comfortable. I'll bring her out."

We sat down, and I noticed we had the porch all to ourselves.

My stomach felt queasy. Jittery. Either my quest to discover Isabelle's identity was about to advance (beyond her first name) or stall out, once again.

Minutes later, the glass door opened. Pushing a wheelchair onto the porch, Kelsie rolled Grace Carson who had a colorful crocheted blanket draped over her legs. The nurse positioned the wheelchair facing Madeline and me. She stepped on a pedal to lock the wheels.

"I'll check on you young ladies soon," Kelsie said, walking away.

We spent the first five minutes covering small talk: weather, our occupations, and where Madeline and I both lived. She was familiar with lot 16 and the fact that it had been part of the original Williams Farm and sold (to Dex and me) a year ago. The conversation smoothly segued to our research at the library and how the librarian thought that *she,* Grace Carson, had taken the Williams' family photo which curiously included *two* teenaged girls, instead of their one.

"Well, dear? Where's that picture you're wondering about?" Miss Grace asked. "I can't tell you who the other girl is without seeing the photograph in question."

I reached into my back pocket and pulled out a folded photocopy. I opened and flattened the sheet of paper before handing it over.

"Indeed," Miss Grace said. "I took this photograph on June twenty-fifth, a sunny Saturday in 1955. I was eighteen and had graduated from high school two weeks earlier. The Williams' photo shoot was my first assignment as a photographer for *The Herald.*"

Sharp as a whip was right. Miss Grace's mind was snappy quick.

She held the paper at arm's length. With her other hand, she pointed to the girl on the left who stood closest to Vivian. "This is Victoria. We went to high school together, although she was two years younger. When I took this photograph, she had just finished her sophomore year."

"What about the other girl?" Madeline asked, beating me to it. "Do you know who she is?"

"Mrs. Williams's step niece. See, Vivian Williams's sister, Louise, married Daniel Taylor—his *second* marriage. His first was to a divorcee with a child. But then his first wife died of diphtheria, a dreadful disease. As a widower with a stepdaughter, Daniel met Louise in Unityville. One instant happy family. They adopted Daniel's stepdaughter sometime after. Gave her the same last name.

"In the summer of 1955," Miss Grace continued, "their daughter stayed at the Williams Farm to work. Poor child."

"Do you remember the girl's first name?" I asked, trying not to sound too eager.

"You read the caption under this photograph, didn't you?"

"None existed. It had been cut off. Both in the newspaper clipping *and* microfilm."

"Interesting," she said. "Her name was Isabelle. Isabelle Taylor."

My palms became sweaty. My fingers trembled.

"Are you all right, dear?" Miss Grace asked.

"I'm fine. Thank you," I said, nodding. "Can you tell us more about Isabelle?"

"When I was on the farm to take this photograph, I could tell Victoria and Isabelle were very close. They were both smart and beautiful." She smiled. "In fact, they could've passed as twins. They were only a year apart. Victoria was sixteen. Isabelle, seventeen.

"Victoria had always kept to herself in school, so she finally had a best friend. I was happy for her." Miss Grace's lips thinned. "But Isabelle was from Unityville. She was only at the farm for seven weeks. To this day, not much else is known about her."

"Earlier," Madeline said, "you referred to her as *poor child*. Did something happen?"

"You read my article in the archives, didn't you?"

Madeline and I shook our heads no.

"Sadly, Isabelle Taylor disappeared," Miss Grace said. "Disappeared from Unityville on July twenty-third, 1955. Gone without a trace. She's presumed dead, of course."

I locked eyes with my sister, hoping my expression didn't look like a victory lap.

"Are you sure she disappeared in Unityville?" I asked, guessing that ghosts probably haunted places which had something specific to do with their deaths.

"Police from Unityville and Boulder conducted investigations back then. I remember the inquiries well. Townsfolk were interviewed. Including me.

"Turns out," Miss Grace continued, "that Isabelle Taylor took a train to Unityville on the day she disappeared. Witnesses saw her purchase the ticket the day before and then ride the train on the next. She was even spotted getting off at the station in Unityville."

Miss Grace stared blankly at her lap, rubbing her hands together.

"Isabelle had never told her parents she was returning for an overnight visit," she added. "Consequently, the Taylors weren't at the train station to meet her. The poor dear vanished."

"I wonder why your article wasn't in the archived collection?" I asked. "The librarian told us that Vivian Williams was a meticulous historian."

"Indeed, she was," Miss Grace confirmed. "But being good at managing details doesn't always imply you share them all. Virgil and Vivian Williams were devoted to this county. Invested in it. And the last thing they wanted was to have the county's reputation, or their family's reputation, linked to a tragedy. Especially one involving their missing step niece."

"It's almost as if Isabelle was wiped from Wayne County's history," I said. "Except for this caption-less photograph."

She raised her wrinkled eyebrows and tilted her head as if I was finally catching on.

"Now you understand how some rural counties worked in the old days, my dear. The powerful protected their interests."

"I'm guessing the Williamses were investigated and cleared?" Madeline asked.

"Yes. If I remember correctly, Mr. Williams was with Victoria at a chicken auction. Mrs. Williams was in Honesdale at a hardware store buying a tractor part or some such contraption. Vincent, also a teenager, was running the farm in their absence. And their youngest, Vaughn, was away at camp with the 4-H Club. Everybody's alibis were verified."

Two flies swarmed around my face.

Annoyed at their interference, I swatted at them.

32

MY CURIOSITY SHIFTED from Isabelle Taylor to the Williamses: that they would place the county's reputation above the importance of broadcasting a missing teenager. *Their* step niece! Someone who had spent seven weeks in Boulder, at *their* farm, before disappearing in Unityville.

Callous was the word that popped into my head.

Was that why Isabelle wanted a break from the farm? Because her step aunt and uncle were cold hearted?

"Can you tell us more about Vivian and Virgil Williams?" I asked Miss Grace. "What were they like?"

"Both were pillars of our county, though perceived differently, if I may say so," Miss Grace started. "Mrs. Williams was beloved. Gracious and altruistic. Industrious, as well. If she had to roll up her sleeves and get dirty, she did so without complaint, always wearing the smile of an angel. Her reputation was beyond reproach and has only strengthened since her passing.

"If Mrs. Williams was the sweet filling of a pie," she continued, "Mr. Williams was the buttery crust. I was seventeen when I first met him. His eyes were large and the bluest of blue. Hauntingly engaging. When he locked his gaze with yours, it was impossible to look away. I often felt he enjoyed making women feel uncomfortable.

"His other features were equally disarming," Miss Grace continued. "His hair was prematurely white, but in a youthful way.

When he frequented Honesdale, he was flawlessly polished and debonaire. Divinely charming. And underneath his tailored wardrobe, every woman knew he had a muscular physique worthy of an impure thought."

"He sounds dreamy, but was he as revered as his wife?" I asked.

"Mr. Williams had an edge about him," she said. "An arrogance that distanced him from politicians who ran the county. Since he was a man of wealth and brains, he didn't need county leaders in his pockets. Mr. Williams only flexed his muscles about the county's public libraries. He was passionate about them. About reading. Lucky for him that politicians didn't care much about our libraries."

Miss Grace seemed to like directness, so I didn't hesitate.

"Did the Williamses have a good marriage then?"

"Mr. Williams flirted with women all the time. His wife turned a blind eye," she answered. "Gossip suggested her husband was either remarkably faithful or expertly discrete. Regardless, my sources told me the disappearance of Isabelle had deeply affected the couple. Individually changed them. Right up to their deaths."

"About Virgil's death," I said. "His obituary was accessible online and in the library's archives. But there were no other articles about the car accident. As a photographer for *The Herald,* were you privy to the circumstances of his accident on Belmont Bridge?"

"I was a reporter by then," she clarified. "And yes, there was more to the story than was published. Mrs. Williams was very influential, and as I mentioned, our county adored her. Grieved for her. My editor wouldn't allow any disturbing details to be released."

Madeline shooed at some flies.

Now was not a good time to be distracted by pesky insects. I was desperate to learn as much information as I could from Miss Grace. She was a fountain of knowledge.

"Please. Go on," I urged.

Madeline nodded in agreement.

"I had interviewed a nurse caring for Mr. Williams in intensive care at the hospital in Honesdale. I haven't thought about this in decades, but I remember. Mr. Williams was barely alive after his car had careened off the bridge and into water. The nurse told me, off the record, that Mr. Williams had uttered one word before being placed on a ventilator. Happens to have been his last word."

I leaned forward in my chair. "Yes?"

"The name of his step niece. He had whispered, *Isabelle.*"

I would've expected a dying man to utter his wife's name. Or those of his children.

"That's perplexing, isn't it?" I asked.

"I discreetly inquired about it with Mrs. Williams. She confided in me that her husband had been tormented by Isabelle's disappearance, as was she. They were devastated, the whole family was, that Isabelle had never been found, dead or alive."

A few more flies buzzed around us.

I also heard loud chirping.

Glancing at the swath of trees to our left, I was shocked. Branches were littered with ravens. A déjà vu anomaly, reminding me of when ravens had overtaken the woods beside my greenhouse.

I felt as though I was in high school taking a timed test—right when the timer was seconds from sounding. And I hadn't even finished answering the questions.

Tick, tick, tick.

I couldn't let flies and ravens interfere. Miss Grace had to know about my encounters with Isabelle, about how her ghost wanted me to find clues (associated with her death, I presumed). And if I didn't, she'd hurt me and the ones whom I loved. In fact, she already had.

Speaking without any pauses, I shared my story.

Miss Grace listened intently. Her expressions weren't of judgment or disbelief. Rather, she looked genuinely concerned.

I understood why she was one of the nurses' favorite residents.

"Truth always finds daylight," she finally said.

More flies swarmed around us.

Birds screamed in the distance.

The glass door opened, and Kelsie hurried onto the porch.

"We need to end your visit," the nurse said, swatting at flies.

Kelsie pointed to a chair on the deck, about three down from where we sat. The chair was coated black with flies.

I had been so absorbed in telling my story that I hadn't noticed. The chair reminded me of what had happened to my paddle board on Boulder Island.

"Flies are everywhere, and birds are amassing," Kelsie continued. "They're acting strange. Aggressive. Everybody needs to get inside or to their vehicles. Visitations are over."

Madeline stood from her chair. Creases on her forehead meant she was ready to leave.

"I was hoping for your advice, Miss Grace," I said, trying to ignore the blasted *tick, tick, tick* in my head.

"That'll have to wait for another day," Kelsie insisted, unlocking the brakes on the wheelchair.

"No," Miss Grace snapped, getting everyone's attention, especially her nurse's. "I'm not afraid of flies or ravens. Nora needs my help."

A few flies kamikazed into Miss Grace's curly white hair. She didn't flinch.

Kelsie began to pick the flies from her scalp. "Please hurry."

"Victoria is still alive," Miss Grace said. "I'm not sure how lucid she is, but it's worth a try. She's a resident of Mountain Manor on the outskirts of Honesdale. She knew Isabelle best."

CRACK...

A raven crashed into a nearby window.

The bird dropped onto the deck, twitching as life fleeted.

"It's dangerous out here, Miss Grace," Kelsie warned. "I insist we go inside. And our guests need to leave. Get to their car. Now."

"A Ouija board, dear," she said, nearly out of breath. "Use it to ask Isabelle questions. About what happened to her."

Her nurse wheeled her to the glass door and entered the code. The door opened.

"Do what police never could," Miss Grace added. "Solve this mystery once and for all."

They entered the building, and the door closed behind them.

Madeline and I ran off the porch steps toward the parking lot, shielding our faces from the bombardment of flies.

33

Monday, July 28, 2025
Wayne Memorial Hospital: Honesdale, Pennsylvania

TWO WEEKS AND two days after Isabelle pushed Dex down the basement stairs, fracturing his neck and arm, my husband was going to be medically eased into consciousness. No more induced sleep. And his orthopedic surgeon *hoped* I'd be bedside as Dex opened his eyes in the early morning hours. There, to help calm him. To provide some visual normalcy in the sterile ICU environment.

Hoped? More like...*try and stop me!*

Every day since he had been assaulted and hospitalized, I had visited him. I could never fathom missing a single day, let alone the moment he was scheduled to wake up.

I had arrived at Dex's ICU room at 7:00 a.m.

Minutes ago, as I clasped his left hand, his eyes fluttered open. And when I whispered his name, he squeezed my fingers. *Squeezed!*

If I was supposed to be stoic, I had failed.

My tears overflowed. Dex was my partner, my friend. My forever love. And he had just moved *below* his neck!

Initially, we just stared at each other. God how I loved this man.

After we spent a few minutes voicing our hellos, Dr. Saddler introduced herself and updated Dex on his injuries and what was planned for the day—mostly testing. Could he bend his knees? Wiggle his toes? Of course, he'd have another MRI. And he'd meet with physical and occupational therapists for the first time.

"A busy day is ahead, Mr. Bliss," the doctor announced.

Dr. Saddler asked if I'd return at 3:00 p.m. She'd know more about his prognosis then.

"Afterwards," she added, "you can have some alone time with your husband. How does that sound, Mrs. Bliss?"

Making me leave...*sucked,* but I wondered if anyone else had ever had the nerve to admit it. To protest out loud. My guess was that no one had, so I smiled and kissed Dex goodbye.

To make the time pass more quickly, I drove to the farm and finished my chores before heading back to the hospital.

I entered my husband's room on time. Dr. Saddler was already talking to Dex, but she graciously moved aside so I could stand on the left side of his bed and hold his hand again.

For the next ten minutes, she reviewed how the testing had gone. Dex could bend his knees and move his toes. His neck and arm fractures were healing beautifully. A full recovery was expected, with no paralysis!

"Before dinnertime," she said, "he'll be moved out of ICU and onto the third floor."

Once again, tears streamed down my cheeks.

My relief was overwhelming.

"How soon before Dex transfers to a rehab facility?" I asked her.

"As early as this Friday. And then rehab takes six to eight weeks, with absolutely no shortcuts."

After Dr. Saddler painted a picture of the intense regimen rehab would require, she left the room, closing the glass door behind her.

I pulled over a chair next to the bed and sat. Dex, who wore a complicated neck contraption, couldn't turn his head to look at me, but we adjusted quickly.

"How are you and the baby?" he asked. "Feeling okay?"

It warmed my heart that *we,* not just me, were on his mind. I told him I was seven weeks pregnant now, and my first appointment with the OBGYN was next week.

"I hope Madeline is still staying with you at the farm," he said.

"She went home last week. But if I need her, she'll come back."

After farm updates, our conversation switched to the ghost.

I recapped the research Madeline and I had conducted, from my googling the Williams' obituaries to our library visit where we discovered a 1955 photo of the Williams family. A photo which included a mysterious girl. *That* finding led to our meeting with the photographer, a senior resident at Wellspring, who identified our ghost as Isabelle Taylor, step niece of Vivian Williams.

"Our visit with Miss Grace had to be cut short," I explained. "Visitors were forced to leave because flies and ravens had invaded the campus. It was crazy."

"Didn't flies coat your paddle board when you and Madeline paddled to the island?"

"Yes. And when we were at Wellspring, they covered a chair. So thick, it looked like the chair was painted black."

"Not surprising," he said. "I remember hearing the Department of Agriculture had bred and released flies to eat the spongy moth larva. Now look what we're left with. Too many flies."

"Not sure that's why. At least, not in this case. Turns out, flies are attracted to electromagnetic fields."

"The same can be said of flies and cow dung. We live in farm country, Nora."

"When ghosts are present," I said, ignoring his snarky skepticism, "they create an electromagnetic field. I read about it. And flies are sensitive to EMFs."

"What you're suggesting is that while you were at Wellspring, meeting with this...*Miss Grace,* a ghost might've been around you? And flies were attracted to the paranormal activity?"

"Could be," I said, shrugging and hoping I didn't sound too paranoid. "In fact, it's very possible."

"And your theory on the ravens?"

"They're drawn to the intersection of life and death. In other words, drawn to ghosts."

"Listen," he started, and I wondered if he'd launch into a condescending lecture. "We both agree our farm is haunted. I haven't forgotten how I got here. But we also shouldn't go *from*... never acknowledging ghosts *to*... thinking they're the cause of every single odd phenomenon."

"My argument," I countered, "is we should at least consider that two strange occurrences, happening near one another in proximity and time, may be linked. That's a logical assumption."

"I hear you," he said. "I guess our ultimate dilemma is deciding what we're going to do about it."

"Madeline thinks we should sell the farm. Right away. Before anyone else gets hurt."

"What do *you* think?"

I was surprised Dex was genuinely collaborating. Then again, I knew firsthand how a traumatic event could rock a person's foundation. Could affect their outlook. Their behavior.

"Selling might be the best solution," I said, "but let's wait to decide until you get home."

We agreed that's what we'd do.

"Are you comfortable staying at the farm? In the interim?" he asked. "If not, we could sell the chickens back to Roxy. You could rent a place in town. Closer to the rehab facility."

Oh dear God! Hearing the suggestion made me realize I was *not* ready for that. Not even close. I adored my flock, my Biddy. Frankly, I also loved Windy Hill Farm, troubled as it was.

"I'll be fine," I said. "I'm no longer naive about Isabelle and her trickery. I'll stay alert."

"What's next then?" he asked.

"Miss Grace suggested I speak with Victoria—the Williams' eldest child who's still alive. I'm scheduled for a visitation next week, except her nurse says she's very weak. Still, I need to try and speak with her. Victoria was close to Isabelle and might give me insight into her motivations as a ghost." I swallowed. "And *umm,* Miss Grace also suggested a Ouija board."

"Isn't that a talking board for spirits?"

"Yes. And Miss Grace thinks asking Isabelle direct questions via the board would be helpful."

"Not a good idea," he said, sounding stern. "Those boards can open a portal into the spirit world. No way. Too dangerous."

"The portal is already open. Right?"

"I'm not sure how all this works, Nora. Neither are you. But when you stick your hand in fire, you will get burned. If Sunday School ingrained one fear into me, it's that the underworld is consumed in fire. The door to Hell needs to stay closed. Period."

"Isabelle seems desperate. Angry," I said. "But is she *evil?*"

"If you were lying on this hospital bed, you wouldn't have any doubts. Believe me."

Yikes. I didn't mean how that had sounded.

I apologized and Dex understood.

"We're on the same page," I assured him. *"Yes* to visiting Victoria. *No* to a Ouija board."

A nurse entered the room.

Time to move Dex out of ICU.

34

Tuesday, July 29, 2025
Windy Hill Farm: Boulder, Pennsylvania

I GOT OUT of bed during Omelet's crowing. My plan was to finish chores as early as possible. I couldn't wait to visit Dex in his new hospital room. Hopefully, he had slept well last night, especially since he knew his fractures hadn't resulted in any paralysis.

I certainly had. The fact that he would fully recover had lifted a heavy burden from me as well, enabling me to be lulled into a much needed deep sleep.

Less stress might restore my creativity, too.

My boss, Cecelia, had noticed my drained temperament reflected in mediocre designs and average work output (her words). Given Dex's injuries, she understood, "of course."

I couldn't disagree with her unflattering assessment. Worrying if Dex was ever going to walk had consumed most of my energy. Not to mention being haunted by a ghost whom I was researching. A ghost who kept me on guard 24/7, though I didn't dare tell Cecelia about Isabelle.

Never mind I was also in my first trimester.

Add farm chores into the mix and my priorities made sense. When it came to getting my attention, work ranked last. D&B's design projects could always be put off for another day. Another time. In contrast, feeding the chickens and watering trees in the orchard and plants in the greenhouse had to happen like clockwork. Or else, they could die.

No wonder that as far as Cecelia and D&B were concerned, I was a hot mess. Fixing that perception would have to wait.

Right now, eating was more important.

Before tugging on my Muck boots, I needed to consume a balanced breakfast. Madeline would interrogate me on what I had eaten during her daily check-in.

Outside, the ground was saturated from last night's rain. My boots squished with each footstep as I headed to the chicken coop carrying my bucket of chicken feed and sliced apples. Omelet was already strutting up and down the long, enclosed run. A few hens—Pricilla, Daphne, and Sally Mae—pecked at the grass behind him. They clucked as I approached.

I sprinkled their food on the lawn beside the coop.

Still no Biddy?

Weird that she wasn't among the hens watching me spread their meal on the grass. She always greeted me at the gate. Then again, she was confident in our routine. My hen understood she was the only one in the flock invited to stick to my heels as I traversed the farm accomplishing chores. The only one who was allowed inside the house. Who had a crate in the bedroom for overnights. And two bowls sitting on a monogrammed rug in the kitchen.

I imagined raising my right hand in front of a judge. *Guilty as charged.* My hen dog was undeniably spoiled.

As I was about to swing open the gate, a roar began to build in the valley below our property. I pictured the gust racing across the lake, forming white caps on the water, before shooting up the hillside. The leaves in nearby trees were as familiar with the freakish wind as I was. They began to twirl in nervous anticipation.

Omelet and the hens raced beside the hutch for protection.

Windy Hill Farm was true to its name.

The wind arrived like a waterless wave, crashing into me as I clutched the gate. My bangs thrashed around my face. My T-shirt flapped violently against my skin.

As usual, sounds of wailing traveled with the gust. I wondered if the tormented crying was somehow naturally created. Or if Isabelle's spirit was anguishing over what had happened to her at the age of seventeen. Anguishing over the circumstances of her disappearance.

Of her death.

Then again, Dex had reminded me that the supernatural shouldn't be blamed for every strange thing happening on our farm. What had the engineer concluded about that damn sinkhole? I remember: *Shit happens.* The truth could be simple. And unexplained.

Once the wind fled eastward, I opened the gate. Omelet and his feathered harem left the run to gobble up their feed. More hens joined in the exodus. After giving them time to roam freely, I'd regather them after I showered and was ready to leave for the hospital.

As the hens left the hutch and exited the run, I counted heads.

Eight, nine...

I was one short: Biddy. What was she up to?

Opening the door to their enclosure, I looked inside.

There she was.

My hardworking hen, perched in the nesting box on the top shelf, was undoubtedly laying eggs while the rest of the flock took care of their hungry bellies.

"Time to take a break, Biddy. Let's head to the greenhouse. I'll give you a zucchini to nibble on."

Her head was tucked down on her chest. She didn't move to the sound of my voice.

Sweat instantly beaded on my forehead.

My stomach felt squeamish. I swallowed hard.

Biddy might be sick.

I walked into the hutch and reached up to bring her down.

The moment my fingers touched her sides, I knew.

"No, no, no!" I cried.

Biddy's body was hard. Cold.

The most precious hen in the world was...*dead.*

I clutched her and brought her to my chest. "My precious hen," I sobbed, trying to breathe. Intense sadness constricted my throat.

That's when I noticed.

Her neck had been snapped. A bone protruded from torn skin below her head.

I remembered Cinnamon. Her neck had been broken similarly.

Back in June, I had blamed Richard Peter for killing Cinnamon, not believing him when he had denied it. Now I realized the common denominator had always been...*Isabelle.*

Wiping my runny nose with the heel of my hand, I sniffled hard.

Isabelle *was* evil. To the core.

Anger and torment hadn't caused her to push Dex down the stairs "accidentally" injuring him. She had tried to *murder* him, and he had only survived because of fate or luck.

Dex was right.

How could I have entertained any excuses for her behavior?

Isabelle was similar to "Mr. Hostile" at Union Station. Both may have had unfortunate pasts, but both were cold blooded, hellbent on killing others.

"I'm going to get rid of you, Isabelle Taylor," I shouted.

Each time I exhaled, a misty plume formed.

Goosebumps spread over my forearms.

"I'll force you back through the gates of Hell. Watch me!"

The window in the hutch cracked like ice.

35

WHEN I CLIMBED into bed, my eyes were raw from crying over Biddy's death. Over her *murder*.

The house was deathly quiet. Dark, too, except for light creeping in from the bathroom's nightlight. The countryside seemed frozen in time. Paused, as if a blanket weighed down with moisture had been draped over it to keep every living thing motionless.

Dense fog was like that.

I wondered if excessive moisture prevented crickets from chirping as they rubbed their wings together. If thick humidity dampened the desires of tree frogs and whippoorwills to call out to potential mates. And if heavy mist disabled a bat's sonar from working in flight, thus keeping them "grounded" and silent from their nighttime chittering.

The atmosphere was hushed like a windless graveyard.

Appropriate for my grief.

Losing Biddy had crushed my spirit. Made me feel morbid. Reminded me once again that the innocent, the vulnerable, could get hurt. Could die.

First, Dex. Now my pet.

Some people might question what all my fussing was about when it came to Biddy.

She was only a hen, they'd say. One of billions. I'd have to accept the facts: Over 30-million chickens were "processed" each day in the U.S. to feed our population. Bottomline, chickens had a noble

143

purpose in society. Death was part of their sacrifice.

They'd tell me to get another hen in her place. Problem solved.

Only, hearts didn't work logically.

Hearts bonded. Got attached. Loved.

Hearts got broken.

I grabbed another tissue from my nightstand and blew my nose.

Earlier, when I shared the news with Dex during my visit at the hospital—that Biddy's neck had been broken and I had buried her beside the orchard, next to Cinnamon—he suggested we purchase a small, inscribed headstone for her grave.

My husband got it. He got *me*.

I wished Dex was lying beside me now. Instead, his side of the bed was cold. Vacant, but thankfully not completely void of protection. Reaching under Dex's pillow, I felt the cool metal of his loaded pistol.

Since his hospitalization, I hadn't felt the need to place his firearm within arm's length at night, especially since Richard Peter had been recaptured and our ghost was immune to bullets. Tonight was different. I felt alone. And the fog with its eerie quiet had only accentuated my isolation. *That,* and Biddy wasn't in her crate cooing or clucking before I drifted off to sleep.

In my cocoon of stillness, I must've fallen asleep.

Ironic that movement woke me up.

Dex tugged on the sheets. Near my feet.

"What?" I whined, trying to clear my head from my dreamy state.

More tugging.

"Can't *you* close the window this time?" I asked, feeling groggy. "I'm so tired. Just let me sleep."

My brain heard my words and started to challenge their logic. *Wait. Wasn't Dex at the hospital? Wasn't I alone in the house?*

Adrenaline surged through my veins. My pulse spiked.

In a seamless motion, I grabbed the handgun while sitting up in bed. I blinked rapidly to help me focus.

Isabelle.

Isabelle stood at the end of my bed in her wet dress, no doubt dripping all over our wood floors. She clearly wanted my attention and now she bloody well had it.

"Get out," I spat. "Leave."

She pointed down the dark hallway leading out of our bedroom.

"Forget it! I'm not following you."

She shook her head like that's not what she meant. She pointed to the hall again.

Our blasted television began blaring from the great room.

Herrrrrr…

Someone had plugged in the cord and turned it on.

How could that be?

Isabelle was here. In the bedroom.

With the sound, she moved away from the bed and hall doorway until her back pressed against the wall beside my window. She continued to shake her head.

Even in minimal light, her expression looked worried. Her eyebrows had pulled together. Her eyes were the size of saucers and her blueish lips quivered.

Was she worried or was her expression more like…*terrified?*

Something wasn't adding up.

"Are you afraid?" I asked her.

She nodded rapidly and pointed toward the hallway again.

The television continued to hiss from the great room.

I decided to ask the same question I had posed once before. It was on the night she had appeared on our deck. *The* night I had followed her to Boulder Island by paddling on my board.

"Are you by yourself?"

Before, her answer had been a nod. A yes.

This time, she shook her head. She was *not* alone.

A door slammed somewhere on the other side of the house, followed by another door and one more after that, as if the intruder was looking for something. Or *someone.*

My heart thundered in my chest.

The danger around me was palpable. Charged and crackling like electricity. Making the hair on the nape of my neck rise and stiffen.

The television turned off.

Maybe that was a good sign.

Maybe the intruder had decided to leave.

Isabelle took two steps off the wall, still keeping her eyes focused on the door to the hall. Still looking hesitant.

In the quiet, I heard footsteps coming toward us from the great room. Slowly. Deliberately. Growing louder as they approached.

I cocked the hammer on Dex's handgun.

Isabelle slammed her back against the wall again, making a thud and knocking a hanging picture off the wall.

When the frame hit the floor, the glass shattered.

Footsteps continued to get closer.

Isabelle disappeared.

With my left hand, I aimed the pistol's barrel at the doorway. With my right, I reached over to my nightstand and turned on my lamp.

When light lit the room, the steps stopped.

The hall was empty.

Although I couldn't see anyone, I could detect a presence.

"I'm alone," I said, shivering and seeing my frosty breath. "So get the fuck out of my house."

My bedroom door slammed shut.

Every inch of my body convulsed in fear.

Whatever entity was inside the house, on the other side of the door, it made my blood run cold.

Deeply inhaling, I tried to calm my ragged breathing while figuring out the meaning behind what had just happened.

Clearly, I had misjudged what was occurring on our farm.

Isabelle was the one being haunted.

A ghost tormented by another ghost.

One who was vicious. Who would hurt anyone in the way.

For the first time, I understood.

Isabelle needed *my* help to free *her* from the terror.

36

I WAS IN no rush to inspect the house. I wanted to regain my composure first. My breathing remained rapid and shallow. My hands continued to shake and my mouth was dry.

Fear still pulsed through every blood vessel.

After what just happened, I had no doubt another ghost was in the mix. One who was different from Isabelle. This other ghost was sinister. Treacherous and menacing.

Don't ask me why, but in the beginning (after I realized Isabelle was a ghost), I mostly felt intense anger and frustration toward her. *Why was she hurting us while desperate for our help? Why did she always disappear before clarifying what she wanted us to find?*

I finally had some answers.

Isabelle wasn't the one hurting us. She seemed as afraid as we were because whoever was haunting *her* was terrifying. Naturally, she vanished in the presence of her archenemy.

De-cocking Dex's pistol, I placed it back under his pillow and thought back to my earlier encounters with Isabelle.

The very first time I had followed her into the lake, I nearly drowned. When I looked underwater in the moonlight, I remembered seeing Isabelle. She had pointed down to the darkest water, below my knees, to where someone unseen had been tugging on my moc shoe. Someone, whom I assumed had been *her*.

Yet, after she swam away, I continued to be pulled under.

Now I realized the truth.

The entity clutching onto my foot *couldn't* have been Isabelle.

I also thought back to the wrist incident which took place at the sinkhole on Boulder Island. After the ground rumbled and I dropped my flashlight, I heard footsteps around me. If they had been Isabelle's, which I was certain they were, then someone else had violently grabbed me at the sinkhole seconds later.

In terms of Dex's accident, I still believed Isabelle had left the wet trail leading to the basement. But I had blamed her for pushing my husband down the stairs and breaking his neck. Now, it was more likely she hadn't been responsible. Instead, the ghost pursuing Isabelle, *hunting* her, was probably following the same wet path as we were. When Dex got in the way, the other ghost had forcefully pushed him.

Would I have been more cautious if I'd known there were *two* spirits? Then again, what ifs weren't helpful. Hindsight never changed what had already taken place.

All I could do was move forward with caution, despite my mission suddenly mushrooming into something exponentially harder. Not only did I need to find clues which might reveal what happened to Isabelle Taylor on July 23, 1955, but I needed to discover who was haunting her and why. Was Isabelle's disappearance the event which connected them?

Even then, figuring out those mysteries would only be halfway to a resolution. Once I knew how the puzzle pieces fit together, I'd have to help Isabelle find peace.

No matter what, I absolutely *had* to expel both ghosts from the property. Windy Hill Farm wasn't big enough for the four (rather, five) of us.

All this, while insuring no one else in my family became collateral damage. All this, while maintaining my workload—visiting Dex, completing farm chores, and designing campaigns for D&B. All this, before Dex came home from rehab and we began deliberating on whether to keep or sell the farm.

Grabbing my cellphone from the nightstand, I studied the calendar. Dex was slated to return home to the farm on September 19th. Fifty-two days from today.

I had to accomplish my goals before then. Every single one.

Next on the agenda was visiting Victoria (Virgil and Vivian Williams' daughter) at Mountain Manor on Monday. Although Victoria was now 86 years old and failing, I hoped she would be conscious and willing to talk with me.

I glanced at the floor between my bed and the window. When Isabelle slammed into the wall, the hanging photograph of Dex and me at our wedding had fallen to the floor. Glass in the picture frame had shattered when it hit the floor.

To avoid stepping on glass shards, I scooted off the bed on Dex's side. I'd sweep up the mess after I inspected the house, making sure it was empty of all other entities, except me.

As I walked to my closet for shoes, I didn't feel the familiar iciness that seemed to accompany paranormal activity. My breath was invisible again. And steadiness had returned to my muscles. No more trembling.

My days of being immobilized in the face of danger were gone.

My determination was fierce.

The only unknown was if my newfound resolve could prevail over spirits from the afterlife.

The living versus the dead.

I'd know in 52 days.

37

Monday, August 4, 2025
Mountain Manor Senior Care: Honesdale, Pennsylvania

"VICTORIA IS TRANSITIONING," the nurse told me, as we stood outside of Victoria's closed door to her private room at the Manor. "She hasn't woken up since Saturday."

"Transitioning?" I asked.

"Her body is slowly shutting down," the nurse explained. "It's preparing to transition from this life to the beyond." She leaned toward me and whispered, "Translation: from this life to *Heaven*. But there are sensitivities these days." She rolled her eyes.

"Oh. Wow." I wasn't sure what to say about the *transitioning* part. My own parents were killed instantly at an intersection when a dump truck ran a red light. Consequently, gradual dying wasn't a process I was familiar with. "Will I disturb her?"

My question substituted for my authentic reaction which was utter disappointment, given Victoria wasn't conscious to speak with me.

"Not at all," the nurse answered. "Many believe the body is simply a vessel. The spirit is very much alive so she can hear you, deary. Knowing Victoria, she'll appreciate the company. She's a hoot."

The nurse opened the door, and I was assaulted with a septic odor—bleach and rubbing alcohol if I had to guess. Victoria was lying on a hospital bed to the left of the doorway. A white blanket was pulled up to her chest and her arms were folded over her breasts, crisscrossing at the wrists. Her hands were marked with sunspots and bulging veins. On her face, Victoria's skin had drooped to the sides of her jawline, leaving the contours of her skeleton disturbingly visible. Her lips were dried and cracked, and yellowing teeth peeked through. Her eye sockets were dark. Curly white hair was splayed out on the pillow like knobby fingers.

Aging was cruel.

I remembered the family photo that Miss Grace had taken in 1955. Sixteen year old Victoria was beautiful then. Her youthful self had high cheekbones like her parents. Wide eyes. A pretty mouth. And long blonde hair pulled back into a braided ponytail.

The nurse took a wet sponge and dabbed Victoria's lips with it.

Across from the bed, in between two windows that overlooked flowering bushes brightened by late morning sunlight, was a bookshelf filled with books and magazines.

I meandered over to inspect her collection, wondering what genres she preferred.

"Victoria was always an avid reader," the nurse announced, now placing petroleum jelly on her patient's lips.

I noticed three hardcover journals stacked on one shelf. Excitement washed over me.

"Are these *diaries?*" I asked, hoping not to sound eager.

The nurse stopped what she was doing and looked over at me. "They are. Her son, Ross, found them a couple months back. Brought them in when she was still able to read."

A rush of adrenaline made my knees quiver.

"Do you think she'd like me to read them aloud to her?" I asked.

"She loves to be read to." The nurse stood. "But since the diaries are personal, I'd better check with her son first. Ross is a lawyer in town, if you know what I mean."

"Never mind. I don't want to be a bother. Thank you, though."

In truth, maybe I could sneak a peek when I was alone with Victoria. No need to involve a lawyer because if he said no, taking a look anyway seemed *way* more dishonest.

"No bother at all, deary. Just give me a minute." She opened the door. "He's real good at getting back to me."

In an exhale, Victoria made a loud rattling sound. I flinched.

"Don't let that bother you," the nurse said. "All part of transitioning."

She closed the door, and I was alone with Victoria.

I didn't move from my spot by the bookshelf. Instead, I listened carefully to the nurse's footsteps which were getting fainter as she walked down the hallway.

Selecting the top journal, I flipped through its pages. The handwriting was slightly crude. Juvenile in appearance. Thankfully, I found a date: 1953. Too early. Victoria would've been 14 years old. I wanted to see entries from the summer of 1955 when Isabelle visited.

New footsteps paused outside the closed door.

I stopped breathing.

My heart nearly exploded in my chest.

My knees felt like they might buckle.

Do something!

I quickly placed the journal back on top of the stack. More like threw it back. Hot potato fast. Then I grabbed a magazine and started to page through it, hoping to look natural if the nurse opened the door. I took a deep breath. My fingers were jittery now.

The footsteps continued down the hall.

Oh dear God. I never could've been an intentional burglar.

With quiet returning, the coast seemed clear again.

I decided to peek at the bottom journal, skipping the middle one. Most people stopped using diaries in their mid to late teens. At least, that's what I had done. Maybe the bottom journal was the oldest.

After pulling the journal from its pile, I began to page through it, searching for a date.

I found one: March 3, 1955.

This diary was written in the right year.

Flipping forward, I found an entry in June, but time wouldn't allow me to read it now.

I grabbed my cellphone from the back pocket of my shorts. I'd snap a few photos of the pages, and no one would be the wiser. Unless I got caught.

My heart thumped like the cylinders of the Titanic when the engine room got the order for full steam ahead. My palms were clammy, so I wiped them off on my shorts.

Placing the open journal on the bookshelf's countertop, I snapped the first photo. I turned pages and clicked several more shots.

My luck had to be running out, so I closed the diary and pushed it back under the pile.

I stuffed my cell into my pocket and grabbed a book: *Anne of Green Gables*.

In the nick of time.

Victoria's door swung open as the phone rang, igniting my nerves. Making me flinch.

"Ross wants to speak with you," the nurse said, sounding like she had run a marathon. Panting, she picked up the phone's handset and gave it to me.

"Hello?" I asked, not sure why I made my greeting a question.

Ross introduced himself before telling me that "Mother" hadn't gotten visitors in several years. And out of curiosity, why would I be interested in reading her diaries?

I explained that Dex and I had purchased lot 16 and we were interested in learning all we could about the history of the Williams Farm, for nostalgia and appreciating the roots of our community. Perhaps reading the diaries back to Victoria would be engaging for both of us. However, I completely understood if he felt uncomfortable about it. I was a stranger, after all.

Internally, I certainly wasn't proud of myself. Deceiving Victoria's son wasn't something I was comfortable with. It came down to *"desperate times call for desperate measures."*

"I've never read them," Ross confessed. "But as long as you don't remove the diaries from Mother's room, I can't see the harm."

After the phone call ended and I told the nurse permission was granted, she frowned.

"So sorry, deary. Reading to Victoria will have to wait for another time. We're required to move patients who can't move themselves. No matter what stage someone's in, bed sores must be avoided. After that, our pain management team is scheduled to drop in."

We agreed that an earlier visit tomorrow would work better.

My next stop was visiting Dex. Three days ago, he had been transferred from the hospital to Good Samaritan Rehabilitation Center and we had plans to eat lunch together.

38

DURING MY EARLIER lunch visit with Dex at the rehab facility, I had avoided the topic of Isabelle and anything or anyone related to her mysterious story.

The restricted topics included my epiphany that there was another ghost. As well as my cellphone snapshots of Victoria's diary pages which I had taken (more like *snuck*) at Mountain Manor.

Instead, Dex and I had spent our time talking about our raspberry. That's how big our baby was at eight weeks, according to my OBGYN. A half-inch!

We couldn't resist gazing at the black and white photograph taken on Friday during my first ultrasound of our little berry. An appointment my husband obviously couldn't attend.

Now that I was home and the house and farm were buttoned up tight for the night, I could give my undivided attention to Victoria's diary from 1955. Correction: *partial* diary. I had only taken a handful of photos before the risk of getting caught had become too great.

After disconnecting my cellphone from its charger, I climbed into bed, ready to read until my eyes closed.

Clicking on the icon for my phone's photo albums, I scrolled to find the first photograph I had snapped, wanting to read the entries in chronological order.

I enlarged the picture on my screen.

154

FIND THEM

After breakfast, Father insisted we finish chores while he drove the truck to pick up my stepcousin Isabelle at the train station in Carbondale. Not even Mother was going. She had to harvest a chicken for a fancy supper tonight. "A welcoming celebration," she'd said.

Isabelle is going to stay with us until late August, providing another set of hands on the farm. I look forward to her help. Less chores for me.

The last time I saw my stepcousin was visiting Aunt Louise and Uncle Danny in Unityville two Christmases ago. "Stepcousin?" I couldn't understand why everyone, including me, still called Isabelle "step" this and "step" that. Aunt Louise and Uncle Danny had adopted her. Stepdaughter, step niece, and stepcousin should've died right then, but I guess old habits are hard to break.

During our holiday visit, Isabelle was 15. She suffered from "growing pains." That's what Mother called them. Isabelle's complexion looked like a snowcapped mountain range. (I can thank Vincent for that visual.) And if her face was part of the Alps, her chest was a flat, barren valley. (Vaughn's two cents.) Brothers can be mean. In my opinion, Isabelle was a caterpillar turning into a butterfly. That's how I saw myself a year back. Not that anyone acknowledged my transformation over the school year. Riffraff still teases that I smell like chicken droppings. But pretty girls make boys with newfound growing pains feel insecure. (You're welcome.)

155

Oh fudge. Mother's footsteps are coming. I'm late to report for chores. Until later...

Entry 2:

The mystery about Isabelle is answered. When the rest of us came outside to greet her, smiling Father rested his hand proudly on his step niece's shoulder before nudging her forward toward us, like...look at the beauty I found at the train station. Isabelle curtsied and said, "Pleased to see you all again."

She is a butterfly all right. Her eyes are pale blue, and her blonde hair flows over her shoulders. Her skin is silky. And her barren valley has grown two perky peaks. Unexpected, but we look like we are related now.

Vincent seemed angry at Vaughn's googly eyes. He said Vaughn should take a picture so it could last longer. Vaughn threatened back with a knuckle sandwich. If you ask me, they were both acting like immature babies.

After the greeting, Isabelle ran into my arms, and I knew we were going to be fast friends. I don't have many friends in school or from nearby farms, so maybe this summer I'll finally have my own friend. How I long for a confidante!

I liked Victoria right away. She was confident and compassionate. And her words sparked memories of my own growing pains which included metal braces and a palate expander which made me lisp. Not to mention when the silver streak grew in my hair. Kids called me *freak* and *grandma*. Mom had always described puberty as "character building" to which I'd reply that I had enough character to build another Empire State Building, thank you very much.

Sliding the first photo to the left, I began to read the second, hoping the entry might start enlightening me as to what eventually happened to Isabelle. Even a hint would help.

Sunday, June 5th, Entry 1:

Isabelle and I talked endlessly last night after the lights were turned off. (She is sleeping in the other twin bed in my room.) We spoke about her not knowing her birth father, her mother's cancer, taking care of her stepfather after her mother died, meeting Aunt Louise for the first time, attending a new school in Unityville, and being adopted and changing her last name.

In comparison, my life is...BORING. But since she is an only child, she's eager to learn what it's like to have two brothers. She finally admitted she thinks Vincent is cute (though he is two years younger than her). I warned her I might barf if she talked like that. We laughed until we fell asleep.

After church and lunch, Isabelle and I started to walk around the entire lake. About halfway, we heard the thunder of horse hooves. Father. On our day of rest, he wanted to show Isabelle the farm in its entirety.

Father asked me to hoist her up. He scooted back on Midnight's rump so she could sit in the saddle. I did what I was told. Isabelle wondered out loud if I minded and if we could resume our walk tomorrow. That was very sweet, but she had a lot to learn about how our farm operated. Isabelle had no choice but to go with Father. Our walk was over whether I minded or not. With his arms around her holding the reins, they cantered off and that was that.

Entry 2:

Sunday dinner was awkward. Vincent was angry. Father had not returned with Isabelle until sunset. During his absence, Vincent had to move grain from the main silo to the feed bins at the end of each poultry barn—all by himself. Vaughn couldn't have helped. He had been mowing dormant fields. And I was mucking out poultry barns. Father simply pointed out that the farm is 2,000 acres and Isabelle needed to know the property. Mother's fist pounded the dinner table once, meaning the discussion was over.

When it was time to leave the table, Isabelle stood and clutched the chair and grimaced. She explained she had never ridden horseback, let alone for hours on end. She was sore to the point of tears. I felt bad for her.

Vincent stormed off. Could he be jealous of the time Father got to spend with Isabelle? Or was he still steaming about his added workload?

Isabelle is clearly the prized new chicken whose attention everyone seeks. Except maybe Mother. She always remains dutiful and never bothers with what she refers to as trivial distractions.

I wasn't sure if it was strange that Virgil had spent so many hours with Isabelle, like maybe four to five if the entry was accurate (spanning after lunch to sunset). I had no clue what constituted a reasonable amount of time to ride double around the Williams' 2,000 acre farm. But in that time span, Isabelle would've needed to go to the bathroom. Right? (At least, that would've been the case with my pea-sized bladder. Which was why I thought of it.) Anyway, going to the bathroom behind a tree, with an adult nearby, would've been embarrassing.

After June 5th, I read two more entries.

At some point, my eyes must've closed.

I woke up disoriented. The lights were still on.

My cellphone was face down on top of the bed. I grabbed it and my heart sank.

The screen was cracked. Shattered. And not just the glass protector. Fissures deeply penetrated into the guts of my cellphone.

I tried turning on my device, predicting the exercise would be futile. I was right. My phone remained lifeless. Dead.

Unbelievable.

And disconcerting, to say the least.

Right now, unwelcomed entities could come and go anywhere, as they pleased. There had to be *something* I could do to place limits on them in my own home.

I needed to remember to google if there was a way to create a safe space. One that warded off paranormal activity.

Bottomline, I needed to be able to sleep peacefully without having my things destroyed.

Without worrying about being attacked.

39

AS I FOLLOWED Victoria's nurse down the hallway, my mind drifted to my cellphone—noticeably absent from my back pocket. I had stopped by the local retail store of our wireless provider to drop off my destroyed device before heading to Mountain Manor.

The store would have a new cellphone ready for me by the end of the day. I'd pick it up on my way home from visiting Dex. Fortunately, all of my data had been saved, given it had been backed up in cyber storage.

An added bonus: Insurance would cover my replacement. For the cause of my phone's irreparable damage, I had reported *"our tractor ran over it"* because I doubted the warranty would've covered *"an angry ghost didn't want me reading Victoria's diary."*

Ghosts didn't exactly inspire honesty from their hauntees.

In fairness, the blame partially fell on an unbelieving public. They weren't quite ready for the truth when it involved the paranormal. I should know. Before moving to Windy Hill Farm, Dex and I were members of *that* public.

Walking in front of me, the nurse glanced over her shoulder. She said something, but my daydreaming was louder than my active listening.

"I'm sorry." I cupped my hand behind my ear. "Could you repeat what you just said?"

"Sure, deary. I'm afraid Victoria is worse."

"Has she woken up since I left yesterday?"

"The next time Victoria wakes," the nurse whispered, "will be at the Pearly Gates."

"I won't stay long. I'll do a little reading and then let her rest."

The nurse opened the door and moved to the side for me.

I walked into the room.

"Sounds lovely, deary." She nodded toward the phone on the nightstand. "Call the nurse's station when you're done visiting. Or if you need me."

The nurse wasn't exaggerating about her patient's condition.

Victoria's skin color had shifted from a yellowish hue to ashen gray. Her eye sockets were as dark as charcoal. Her lips were thin, stretched to a grim frown. Death wasn't just knocking; it was already inside, packing up her things.

The nurse closed the door.

I was alone again with Virgil and Vivian Williams' daughter.

"Good morning, Victoria," I said, walking to the bookshelf. I grabbed the bottom journal. "I'm going to read to you from your diary. The one from 1955."

With the journal tucked under one arm, I dragged a chair across the floor to Victoria's bedside. Sitting, I paged through the diary until I found an entry of interest beyond what I had read last night.

"Tuesday, June fourteenth. Entry number one," I read out loud. "Isabelle has been with us for over a week and my hopes have come true. She is hardworking and smart. Funny, too. Best of all, she's the closest friend I've ever had. Except, she keeps secrets from me. I'm not terribly angry with her, though. My feelings are more wounded that she doesn't trust me enough, but in all honesty, I harbor a few secrets as well. It's only fair to extend some understanding.

"For the last couple of nights, I thought Isabelle had been going to the bathroom in the middle of the night. I had always fallen back asleep before she returned so I never really knew. Until last night when I learned the truth.

"Isabelle has been sneaking out at night. From the window, I watched her dash toward the lake in her nightgown. Who could she be meeting at night? Vincent? Vaughn? A farmhand?

"I had to investigate," I continued reading. "I wanted to learn if

161

one of my brothers was also missing. (Vaughn's bedroom is across the hall from mine.) So last night, I tiptoed to his room and creaked open his door, peeking inside. My youngest brother was in bed, sleeping soundly. As I closed his door, I heard footsteps and nearly barfed. *MOTHER!*

"Mother demanded to know why I was out of bed. 'I heard a noise,' I answered, 'but everything seems fine.' Then she asked me a question which I could not answer honestly. I was thankful Mother couldn't see my eyes in the darkness. She asked me if Isabelle was in my bedroom, asleep. 'Yes, Mother. Of course she is,' I lied. I held my breath, unsure if she would accept my claim or seek visual confirmation. To my relief, Mother didn't challenge me. But she promised I'd get spanked with the switch if I roamed the hallways again. And that was that.

"This morning, I insisted Isabelle tell me whom she was meeting at night. She became upset, sobbing and begging me not to press her on the matter. I agreed to let her keep her secret for now."

I paused from reading to reflect on the entry.

The Williams' farmhouse must have been situated on the grounds immediately east of our lot, adjacent to our corner parcel.

I could picture Isabelle racing toward the hillside overlooking the lake. After all, I had followed her ghost several times as she sprinted in that direction on her way to the water and Boulder Island.

Turning a couple more pages in the journal, I found another passage of interest dated June 18th, a Saturday.

"Last night," I resumed reading aloud, "before Mother came to my bedroom to turn off the lights, I gave Isabelle a present...my gold, heart locket necklace. (Isabelle always admired the necklace when I wore it.) I want her to have it so she thinks of me after she returns home to Unityville at the end of the summer.

"When Isabelle unwrapped the gift tucked within the folds of my handkerchief, her eyes widened. She opened the locket and read the inscription: *'Forever in my heart. Love V.'* As expected, Isabelle wanted to know who in my family had given *me* the necklace. She guessed Vincent or Vaughn because a parent would have signed Mother or Father. I refused to divulge the answer, as she would think of them instead of me. *'V' is for Victoria* is all I would say.

"My only stipulation to Isabelle," I continued to read from Victoria's diary, "is that she keeps my gift a secret while she's at the farm. I suggested she hide the necklace and locket with her diary. (Should the truth be discovered, I explained, I would be beaten with the switch because I gave her a gift that had been given to me.)

"I also assured Isabelle that if anyone questions me about the necklace's whereabouts, I will admit that I lost it in one of the fields. Which one, I do not know.

"Mother's footsteps were coming down the hall and Isabelle quickly shoved the necklace under her pillow. We giggled at the excitement of having our very own secret. One, just for us."

A cold, boney hand clasped my wrist and squeezed.

I gasped in horror.

Victoria's eyes were open, but I was certain she couldn't see. Her irises were milky white. And her breath smelled like soured milk.

"Never tell," she hissed. "Never tell."

My heart thundered in my chest.

Never tell...about the necklace?

Victoria's hand dropped from my wrist and her eyes closed. Her chest rattled as air escaped from her lungs.

I called the nurse's station, requesting that Victoria's nurse come to her room right away.

When the nurse arrived, I explained that Victoria had woken up for a second.

"Did she say anything?"

"She moaned. That's all."

Oh dear God. I was lying again. But revealing what Victoria had actually uttered might cause needless angst for her nurse and son Ross. Why would I want to do that when Victoria's life was barely clinging to its sunset?

The nurse placed the disk of her stethoscope on Victoria's chest.

"Her heart is racing," she announced. "Best we end your visit."

40

Thursday, August 7, 2025
Mountain Manor to the Johnson Residence

I STOOD AT Mountain Manor's front desk in disbelief as Victoria's nurse delivered the news. Victoria had died yesterday.

I mean, I shouldn't have been shocked. Her nurse had been straightforward from the beginning. And even on Tuesday, Victoria had looked as if death was imminent. Still, I had hoped for more time with her. *With her diaries,* if I was honest.

"If it's all right, may I spend a few moments in her room, alone?" I asked. "To sort of pay my respects?"

The possibilities were spinning in my mind. With my new cellphone, maybe I could snap more photos of diary pages.

"Victoria's room is already occupied, deary. The cycle of life is a revolving door. When someone leaves, another enters." She leaned in and whispered, "We call it job security."

Maybe Plan B would work. I asked if I could have Ross Johnson's contact information. The answer was no. Privacy regulations. But at least the nurse offered to contact Victoria's son to give him my number, in hopes that he would call me.

Lo and behold, as I drove out of the parking lot, my phone rang. A local number displayed on my dash's control panel screen, and I hoped, *prayed,* the caller was Ross.

My prayers were answered.

After extending my condolences, I explained I had enjoyed reading to his mother. The family history in her diaries made me appreciate our homestead even more. Dex and I felt part of the Williams' legacy. I only wished I had gotten through all the journals.

I paused, applying an effective marketing strategy. The momentary silence provided extra time for my implied request to ferment.

"Oh," Ross said. "Would you like to borrow them for a bit?"

Even better, he invited me to stop by his townhouse to pick them up. In a half hour. Of course I agreed.

Ross's home was located in downtown Honesdale. According to my GPS, it was just eight miles from the Manor.

After I parked, I walked up the brick walkway and steps and knocked on the arched door which opened right away.

Having hair peppered with gray, Ross looked to be in his late 50s, early 60s. He invited me inside, hoping I'd agree to have tea in the sitting room. Before I even answered, he started walking down the hall. Apparently, he knew a few marketing strategies himself. Perhaps marketing and lawyering weren't that dissimilar.

In the sitting room, he directed me to sit on a simple Shaker-styled couch. Already on a tray (on top of a round table) were a porcelain teapot, matching cups and saucers, sugar cubes in a small crystal bowl, and cream in an ornate pitcher. Clearly, when it came to having tea, *no thank you* had never been an option.

A plume of steam escaped from the teapot's spout.

I marveled at the old fashioned-ness of having tea in a sitting room. Victoria must've instilled the formal ritual in her children.

As I prepared my tea, I wondered what Ross really wanted. Maybe he had second thoughts about loaning me his mother's diaries.

"You know," Ross started, "no one even knew Mother's childhood diaries had survived the fire. We thought they had been destroyed in 1986 when the farmhouse burned to the ground."

"Where did you find them?"

"The location was curious, too," he admitted. "Mother's diaries were in a safety deposit box at a bank where my sisters and I never even knew she had an account. With her failing health, she had forgotten to pay this year's rental. Naturally, the bank reached out to me since I live close by."

I sipped my tea, trying to display a neutral expression.

"As I mentioned," he continued, "I've never read them. My older sisters haven't either. I'm curious. Are the contents… *interesting?"*

Time to downplay the truth again. And I'd do it without guilt. I reminded myself that the origins of the supernatural havoc affecting Dex and me stemmed from *their* family's unresolved shit (back in 1955). My deviations from the truth were warranted. My husband's fractured bones proved it.

"More than interesting," I answered, "they are historically informative. Despite her youth, your mother was well versed in the area. Something my husband and I are determined to become."

Hopefully, Ross wouldn't ask for an example. I'd mention factoids about the library if he did. After all, Ross's grandmother donated the building which still houses the local library. Surely passion for libraries had trickled down from Vivian to Ross's mother, Victoria.

"Our legacy started in this county," he said. "My grandmother, Vivian Hall, moved to Boulder in 1938 after marrying my grandfather, Virgil Williams. He was born and raised here."

Ross reached for a clipboard on a stack of books. A document was clipped to the board.

"Since I'm not familiar with the content of the diaries," he said, "I'd like you to sign a non-disclosure agreement. Our family doesn't want to see Mother's private musings printed in a newspaper or book. Or online. Not that those are your intentions. This agreement simply makes it binding that her entries, in part or in their entirety, are to remain private. Out of the public's eye. As well, no photocopies or photographs, or replications of any kind, are to be made of the entries."

His request seemed fair enough, though to comply, I'd have to delete the photos I'd already taken. Not a problem. My only goals were to solve the mysteries behind Isabelle's disappearance and to learn why a ghost was haunting her. And afterwards, to rid their spirits from our farm. Nothing more, nothing less.

I read and signed the document.

Ross handed me the journals as he stood from his chair. "Before you go, would you like to see some old family photos hanging in our library room?"

I eagerly popped up from the couch. "Would I ever!"

He walked down the hallway and turned right as I followed.

The library included a built-in bookcase that encompassed one entire wall, complete with a sliding ladder since the ceiling was 12-feet high. The shelves were packed with hardcovered books, most of which were leather bound.

Another wall was wallpapered with family photos in frames of different shapes and sizes. Because of my visit to the Honesdale library over three weeks ago, I was already familiar with the "who's who" in the Williams family.

I was instantly drawn to a color photo of Virgil. He was standing outside in natural light. Miss Grace was right. His eyes were neon blue. A few freckles dotted his cheeks which were well defined. His skin had been tanned by the sun. And his dimples were dreamy.

Virgil Williams was painstakingly gorgeous, in a conflicted sort of way. His looks caused an internal battle between wanting to drool (while gawking) and desperately trying not to embarrass oneself.

Ross pointed to several framed photographs and explained who had been pictured, sharing the story associated with each print. I noticed a close-up of Victoria and Isabelle. The photograph had probably been taken in 1955, the summer Isabelle disappeared. Sure enough, Victoria wore a heart locket and chain around her neck.

Actually *seeing* what I had read about sent shivers down my spine. The past was being validated in the present. And like it or not, I really was a part of the Williams' legacy, though certainly not by choice.

"Pretty necklace," I said, guessing it was the same one Ross's mother had secretly given to Isabelle. "Looks like an heirloom which would've been passed down through generations."

I had cast the line on my fishing expedition.

"Mother lost the necklace as a teenager. Somewhere in a field. It was never found." He winked at me. "If you come across it on your land, please let me know."

"Who is this?" I asked, pointing to Isabelle and pretending I didn't recognize her.

"Isabelle Taylor," Ross answered. "She was Mother's stepcousin through marriage. My grandmother's step niece."

"She and your mother look alike. Beautiful. Are there more photos of Isabelle?"

"Just a family photograph taken in 1955." Ross extended his index finger in the photo's direction. This print was the original so it wasn't pixelated like the newspaper photo archived at the library.

"Unfortunately," Ross continued, "Isabelle disappeared from her hometown—from Unityville—about four weeks after this picture was taken."

"Disappeared? How awful. Was she ever found?" I asked.

"Tragically, no. Her mysterious disappearance always haunted Mother."

Victoria and I had quite a bit in common as far as being haunted was concerned.

In fact, I wanted to ask Ross if anyone in the family had ever seen Isabelle's ghost. I thought better of it, though. I didn't want to broach a potentially sensitive subject that might lead Ross to believe I was unstable. He needed to trust me with his mother's journals.

Several flies began swarming around our heads.

"You can leave the farm," Ross said, swatting at them, "but the farm never leaves you."

How right he was.

41

Thursday, August 7, 2025
Good Samaritan Rehab Center: Honesdale, Pennsylvania

AFTER I DROVE away from Ross Johnson's townhouse with Victoria's three journals stacked on my passenger seat, I worried about returning to the farm without having established a safe space *if* that was even a thing. Ross may have joked that the buzzing flies were reminiscent of farm life (perhaps implying they had tagged along with me), but I had a different interpretation.

Flies and goosebumps were telltale signs that a spirit was present.

I arrived at Good Samaritan for my visit with Dex. After parking in the lot, I remained in my car to conduct some research on my cellphone. I googled *how to protect a room from ghosts.*

The list I found was surprisingly comprehensive:

1. Add salt to your cleaning solution and spread it on your floors, being sure not to miss corners. Let the solution dry, forming a white, salty coating.
2. Place small bowls filled with salt in each corner of your room and on windowsills. On top of vents, too.
3. Place a line of salt parallel to the thresholds of each door leading in and out of the room.
4. Put small bowls of Holy Water on windowsills and on each side of a door frame (for doors leading in and out of your room).

5. Tape a handwritten poster on both sides of doors. If Christian, write: "God is a shield to those who take refuge in Him." (Adapted from Proverbs 30:5) (Click links for passages in other religions.)
6. Burn white sage in the room (called smudging).
7. Purchase a salt lamp and keep it on.

NOTE: These measures will provide temporary relief from apparitions within fortified spaces but will not <u>remove</u> paranormal activity from the entire home. Room protections must also be reapplied as needed. For permanent evictions, please contact specialists in the clergy or a paranormal professional.

Salt? I wondered what properties made it so powerful at warding off ghosts and the supernatural.

I googled the mineral's connection to the supernatural and found a link to the website of a renowned medium named Dr. India Cloud. Apparently, she was acclaimed for communicating with spirits.

Good to know. I mean, after I solved the mysteries involving Isabelle, I might need her professional help to permanently evict the ghosts haunting our farm. And Dr. Cloud's home city was none other than…Baltimore. So, close enough.

On the medium's homepage was a photograph of her. Her smile looked kind and energetic. Her red hair was long and wild, abundant with curls (reminding me of Roxy, our chicken liaison). Above her freckled cheeks, she wore large glasses framed in robin-egg blue.

Under Dr. Cloud's photo was a caption listing her academic credentials, including her most prestigious: PhD in Paranormal Science from the University of Arizona.

Who knew that degree even existed?

I read her blog about salt and ghosts.

Her explanation on their connection was succinct: *"Energy and heat accumulate in the corners of a room. Ghosts absorb energy and heat to manifest. Salt absorbs energy and heat. Place salt in the corners of a room and voila! Ghosts can't manifest."*

Dr. Cloud also claimed that salt's ability to purify and heal contributed to its preventative properties against supernatural manifestations such as ghosts.

My to-do list for the rest of my day became crystal clear, starting with my visit with Dex. My goal was to bring him up to speed. I hadn't exactly told him about the second ghost, the one haunting Isabelle. *The* scary, evil one responsible for his injuries.

There was no longer any reason to withhold the truth or my plans moving forward. He was well enough, and I was strong enough. And he'd feel better knowing I was going to fortify our bedroom against unwanted paranormal visitors—*both* of them.

After we spent time together, I'd leave and go shopping for supplies because in my kitchen pantry, I didn't have an abundance of salt on hand. Nor did I have poster paper or a salt lamp. Or white sage for that matter.

I'd be able to find everything on the list except Holy Water. *That* had to wait until Sunday. I'd request the blessed water then, from the minister at White Oak UMC, the church closest to our farm.

Tonight, protected from ghosts invading our bedroom, I'd continue reading from Victoria's 1955 diary in hopes of learning more about Isabelle's disappearance.

My plan was a good one.

I got out of the car and locked it. I caught myself looking around for swarms of flies. There were none. No ravens either. Not even one goosebump prickled my skin.

Walking toward the front doors of the rehab center, I smiled.

Everything was under control.

42

STANDING ON THE hallway side of our bedroom door while looking inside the room, I took a deep breath, admiring my work. The time was 9:00 p.m. My exhaustion made it seem later. Despite my heavy eyelids, I still hoped to read Victoria's 1955 journal before I fell asleep.

No matter what, I needed to focus on the progress I had already made. In. One. Day.

My safe space was a mere step in front of me. The achievement generated a feeling of reassurance. Empowerment, too. Like the posters taped on the door promised: Once in my bedroom, I would be shielded from ghostly harm.

I was resolved in my belief that the applied protections would keep me safe. A smidgen of doubt, even as thin as a threadlike fissure, might jeopardize my security. Tiny breaches could eventually destroy a dam. Not a risk I was willing to invite.

Anyway, throughout humankind's history, *believing* (having faith) had helped overcome ridiculously dismal odds, so that was the truth I wanted to tap into.

After returning home from visiting Dex and then shopping for supplies, I had left Victoria's journals in the car, hidden under my rain slicker, while I embraced my *busy*. I ran around in every direction, like Biddy used to do when she spotted me holding a cracked zucchini about to become her treat. *Busy* meant farm chores came first, followed by unloading shopping bags from the car. Afterwards, I prepped the supplies I'd bought before "sealing" my room and bringing the journals inside. And in between, I managed to eat a healthy dinner.

Now that I had finished, our bedroom looked bigger.

Around sunset, I had rolled up all the area rugs and stashed them inside the laundry room. I moved chairs from our room into our walk-in closets. And as directed by the instructions I'd found on the Internet, I whitewashed our wood floors with a salt solution. The thin coating of salt would likely destroy the finish, but Dex had agreed with me that floors could be replaced; lives couldn't.

A thick line of salt ran along the threshold of the door leading into our room from the hall. Instead of bowls of Holy Water (which I'd get soon), I had temporarily placed two bowls filled with salt on each side of the door frame. Plus, bowls of salt were in every corner, on every vent, and on the sills of both windows.

Still standing at the doorway, I watched as a misty plume of earthy-smelling smoke wafted upwards from the incense smoldering within a ceramic dish placed on my windowsill.

Turns out, the largest nursery in the area included an aromatherapy retail store on its grounds. Inside, the nursery sold homemade candles, soaps, oils, and incense. I purchased white sage incense which the salesperson assured me had been grown organically and shipped from California but had been dried on the premises recently.

I had replaced the regular lamp on my nightstand with a salt lamp. Large rocks of Himalayan salt glowed pink from the lit bulb hidden in the lamp's center.

The transformation of my bedroom was visually potent.

I wondered if walking over the salt-line threshold, taking just one step, might affect me like fictional time travel…the feeling of leaving chaos behind to enter a fortified bubble. The classic character Dorothy and her small terrier came to mind; the time when her bedroom was safe and intact despite being embedded in a tornado.

The journals were on my bed, beckoning to share their secrets.

Nothing else was left to do except to read them.

Every door was locked, every window closed.

I had already changed into my pajamas and made my two nightly calls, one to my sister with updates and the last to Dex for our bedtime goodnights.

Yet, I was stalling, and my thumping heart knew why.

My security was undoubtedly going to be tested.

I walked over the salt line and gently closed the door behind me.

Climbing into bed, I selected Victoria's 1955 journal. My fingers were shaking as I paged through the entries until I found one written the night before Isabelle's disappearance.

Friday, July 22nd, Entry 1:

Isabelle is sound asleep now.

She wasn't herself today. She had braided her hair like mine, instead of wearing it loose. But she had done this before for our family photograph. We wanted to look like twins. So her hair wasn't what had me worried. She seemed distracted. While we collected eggs from the layers' hutch, she was distant. She didn't talk. Or smile. Her cheeks were blotchy. Had she been crying?

When I insisted she tell me what's been wrong with her, she finally admitted that she is homesick. In fact, while I had been mucking horse stalls, Father had driven her to the train station to buy a ticket for early tomorrow morning. (Why the ticket couldn't be bought then, I do not know. Perhaps the booth isn't open at that hour.)

With the news, my heart had nearly exploded. But Isabelle assured me her departure was only for an overnight. She was grateful Father had suggested a visit home. Being apart from her own adopted father was difficult. They had gone through so much together and had formed a true father-and-daughter bond. Seeing him would be the medicine she needed.

I was only half kidding about medicine because Isabelle might actually be ill. After we had collected eggs, she barfed on the grass. She blamed it on a smell clashing with her stomach. (She'd get used to farm life.)

Dinner felt strange, too. No one spoke much. Everyone seemed preoccupied. It was as if they all knew something that I didn't. Well, everyone except Vaughn. He had left for camp last Sunday with his 4-H Club.

Isabelle's suitcase is packed and waiting at the foot of her bed. She didn't want to talk to me tonight either. She had changed into her white dress before bed (less chance of waking me at dawn). Now her eyes are closed.

Mother never came to turn off the light, even though she had done so ever since Isabelle had arrived on the farm.

I need to close my own eyes. While Isabelle heads home to Unityville on a train, Father and I will be driving to a chicken auction some 11 miles west of Unityville, in the town of Hughesville.

Why Father and I can't drop Isabelle off at her parents' house makes no sense. Surely, she doesn't have to be home at the crack of dawn.

Friday, July 22nd, Entry 2:

An hour ago, I woke up when Isabelle snuck out of the room. Brightened by moonlight shining across our lawn, I waited beside the window in hopes of seeing her running toward the lake. Which I did...her long hair was loose now and twirling as she ran in her white dress. Only this time, she was holding some sort of box.

Since Mother always catches the rule breakers, I dared not turn on the light or sneak out of my room. Instead, I grabbed my flashlight, determined to look for clues among all of Isabelle's things.

I picked up Isabelle's suitcase and lifted it onto my bed. Unclasping the latch, I opened it like a book and began paging through the layers on both sides. I hoped to find her diary to reveal the truth about what she has been doing every night.

To my astonishment, she hasn't included her diary among the items she is taking for the overnight with her parents. Another oddity. With my heart racing, I carefully repacked her belongings and returned her suitcase to the foot of her bed.

Drawers and closet shelves were next. My inspection yielded nothing. Nor did looking under her pillows and bed or in between the mattress and box spring.

Isabelle's diary is not in my bedroom.

I cannot wait any longer for Isabelle to return. Tomorrow will be a long day. Until then...

Victoria's entries hinted of several things being amiss.

In fact, I found myself asking the same questions Victoria had penned in her diary.

It made no sense why Virgil and his daughter couldn't have driven Isabelle home on their way to Hughesville. Why did Isabelle *have* to take the train? And why so early?

Sneaking out at night seemed to be habitual for Isabelle. If she was meeting someone, I hoped it was Vincent. At least he was close to her age. But a tiny voice whispered a name I could scarcely contemplate…Virgil, described by Miss Grace as the "buttery crust" whom women swooned over. A man who caused his wife to turn a blind eye.

Lastly, where was Isabelle's diary? Could it have been in the box she was carrying that night? Or had someone in the family taken it?

I needed to continue reading.

Saturday, July 23rd, Entry 1:

When I awoke at dawn, Isabelle and her suitcase were already gone. Her bed was made and draped across the bedspread was my white dress. Mother. Her way of controlling what I wear.

Except for the chicken auction, the day was a total nightmare. And it started before my breakfast. Apparently, before I was even awake.

While it was still dark, my parents told me Isabelle ate her breakfast with them. During their conversation, Isabelle claimed that driving to Unityville was faster than taking the train. A friendly disagreement ensued. Father told me Isabelle was still laughing about it when he dropped her off at the station. Laughing, because Father planned to prove her wrong for the fun of it.

During my own breakfast, Father outlined his plan which regrettably involved ME.

He wanted ME to take the train to Unityville and time my trip. He already had my ticket (which he had bought after dropping Isabelle off at the station). He predicted the train ride would take one hour and 20 minutes while the drive would take 10 minutes MORE. Isabelle had predicted the opposite: that the drive would take 10 minutes LESS than the train ride.

Turns out, Father had to stop at the hardware store in Unityville anyway. So, he'd time his road trip to compare with mine. After I got off the train, he'd pick me up in the alley at the edge of town.

I became angry and softly voiced my protests while trying to sound respectful. Why did I HAVE to take part in a bet that I didn't care about? For a dispute over a trivial difference? Why couldn't Isabelle just report how long her ride had been? And if we were stopping in Unityville anyway, why hadn't we simply driven her there?

Mother claimed she promised Isabelle her favorite pie if her prediction was right. In fact, Mother thought Isabelle would win the bet so she'd start baking the pie while we were at auction.

Father, who looked very tired, addressed some of my questions. He explained that a specialized part on our tractor had broken after Isabelle left. Needing to stop in Unityville was a new development. Mother was also going to a hardware store in Honesdale to look for the same part. It was that important.

Since Father and I were already heading to Unityville, there was no reason not to play along.

Count Vincent out. He threw down his napkin and stood, causing his chair to squeal across the floor. He stormed outside to start his chores. No one threatened to use the switch on him. He was merely acting "like a man."

I wish I could react like Vincent, but I am forced to obey and act like a lady. So I rode the stupid train to Unityville and Father picked me up in the alley.

Victoria's entry reminded me that being a minor could have major disadvantages (especially when the minor was also a female in the 1950s). Children could be forced to obey their parents even when their demands were bizarre and unreasonable, even when their demands were probably designed to cover something up.

Something *bad*.

I didn't need to be a homicide detective to predict that Isabelle Taylor had never gotten on that bloody train. Her ghost wasn't haunting Unityville. It was haunting Windy Hill Farm.

Virgil and Vivian Williams had clearly executed a well planned ruse, knowing their eldest child (their only daughter) would have no choice but to play her part.

But which member of the family had actually killed Isabelle?

And why?

43

Thursday, August 7, 2025
Windy Hill Farm: Boulder, Pennsylvania

PLEASE, PLEASE, PLEASE let one of Victoria's entries hint at what happened to Isabelle.

My eyelids were getting heavy, but I couldn't stop reading even though the time was approaching midnight. I listened for noises beyond my closed door. Everything was quiet, and I smiled. My protected sanctuary was working, so I turned another page in Victoria's diary.

Sunday, July 24th:

I miss Isabelle terribly and have occupied myself by doing extra farm work. I was too exhausted to write my bedtime entry last night.

By the way, Isabelle won that stupid bet. Driving to Unityville IS faster than taking the train. Mother's blueberry pie sits on the kitchen counter, but still no Isabelle. Father says we'll call Aunt Louise tomorrow. "There's no sense in pressuring Isabelle. Besides, the cure for homesickness is being home," he lectured.

180

FIND THEM

Monday, July 25th:

Mother insisted I call Aunt Louise about Isabelle. She even told me what to ask: "Has my stepcousin changed her mind about coming back?"

But Aunt Louise knew nothing about Isabelle visiting home for an overnight. NOTHING!

She immediately got Uncle Danny who started yelling questions at me over the telephone. I gave the handset to Mother. I am too young for this. My brain will turn to jelly with too much stress.

Isabelle, my best friend in all the world, is missing.

Tuesday, July 26th:

I refused to get out of bed today. Isabelle has still not been found, and the police have been notified.

Two hours ago, I heard footsteps coming down the hall. Mother and Father came into my room. They wanted to have a serious discussion with me. Investigators are going to come to the farm to question us.

They told me witnesses confirmed seeing Isabelle riding the train and then getting off the train in Unityville on Saturday morning. And since Father never purchased a tractor part at the hardware store in Unityville, and no one saw us, they think it's best (for my sake) that I don't mention riding the train at all. "Why complicate matters which could delay finding Isabelle?" Father had asked me.

Father explained that he will tell the police that I was in the truck the whole time. We had driven straight through to Hughesville for the chicken auction. If I said otherwise, I could get him in a lot of trouble. Who knows, Father might get arrested for lying. The farm could be lost forever despite the truth (that Father is only trying to protect me from an innocent coincidence).

My parents were clear: I can't tell anyone about my train ride. Ever. Or about Isabelle's bet with them.

However, police should be told that Isabelle was homesick. She bought a train ticket on Friday. Rode the train on Saturday morning. (The exact time isn't certain, as she could've missed getting on the first train.) And she wasn't discovered missing until Monday after I had telephoned Aunt Louise.

I asked questions. Could witnesses have mistaken me for Isabelle when I rode the train on Saturday morning? And also when I got off the train in Unityville? Our hair styles and dresses were nearly the same. And everyone says we look like twins.

Father had enough of what he called my insolence. He made me write "Never Tell" 200 times. I was not allowed out of my room until I did so.

It was then that I realized how much I hate my parents.

Victoria's mention of *Never Tell* sent chills spiraling down my spine. I vividly remembered her saying those exact words to me after she grabbed my wrist at Mountain Manor.

I turned the page in her diary and couldn't believe my eyes. The page was blank. As were all the pages that followed. In fact, nothing else had been written.

Tuesday, July 26, 1955, marked Victoria's last entry.

Obviously, Victoria had intentionally kept her diaries hidden from her family for decades by storing them in a safety deposit box that was unknown to her family.

I flinched.

From my bedroom, I heard the *herrrrrr* of our television in the great room. Even though I kept unplugging the blasted thing, it was to no avail. I smiled anyway. A victory smile if I was being honest. With my door closed, the sound wasn't loud enough to interfere with my sleep.

My safe space was amazing. Well worth the effort.

Placing Victoria's journals on my nightstand, I wondered what my next step should be. Without more entries, how could I find out what had happened to Isabelle?

BANG...

I had celebrated too soon.

Loud banging, I mean *really* loud and violent, resonated from the kitchen. That damn ghost was slamming my cabinetry drawers! Pots, pans, and silverware were clanking over the constant static of the television.

I heard my dishware, stacked on open shelves, crash and shatter on the floor.

How dare that ghost try and take over my house.

I was seething. My body temperature, boiling.

I leapt out of bed and that's when I noticed Isabelle standing outside my window. She vigorously shook her head as if warning me not to respond. Droplets of moisture escaped from her soaked hair and beaded on the glass before racing downward like tears. Her breath left frosted condensation on the window.

"You wanted help," I snapped, "and this is me helping."

What Isabelle didn't understand was that I was no longer the woman who remained passive (and vulnerable) in the face of danger. I had changed. And I wasn't going back to my former self at Union Station.

I grabbed a tablespoon worth of salt with my left hand. Just to be on the safe side.

The minute I opened the bedroom door, the volume of noise assaulted me. I looked down at the line of salt marking the threshold. If I needed to retreat into the bedroom, I wanted to make sure the barrier had not been breached. Thankfully, it was still intact.

Confident, I stepped over the salt and tiptoed down the dark hallway. At the end of the hall, I flipped the light switch to turn on the recessed lighting in the kitchen.

What an unbelievable mess.

Broken dishes and cups were strewn across the floor. My ceramic canisters of flour and sugar had toppled over, making half of my kitchen look as if a dusting of snow had accumulated.

The overhead lights began to flicker as goosebumps erupted on my arms. Seriously?

"Leave. My. House," I snarled, my words traveling with mist.

The television blipped off.

Nothing moved.

There was no hum from the refrigerator. No ticking from our wall clock. Or air hissing through vents.

Our house was holding its breath.

I even wondered if blood had stopped coursing through my veins.

Maybe the absence of sound meant the ghost had heeded my demand and left.

Or maybe not…

My heart pounded into action.

On the floor, footsteps appeared in the dusting of flour.

Footsteps *without a body*.

And they were heading in my direction.

Turning, I took off running toward my bedroom.

I could make it. I *had* to!

Halfway down the hallway, in the dark, I rolled my ankle and fell to the floor. On impact, my fist flew open. My small handful of salt launched toward my bedroom.

Oh dear God. Why had I left my safe space?

I scrambled to get onto my knees.

Footsteps and breathing were behind me. More like, on top of me!

FIND THEM

The ghost grabbed my right ankle and yanked hard, causing me to slam back down, flat on the floor. With a tight grip, the ghost began pulling me toward the kitchen. Dragging me down the hallway and away from my bedroom.

With my right hand, I seized hold of the trim framing the laundry room door. But the ghost twisted my ankle, and I yelped in pain. My fingers slipped off the trim and the ghost resumed dragging me even farther from my safe space.

A log in the rapids: I needed one to save myself.

A strategy crystallized.

I rolled onto my back, kicking at the pressure on my ankle.

The ghost's grip didn't falter.

Maybe my sweaty palm still contained some salt residue.

I jolted upwards, bending at my waist in a power sit-up. I grabbed my right ankle, hoping to make salty contact with the ghost.

The ghost released me.

Knowing my freedom would be short lived, I clambered to my feet and darted to my bedroom. High octane adrenaline fueled my burst of energy.

Footsteps were behind me.

Closing in.

Every joint, every muscle, every cell was giving their all to get me to my bedroom.

Just four more feet...

I barreled over the salt threshold and slammed the door shut.

Some of the salt marking the threshold had scattered with the force, and I dropped to the floor. With trembling fingers, I repaired the line.

The ghost pounded on my door.

BANG.

BANG.

BANG.

I held my breath...

Until I convinced myself I was safe enough to inhale.

44

SALT BOMBS. HAD someone already invented them as standard issue when fighting against the sinister factions of the paranormal? Or was I the first?

Streaks of orange sunlight streamed in through the sliding glass doors in the great room.

At the kitchen counter, I sprinkled fresh strawberry slices over two salads. Madeline would be arriving any minute for dinner.

My sister's salt bombs, four of them, were lined up on the kitchen island, ready for her.

After I was dragged down the hallway and my salty palm repelled "V" (Virgil, Vincent, or Vivian—the most likely suspects in Isabelle's death), I learned to fully appreciate the power of salt. *Salt* had forced the ghost to release my ankle. And since cowering 24/7 inside my safe space wasn't an option, I decided to equip myself with two homemade varieties of salt bombs. That way, no matter where I was on the farm or in the house, deterrents were at my disposal.

When considering vessels for my salt, the word *vessel* reminded me of four ornaments Mom had given me at Christmastime. They were small glass balls, delicate because of their thin glass. Each ball encapsulated one tiny, intricate sailing ship.

After popping the corks, I filled the ornaments with salt, burying their ships. Once resealed, I attached ornament hooks. I hung two salt bombs on each twine necklace I had made and crimped the hook ends to secure them. One necklace was for me; the other was for Madeline.

If V attacked, the balls could easily be detached and thrown. They'd shatter on impact, spreading their payload.

I made the other variety of salt bombs from four plastic bottles, measuring three inches in length, that I'd purchased to accommodate my hair products for overnight traveling. Now filled with salt, the flip-cap bottles could be tucked in a pocket and easily accessed.

For Isabelle, the salt bombs wouldn't prevent her from appearing outside of my safe space because the weapons would remain sealed until deployment.

I was startled at the sound of knocking at my front door.

My nerves were on edge.

If I was being completely honest, I had lured my sister into having dinner with me over false pretenses. Although we would certainly "catch up," I had something else in mind. Something that included risk. And flat out danger.

First things first. I explained the need for salt bombs as Madeline entered the kitchen.

She armed herself without hesitation. After all, she was well aware of the horror inflicted on Dex. In addition, she had seen the bruise on my wrist.

When I mentioned I had converted my bedroom into a safe space, she scowled. Major alterations to the house, she warned, indicated the problem was escalating. I couldn't argue, but at least I had applied precautions to stay safe while pursuing a resolution.

As we finished dinner, I got up from my stool and retrieved the real reason for having my sister over. I placed the heavy rectangular box on the kitchen island and waited for her reaction.

"Why do you have that?" she snapped. "Dex warned you. And you agreed not to."

Dex didn't know I had overruled our initial joint decision. But with Victoria dead and the rest of her diary blank, I needed to get information directly from Isabelle.

Only 41 days remained until Dex came home and we'd decide on keeping or selling the farm.

The Ouija board was the only quick and easy communication tool

I could think of.

Knowing what happened to Isabelle was instrumental in ridding our home and property of ghosts. For that outcome, I was willing to take risks.

Hoping she'd support me, I stated my case to my sister.

"I have no clue how to use a Ouija board," Madeline admitted. "Let alone...*safely.*"

"But I do. I've read the directions. And I'll read them to you. Then decide. Deal?"

She nodded as I lifted the lid from the box and grabbed the printed instructions. I read each step, each warning, and then recapped the most important.

"Ouija boards shouldn't be used alone," I said, "which is why I need your help. If you agree, I'll ask the questions. We'll work together to spell out Isabelle's answers." I pointed to the last rule. "The most important rule is to say goodbye when the session is over. Closing the board is crucial."

"What happens if something goes wrong?" she asked.

"Salt bombs, for starters. And if we have to make a run for it, head to my bedroom. Make sure you still have one bomb left in case we encounter trouble on the way."

Adrenaline made my fingers tingle. My body was preparing for a potential battle.

"Where do you plan on holding the session," my sister asked. "Here? In the kitchen?"

"The den."

She briefly closed her eyes. I could sense her internal battle.

"Do you have questions prepared?" Madeline asked as she stood.

"Yes." I retrieved the list from my pocket. "Let's do this."

Returning the lid, I picked up the Ouija box and headed to the den, located on the opposite side of the house from my safe space. I opened the door and flipped on the light switch.

I had placed a round table in the center of the room. Two chairs were positioned across from each other so my sister and I could face one another. We'd each be able to see the door (which I would close). I had also drawn the curtains on the only window in the room and placed several thick candles on end tables and on top of the desk.

FIND THEM

I gave my sister a handheld lighter. "Would you please light the candles?"

While Madeline lit the wicks for our light source, I set up the wooden board and planchette in the middle of the table. I included a small tablet and pen. And a flashlight in case the candles were snuffed out.

The room was ready.

I turned off the lights and closed the door.

My sister and I sat down at the table.

The situation became uncomfortably *real.* The danger was palpable. Nevertheless, I instructed Madeline to lightly place the tips of her index, middle, and ring fingers from each hand on the planchette. I did the same on the other side of the wheeled plank.

The candles flickered as if there was a light breeze.

Thank goodness we were armed with our salt bombs.

I posed my first question.

"Isabelle Taylor. Are you here with us?"

45

NO ANSWER WAS spelled out on the Ouija board. The planchette remained still as Isabelle simply appeared in response to my *are you here* question.

I heard my sister's breath catch. Saw her eyes widen. Not a surprise since this was the first time she was seeing Isabelle's ghost.

"She looks so human," Madeline whispered, with a misty plume fleeing from her mouth.

"And heartbreakingly tragic," I added softly.

Isabelle was deathly pale. Her eye sockets were dark as charcoal.

Even still, I could picture Isabelle on the final night she had snuck out of Victoria's room...*alive*. She had been clothed in the white dress she was wearing now. But instead of being drenched and dripping on our den's carpet, I imagined her full skirt flapping in the wind as she ran by Victoria's window toward the lake. Instead of being snugly lassoed around her neck and covering her dress's neckline, the flowered sash had probably been tied and ribboned on her waist. Her blonde hair would've been shiny and absent lake grass. Her ankles, free from painfully raw and purple bruises.

"My sister and I want to help you, Isabelle," I started. "But first, we need to understand what happened to you. I'll ask you questions. All you have to do is spell out your answers by moving this planchette which sits on tiny caster wheels."

I glanced at the wooden pointer where my fingertips and my

190

sister's fingertips lightly rested. "There are letters of the alphabet printed on the face of this board, along with numbers, too.

"Please come closer so you can see them," I urged.

Isabelle approached our table, and I saw Madeline's body and fingers tense.

"I'll start by asking yes or no questions," I continued. "See how the board has YES already spelled out in the upper left hand corner? And NO in the upper right?"

Isabelle nodded.

"Just move the planchette to either side for yes or no answers. Then return the pointer to the middle of the board for the next question. Does that make sense?"

The pointer rolled across the shellacked board. It stopped at YES before gliding back to the middle.

Our fingertips were along for the ride.

"Good," I said, wondering if she'd stay long enough for me to ask all my questions. I had decided to proceed chronologically, which would take more time because I wanted her to feel comfortable and safe. If she was stressed and disappeared, our session would be over.

I shivered. The den grew colder by the second.

"When we're done, either one of us can move the planchette to the word GOODBYE. Are you ready to start?"

YES

"Are you the only ghost here?" I asked.

Isabelle scanned the room. The pointer moved to YES and went back to the middle.

"Did you buy a train ticket to Unityville on Friday, July twenty-second, 1955?"

YES

"Were you planning to visit your parents for an overnight stay?"

YES

"Did you ride the train to Unityville the next morning, that Saturday, as planned?"

The planchette raced across the board and pointed at NO.

"Why not?"

The planchette began pointing at letters. When my sister was able to combine the letters into words, she relayed the answer out loud.

191

"I…was…murdered," Madeline stated.

Dozens of questions bombarded my thoughts, but I couldn't put off the most important.

"Who murdered you, Isabelle?"

The planchette started to glide, pointing at letters.

V…I…

Isabelle stopped moving the wooden device and looked at the den's closed door.

My anxiety amplified.

"Finish, Isabelle! Tell us who murdered you!"

"Vi" wasn't enough. The names of all three suspects started with those letters.

The doorknob turned.

The door flew open with a force that blew out several candles.

Isabelle faded until she disappeared.

The sound of footsteps crossed over the door's threshold.

"What should we do?" Madeline whispered, her fingers trembling on the planchette.

I didn't want to stop asking questions because I suspected that the invisible entity who had just entered the den was Isabelle's murderer.

"Who has joined us?" I asked. "Please spell out your name."

The planchette started moving.

Our exhales were plumes of dense white mist.

Madeline was silent as she studied the letters and attempted to combine them.

"I didn't catch the name," I admitted, looking at my sister.

A tear raced down her cheek.

"What?" I pleaded. "It's okay. Tell me who's here."

"The answer was…*LEAVE OR DIE.*"

An explosion of adrenaline, mixed with anger and fear, swept over my body. I expected a name, not a threat. I wanted to scream a rebuttal like, *"This is my house; YOU leave,"* but fear began to concentrate in my veins and muscles, diluting the fight in me.

The preprinted GOODBYE on the Ouija board was my log. My way to regain control.

"Goodbye," I yelled, forcing the planchette onto the board's closing statement. "This session is closed."

Like a strong breath released over a birthday cake, all the candles in the room extinguished.

The den became pitch black.

I felt angry hands on me. They pushed me over and my chair slammed down with me.

Madeline screamed.

I heard her chair crash onto the floor.

"What should I do?" my sister cried. "I'm scared."

"Hurry! Sprinkle salt on yourself from one of your bombs."

With a shaking hand, I grabbed a plastic container from my pocket, flipped the cap, and dusted myself with salt. Hopefully, Madeline was doing the same.

Snap, snap, snap.

Something was being destroyed. Broken.

Was it the board? Furniture?

Something crashed against a wall.

I held my breath.

The room became still. The blackness enveloped us.

On the floor, I didn't move until I was fairly certain my sister and I were alone again.

After a minute, I stood and patted the tabletop with my hands. Finding my flashlight, I turned it on and swept the light beam around the room. No entities seemed to be present.

I helped my sister off the floor. Then I headed to the door and flipped on the light switch.

The Ouija board and planchette were no longer on the table. The wood they were made from had been snapped and splintered into a dozen pieces. They littered the carpet. And now there was a deep indentation in the drywall where one board piece had slammed into the wall.

"What the hell just happened?" Madeline asked, breathing heavily.

My sister's comment seemed less of a question and more of an expression of disbelief, but I answered her anyway.

"Isabelle's murderer doesn't want us to know their identity."

"Understatement of the century," she gasped.

46

Saturday, August 9, 2025
Windy Hill Farm: Boulder, Pennsylvania

AFTER THE OUIJA board ordeal, Madeline reluctantly agreed to spend the night. No guest room this time. Instead, she'd sleep in the safe space with me, protected from all things *supernatural.* Not going to lie: Having my sister with me was much needed support.

Paranormal investigating was exhausting.

My muscles felt like I had run a full marathon.

A warm bath was what I needed to further dilute the adrenaline which lingered in my bloodstream, making me tense. And my sister agreed to provide me with some private time so I could take one before we turned off the lights for bed.

"Make sure the water's not too hot," she cautioned. "Keep it lukewarm for the baby."

"Good reminder. And what are you going to do while I unwind?"

Madeline reached into her purse, fumbled around, and pulled out a hand rolled cigarette. She smiled and twitched her raised eyebrows. "I'm going to smoke a joint on your patio."

"I thought I told you to stop smoking that stuff."

"Now who's the mama bear?" She winked. "Seriously. Relaxation isn't exactly your farmhouse's forte. So I've come prepared."

"You're armed with your ordnance, right? In case 'V' shows up?"

My sister pulled out her necklace ornaments from under her collar and then felt for her remaining plastic bomb stuffed in her pocket. "Check."

I took off my salt bomb necklace and laid it on the bed. "I'll make more tomorrow."

As Madeline walked over the salt threshold and into the hallway, she turned and looked at me. She gave me that *I love you* look. "Holler if you need me, little sis."

When my soaking tub was filled, I undressed, leaving my clothes on the bed. I dimmed the lights in the bathroom and carefully lowered myself into the tepid water. I could practically hear my muscles and bones releasing an elongated *aah.*

I rested the back of my neck on the tub rim and slowly exhaled.

Wait.

Was the mist escaping from my mouth just foggy humidity from the warm air?

I sat up.

Goosebumps erupted on my arms.

I was confused. How could a ghost have entered my safe space?

The lights started to blink. Not sporadically, but rhythmically. Creating a strobing effect.

On, off. On, off. On, off.

I wanted to stand up, to jump out of the tub and race to my salt bombs on the bed, but the flickering lights were mesmerizing.

Hypnotizing.

Was Isabelle's murderer finally going to appear?

Knowing their identity would be a significant piece of the puzzle.

In between blinks of light, I watched with curiosity as my navy towel (hanging on the rack) began to flutter like the wind rustling a sheet on a clothesline.

My towel dropped onto the tiled floor. In between every flash of light, it seemed to inch closer, reminding me of still frames shown in succession to create animation.

Was this real? Or was my exhaustion playing tricks on me?

Mist continued to billow from between my lips.

My towel was near the tub now.

I couldn't look away.

I remained staring. Intrigued. Wondering what came next.

A voice inside my head screamed for me to snap out of it. *To think quickly and act quickly.* But I was frozen. I was back to being the woman at Union Station. The one who watched "Mr. Hostile" push her onto the train tracks. The one who did nothing to stop him.

What happened to the fierce woman who fought and saved herself from Richard Peter?

I gripped the sides of the tub and shook my head, forcing myself to wake up from the trance I was in.

The bathroom door slammed shut.

The lights turned off completely.

My mind searched for answers on why my safe space wasn't working. Where could I have gone wrong? I pictured the Internet instructions I had followed.

The directions specified: *"Place a line of salt parallel to the thresholds of each door leading in and out of the room."*

Each door.

That's where I screwed up.

The bathroom was a separate room, and I hadn't fortified it.

Ghosts didn't need hallways to enter a room. They just needed salt-free spaces to appear.

Oh dear God. I was processing again. Which meant I wasn't *acting.*

Bah-boom. Bah-boom. Bah-boom.

My heart was steps ahead of me. It pounded to break out and flee the bathroom.

In the pitch black, I couldn't see my towel being lifted off the floor and dropped over my head. But I felt it. Followed by strong hands pushing me down under the water.

Drowning me.

I thrashed and kicked.

My lungs screamed for air.

Leaving the bathroom unfortified might be the end of me.

The end of *us.*

I was fading. Losing the battle.

An image of my sister popped into my head. An image of her finding me submerged underwater. She'd peel back the towel to find my find my eyes wide open. She'd know. I had to keep them open, searching for signs of hope—even in the darkness. Even as life lifted from my body. Death was not something I wanted to give in to.

Wait.

I heard something. Something at the door.

My sister. She was banging.

Even submerged, I could hear her.

"Are you okay?" she screamed, beating on the door.

Maybe I could rally. Maybe it wasn't too late.

I clawed at the towel over my head.

If I didn't get air soon, I would pass out.

CRACK...

Madeline must've kicked in the door.

The next thing I knew she lifted me up and pulled the drenched towel off my head.

"Breathe!" she shouted.

Air never tasted so good.

I breathed in, breathed out. Breathed in, breathed out.

My lungs took several minutes to recover.

At last I could wrap my arms around my sister. I explained, in between sobs, what had happened and how I hadn't properly protected the bathroom or our walk-in closets.

"You saved me, Mad. I'm so grateful."

She stroked my wet hair. "Thank God for the bombs. I threw one ornament on the floor and used the other bomb to dump salt into the bathwater. They worked." Then Madeline added in a whisper, "But you need to leave this house, Nora."

"What I *need* to do is fortify all connected spaces to the bedroom, like the directions specified."

"And then what?"

"Then I bring in professional help."

47

Tuesday, August 12, 2025
Windy Hill Farm: Boulder, Pennsylvania

PSYCHIC MEDIUM AND paranormal scientist India Cloud was more than happy to stop by the farm on her way to Seneca Lake, in upstate New York, ahead of a weeklong vacation. She admitted to me that her typically heavy work schedule had already been cleared for her trip, so the timing couldn't have been any better.

Of course, her consultation wasn't free. Not to mention the upcharge for an expedited onsite visit. But if Dex and I decided to remain at Windy Hill Farm, did we really have a choice?

I had to resolve this paranormal infestation. Dex would be coming home in 38 days.

Dr. Cloud arrived around 10:00 a.m.

When I opened the front door, I was greeted by a woman who projected an aura of fidgety energy as if she had gulped a pot of high-test coffee and chased it with an energy drink. Her red hair was equally wild and curly. Both her tunic (with deep front pockets) and large framed glasses were Irish green. Silver crosses, adorned with emeralds, hung from her loop earrings and she wore a large matching cross pendant on her necklace.

She brought nothing else with her. No briefcase. No purse. No devices that I could see.

I invited her inside the house. Before closing the door, I glanced outside, curious what type of vehicle she drove, but I only saw my Tesla and Dex's hybrid SUV near the garage.

"I parked at the base of your driveway. *Umm,* down the hill," she answered, even though I hadn't verbalized my question. "I like to walk in," she added, "to feel a property's vibe."

Nervously smiling, her eyes shifted from right to left, to her feet.

"Socially awkward" was my conclusion. Which made sense. Talking to most spirits was probably easier than chit chatting with the living. Surely the dead made less judgments. I couldn't imagine a ghost labeling India Cloud as I just had.

I shut the door and pointed in the direction of our great room.

She followed me in.

A tray topped with ginger tea and sugar cookies was on the coffee table. Our windchimes were pleasantly vocal from the patio. With a steady breeze and bright sunshine, I had opened the windows and sliding glass doors to enjoy the crisp mountain air. There wasn't a hint of humidity.

In northeastern Pennsylvania, fall's seasonal changes didn't wait for September.

"Did our property's vibe convey anything, Dr. Cloud?" I asked.

"Please. Call me India," she said, making herself comfortable on the couch.

I sat across from her in an overstuffed chair.

"Umm," she continued, "there's a lot of history on this parcel."

I didn't find her analysis particularly insightful. Her comment was true for *all* land, right?

But then she added, "I hear a young woman's cries in the wind."

Okay, *that* statement caused goosebumps to rise on my skin. Not from the chill of paranormal activity. More from the fact that someone else, a *professional,* could hear what I heard (*without* me telling her about the phenomenon first).

Most importantly, she wasn't trying to dismiss the wailing.

Her validation instantly opened my flood gates. Information about all the strange happenings at Windy Hill Farm poured from my mouth. I barely took a breath in between my retellings of each paranormal intrusion or in between my explanations of the research I had conducted on Isabelle Taylor and the Williams family.

When I concluded my oral report and sought her initial assessment, India agreed with me that if I could discover what happened to Isabelle (if I could bring forth a degree of justice), her spirit would likely find peace, allowing her to transition to her eternal resting place.

"A battle is occurring on your property," India said. "The ghost you call V is trying to prevent Isabelle from enlisting your help to expose the truth about her disappearance and death. But Isabelle won't rest until the historical record is accurate. Until her body is found and her killer has been publicly identified.

"My guess," she continued, "is that Virgil Williams and his wife knew or suspected there was culpatory evidence hidden on this parcel. Why else would the Williamses refuse to sell it? Why else would Isabelle ask you to *FIND THEM?*"

"Your theory makes sense while Virgil and Vivian were still...*alive*," I countered, "but this long after their deaths? Why would V *care?* I mean, even if authorities were able to confirm that V had murdered Isabelle on this land seventy years ago, they can't arrest a ghost."

"*Umm,* motivations are what's keeping V here. Research shows that if a spirit hasn't passed on from this dimension, what motivated them in life will motivate them in death."

Actually, I had read something similar in my own research.

India's comment also reminded me of what Miss Grace had said about the Williams family, about what motivated them in the 1950s.

"A photographer who knew the family," I said, "made a point of telling me Virgil and Vivian were devoted (her word) to protecting the reputations of their family and this county."

"One of the Williamses is still driven by those motivations. Is still trying to keep old secrets buried," she concluded. "Let me ask you about their children. *Umm,* you told me Victoria recently died, so clearly, she isn't V. What about Vincent? Alive or dead?"

"Vincent died young. Forty years ago. At the age of forty-five. A heart attack like his mother," I said. "Their youngest, Vaughn, is still alive in a retirement home. New Jersey, I think. In fact, Vaughn's son, Duncan, was the one who petitioned the court to overturn the restriction on selling the lot, a directive (a trust) carried over from Virgil to Vivian's will. And then to the wills of their children."

"I'm not at all suspicious about Vaughn," India said. "You told

FIND THEM

me he was at camp when Isabelle was murdered. Besides, he's still alive. Then there's his name; it doesn't start with Vi."

I appreciated her ability to organize all the facts into crisp little chunks. That allowed her to "file" the irrelevant ones. Sometimes in my brain, information oozed together into one big blob.

"The good news is," she continued, "once the truth is revealed, the reason for both ghosts to remain here will be mitigated. The truth should set each of them free."

"Sounds simple enough, but I'm stuck. I'm not sure what my next step should be. Meanwhile, the level of danger keeps ramping up."

India sipped her tea. "There's a connection between the *FIND THEM* messages and the sinkholes. The fact that you've been led to *two*—here and on the island—isn't a coincidence."

"But nothing was found under our sinkhole, and our engineer used ground penetrating radar."

"If your sinkhole returns," she said, "which wouldn't surprise me, don't ignore it. Something small might be buried there—a time capsule, a weapon, that sort of thing."

"And the sinkhole on the island?" I asked.

"Seek permission to have your engineer use GPR on that site. *Umm,* perhaps at your own expense. Make it harder for local authorities to deny you. If and when remains are found, law enforcement will be required to exhume them."

Exhume them...the possibility that Isabelle's murdered body could've been buried in dirt on Boulder Island, decaying over the decades until just bones remained, made me shiver.

India pulled a few business cards from her tunic's pocket and handed them to me. "Feel free to invite law enforcement to contact me. I've worked with detectives on cases before."

"You must feel strongly that Isabelle's body is nearby," I said.

"Of course. Through the Ouija board, she told you herself that she never rode the train home. That she was murdered. And she's asking for your help. Wailing that she cannot rest until the past is unearthed."

A lump formed in my throat, and I swallowed hard to try and push it back down.

"Can you tell me who V is?" I asked. "It would help me knowing who killed Isabelle."

An instant chill pervaded the air around us.

BANG...

Every window in the great room slammed shut.

Our open sliders raced along their tracks until they crashed closed against their frames.

The energy released caused the room to shudder.

My trinkets on shelves trembled and vibrated.

Picture frames tilted on the walls.

I jolted up from my chair, clutching a salt bomb ornament hanging from my necklace.

India remained seated on the couch, carefully returning her empty teacup to the coffee table. She slowly stood and reached into the other pocket of her tunic, retrieving a glass vial of clear liquid.

"Holy Water," she announced sternly, as if stating a warning to the ghost.

A frigid gust raced past me toward the kitchen, rustling my bangs before racing out of the open window over the sink. At least, that's what my curtains seemed to indicate.

The temperature in the room returned to normal.

"Keep in mind, *umm,* spirits have triggers like humans do," India said. "Don't change what you're doing, what you're seeking, just don't announce it. Don't make your intentions so obvious. Not unless you're prepared for an aggressive reaction. One that may cause you harm.

"And to address your question," she continued, "V is advanced, able to mask his or her identity. So instead, try to focus on the clues, the evidence. Let them quietly reveal the truth."

Walking to the kitchen island, I grabbed my shopping-list tablet and a pen. "When this mystery is solved, do you...could you..." I said out loud, before writing on the tablet: *conduct an exorcism?*

India smiled while reading my handwriting. "You're a quick learner." She locked eyes with me. "About conducting the *e*-word. Generally speaking, no. It would tarnish my reputation in the afterlife. Spirits don't, *umm,* want to trust and communicate with someone who has the know-how and skills to banish them. Too risky. But I'll ask around with my living colleagues."

I thanked India for being so helpful and walked her to the foyer.

"You're closer to a resolution than you think," she said, as she exited the front door. "Just be careful." She smiled, but not in a happy, cheery way. More like kindness mixed with concern. "By the way," she added, "your salt bombs are a clever idea. I'll have to make some for myself. *Umm,* for the bad actors. The ones like V."

Waving goodbye, I closed the door.

My next step was to call Evan, the engineer who had repaired our sinkhole.

If I could obtain a permit, I needed to know if he would even consider scanning the middle of Boulder Island using GPR.

48

I SAT ON an uncomfortable wooden chair across from Detective Gilbert's desk which lacked any evidence that he might be swamped with police work. In fact, there was only one manila folder on his desk and I had managed to read the tab: *End of Summer Barbecue.*

The escape and capture of Richard Peter had to have been the department's most significant case since the disappearance of Isabelle Taylor in 1955.

I considered this likelihood to be a positive talking point for the Boulder Police Department because, in my opinion, overwhelmed law enforcement suggested that *something* was amiss. In contrast, departments which had time to plan seasonal barbecues with their community meant they were doing *something* right.

Detective Gilbert had an office the size of a walk-in closet. In his 50s if I had to guess, he was blessed with a head full of wavy, sandy blond hair. He had a thick handlebar mustache—its tips curled and pointed upwards. His skin was tanned and weathered. Not a surprise since a fish mount (a largemouth bass or something similar) hung on the wall behind him. The department's name and GILBERT were embroidered in black on the left side of his khaki shirt.

Opening a desk drawer, he withdrew a tablet and pen and placed them on the desk.

"You're a brave woman, Mrs. Bliss," he started.

Oh great.

He was probably going to mention *The Nightmare at Union Station*.

"I was a member of the team who responded to your 911 call," he added instead. "The team who apprehended Richard Peter on your property two months ago."

I released the breath I had been unconsciously holding. Not that either notoriety was positive, but at least with Richard Peter, I had fought back.

"Thank you for helping me," I said. "You all saved my life."

Detective Gilbert sat back in his chair and tilted his head while assessing me. He didn't say a word.

I instantly felt uncomfortable. It seemed like he was trying to figure out what secrets I kept close to my chest. Secrets, he might be interested in knowing.

"You and your husband have had quite a bit of bad luck out there," he stated. "At your place."

Trying to gauge what he thought about town rumors regarding lot 16, I blurted out, "As locals like to point out, our land is haunted. So bad luck comes with the territory."

"I was sorry to hear about Mr. Bliss's accident. How's he doing?"

Detective Gilbert wasn't giving an inch about his stance on paranormal activity, unless avoiding the subject altogether meant he wasn't a believer.

"Better," I answered. "He's in rehab now. He'll be back home in mid-September. Thank you for asking."

The detective glanced at his watch. "What can I do for you today? My time is limited."

"With all the bad luck and local rumors," I continued, "I decided to investigate the history of our parcel at the Honesdale Public Library. I've also interviewed Grace Carson who used to photograph the Williams family in the mid-1950s. In addition, I spoke to Victoria Williams Johnson before she died. As well as to her son, Ross."

I wouldn't mention that Victoria, on her deathbed, wasn't capable of speaking back to me (other than her eerie *Never Tell* chant). Or that I had temporary possession of her diaries.

"Are you a reporter, Mrs. Bliss?"

"No," I said with a slight chuckle. "My profession is actually in marketing and design."

"Not to sound rude, but why would your casual research be of any interest to me and this department?"

"I stumbled across Isabelle Taylor who supposedly disappeared in Unityville. Back in 1955."

"What with my extensive experience and all," he smirked, "I'm guessing you've intentionally chosen the word *supposedly*. Is there a point you'd like to make?"

No more beating around the bush or he'd end our meeting.

"There's a sinkhole in the middle of Boulder Island, Detective Gilbert. Based on my research, I believe there's a strong possibility that Isabelle Taylor's body is buried there. And if I'm right, her seventy year old cold-case would be one step closer to being solved."

Detective Gilbert leaned forward, placing his forearms on the desk. "As I see it, Mrs. Bliss, there are three problems."

"Oh?"

"First off, Boulder Lake State Park is a wildlife sanctuary. If you've been on the island, you've trespassed on state land." He wrote my name down on his tablet, no doubt to intimidate me. "Second, a city slicker's hunch on a seventy year old missing persons case carries no weight in these parts. And third, even if this department wanted to have a look-see into this farfetched *possibility* of yours, we've got no funds in our budget for it."

Detective Gilbert stood up from his chair.

I remained seated—my only option to counter his powerplay.

"My husband and I are willing to pay for a non-invasive process that won't disturb the sanctuary and will be able to prove or disprove my hunch. It's called ground penetrating radar. The device looks like a lawnmower. I know an engineer who specializes in GPR and is willing to do it at no cost to anyone but my husband and me. All I need from you is a permit."

"Except, that's a state matter," he said. "And we're a county department."

He took two steps to the door.

I remained seated. "So you don't know anyone at all with state jurisdiction who could help?"

"Our time is over, Mrs. Bliss."

"Okay. I understand."

I finally stood and walked to him. I reached out my hand for a shake and he accepted.

We were at his office door.

"I appreciate you taking the time to hear me out," I added.

"My pleasure." With raised eyebrows, he smiled, maybe confused I was giving up so quickly.

"I'm heading to Scranton," I announced. "I've already scheduled a Plan B. Just in case."

"What might that be?" he asked, trying to sound bored. "If you don't mind me asking."

"Not at all." I had cast a line and he was biting on the hook. "I have a good friend there. We know each other from D.C.

"Maybe you've heard of him," I continued. "Jim Stevens? A WSET broadcast reporter?"

I was embellishing, of course. Speaking to my "good friend" one time about our sinkhole and his boss knowing about my accident on the train tracks did not constitute a friendship.

Nevertheless, *angler* Gilbert must have realized I had just snagged him. I had figuratively yanked on the line and was reeling him in by introducing the implied threat of speaking to a reporter.

I was more than aware most of the people I interacted with in business felt uneasy about news reporters. But their angst wasn't mine. Journalists simply wanted to investigate in order to discover, validate, or disprove details. Their carrot was the truth.

"Will you, by any chance," he said, sounding cautious, "be mentioning our meeting?"

"Why wouldn't I?" I shrugged. "I offered to pay for an environmentally safe procedure to help with an old cold case, one long forgotten and never solved by this department or the one in Unityville, and you weren't interested. Anything I left out?"

"Look. Before you meet with him, let me see what I can do about getting a permit."

"Really? You'd help a city slicker like me?"

"Careful with the sarcasm, Mrs. Bliss. I might change my mind."

49

DEX WAS HALFWAY through rehabilitation for his neck, arm, and general strength.

I was immensely proud of his progress. Watching him regain his flexibility, session by session, made me appreciate the enormous gap he was closing—from intense pain and a fear of moving to fighting for each increment in his ranges of motion, regardless of discomfort.

My Viking was kicking ass and taking names.

After today's physical therapy, his PT trainer snapped on Dex's neck collar and gave us the thumbs up so we could walk down the hallway toward the dining room.

"Let's sit with Oscar for lunch," Dex said. "If he's already seated."

There was never an empty table for us to sit privately. At least Oscar, who had shattered both his legs in a motorcycle accident, was the closest to Dex's age. Oscar was 48 and Dex, 31. But since most patients were in their 70s and 80s, *closest* was acutely accurate.

At the entrance to the dining room, Mrs. Tilghman, dressed in her fluorescent pink bathrobe and dining beside her portable oxygen tank, waved at Dex. She had a crush on my husband, apparently saving her sugar-free chocolates exclusively for him.

In one's golden years, cures for loneliness came with no age limits.

We spotted Oscar. He sat at a round table in the back corner.

Nodding, we smiled at Mrs. Tilghman as we meandered around tables, wheelchairs, and walkers, heading toward Oscar. A few patrons tapped Dex's butt as he passed, accompanied by spicy encouragement which was locker room worthy.

After we sat down and received our meal of chicken piccata (rehab style without capers—also meaning the chicken was diced into small bites and nothing was salted), our conversation drifted into Oscar's childhood. He grew up in none other than…Boulder.

"You live on part of the old Williams Farm," he said, stroking his white goatee beard. "You might appreciate this story."

Not going to lie. Oscar had my attention.

"In high school, my freshman year, I wrote a paper about the five curses of the Williams Farm." He chuckled. "Mrs. Queen gave me a D, man, so it's always stuck with me.

"When you fuck with karma," he continued in a whisper, "it'll high side you on the asphalt. Trust me. This, right here, is my bad karma for cheating on Mildred. My *ex*-wife now."

"Curses?" I asked, hoping his story was going to be about *them* and not about his teacher or poor grade. Or his failed marriage.

"Yeah," Oscar mumbled with food in his mouth. I waited patiently as he chewed and swallowed. "The Williams' bad karma started with the disappearance of their step niece back in 1955." He paused and looked up. "Her name's on the tip of my tongue…"

"Isabelle Taylor," I said.

Oscar looked at Dex. "Pretty *and* smart. Good job, my friend."

I should've guessed Oscar was also from that special planet: Mars.

He sipped his iced tea. "Two years later, Mr. Williams dies in a single car accident on Belmont Bridge. Never found out what the cause was. But my mother knew this ICU nurse at Wayne Memorial—you know, right here in Honesdale. The nurse told my mom that Mr. Williams's last word was…*Isabelle*. Head scratcher. Am I right?"

Miss Grace had told me and Madeline the same thing when we visited her at Wellspring.

"Anyway," Oscar continued, "things quieted down with the family for a spell. Until 1974 when their youngest son, Vaughn, got institutionalized for early onset dementia. I'm talking *early*. Vaughn was thirty-two. In his prime."

No wonder Vaughn's son, Duncan, petitioned the court to sell our parcel. Having his father institutionalized for 50 years had to be economically debilitating on the entire family.

"That was curse number three," Dex said. "What came next?"

"Vincent, their eldest son and middle child, dies in 1985 while living at the farmhouse."

"Heart failure. Right?" I asked.

"That's what his death certificate reported. Locals suspected something else. Rumor was that Vincent had been *scared* to death. Literally. Apparently, his missing stepcousin (this *Isabelle*) was haunting the crap out of him and his mother. Turns out, my Pops knew the coroner who did the autopsy. Said Vincent had a frozen look of terror on his face. When I turned fifteen, Pops held nothing back in his description. Gross stuff like his lips were drawn back exposing his gums, as if his skin had shrunk from fear."

Oscar's disclosure that Vincent was living at the farmhouse at the time of his passing was new information. Also interesting were the rumors swirling that Vincent's death might have involved *unexplained* circumstances, much like his father Virgil's car accident.

One thing was certain, Oscar was filling in some voids after Victoria's diary had gone blank.

"Why was Vincent living at the farmhouse anyway?" I asked.

"He moved back home in 1983 to help his mother. She had a documented weak heart. But she was sixty-five then. Vincent was some twenty years younger and healthy as an ox."

"The farmhouse burned in 1986," I said. "Is that the fifth curse?"

Oscar smiled with a piece of lettuce protruding from his closed lips. I watched as he sucked it into his disposal, grinded it up, and then swallowed. The guy was an eating machine.

"Yeah. The fire marshal attributed the blaze to an airborne ember. All I know is a lot of damning evidence might've been lost the day that farmhouse was reduced to rubble."

I sipped my water. "Like what?"

"Vivian Williams kept her diaries in that house. Diaries which gave details about how the curse started—the point in time when all the family's gremlins came out of the woodwork. *That* moment was Isabelle, when she arrived at the farm for the summer." He loaded his fork with his last bite of chicken. "Victoria was the only one spared from the drama. From the curse. She died like what…"

"Nine days ago," I finished, finding it comforting that Isabelle's best friend had not been directly affected by the curse. (Which actually sounded less like a curse and more like paranormal revenge.)

"Hot diggity, Dex," Oscar cheered, way too loudly. Heads turned. "Your wife, here. She knows her shit."

I ignored Oscar's patronizing banter. Instead, I was disappointed that Vivian's diaries had been torched with everything else in the farmhouse. What secrets they could've revealed.

"Don't leave us hanging," Dex countered. "Why did you get a D on your paper?"

"The writing assignment was supposed to be non-fiction," Oscar said. "Mrs. *Royal Bitch* Queen classified my paper as fiction. *Fantasy*, I think she called it." He shrugged.

I needed to redirect the conversation back to the Williamses. "What role did the family have in Isabelle's disappearance?"

"*Aah.* That *is* the question. And I think the answer comes down to problem management."

"How so?" I asked.

"Pardon my bluntness, but I think either Virgil or Vincent was boffing the step niece."

Oscar paused, perhaps waiting for a shocked reaction. When he didn't get one, he continued.

"They both had reputations as playboys. Maybe the Mrs. found out and one of the men terminated the problem. Authorities didn't challenge the family's alibis. That's because the Williamses were prominent. With deep pockets. Townsfolk looked the other way, man." He stroked his goatee again. "All would've been shoved under the rug for eternity, except…"

The lights in the dining room flickered.

"Except, little miss step niece came back to haunt them." Oscar put his fork down on his empty plate. "Yuppers. That young lady was the beginning and end of the five curses."

Dex and I glanced at each other. We knew the hexes were still accumulating.

And Isabelle wasn't the only ghost adding to the sum.

50

Monday, August 18, 2025
Honesdale Public Library: Honesdale, Pennsylvania

AS I APPROACHED, Jennifer opened the front door to the library. She had called me over the weekend, having found an interesting archive she thought I'd want to see.

Consistent with the first time I had met her, Jennifer was a ray of sparkling sunshine, a radiating buzz of over the top positivity. Dressed in another cheery sundress (this one decorated with happy bumble bees flying in every direction), she greeted me as if we had known each other since elementary school.

Don't get me wrong. I appreciated exuberance. But I had lived in a city most of my adult life. *That* level of jolly was an advertisement for naivety. In other words, an invitation to get robbed.

In the city, even minding one's own business could land someone face first on the tracks.

After exchanging pleasantries, Jennifer led me upstairs to the same room where Madeline and I had reviewed the archives for the Williams family. Several letters and a photograph of a woman were resting on top of the rectangular table in the center of the room.

Jennifer closed the door.

Reaching for the picture, she handed it to me. "This is Ester Bramwell," she said. "Miss Bramwell was an at-large member of the Wayne Library League, back when Virgil was chair."

The youthful woman in the photograph looked lovely, having wheat colored eyes, a full bottom lip, and wavy black hair.

Jennifer picked up a handwritten letter from the table.

"I've been organizing archives," she explained. "For an upcoming Library League ball. A fundraiser. And I came across this letter. Read it, if you don't mind. I found it...*curious.*"

November 6, 1954

Dear Miss Bramwell,

I am requesting your letter of resignation immediately. Your advances toward me are inappropriate, scandalous, and will not be tolerated. I am completely devoted to my beloved wife and family. They are my world.

With your resignation and complete discretion regarding this matter, the Library League will furnish you with a positive employment reference to be used in any other state, save Pennsylvania. However, refusal to accept these terms will result in termination for sexual misconduct. Your reputation would be irreparably tarnished.

I expect a letter of resignation by the end of the day. Please sign the attached agreement of terms.

Virgil Williams
Wayne Library League Chair

"I've had several people tell me Virgil Williams was a playboy," I said. "Makes me wonder who actually initiated the advances."

I returned the letter to the table. "I'd place my bets on Virgil. Is that what piqued your curiosity? The person who instigated the misconduct?"

"No," she said. "There are inconsistencies in the handwriting."

"Oh? In what way?"

"I'm certified in handwriting authentication," Jennifer said. "I've been schooled to identify the distinctive features of someone's penmanship." She tilted her head and raised her eyebrows. "With computers, it's a dying art. But I was drawn to it anyway because now I can verify the authenticity of penned archives in the library. Then there's my uncle. Sometimes he needs my expertise, too."

Seemed like more information than I needed.

I got it, though. She was proud.

With Ester Bramwell's letter back down on the table, Jennifer slid it flush against another letter from Virgil.

"Compare the r's in both letters. In the second, r's are wider, more distinct. And look at the descender loops in the f's, g's, and y's. The loops are wider and longer in the second letter."

"Are you suggesting Virgil didn't write the letter to Ester Bramwell? But why would that be unusual? Couldn't his secretary have written it for him?"

"Not likely," she said. "This would've been a scandal in those days. And the fact that this discovered letter is the only historical mention of the alleged *impropriety* means that the reason behind Ester Bramwell's sudden resignation was, indeed, kept under tight wraps."

"Who do you think wrote the letter then?"

She slid over the other two letters.

"My radar started beeping when I read the line: *I am completely devoted to my beloved wife and family. They are my world.* That struck me as odd in a termination letter, especially from a man with infidelity issues. My intuition suggests that someone who wanted to desperately *believe* in their husband's or father's devotion might've included a statement to that effect. So I pulled two archived letters— one from Vivian and Vincent—and analyzed their handwriting."

"Vincent?" I asked. "How did you get a letter sample from him?"

"He was also a volunteer here. Started when he was twelve. Passion for our libraries was a family affair." Her cheeks flushed crimson. "Sorry for the poor choice of words."

"How old would Vincent have been in 1954?"

"Fourteen. Old enough to write this letter." She pointed at the two samples proving her point. "Take a look. You'll notice that Vivian and Vincent have nearly identical penmanship. Their r, f, g, and y's match the writing in the letter to Ester Bramwell. My opinion is that either one of them was the likely author."

I remembered Jennifer had positioned herself on the *"conservative side"* about why lot 16 was never to be sold. *"Wanted to preserve their slice of heaven,"* she had told me. I was curious if she was figuring out that the Williams' nirvana was a smoke screen. An illusion.

"What do you think it means?" I asked, wanting to hear her take.

"Forging a letter is an intentional act of deception," she said. "It tells me the family knew each other's indiscretions and were willing to...*intervene* to ensure their secrecy. It tells me that whoever wrote this letter wanted Ester Bramwell to leave. To be gone from the League, from the area, whether Virgil wanted that outcome or not.

"Strange," Jennifer continued, "how one unsavory revelation can cast doubt on every other aspect of a family. Even on a family as revered and influential as the Williamses."

She was speaking to the choir.

"You're realizing the family wasn't all rainbows and puppy dogs," I said. "They hid a dark side. One with fangs."

She nodded. "I encouraged my uncle to apply for that GPR permit. For Boulder Island."

"Wait. What?"

"My uncle. Detective Gilbert from the Boulder Police Department." She chuckled. "I know. We don't exactly look related. He married my aunt who was a widow."

I blushed. "My surprise was about the permit, not about your family resemblance!"

"Or lack thereof." She winked.

"So you spoke to your uncle about my request?" I asked.

"He talked to me about your visit to his office *before* he knew I had met you. Anyway, he'll be reaching out to you soon. You'll be pleased, I'm sure." Smiling, she gathered the letters and photograph, placing them into a neat pile. "I predict the Williamses have more indiscretions that need unearthing."

I had a prediction, too.

Jennifer and I were going to be fast friends.

51

MY FINGERS TREMBLED from nervous energy.

Evan was on his way to the farm. He wanted to share results with me before dropping them off at the Boulder Police Department. During his visit, he'd also collect his check which waited for him on the kitchen countertop.

Jennifer had been right. Her uncle, Detective Gilbert, had called me the day after my visit to the library, confirming he had obtained a time sensitive permit from the state. The permit green-lighted Evan, our sinkhole engineer, to perform GPR in the center of Boulder Island at the spot where the ground had sunk in the shape of a grave. With a limited window of time to complete the job, Evan had immediately scheduled the project and taken care of it two days ago.

Hence, the thank you basket of fresh eggs, home baked bread, and strawberry jam beside the check.

I closed my eyes.

If Isabelle's body *had* been buried there, finding her remains might be a significant step to ending this nightmare. Dex and I could return to living our best lives, preparing for our expanding family.

Please, God.

Praying that human bones were found seemed counterintuitive.

However, it wasn't like there was a chance that Isabelle had run off 70 years ago to Turks and Caicos and was now, in present time, sipping a pale pink Koo-Koo Cabana on an island beach at the age of

216

87. As India Cloud had reminded me: Isabelle had already told us via the Ouija board that she had been murdered when she was 17. *Murdered* by someone whose name started with Vi.

Isabelle's body was somewhere. Somewhere close.

I flinched. The knock at the front door startled me.

Lost in thought, I hadn't heard Evan's truck pull up to our garage.

Opening the door, I couldn't help staring at the large manila envelope in Evan's hand. Other details were less attention grabbing, like his plaid shirt, faded jeans, and leather belt with a big silver buckle. No doubt he was packing a firearm under his right pantleg. After all, he was a member of the Wild, Wild West pistol posse.

Duke, his black Lab, stood beside him, wagging his tail.

"Come on in," I said. "Your pup, too."

"*Aww,* that's nice. Thank you. But Duke loves the outdoors." He glanced behind him toward the chicken coop. "Unless your flock is roaming the grounds?"

"Still in their hutch," I said, standing to the side, inviting him in.

Duke ran off as I closed the door and led the way to the kitchen.

Evan appreciated the basket and pocketed the check.

My heart accelerated as he opened his manila envelope.

He pulled out printed color images, arranging them on the kitchen island's countertop.

"I used the same technology as with your sinkhole," he started. "The device sends pulses of electromagnetic energy into the ground and the software displays anomalies with contrast."

"Contrasts in color are how you spot objects underground?"

"And distortions." He nodded. "Curious. What do you see?"

I studied the prints as I clenched my teeth.

Distortions. Color changes. They stood out.

I pointed to a print. "Looks like there's something under there."

"You're right, Nora," he said, running his finger over the visible distortions. "I believe those anomalies are bones. From my experience, I'm predicting *human* bones."

A wave of nausea crashed in my stomach and raced up my throat.

I darted to the sink, leaned over, and gagged. How embarrassing.

"Are you okay?" he asked.

Wetting a paper towel, I dabbed my mouth and lips. "I'm sorry." I straightened up. "We're going to start telling people outside of our immediate family. I guess you'll be the first." I smiled. "I'm twelve weeks pregnant. When I get overwhelmed, this is what can happen."

"You're having a baby. Cool beans! I'm excited for you and Dex. Congratulations!"

"Thank you, Evan." I walked back to the kitchen island. "The police department will be required to oversee this now. Right?"

"Absolutely. It's a forensics issue now. Hopefully, they can match the remains with that missing girl from the old cold case you told me about. What was her name again?"

"Isabelle Taylor."

A horrible shrill pierced my eardrums.

It was followed by desperate yelps.

"Duke!" Evan yelled.

Racing to the front door, he flung it open.

His Lab bolted inside. The ridge of black fur running along his spine stood erect. His ears were pinned back. Tail tucked between his legs. And his entire body quivered.

Evan immediately dropped to his knees and began assessing his dog, undoubtedly looking for injuries.

The temperature in the foyer dropped.

Plumes of mist streamed from our mouths.

The front door slammed shut, with no one touching it. No one visible anyway.

Whimpering, Duke scrambled on the wooden floors to distance himself from the door. As he bolted, he knocked into Evan who lost his balanced and fell over onto his side.

Lights flickered.

Windows in the kitchen and great room slammed shut.

From my necklace, I grabbed an ornament, this one filled with blessed water. I hoped to mimic India Cloud's confidence. "Holy Water," I announced.

A wind swooshed by us.

It funneled out through an open sliding glass door, causing the screen to rattle and shake.

Duke viciously barked, spraying drool from his jowls.

With the ghost's departure, the house began to calm.

Evan stood and brushed off his knees.

"Tell me you know what's happening," he said.

There was no need to hide the truth. Not with the man who had discovered buried bones—those most likely belonging to Isabelle.

"Our property is haunted," I admitted. "And it has everything to do with Isabelle's unresolved murder back in 1955."

"Not going to lie, Nora. You and Dex need to get the hell away from here."

52

Friday, August 29, 2025
Windy Hill Farm: Boulder, Pennsylvania

SHIT DE LA shit.

My boss Cecelia, whom co-workers secretly labeled the stiletto queen, called me at the crack of dawn while I was feeding the chickens, wearing my farm dirties (otherwise defined as soiled clothes worn repeatedly for chores). My outfit was accessorized with my mud-encrusted Muck boots.

Shoes seemed symbolic of my journey. They visually epitomized where I'd been versus where I was. The irony.

Apparently, Cecelia had visited a client in Allentown yesterday and had plans to stay the weekend with her parents in Bethlehem. Since she was "in the area" (quite a stretch because the farm was an hour and a half away), she wanted to surprise me by popping over.

A visit, I was not remotely prepared for.

Which made me wonder. Had she *planned* to catch me off guard?

Cecelia would be arriving at 9:00 a.m. so I didn't have time to dwell on her possible motives. Bottomline, she was as addicted to punctuality as she was to seven inch heels.

I hadn't experienced this level of pressure since…*since* I had been standing on the platform at Union Station, 15 months ago, waiting for my late train.

I showered and dressed as quickly as I could.

Gazing at myself in our bathroom's full length mirror, I looked acceptable. I wore a stylish, untucked silk blouse (shimmering silver), paired with flared, black silk slacks. I always liked how this outfit matched my hair and silver streak. I finished my look with large, silver looped earrings and heeled sandals. Not to mention, I wore a tiny vial of Holy Water attached to my necklace which was undetectable under my blouse. (Salt bombs would've created a bulge.)

For an outfit that had been appropriately casual for office hours at D&B's Baltimore studio, it felt majorly dressy and uncomfortable now. Again, the irony.

Before heading to the kitchen, I made sure to close the door to our bedroom. Cecelia did not need to see my safe space. I didn't want to become the center of juicy gossip at the office.

Speaking of my ghost free zone, I prayed the whole house would remain quiet during Cecelia's impromptu visit. But since ghosts didn't give a rat's ass I hoped Cecelia and I could chat and eat defrosted crumpets in peace (especially since Cecelia was my boss), I sprinkled salt on the rug and couch in the great room. To season my prayers.

Adding to my anxiousness, severe thunderstorms were forecasted to arrive in the area around noon. Would she still be here by then?

I was arranging freshly clipped flowers in a vase when I heard knocking at the front door.

Swallowing hard, I begged myself to act naturally.

If I had never left office life, seeing Cecelia would've been easy peasy. But I had removed myself from the employee environment when I relocated and started working remotely. Which meant, this visit would feel more like *an interview*. Mostly awkward and disjointed.

Calm down. This was Cecelia, not some stranger.

I opened the door to my boss dressed in a pencil skirt, a posh tunic blazer, and red stilettos, holding a purse-styled briefcase. Her skin was blemish free and pale, as if she only came out at night.

After exchanging niceties, starting with a peck on each cheek, we settled in the great room, side by side on the couch, in reach of the ginger tea, crumpets, and jam—all plated on the coffee table.

"You've got circles under your eyes," she started.

I had forgotten how direct Cecelia was. She spoke what was on her mind, even when her thoughts didn't need to be shared. She was blunt and expected blunt back. It went hand in hand with efficiency. Or so she pontificated.

"Not surprising, really," I countered. "My husband's in rehab for his broken neck and arm. I'm managing the farm on my own. And keeping up with my design work for you."

"*Keeping up* is why I'm here, darling." She placed her palm on my knee for a second. Her way of showing empathy. "You're not."

"Excuse me?"

"I'll make my point succinctly. This arrangement isn't working. Your output has slacked and your submissions, well, they lack what D&B has come to expect from you: uniqueness."

All I could do was stare at her in disbelief.

My world continued to spiral downward.

Dex had nearly been killed. Biddy had been murdered. Cinnamon, too. Our house and property were a fucking ghost depot. And now *this?* I was losing my freaking job?

Compassion. Understanding. Pity. I needed Cecelia to feel those emotions when she considered my circumstances.

I didn't want to play the pregnancy card, but I was suddenly drowning in an ocean of desperation and there was no log to grab onto to save me from this moment. The white water was raging and tossing me uncontrollably.

My chest tightened.

I placed my hand over my heart and tried to breathe.

"I'm pregnant," I managed to whisper. "I need the money and health insurance. I'll do better. I promise."

Cecelia moved her hand onto my back and rubbed it. "Relax, Nora. Please, darling. You should know by now; we are not heartless. Hear me out. We have a plan."

A *plan?*

I closed my eyes and attempted to regulate my breathing. Tears raced down my cheeks, ignoring my efforts to hold myself together.

"We know how exceptional you are," Cecelia stated. "At the same time, we also have to maintain our reputation as an agency. Family matters, including pregnancy, are no excuse for sub-par work."

I instantly felt guilty for bringing up my pregnancy. Indeed, my "plum" was not to blame.

In truth, my declining work performance had to do with the priorities I had placed above my work responsibilities. Sure, pregnancy was at the top now—as it should be regardless of what Cecelia thought. But I had also squeezed in plenty of others. And those were all *choices.*

"Are you firing me?" I asked.

"Not quite." She reached into her briefcase and pulled out some papers. "We're placing you on a yearlong leave of absence. No pay, but you'll maintain your health insurance and 401-k account. Hopefully in twelve months, you'll be over this…this rough spot."

Could Cecelia's plan be a blessing?

In 12 months, our baby would be six months old, no longer a newborn. By that time, I wouldn't be distracted by ghosts (they'd be a thing of the past…hopefully). Dex would be working again. We'd all be back on track.

"Your leniency and understanding are deeply appreciated," I said. "And I regret my work hasn't met D&B's standards. I'm sorry."

"This temporary solution will benefit us all, darling." She tapped my knee. "Look over the papers. Sign and mail them to me."

The house rumbled, strong enough to make the light pendants sway (those hanging from the beams above us). One of the guest room doors slammed shut.

Cecelia flinched.

My smartwatch read 9:45 a.m. Too early for the forecasted storms, but it was the only excuse available to me. Cecelia lived in the *everything has an explanation* camp. Like I used to.

"This house is funny," I said, making my tone carefree. "There can be a nasty thunderstorm in Honesdale, and we feel the reverberations on Windy Hill Farm."

Cecelia glanced out a window at the sunshine. "How far is Honesdale from here?"

"A good ten miles. Over some mountains."

As a crow flies, the distance was close, weakening my claim.

Cecelia raised her eyebrows but didn't press the issue. Instead, she rubbed her arms as if chilled and ended our meeting, stating she had to head back to Bethlehem.

Interesting how my tolerance for the paranormal had changed. These days, it took something far more dramatic to frighten me.

53

Saturday, August 30, 2025
Windy Hill Farm: Boulder, Pennsylvania

THUNDERSTORMS CONTINUED WELL into the dark, predawn hours of Saturday. The electricity had shut off sometime after midnight. The only light coming into the bedroom was from lightning flashes strobing through the windows.

Rain pelted the glass.

It sounded like a thousand fingertips tapping for my attention.

Talk about being restless.

My mind wasn't thinking about any *one* thing. It was bombarded with snippets of every single issue affecting me. The fragments were bouncing around in my brain like heated molecules about to burst into vapor. *Did Virgil want Ester Bramwell to move away after their affair was discovered? Or did his jilted wife or son write the termination letter as a demonstration of force? Who had Isabelle been meeting at night? And when would I learn if the bones found on Boulder Island were hers?*

Thunder rattled the window.

My thoughts shifted to the financial hardship facing Dex and me. *Did we have enough savings to even afford Windy Hill Farm when neither of us were bringing in paychecks?*

Time for another toss and turn.

I rolled toward my window and gasped.

Isabelle.

All my random thoughts evaporated.

Isabelle stood on the other side of the glass.

224

The wind and rain were battering her. Drenched, her white dress clung to her body.

With her finger, she wrote backwards on the glass, maybe so I could read the words, but each letter raced away, undefinable.

I got out of bed and jogged to the window.

"Write the letters again," I urged.

Isabelle did, and like the first time, they washed away as quickly as they were written. But when she traced the first letter, it was recognizable: the letter F. And that was all I needed to know.

"FIND THEM, right?" I shouted.

She nodded.

"Find what, Isabelle? *Show* me!"

Isabelle's eyes rolled upwards until her irises were hidden behind her open eyelids. I could only see the whites of her eyes as they quivered in their sockets.

Her whole body began to shake. To convulse.

I felt the rumble underneath my bare feet first.

The house began to tremble.

Gently at first. And then more aggressively.

Even with the bedroom door closed, I heard plates and glasses crash onto the kitchen floor.

The walls shuddered violently.

A booming crack made me cover my ears.

Oh dear God! She was going to rip our house apart.

"Stop it," I yelled. "Please!"

Her eyes returned to their normal position. She stopped shaking.

Gazing at me for a second, she turned and pointed behind her to our backyard.

Then she disappeared. Vanished.

I darted to my nightstand and grabbed my flashlight.

As I ran toward the bedroom door, I double checked that I was wearing my salt bombs around my neck (which I was). I turned the doorknob and opened the door.

Stepping over the salt threshold, I raced down the hallway and turned left into the open space between the kitchen and great room. I maintained my pace until I entered the foyer.

On the shoe tray by the front door, I grabbed my Muck boots and tugged them on. With my adrenaline surging, I didn't care about getting a raincoat or umbrella.

I was desperate to see what Isabelle had pointed to, though I had a good hunch. India Cloud's words echoed in my head: *"If your sinkhole returns,"* she had said, *"don't ignore it. Something small might be buried there."*

I opened the front door and went out into the storm. Dex's T-shirt flapped against my skin. The rain was furious, hitting my arms and legs like tiny, stinging slaps.

Running toward the left corner of the house, my boots sloshed in pools of rainwater. I turned and headed to the back of the house, to the seeded lawn behind our bedroom where our sinkhole used to be.

A lightning bolt flashed nearby.

Dangerously close.

It was followed by a deafening crack. Then a boom.

Somewhere in the woods, no doubt, a tree had been struck, causing it to fall to the ground.

The entire night was restless.

Beyond angry.

A driving gust crested our hillside. Isabelle's cries traveled with it.

Goosebumps erupted on my wet skin.

My T-shirt clung to my skin.

Clicking on the flashlight, I shined the light beam over the ground, moving it from left to right and back again, scanning the yard.

Until I found what Isabelle had been pointing to.

The sinkhole. It was back.

And I knew what I had to do in the morning.

54

Saturday, August 30, 2025
Windy Hill Farm: Boulder, Pennsylvania

WHEN OMELET CROWED his morning alarm, rain still pounded on the roof and against our bedroom windows. Outside, an overlay of saturated grayness darkened the landscape. And the wind pushed and shoved at trees and bushes like an impatient bully.

My weary body longed to stay snuggled in bed, but adrenaline overruled my physical exhaustion. Rain or shine, I needed to recharge and discover what was hidden under that blasted sinkhole.

I wouldn't stop digging until I found something. Today needed to be the beginning of the end for the ghosts of Windy Hill Farm.

Of course, chores came before everything else.

During more than one downpour, I fed the chickens and collected eggs. I watered the plants in my greenhouse and picked ripened veggies. Thankfully, nature was feeding the orchard and my flower beds for me.

By the time I finished chores, the rain and wind had subsided, replaced by a thick mist growing over the lake. There were no birds flying in the murky skies or chirping from the trees. Like me, they knew what was coming.

Fog.

It would continue to swell until it crested the hillside and enveloped our property, spreading and becoming so dense that I wouldn't be able to see two feet in front of me.

Which meant I had to hurry.

I wasn't the greatest backhoe operator to start with. Dex had taught me, and I was adequate enough. But certainly my skills would diminish with reduced visibility.

Inside the house, I grabbed my overstuffed key ring. I smiled thinking of Dex. He managed keys differently than me. He had a separate key ring for every area on the farm. Me? I clumped them all together. One large ring was easier to keep track of than three.

I got the backhoe from the barn and drove it to the sinkhole behind our bedroom. My plan was to use the digging bucket to move soil. And if I needed to, I could use the hammer attachment to help break up the concrete and rebar, *if* Isabelle hadn't already done that with the freaky strong tremors she had conjured up.

The lake was already blanketed in an opaque cloud.

Foggy fingers crept over the hilltop.

I positioned the digging bucket and nearly panicked. I had forgotten to stuff my vial of Holy Water into my sweatshirt's kangaroo pocket. I groped for my necklace under the thick cotton. Thankfully, I still had two salt bombs attached. I was good.

Thirty minutes later, discouragement started to set in.

Five loads of dirt were piled in a mound, accompanied by a few chunks of cement and rebar. As I dumped each load, I had carefully watched for debris among the dirt. Debris, which might resemble an artifact such as a time capsule or weapon as India had suggested.

I had found nothing so far.

The only thing advancing was the fog. Mist had rolled over our property, leaving beads of moisture on me and the backhoe.

Visibility had been cut in half.

When I dumped the sixth load of dirt, I spotted something solid. Probably a rock or as our construction manager had always joked about, petrified dinosaur dung. I turned the key in the ignition to off, pulled it out, and stuffed the key ring into my sweatshirt's pocket.

No matter what, I'd have to stop digging until the fog lifted. It had gotten way too thick.

I walked to the dirt pile. Sure enough, a corner of something solid poked out from the soil. Still, my heart contradicted my head. My heart pounded, excited I might be making major progress, while my brain warned me that hitting the jackpot was wishful thinking.

FIND THEM

Pulling the item from the dirt, I discovered it was a metal box.

I instantly remembered part of an entry from Victoria's diary, written on the last night of Isabelle's life, when Victoria saw her best friend, her stepcousin, running toward the lake.

> Brightened by moonlight shining across our lawn, I waited beside the window in hopes of seeing her running toward the lake. Which I did...her long hair was loose now and twirling as she ran in her white dress. Only this time, she was holding some sort of box.

Now my heart jackhammered in my chest.

Isabelle had been holding...*a box*. Most likely, *this* box!

Were there items inside? Was this what Isabelle meant when she urged me to *FIND THEM?*

I tugged to lift open the lid, but it was stuck—sealed with time, moisture, and rust.

Buzzing caught my attention.

If I had to guess, the sound came from the lake or Boulder Island. In the stillness of the fog, the noise resembled a chainsaw churning through the air, getting closer and closer.

The fog was fully developed now. I couldn't even see the backhoe which was less than 10 feet from the dirt mound. I knew our property inside and out, but disorientation caused by a blanket of fog could turn everything familiar into an impossible maze.

I needed to get inside the house.

Closing my eyes, I pictured my surroundings. I knew when I faced the dirt mound, the backhoe was located behind me. And once I found the machine, then the patio would be in a straight line from it. From the patio, I'd enter the house through one of the sliding glass doors leading into the great room.

The buzzing became deafening.

Could the sound be coming from...*flies?* Similar to the massive swarms Madeline and I had encountered on Boulder Island and at Wellspring?

229

I touched the bulge from one of the salt bombs attached to my necklace. If paranormal activity was activating a fly frenzy, would deploying my bombs neutralize them?

Focus. Take one step at a time.

Excessive processing had a habit of immobilizing me.

Getting inside the house had to be my singular objective for now.

Several steps later, I found the backhoe.

Good. Now I was on my way to the patio.

Weird, but I felt like I should drop on all fours. To crawl instead of walk. Being closer to the ground seemed like a safer option, but *childish* came to mind. *That* and overreacting.

I forced myself to stay upright but to inch forward. Oh so slowly.

Gray flagstone under my boots meant I had made it to the patio.

Concentrating on each step had consumed my attention. But now, as I regained my bearings, the shrill of buzzing stopped me in my tracks. It sounded so close.

Clutching the metal box, I looked behind me.

Emerging from the fog was a swarm of flies in the shape of a body. Male or female? I couldn't tell. All I knew was that the translucent figure was comprised of hundreds, if not thousands, of flies. And the mass was coming toward me, reaching for me with its black, insect arms.

Fear produced a metallic taste in my mouth.

I bolted to where I thought the sliding glass doors were. In the dense fog, I crashed into one of them, smacking my head against the glass. Damn it to hell that hurt.

With a trembling hand, I clutched the handle and tried to open the sliding glass door.

Are you kidding me? It was locked. All of them were.

Reaching into my sweatshirt pocket, I pulled out my crowded key ring. Oh dear God! Finding the match would take too much time.

In fact, the only one that stood out was the key card to my Tesla.

I glanced over my shoulder again.

The figure's fly fingers were stretching toward me. Closing in.

And I knew. I knew this bastard of a ghost would kill me in a heartbeat, like maybe forcing flies down my throat to block my airway or something unspeakable like that.

I ran.

My electric vehicle. It was parked around the corner of the house. In front of the garage.

I could find refuge inside my car. Drive away, even.

If only I could find my EV in the fog.

A vibrating, buzzing hand wrapped around my ankle and yanked hard. I fell to the ground, chest first. On impact, I felt the thin glass of my salt bomb ornaments shatter. Shards pierced my chest, and I felt warmth spread in the fabric of my T-shirt. *Warmth,* as in blood.

At the same time I hit the ground, the metal box released from my hand and tumbled away from me, swallowed by the fog.

Mimicking the playbook from my first ankle confrontation with this ghost, I rolled onto my back while reaching under my clothes. Salt had emptied and collected inside my bra, forming sticky clumps with my blood. I scraped what I could from my skin, which included glass fragments, and flung the mix at the fly figure.

The whirling form scattered into chaos as flies abandoned their bodily positions.

The disruption gave me time to scramble to my feet.

Bolting to where the box had rolled, I bent down and grabbed it without stopping my momentum.

Thank goodness I spotted my Tesla.

With my free hand, I fingered the edge of the key card in my sweatshirt pocket and pulled it out, along with the key ring.

The figure had reorganized as I arrived at my car.

Shit, shit, shit.

Touching the key card to my driver's side window, the car door unlocked. I threw open the door and launched myself inside. Slamming the door shut, I pressed the lock icon on my control panel screen and then tossed the box in the passenger seat.

Closing my eyes, I took several deep breaths.

Darkness rolled across my closed eyelids.

Confused, I opened my eyes.

Every window on my EV was completely covered with flies.

55

I SAT IN near darkness inside my car. The windows were blanketed with layers of flies—one black, twitching layer on top of another. The only light came from the screen on my EV's digital control panel.

I activated the windshield wipers.

Swarms of flies took flight to save themselves. Others were crushed by the oscillating blades, reduced to blood and guts smearing and blurring across the glass surface.

Maybe wiper fluid could help restore my view. After pushing the wiper button a second time, blue liquid sprayed over the entrails.

One streak of clear glass began to form, but the fog still enveloped my vehicle, making it impossible to see anything at all. Especially an invisible ghost.

At least some natural light had seeped into the interior despite flies covering the exterior of my side windows and rear windshield.

My car started shaking. Violently.

My heart felt like a stampede of bison.

When was this spirit ever going to leave me alone?

Leave our farm forever?

SNAP...

I watched helplessly as my left windshield wiper was ripped off by an indiscernible force. The wiper flew through the air until the mist made it disappear. My brain had trouble processing what was happening. And then the right wiper met with the same fate.

What if the ghost tried to materialize inside my vehicle?

Salt. I kept a container of salt on the passenger side floor.

My EV continued to shake as I grabbed the dispenser.

Pouring salt into my hand, I tossed the tiny granules across the front and back seats.

Overwhelmed by an instinct to flee, I fastened my seatbelt. Placing my foot on the brake, I started my vehicle and shifted the gear lever into reverse. The camera on my rear bumper showed the view behind me on my control panel screen. It also helped that our driveway was a straight line until the massive white ash where our pavement turned down the hill.

I held the steering wheel steady and floored the accelerator.

Some of the flies blew off as I sped. Most didn't.

The fog was less dense the farther I got from the lake.

At our ash tree, I turned the wheel, stopped the car, and shifted into drive before racing down our driveway.

I managed to get to the main road and wondered where I should go. I didn't have my purse or cellphone. And I was dressed in my dirties, limiting my options.

At least the fog continued to lift. The treetops were swaying, which meant wind had come to the rescue.

White Oak United Methodist Church was up ahead, the same church which had given me a supply of Holy Water.

I turned into the driveway.

As luck or divine intervention would have it, a cleaning van plastered with colorful decals was in the parking lot. At the church's main entrance, a woman was about to go inside.

Stopping my car, I grabbed the metal box from the passenger seat and gingerly opened my door. I got out slowly, praying I wouldn't disturb the flies in the process.

The woman couldn't help but notice me.

"You can't come inside, honey," she said, looking down at me from the landing at the top of the steps. "The church is closed. I'm here to clean for tomorrow's service." She studied me for a second and her eyes widened. "Oh my. Do you need the pastor? Or maybe an ambulance?"

I looked down at my sweatshirt to see what had caused her

alarmed reaction. Blood had seeped through my T-shirt *and* sweatshirt, joining the mud stains I had acquired when the ghost forced me to fall on the moist ground.

"I'm hoping to go inside the sanctuary," I said. "Hoping to borrow a phone to call my sister. I'm having a problem." I nodded toward my car. "My windows aren't tinted. Those are flies."

The woman crossed herself, obviously aware of Christian symbolism regarding flies.

She looked inside the church and then back at my car, as if torn about what the best decision might be. After all, the business side of a church included hours of operation.

"Hurry," she said at last. "Come inside."

Whether it was her invitation or a coincidence, I didn't know. All I knew was that across the road, a new and larger cloud of flies emerged from the woods at the same time the flies on my car windows lifted from the glass.

The buzzing chainsaw was back.

"Run!" the woman urged.

Clutching the box, I leapt up the steps, skipping over two or three at a time. I propelled myself across the church's threshold as the woman slammed the door shut.

Flies bombarded the double doors from the outside, sounding like a barrage of BB gun pellets striking the wood.

Before long, the insects began to cover the stained glass windows of the church.

The woman handed me her cellphone.

"The flies will leave soon," she said, sounding confident. "Evil gets bored when we won't let it in."

She grabbed the mop which had been propped against a pew. "I've got restrooms to clean. Holler if you need me, honey."

I called Madeline and briefly explained my situation in a whisper.

My requests followed.

Ordnance reinforcements. That's mainly what I needed my sister to bring to the church: her extra salt bomb ornaments (since mine had been crushed), as well as her spray bottle of Holy Water.

In addition, I begged her to spend the night at the farm so we could explore what was inside Isabelle's box. I didn't want to be alone. I was exhausted and anxious.

"Be there in about an hour," my sister said. "But I'm going to be frank with you. I can't wait until this nightmare is over. Either by you moving out or sending that evil ghost back to hell. Don't take this the wrong way, but you have a baby to think about. To protect."

I rubbed my belly.

I had never stopped thinking about my plum. Raising my baby in a safe place was paramount. It was what I was fighting for. Running from place to place to avoid danger didn't sound like a reasonable option anymore. Not since I learned that danger could be anywhere.

When the woman came back from cleaning restrooms, I returned her cellphone and sincerely thanked her.

"Glad I could help, honey," she said. "Let me guess. You live on lot sixteen. The forbidden land."

"How did you know?"

"When you've grown up here, you know things. The good and the ugly. I suppose about now, you're finding them out for yourself."

"You mean, that our property is haunted," I said.

"The truth can only be entombed for so long. Eventually, truth finds a way to overcome the forces which caused it to be buried in the first place."

Her words were wisdom.

I shook the metal box. Something was inside it.

Hopefully, it was the truth.

56

MADELINE AND I rushed through farm chores, including the add-ons of hosing off my car, ordering new wipers, and refilling the sinkhole. Afterwards, we wolfed down dinner, closed up the house, retreated to my safe space early, and got ready for bed.

Today marked the first day I hadn't visited Dex. Somewhere from deep within me, acrid guilt bubbled over, burning the sensitive lining of my throat. I felt awful about it.

On the phone, Dex assured me he understood. I shouldn't fret about it, he said. Shouldn't be so hard on myself. Bottomline, I was finally making significant progress on solving the mystery behind Isabelle's murder. He supported my efforts as long as I stayed safe.

I omitted sharing details about today's encounter, like the glass that cut into me after being slammed to the ground by possessed flies. *Safe* wasn't the condition that came to mind.

Regardless, the clock was ticking.

My husband would be home in 20 short days. And as our baby grew in my womb, I wouldn't be able to outrun or fight off our villainous ghost. Nor would I accept the risk.

These hauntings had to end soon.

Immediately after returning from the church, my sister and I had brought the metal box into my safe space and pried it open using a screwdriver and hammer. Two items were inside: Isabelle's diary from 1955 and the gold, heart locket necklace that Victoria had

236

secretly given her stepcousin two weeks after Isabelle had arrived at the Williams Farm.

Both items had been preserved in two, sealed plastic baggies.

I shivered with nervous excitement about the pages Madeline and I were about to read.

Since reading Isabelle's diary out loud might agitate her ghostly nemesis, Madeline and I agreed we'd sit close together in bed and read the journal silently, at the same time.

I lit one end of my white sage incense until it glowed orange and fragrant smoke swirled and undulated from the smoldering tip. My salt lamp was on and my other fortifications had been inspected and replenished as needed, including in the bathroom and walk-in closets.

Situated in bed, supported by an abundance of pillows, I turned the pages until I found the entry I was looking for: the account of Isabelle's arrival at the farm. I nodded *ready* to my sister.

Saturday, June 4th (Night):

Uncle Virgil is the type of man you wish, with all your heart, that you weren't related to.

Of course, we aren't related by blood, just by marriage. But family members shouldn't covet other family members. I'm fairly certain that would be morally wrong unless you lived in medieval times.

Most people who have white hair look old. Not Uncle Virgil. His hair makes his blue eyes glow like he's some sort of superhero. And his freckles and dimples are to die for. Why does he have to be so attractive?

At the train station, Uncle Virgil mentioned how much I had grown up since he last saw me. That he could tell I had become a woman. How special of him to notice.

Driving in the truck on our way to the farm, Uncle Virgil kept staring at me. I pretended not to notice. What else could I do? He placed his hand on my thigh, on my warm skin, and squeezed, letting his hand linger. He promised we would become close. That he couldn't wait to get to know me better.

Something happened when his hand touched me. I felt desire and repulsion at the same time. And mostly confusion. Is Uncle Virgil attracted to me? Or are my emotions trying to deceive me?

When we arrived at the farm, the family was outside to greet me. Vincent looks handsome like his father, only with light brown hair. But he seems angry, as if my staying here might annoy him. Vaughn is all smiles though. Then there's Aunt Vivian. She is a beautiful woman. Her eyes are hazel. Her hair, blonde. And her cheekbones and lips are movie star dreamy! Most of all, she is kind and loving. I instantly felt guilty regarding my earlier thoughts about Uncle Virgil.

Why is growing up so difficult?

The best part about staying at the farm is knowing I'll get to spend time with Victoria. She was right! We do look related. I think we are going to become close friends.

I glanced at my sister. "I dread where this is going."

Madeline nodded, briefly closing her eyes.

Sexual predators were the worst of the worst. The absolute scum of the earth.

FIND THEM

Sunday, June 5th (Night):

I hesitate to document what happened today, but I have never withheld anything. And so I write, dearest diary. Perhaps you will understand and forgive me because I have no one else to talk to or confide in.

After church and lunch, Victoria and I began our walk around Boulder Lake. We only made it halfway before a horse and rider galloped up to us. It was Uncle Virgil and he wanted to show me the entire property on horseback even though I had never ridden in my life!

I sat in the saddle. Uncle Virgil sat on Midnight's rump, on a strap which had leather satchels on each end. He held the reins.

We rode and rode and rode. The property is massive, and Uncle Virgil gave the history of every parcel of the land. Finally, I admitted my legs were ungodly sore. He suggested we take a break under a tree on the far end of the farm. Now I know what the satchels were stuffed with...a blanket, a bottle of wine, and fresh strawberries from the garden.

Sprawled out on the blanket, Uncle Virgil opened the wine and guzzled right from the bottle. He urged me to do the same. "Wine will help lessen your pain." He was right. A warmth washed over me that made me forget. He also insisted that when we were alone, I was to call him Virgil, since we really weren't related. He also asked me about my age. I told him I'd be 18 in 2 months.

Together, we finished the wine and strawberries.

Then the devil struck. Virgil asked if I'd like him to massage my inner thighs to loosen my muscles for the ride back. I don't know why I thought his offer sounded reasonable. Maybe because a man had never touched me before and I didn't know the effect it would have on me. Maybe because the wine was making my thoughts swim.

He asked if I would remove my shorts to make the massage easier. I did it. The way he touched me, gently pulling, pinching, and releasing my skin with his hands sent shivers into new places. His fingers accidentally combed over the front of my underwear. I moaned and he apologized. But he misunderstood. I had never felt anything so good. He smiled then, urging me to relax even more. Exploring is natural...adult to adult, he said.

I had never ever been treated like an adult before, like a woman.

Perhaps if we had stopped there, everything would've been okay. But he asked if he could see me. I didn't know what he meant at first, but his eyes clarified his desire. So I took off my underwear. I wanted to.

When he touched me...there, when he eventually entered me, I was overwhelmed. I felt a passionate hunger that I had always dreamed about. That I had longed for.

He unexpectedly stopped rocking on top of me, asking if he could release himself inside of me, if the timing would allow it. I didn't know what he meant, but I didn't want him to stop. So I said yes. I might have even added...please.

Before we packed up, we agreed to meet every night on the lake's shoreline, after everyone had fallen asleep. He kept a rowboat by the shore, and we could venture out to Boulder Island. We could deepen our friendship. (If only I could share my excitement with Victoria.)

I hated Virgil Williams. And I loathed reading about how he seduced Isabelle who was innocent and naive, desperate for love in any form. At the same time, I was no longer an ostrich. Closing my eyes to her entries wasn't going to erase what happened to her. Most importantly, her writings might identify her killer, might help bring her a degree of justice along with the peaceful rest she deserved.

Isabelle was counting on me.

She had led me to her diary for a reason.

My sister and I continued reading her June entries.

Exhausted, we agreed to turn off the lights after one more.

Monday, June 27th (Night):

I cannot wait until morning to write down what happened tonight. Thank goodness moonlight is bright enough for me to pen new words within your pages. But these words are bleak and comfortless.

My dearest diary, I told Virgil.

He was a bit drunk and we were lying together on a blanket in the middle of Boulder Island, under the stars and moonlight. We were naked and he was on top of me, caressing my cheek with his thumb.

Telling me how special I was. How he was falling in love with me. I remember thinking my world was going to be perfect. We truly loved each other.

When I told him the news that my period was a week late, he froze. His eyes turned wild and frantic. His body became dead weight and I couldn't breathe. It was like he was intentionally pressing down on me. I suddenly felt trapped and scared, desperate for air. I scratched his back. The shock of it made him roll off me and I began to rise to my feet. I wanted to run. He clutched my ankle and yanked me back down onto the blanket. He put his hand on my neck and squeezed and he entered me with a roughness that hurt. I feared that the man whom I loved might...kill me.

His drunken words were the last thing I remembered before passing out: "When you act like a whore, you get fucked like one." His words made no sense. And they were hateful. Not at all reflective of the man I had loved with all my heart since I arrived.

I woke up in the rowboat. He didn't utter a word. I fear he'll never speak to me again.

Instead of feeling loved, I feel sinful. And alone.

"*He clutched my ankle and yanked me back down onto the blanket.*" I could picture the physical act so easily because the ghost haunting Isabelle and the farm had grabbed my ankle and dropped me to the ground not once, but twice.

I whispered into Madeline's ear. "Virgil Williams. He's Isabelle's killer."

57

I WOKE UP when Madeline got out of bed to Omelet's crowing. It was six in the morning. She had to leave early for an appointment with a potential buyer of a house listed in Scranton.

My sister suggested I continue reading Isabelle's diary while she prepared our breakfast. I could catch her up over our meal of eggs, low sodium ham, and fruit salad.

As I watched her walk toward the bedroom door and its salt threshold, my heart thumped hard in my chest. "Mad, stop!" I was having a mini panic attack. "Do you have your bombs?"

She smiled and pointed to them before closing the door and heading down the hallway.

Reaching for Isabelle's diary on my nightstand, I grabbed it, got comfortable, and paged my way to the next June entry which caught my interest.

Wednesday, June 29th (Morning):

Victoria is still sleeping. Not for long. We're expected to get out of bed soon to start our day of chores.

I still have bruises. I'm covering the one on my neck with my hair and wearing socks for the bruise on my ankle.

243

Last night, I waited for Virgil by the shoreline.

Vincent emerged from behind a tree and asked me who I was waiting for. I lied, of course. I said I couldn't sleep and that the lake calms me and feeds my soul. He warned if I wasn't careful, the coyotes might feed on my flesh. I might be dragged into the woods, never to be found.

He approached me until our chests almost touched. Moving my hair away from my neck, he exposed my bruise, as if he had known it was there. Panicked, I explained that their border collie Rooster had jumped on me, excited to play ball. He sneered and said I enjoyed getting things...aroused.

Vincent gives me the creeps. He speaks in riddles. And he always hints he knows more than he should. Worse, threats linger with his every word.

Did Virgil send his son last night to unnerve me? Has the man I love forsaken me?

I can't face my condition alone.

Last night, I was certain Virgil was Isabelle's killer. But now, Vincent seemed just as capable. And just as intentional as his father. He clearly knew about Virgil and Isabelle's nightly routine and he had waited for her. Waited, so he could put her on edge.

I wondered if Virgil and Isabelle's perverted relationship was indeed over, so I read on.

Sadly, her July entries proved Virgil did *not* refrain from his abuses. Their pattern of nightly visits on Boulder Island resumed on July 1st when he professed his love for her: *"a temporary secret to be theirs and theirs alone,"* Isabelle had written.

Mid-month, however, entries suggested their secret was far from being contained.

Saturday, July 16th (Morning):

Last night after our lovemaking, I shared some bad news with Virgil. Someone has read my diary because I use a bookmark and I discovered that someone returned it to the wrong place. Perhaps it had fallen out when the person was reading my journal and they had returned it haphazardly. Or maybe they wanted me to know of their intrusion.

For our sake, I hope the culprit is Vaughn. If it is Aunt Vivian or Victoria, my words will crush them. And if the person is Vincent, my entries will inflame him. Cause anger to ignite beyond logical thought.

Virgil urged me not to dwell on this. He had difficult conversations ahead of him. His wife needed to be told about us. He respected her and didn't wish to rub salt on the wounds she would bear.

Why hadn't I considered the consequences before? I am pathetic. Evil. Selfish. A homewrecker. I never thought about the people who would get hurt. As well, I am in over my head. I need my mother, my real mother. How I miss her and her wisdom.

Virgil saw my pain last night. He wrapped his arms around me. Assured me nothing of value came easily. He confessed his and Vivian's relationship was more of a business arrangement. He only asked that when the timing was right, I let him handle the situation. I agreed. I would speak to no one about it.

Several entries had been handwritten on the day before Isabelle's documented disappearance.

Friday, July 22nd (Morning):

Last night, Virgil shared his plan with me.

I will claim I am homesick and want an overnight visit with my parents in Unityville. Aunt Vivian has agreed to call my mother today to tell her. Then after lunch, Virgil will take me to the train station to buy my ticket. The drive to Carbondale will give us more time to talk.

While I am away from the farm, he'll speak to Aunt Vivian. He'll tell her he is in love with me and I am pregnant. He said things will get messy, but that's what lawyers are for. I shouldn't worry.

For now, the morning sun is shining through the window. I feel queasy. I have to put food in my stomach before I throw up all over the bedroom floor. Time to get out of bed.

Friday, July 22nd (Afternoon):

On our way to purchase my train ticket, Virgil asked if I'd wear my hair in a braided ponytail. For him. He even handed me a rubber band. Whatever. I was too depressed to resist. Not everything has to be a problem.

All was going as planned until we returned to the farm. I was heading to Victoria's bedroom to place my ticket there. But as I walked down the hall, Vincent opened the door (from the inside). Stepping

246

out from the room, he looked startled to see me. I asked what he was doing inside our room and he said he was looking for Victoria.

He must think I'm stupid. "Looking" doesn't require him to enter our room and close the door behind him. I felt a wave of nausea then.

Is Vincent the one reading my diary?

Tonight, Virgil and I will meet ahead of my trip back home. This weekend will be very difficult for the household and he longs for my encouragement.

I am going to keep a secret from Virgil. Not because I don't trust him. It is because I don't trust Vincent. He scares me.

Before I rendezvous with Virgil by the lake, I am going to find a container and bury my diary and necklace in the field next to the hillside overlooking the lake. If something happens to me, maybe someone will find it.

Friday, July 22nd (Night):

During chores when no one was looking, I found a metal box in the barn. It is perfect for you, dearest diary, and for my necklace. I will place you both inside two baggies I got from the kitchen. I'll make sure each is sealed for double protection. Then I'll secure you inside the box. If it rains while I'm away, you will stay dry.

Before dinner, the family went on a horseback ride. I stayed at the farmhouse to pack. But I also took the time to dig up the ground where I'll bury the box. I returned the loose soil back into the hole and covered it with a patch of grass. I would've buried the box then, but I realized that IF I went missing, I had never named (in my afternoon entry) the person whom I suspect. Implying isn't good enough.

On my way to meet Virgil tonight, I'll find the hole I prepared. I'll scoop out the loose dirt by hand, bury the box, and then pack the dirt and grass on top. Then I'll meet Virgil by the water and he'll never know.

I just glanced over at Victoria. She is still reading a book in bed. She hasn't started writing in her diary yet. I love her like a sister and wonder if she'll hate me after she learns the truth about her father and me. Losing her will pain me. I never intended to hurt her. My words seem so naive now. Virgil is her father! And her mother will be devastated! The family will be broken. They will all hate me.

My suitcase is packed. I'm already dressed for my early departure tomorrow morning so I don't wake Victoria. Aunt Vivian suggested it. And Virgil asked me to wear my white dress, his favorite. He said my parents would also be pleased with the choice.

A minute ago, I said goodnight to Victoria and told her that I love her. She made me promise I'd be back on Sunday. But if something does happen to me, dearest diary, you will carry the truth in your pages. Vincent will be the cause of my disappearance.

Goodbye until my return on Sunday...

Tears rolled down my cheeks.

Sunday never came for Isabelle or her pregnancy.

While it was true that Isabelle had made a handful of terrible decisions, what young adult could claim a perfect record? In this case, the mistakes she made had dire consequences (with no second chances) because the moment Isabelle arrived at the farm, predators circled around her. Clearly, she had never been equipped to recognize the warning signs or to protect herself.

In terms of the mystery, there were *still* unanswered questions. I didn't know exactly how Vincent killed his stepcousin or if Virgil and/or Vivian even knew her disappearance and death came at the hands of their middle child (their eldest son).

Despite loose ends, I hoped the revelations, along with the anticipated results of the exhumed bones from Boulder Island, would be enough to convince Isabelle that she had successfully led me to important truths…that she had been murdered on this land. Murdered by her stepcousin, Vincent.

All that remained for Isabelle was to accept her new destiny: her eternal rest.

58

Monday, September 1, 2025
Windy Hill Farm: Boulder, Pennsylvania

DETECTIVE GILBERT HAD called me earlier, requesting to stop by. I heard him knocking at the front door and could see his parked cruiser through an open window in the great room.

Warm oatmeal cookies and tea were already staged on the kitchen island, along with a spray bottle of Holy Water, but the detective wouldn't be privy to its contents. Salt bombs were also tucked under my blouse and hidden in drawers and in nooks and crannies like Easter eggs.

Yesterday, Windy Hill Farm had been free of any detectable paranormal activity. Neither ghost had made themselves known. However, there were no guarantees today would be just as quiet. After all, I suspected Detective Gilbert had asked to visit me because he wanted to share the identification of the skeletal remains found on Boulder Island.

I knew they'd be Isabelle's.

Still, science needed to officially confirm it.

After opening the door and exchanging greetings, I led the detective into the kitchen. I stood at the counter facing the great room while Detective Gilbert sat on a stool across from me.

Since our last meeting at the station, his sandy blond hair seemed shorter. Even his handlebar mustache looked trimmed. And he wore a different uniform—navy instead of khaki.

He eyed a cookie. "Do you mind?"

"Please. And what you don't eat here, you're taking with you."

Smiling, he consumed three cookies at lightning speed, verbalizing his pleasure with *oohs* and *aahs* as he chewed.

He sipped his tea before talking.

"We located the living granddaughter of Isabelle's maternal aunt," he started. "The granddaughter's name is Francis Nelson. Believe it or not, she lives in Unityville, so she was easy to find. Also, Ms. Nelson was quite amenable to our request for a blood sample."

I wasn't great with family trees, especially ones spanning nearly three quarters of a century. "So Francis's grandmother was the sister of Isabelle's birth mother. Am I right?"

"Correct." He eyed another cookie. "Francis and Isabelle are maternal first cousins once removed."

"And that means..."

"They should share some genomic DNA when compared."

"Did they?" I asked.

"Yes. Thirteen percent."

"Is that even enough to prove they were related?"

"Oh, definitely. In fact, the identity of the remains is irrefutable. Thanks to your hunch and...let's call it *persistence,* Isabelle Taylor is no longer missing. She has been found."

Even though I had expected this outcome, a wave of emotions washed over me. Tears welled in my eyes. My lips trembled.

I couldn't imagine the pain and despair, the unrelenting sadness, of losing a child. Of not knowing where she was or what had happened to her. Of having to assume with the passage of time that she was no longer alive.

With my parents, knowing the precise intersection where they were killed in the car accident was hard enough. But I couldn't imagine if they had been in route to a grocery store and mysteriously *disappeared* without a trace.

Somewhere in the afterlife, I prayed Isabelle's mother (who had died of cancer more than a decade before her daughter's disappearance), as well as her adopted parents—Louise and Daniel Taylor, were relieved that their daughter had finally been found.

"You okay?" Detective Gilbert asked. "You've invested a lot of time finding her. Decades after law enforcement had given up. I can only imagine how much this means to you."

I nodded and a tear raced down my cheek.

"Someone buried Isabelle's body on the island, hoping she'd never be found," I said, sniffling. "Did her remains provide any clues about *how* she died?"

"Her hyoid bone was fractured."

"I'm not familiar..."

"It's a horseshoe shaped bone the shape of the lower jawbone. Only, it's smaller and located under the tongue and back in the neck."

"Does that suggest anything? The fact that the bone was broken?"

"A fractured hyoid indicates manual strangulation."

There it was: confirmation that Isabelle had been murdered.

I felt a drop in room temperature.

Detective Gilbert began to rub his arms.

"Not to sound rude, but it's chilly in here," he said.

"We have an overactive AC system," I lied. "At least soon, we'll only be using heat."

He swiveled on his stool to look behind him at our windows.

Damn it to hell. Every window in the great room was open since it was warm outside.

"Using AC with open windows will overwork your system. Big time," he cautioned. "Not to mention, it needlessly inflates your electric bill. I'm sure your husband knows that."

My husband? It might surprise the wise detective that I knew how HVAC systems worked, too. However, now was not the time to prove that I could stand my ground. After all, my little white lie had provoked his lecture.

"Of course, you're right," I said, hoping to sound humble and appreciative of his advice. "Before I forget, are you planning to tell Ross Johnson? About finding the remains and identifying them as Isabelle's? I'm asking because his mother, Victoria, was Isabelle's stepcousin. They were related by marriage and adoption so I'm curious about the department's timing regarding notifications."

"Glad you asked. We'd like to keep this under wraps for a week or two. You know, until we make sure our ducks are lined up in a row. Would you agree to that?"

Would I ever.

I wasn't ready to disclose the truth to Ross, to explain to him that I had intentionally withheld why I was interested, obsessed even, in learning more about his family's history. That my real motivation in reading his mother's diaries was to find out which one of his relatives had murdered Isabelle. And the answer—which was Ross's Uncle Vincent—had been penned in the victim's diary. A diary which he knew nothing about.

While Ross had been generous to me from the start, I had been downright stingy reciprocating anything in return.

"Waiting to go public seems wise," I said. "Anyway, there's no need to rush at this point. Right? I mean, her murderer is probably dead. So I won't say a word until you're ready."

"Any guesses on who killed her? What with your research and all."

Isabelle naming the person she suspected (if she went missing) was damning, for sure. But would law enforcement consider her diary entry as conclusive evidence? Enough to announce the name of her murderer when the department went public? I didn't think so.

A victim's stated suspicion didn't equate to forensic proof.

Which meant, I was also in no rush to disclose I had found Isabelle's diary and necklace. Bottomline, I wasn't ready to part with them. I had to be certain I hadn't missed anything important.

"Well?" Detective Gilbert pressed. "Any idea who might've murdered her?"

"I have a hunch. That's all."

"Your hunches have been pretty accurate thus far, Mrs. Bliss."

"I think Isabelle's murderer was an angry and jealous soul. Not mature enough to process his wild emotions. Someone who also had easy access to Isabelle. Who was related. Who probably acted out in rage before he could stop himself."

"Victims are usually killed by someone they know."

"I'm guessing Isabelle's murderer was her stepcousin, Vincent Williams."

In between the kitchen and great room, Isabelle appeared in her white dripping dress. She looked panicked. Eyes wide with distress. She was vehemently shaking her head. More like, frantically.

"No?" I questioned in disbelief, staring at her image which stood a dozen feet behind the detective.

253

"What do you mean...*no?*" I snapped at her.

Detective Gilbert turned toward the great room again, following the direction of my eyes.

Isabelle disappeared before he could complete his stool swivel.

"Who are you talking to?" he asked, with deep trenches forming across his forehead.

"I...I thought you were disagreeing with me."

That's the only response I could think of because my brain was hiccupping. The room was spinning.

I felt blood draining from my face.

"I'm sorry," I mumbled. "I'm not...I'm not feeling well."

"Easy, Mrs. Bliss." He rose from his stool and approached me. "Take a deep breath. Steady and slow."

I had desperately hoped that unearthing Isabelle's remains and finding her diary and necklace meant the mystery was practically over. That the hauntings would end soon after.

But now, after I had named her murderer out loud, Isabelle wanted me to know her killer *wasn't* Vincent? That her suspicion, penned in her diary 70 years ago, turned out to be...*wrong?*

Maybe finding her items was never intended to be the end-all. They were more like significant pieces to an incomplete puzzle. One that was still in the process of being resolved.

Problem was, I didn't know if I had the energy or the will to continue sleuthing. A deep weariness was all I felt.

Moreover, I had no clue what should come next.

I felt defeated.

Drained.

And the last thing I remembered was Detective Gilbert's arms catching me before he gently lowered me to the kitchen floor.

59

TREES HAD STARTED to turn yellow. The skies were azure blue and a crisp wind kept fallen leaves, those shed early, somersaulting across streets and lawns. Flying in arrowhead formations, Canadian geese were already traveling south as they squawked, sounding like honking horns in the city.

I had fully recovered from my fainting spell yesterday.

The hopelessness which had overwhelmed me (after Isabelle refuted that Vincent was her killer) had been replaced with curiosity. Ross had called me. Apparently, he had found unexpected items in the attic of his townhouse. Items he knew would interest me.

On my way back from visiting Dex, I stopped by his home.

As with my previous visit to Ross's townhouse, he led me down the hall and into his sitting room where tea and petit fours were on the coffee table, ready for consumption. Next to the offerings were two identical books, both one-inch thick and leather bound. The page edges were painted in gold leaf. He had my undivided attention.

"Something strange happened last night," Ross started.

I couldn't help thinking…*welcome to my world*.

"When I got home from work and retired into the library with my Manhattan, I heard pounding upstairs. Loud pounding, as if a construction crew was hammering away. Naturally, I grabbed my handgun and headed to the third floor to investigate."

Pausing, he selected a small chocolate cake from the plate and

255

popped it into his mouth.

My appetite was nonexistent. I had to learn what happened next.

"Upstairs, the overhead hatch to my attic was open," he continued. "I was alarmed. I pulled down the folding ladder anyway and announced to the intruder that I was carrying a loaded gun."

My heart started beating double time.

"Did you call nine-one-one for help?" I asked.

"No. Stupid of me, I know." He sipped his tea. "Anyway, when I climbed the attic ladder, ready to shoot if I had to, what I found instead was a god damn shitshow."

"How so?"

"Boxes were everywhere. Toppled over. Open with their contents spewed all over the floor. It was freezing up there. Mist was literally streaming from my mouth. And there were freaking random puddles of water beaded on top of the boards. For no apparent reason."

I flinched.

"What? Does the water mean something?"

Isabelle. She wanted Ross to find something in his attic.

She clearly wasn't done helping me.

"No," I lied. Now was not the time to change my game plan. "It's just that I can picture what you're describing. It sounds so scary."

"Tell me about it. At any rate, I didn't find an intruder up there. And believe me, I looked everywhere." He picked up one of the two leather bound books. "What I found were these. They were situated by themselves, away from the clusterfuck." Ross rolled his eyes. "Sorry for the language. Hard habit to break."

"Are the books significant?" I asked.

"These are my grandmother's diaries," he said, with wide eyes. "Now you know why I called you. You're interested in this stuff. Eventually, I will be, too. Once my workload lessens."

"Wait. *Vivian's* diaries?" I was still digesting the news. "I thought you said they had been destroyed in the farmhouse fire. In 1986."

"That's what my sisters and I thought. What my mother told us. But remember, Mother also told us *her* diaries had been burned, too. Turns out, my mother's diaries had been hidden in a bank's safety deposit box, as you are well aware."

"How could your grandmother's diaries have gotten *here?*"

"I didn't mention this before," Ross said. "This townhouse belonged to my grandparents. What I'm about to say may sound privileged, I know. But they kept their formal wardrobe here for when they had to attend galas and fundraisers. They also entertained guests here and sometimes spent the night. My grandmother always said she didn't want the perfume of farm life to offend the company she and my grandfather kept.

"When I inherited the townhouse," he continued, "I never took the time to empty the attic. Like I said, *busy.*" He shrugged. "So are you interested in reading them?"

I fisted my hands so Ross couldn't see my fingers shaking.

"I absolutely am," I replied. "Do you want me to sign another non-disclosure agreement?"

"Can we agree that the first one covers everything?"

"Definitely. Thank you so much for trusting me with their care."

Taking hold of the journals, I pressed them against my chest as Ross walked me from the sitting room toward the front door.

"Almost forgot to ask you," he said. "In my lawyering universe, I came across a permit for using ground penetrating radar out on Boulder Island. The requestor was the Boulder Police Department, which I found curious. If my memory serves me, you have a great view of the island from your property." He opened the door. "Have you seen any activity out there?"

Stick to the plan.

As outlandish as it sounded, I wanted to remain loyal to Isabelle. Her ghost was counting on my help to right a tragic wrong. This wasn't over. If I did what she asked, if I continued to follow her lead, then the hauntings on Windy Hill Farm might disappear forever.

"I've been extremely busy," I answered Ross, since that was a condition he understood. "I haven't noticed anything unusual out there. I'll keep my eyes open, though."

"Thanks. I've done some snooping but everyone I've talked to either doesn't know anything or they're keeping what they know close to the vest. That's got my interest piqued even more."

Hopefully, Vivian's diaries would help solve the mystery of Isabelle Taylor...*before* Ross started getting answers.

60

MY FLOCK WAS safely tucked within their hutch for the night.

As I walked from the chicken coop back to the house, I felt the seasons changing in my bones.

The sun cast an orange glow over the lake and a cool breeze nipped at my arms. Soon, my hens would experience the fall molt, a time of rejuvenation due to naturally lower egg production.

Our young apple trees would be dormant as well.

Fall and winter were definitely coming.

Hard to believe that Dex and I had only moved into our forever home a little over three months ago. The span between *then* and *now* had aged me a lifetime. So much had happened. Other than my pregnancy, most of it wasn't good.

My thoughts drifted to Dex's rehab buddy, Oscar, and what he had shared with us. In high school, he had written his class assignment on the five curses of the Williams Farm.

What my husband and I were going through felt like the sixth.

Midway to our front door, I heard the familiar roar building in the valley and racing up our hillside. Sure enough, a gust slammed into me. Isabelle's wailing was along for the ride.

"Stop crying," I reprimanded her out loud. "I'm getting to them."

Them referred to Vivian's diaries.

Surely the journals contained important information or Isabelle wouldn't have made sure Ross discovered them in his attic.

FIND THEM

Ever since I had gotten home, I had tried to remain low-key. To not draw unwanted attention to my plans. Our ghost nemesis, who I now assumed was Virgil (though Vivian hadn't exactly been exonerated) had left me alone since the fly possession incident.

I wanted it to stay that way.

As India Cloud had warned, agitating this "advanced" ghost could have dangerous consequences.

That's why I had purchased more salt and bomb vessels after leaving Ross's townhouse. I needed extra protection in the chicken coop, greenhouse, and barn. Reserves had to be available throughout the farm in case another ghost encounter crushed the supply I wore around my neck.

I entered the house and walked into the kitchen. My purchases from earlier were piled on the kitchen island's countertop. I'd assemble salt bombs soon and ignore the mess until then.

Right now, I wanted to fork down my dinner, lock up for the night, change into my pajamas, and light my incense. Then I could tackle Vivian's diaries.

Methodically, I accomplished my to-do list and was ready to read.

I climbed into bed and opened the first volume which included Vivian's entries dated from 1954 to 1955. My plan was to read every entry, from start to finish. I'd slow down and concentrate on passages which contained clues or addressed one of the loose ends.

I found an entry that required focus.

January 14, 1955:

I cannot bear wearing the necklace any longer—the one with the engraved heart locket professing Virgil's never ending love for me.

Ester Bramwell was the last straw. This morning, Virgil lamented that he continues to regret that Vincent and I made sure, with the termination letter we crafted, that Ester would leave and never return to Pennsylvania.

What kind of husband admits this to his wife?

Virgil crushes my heart with his every word. With his repeated infidelities that torment me.

How many times will I pretend to accept his lies? Or catch him in bed with a stranger at the townhouse? Or discover him missing at a party, only to watch him exit the powder room with another woman? With her lipstick still branded on his neck.

Virgil has taunted me to divorce him. He knows I will never. The children! The farm! Our reputations!

I spoke to Vincent and he agrees. I will give my heart locket necklace to Victoria as an heirloom on her 16th birthday. This way, the necklace will never touch my skin again.

I will remain gracious, for I adore my children. And save for my eldest son, Victoria and Vaughn know nothing of their father's unsavory exploits.

Vincent is the only one who truly knows the demons which plague his father. My son and I have no secrets between us. He is my protector. My confidante. A blessing from the Lord above.

Virgil Williams was a monster. A philanderer. An abuser.
His betrayals had to be heartbreaking. Humiliating for his wife.
Would Vivian learn that her husband's worst self was about to emerge? The *self* that became a sexual predator?
I continued reading entry after entry about the farm (such as which chicken house produced the best results and what equipment needed repair); about the children and their achievements in the classroom and in sports; about the library and fundraisers; and her duties as a wife, mother, and respected community influencer.

In all her entries, Vivian seemed thoughtful, even tempered, and kind. But would her positive qualities persevere when Isabelle came to the farm for the summer?

June 4, 1955:

Isabelle arrived today. It would be dishonest if I did not express my disappointment. When Louise asked if Isabelle could stay the summer, I welcomed an extra set of hands. There is always more to do on the farm than can be done.

I pictured my step niece as the youngster of over two years earlier, the one with growing pains. But the girl who arrived was a breathtaking woman. No child at all. One who resembles Victoria's beauty.

Since Ester Bramwell, Virgil has remained busy on the farm. His indiscretions have been few.

I fear what may happen to Isabelle in our home, as one would fear if a chicken was welcomed into a fox's den.

Vincent shares my concerns, though he clings to anger more than fear. I reminded him that we are to have courage to change what we can. I will check on Isabelle before I retire to bed every night, to make sure she and Victoria are resting peacefully. Vincent will keep an eye on Isabelle during the day, as best he can.

At least Victoria will finally have a close friend, as she has always longed for. With Virgil's reputation, it is of no surprise that families do not allow their daughters to stay at the farm unsupervised. They do not speak of these things loudly, but the whispers can still be heard.

JULIA ASH

June 5, 1955:

One day after Isabelle's arrival, I have already failed to protect her. I do not know how I am to endure this madness. For this wrong cannot be righted. Its wounds will fester for eternity.

How could a mere walk around the lake with Victoria have taken such a despicable turn?

When Vincent and Victoria crossed paths during their afternoon chores today, she mentioned that their father had wanted to show Isabelle the property on horseback. Riding off together, they had left Victoria by the lake to walk back alone. That was nearly three hours ago.

I immediately sent Vincent to check on their whereabouts, to deliver the message that I urgently needed my husband. I prayed it was not too late.

Vincent came back alone.

From a distance, my son witnessed his father and Isabelle lying together under a tree. My husband was... having his way with her. Since Isabelle was not resisting, Vincent could not bring himself to interrupt. As well, her virginity, her innocence, had already been taken.

I do not know what I should do next, only that I surely must act, even though there is so much at stake. So much that threatens this family.

I can no longer turn a blind eye to Virgil's immoral perversions.

61

MY CELLPHONE RANG, rattling my brain. The sound startled me and I opened my eyes. Last I remembered, I had been reading Vivian's diary as night lowered on Windy Hill Farm. Her journal (volume 1) still rested on my comforter. But now, morning sunlight streamed in through the window on Dex's side.

My body had clearly needed sleep.

Another ring. Madeline was calling me so I answered.

"Big, beautiful morning to you, little sis," she chirped.

"Sunny side up," I quipped, mimicking Roxy (my chicken liaison). "And you're so cheerfully caffeinated because…"

"Remember the listing I showed in Scranton on Sunday? Well, I sold it after a bidding war. I've met my quota to qualify for a significant bonus. And it's only September! Naturally, I did some celebratory baking last night."

I smiled. Most people celebrated at a bar with their colleagues. My single sister baked. She trusted the science of baking…if measured ingredients were combined and heated at a certain degree for a precise amount of time, then the picture on the recipe would be the outcome. In contrast, bar encounters came with no such guarantees. A person might think they were getting a spongy angel food cake, only to open the oven and pull out a dry, bland muffin.

"What did you make?" I asked, as my stomach growled.

Over the years, Madeline had become quite the expert baker.

263

"Apple pies. Your favorite."

After chatting, we agreed she would bring my pie over tomorrow morning. I reminded her if I wasn't home, she should use her house key and leave the pie on the kitchen counter. Otherwise, maybe she could stay awhile and help me make extra salt bombs for the farm's outbuildings. But today, I was having lunch with Dex at rehab and realistically, I probably wouldn't get to ordnance production, especially since I also had chores and a lot of reading to do.

"You're still reading Isabelle's diary?" she asked.

I brought her up to speed, making sure I whispered and spoke in riddles to explain that I had moved on to Vivian's diaries. In fact, my sister and I exchanged goodbyes so I could continue reading before I needed to eat breakfast.

Grabbing the diary, I opened it and started where I'd left off.

June 14, 1955:

Every time I check on Victoria and Isabelle at night, they are sleeping in their beds, safe from the fox.

Curiously, Virgil has developed insomnia, claiming to walk the property to ease his anxieties, to clear his mind. He tells me midnight strolls counter his body's refusal to rest, eventually allowing sleep to win the battle.

However, foxes are conniving, always planning their next meal. And so I hid myself on the hillside after Virgil left for one of his walks.

A spying wife knows there is something to find.

I discovered Virgil meets Isabelle by the lake's shore. Using our rowboat, he paddles her to the island to lie with her. In two hours' time, they return.

My heart is broken. I do not know if mending is possible. But I must remain stoic for the children.

FIND THEM

I continued reading, stopping at another important entry.

June 29, 1955:

When a fence is down or something needs repair, Virgil requests Isabelle's help, since she is an extra on the farm. He states his need for her assistance so matter of fact, so innocently that it is nearly forgettable that he is drawn to her as if she were a rabbit in heat.

I would challenge him except her time away allows me to read her diary. She places a bookmark within her journal (the placement always changes). I am careful to return the marker to its designated pages.

Earlier today, I was especially interested in her latest entry since I had spotted a bruise on Isabelle's neck. I learned the wound reflects Virgil's response to her... *news*.

Isabelle claims she is pregnant. My worst fear.

Virgil will not be allowed to leave the house tonight. I will send Vincent to intercede Isabelle. Perhaps an encounter with my son will help her understand that indiscretions involving her and my husband have *not* gone unnoticed.

Perhaps she and Virgil will cease their offenses.

For now, I must think...

Consistent with Isabelle's diary, Vivian's entries acknowledged that Virgil and Isabelle had resumed their affair a couple of days later on July 1st. Isabelle was leery of Vincent now, but that seemed to be the only relationship which had changed.

July 15, 1955:

I was reading Isabelle's diary when I thought I heard footsteps in the hallway. I dropped the bookmark without attending to where Isabelle had placed it. I had no choice but to return it between random pages.

My nerves are not faring well. I may need to task Vincent with sneaking into his sister's room and reading his stepcousin's diary. He has the constitution for it.

One truth stands above all others.

Isabelle must return to Unityville.

Are you kidding me?
The rest of the 1954 to 1955 volume was blank!
Why did Isabelle keep leading me to dead ends?
I grabbed the other volume on my nightstand and frantically fanned over the pages. There weren't any entries dated 1955. They started in 1956 and continued through 1957, offering no clues, not even a mention of Isabelle Taylor. Business as usual was the main theme—information about poultry and egg production, awards, and the children. All standard fare.

Then I remembered something that happened in 1957.

Virgil was in a single car accident on Belmont Bridge. Miss Grace, the family's photographer, mentioned that Virgil's supposed last word before his death was…*Isabelle.* In fact, Oscar at rehab had said the same thing. Maybe Vivian had noted her reaction.

I flipped the pages until I found the entry.

May 13, 1957:

I do not know why Virgil was driving out by Belmont Bridge so late at night.

Though his heart has grown distant from mine.

Authorities claim my husband had a packed suitcase and several filled boxes in the truck. *Could he have been leaving me and the children?* I simply told police that Virgil had been traveling to a poultry auction in Maryland. Even now, I am compelled to cover for him for he remains my true love regardless of how many times he has broken my heart.

He was transported to Wayne Memorial where he underwent emergency surgery, but his prospects of surviving are grave. For that reason, they allowed me to spend some private time with him before placing him on a ventilator and dosing him with even more morphine.

He was groggy but awake. I asked him what had happened. He whispered, and I quote: "I saw her on the bridge. I had to turn the wheel. I couldn't hit her."

"Who?" I pressed. And then a nurse walked in, right as he uttered his answer: "Isabelle."

He must have imagined seeing her.

I gave him a peck on the forehead and told the nurse I had said my goodbyes. Virgil would certainly be traveling on this night. Which direction, I did not know, though it would not be toward a poultry auction.

Virgil died sometime after midnight.

I found the whole entry curious.

Vivian didn't sound like a grieving wife. Nor did she sound like Isabelle's jealous murderer.

I put the volume down.

Frustration wasn't close to describing the emotion I felt.

"If you want me to know who murdered you, Isabelle," I said out loud, practically yelling so she could hear me beyond my safe space, "then write the killer's name down. Or speak it to me. Because you're going to have to do better than this. No more dead ends."

I listened for movement in the hallway or kitchen.

Everything remained quiet.

"DO YOU HEAR ME?"

Oh dear God.

I needed to stop shouting before I provoked the wrong ghost.

62

Thursday, September 4, 2025
Windy Hill Farm: Boulder, Pennsylvania

THE BELL PEPPER from my greenhouse was blood red.

I had moved my cutting board beside the sink so I could look out the window while slicing thin strips of pepper for my breakfast omelet. *That,* and I could avoid looking at the pile of supplies on the kitchen island behind me (the supplies from which I needed to assemble more anti-ghost ordnance for our farm's outbuildings).

When I had walked into the kitchen fifteen minutes earlier, I had taken off my salt bomb necklace and added it to the collection. The rough twine had started to irritate my skin so I had purchased thin ribbon to replace it. When Madeline arrived with my pie, I'd switch out the twine in her necklace as well.

Anyway, I was safe for the time being.

V wouldn't dare attack me with so much ammo in reach.

Speaking of ghosts, maybe I'd be lucky and find that last night (after my shouting and taunting), Isabelle had written the name of her killer on the greenhouse counter…in dirt, like she had originally done to communicate her own name.

Or this time, maybe she'd use eggs in the hutch to form letters and spell out the name of her murderer that way.

I smiled. Now I was being ridiculous.

At least my thoughts paired nicely with the ridiculousness of my outfit. I wore Dex's teal T-shirt which doubled as my oversized night shirt. My yellow cotton shorts weren't long enough to be spotted below the shirt's hem, but they were there. Shaggy, neon pink slippers pampered my feet. And I had thrown on my lime green cooking apron to avoid getting butter splatter on my husband's favorite T-shirt. I was a psychedelic human peacock with tousled black hair boasting a unique silver streak. (If only Cecelia could see me now.)

I continued slicing thin strips of red pepper. My knife was extra sharp. I'd have to tell Dex I was impressed with the quality of our new sharpener. He had recommended the brand.

A shiver raced down my spine.

Brrr. The kitchen was chilly.

Soon, I'd need to turn on the heat at night.

My teapot was on the stovetop. The burner glowed red.

A mug full of ginger tea would warm my bones.

Glancing out the window, I paused my slicing to watch the frenzy of hummingbirds at our backyard feeder. I don't think I ever glimpsed a hummingbird in the city. If the tiny birds were there, I was in too much of a hurry to notice.

Here though, there were eight hummies diving at each other, or hovering with puffed feathers in an attempt to project their dominance. The mightier they acted, the more access they were granted at the feeder. And full bellies were the name of the game. Soon, very soon, they'd all be leaving for their migratory flight to Mexico or Central America.

The whistle on my teapot shrilled.

Without thinking, I tried to put down my knife so I could turn, walk across the kitchen, and take the pot off the heating element.

I gasped.

What the hell was happening?

I felt pressure on my hands. Immobilizing pressure.

The *freeze in place* sort of pressure.

With my fingers splayed, my left palm was plastered flat against the countertop surface. It felt stuck, as if glued.

But my real confusion centered on my right hand. The one holding the knife. I couldn't move it either. Nor could I manipulate my fingers to release the knife.

The teapot continued to scream.

My heart jackhammered in my chest.

A wisp of air tickled my right ear and I felt a push against my back. It was as if someone stood behind me, reaching around me to clasp my hands.

Oh dear God. It was V.

Isabelle's murderer was here.

And all my protections were on the kitchen island behind me.

Panic washed over me.

I could barely breathe. Or swallow. Or blink.

Think quickly. Act quickly.

I needed to remember how I had evolved. How I had changed.

"I'm going to be packing up to leave," I lied. "You win. Dex and I never should've invaded your space. We never meant to."

If V believed me, then maybe the ghost would release me and I could make a beeline to the supplies. Then I could grab my plastic bottle and spray the hell out of the apparition with Holy Water.

V's answer became clear.

My right hand was forced to move until it was suspended over my left, positioning the blade inches above my skin.

"No!" I cried. "I promise. I promise to leave this house. This land. Please don't hurt me."

The shrill of the teapot assaulted my eardrums—they reverberated to the point of pain.

"Please."

Using an invisible force, V thrust my right hand downward.

V's spectral strength was unworldly.

The blade punctured my hand halfway between the knuckles of my index finger and thumb, about two inches from the rounded edge of my skin. The knife didn't stop.

The tip exited my flesh, hitting the countertop's granite.

I screamed.

Blood erupted from the wound like red hot lava.

I screamed again, at an octave that was unrecognizable to me.

Bright red blood pooled under my palm and crept in finger like streams along the countertop.

A wave of wooziness overwhelmed me.

Now was *not* the time to faint.

Using my blood as ink, the ghost started writing on the counter.
If only I could move my hands.
The Holy Water was only two or three arm lengths from me.
I read V's message…

LEAVE OR DIE

Suddenly, I could wiggle my fingers.
I was free from V's invisible grip.
Grabbing the knife handle, I pulled out the blade.
I ignored the blood, taking my first step toward the kitchen island.
Toward my supplies.

63

MY EYES WERE laser focused on the spray bottle of Holy Water. If I could make it to the kitchen island, a mere five feet from me, I could grab the bottle and protect myself from the malevolent ghost.

As I thrust one foot in front of the other, I tried to ignore my self-talk because it wanted to harp on the obvious. That V had just stabbed me. And even though the knife's blade had only penetrated the fleshy part of my hand, next time—which could be any second, V might aim for a vital organ.

I extended my right arm toward the bottle. Reaching. Stretching.

A sob escaped from my mouth.

I had stayed too long in this situation.

Tempted the ghost, and my fate, far too much.

My fingertips touched the plastic of the spray bottle.

Protection was so close.

Before I could clasp my fingers around the bottle, I was yanked back by my apron's neck strap. With force, V changed the direction of my momentum. I was moving away from the spray bottle now. Away from my supplies.

The strap tightened around my neck. Constricted my airway.

Even if I had wanted to, I couldn't have screamed.

At least the teapot did it for me.

I pedaled my feet on the floor in an attempt to gain traction, but the soles of my slippers were too smooth. Too slippery.

273

Anyway, this ghost liked to drag its victims.

My knees buckled.

I clawed at the apron strap trying to get my fingers underneath the fabric. Maybe I could pull the strap away from my skin long enough to inhale. To breathe.

But the strap was too tight. It was crushing my neck.

Is this how Isabelle's hyoid bone had been fractured?

My eyes felt like pinballs about to be launched.

I dropped onto the kitchen floor.

The pressure continued to compress my neck.

No log was in sight. I was by myself in the rapids. Alone. Helpless.

I was fading. My body was giving up. My mind, drifting.

A mist started to swirl in front of me.

The particles condensed like magic.

Isabelle.

She appeared, putting herself at risk in the presence of her nemesis. Of her murderer.

For *me*.

The strap loosened and I gasped.

I leaned over, hacking and coughing. And gulping for air.

When I looked up, Isabelle was gone.

Her nemesis, too. No doubt to pursue her.

I rose from the floor on wobbly legs and immediately grabbed the spray bottle of Holy Water. Racing to the stovetop, I slid my teapot off the burner before turning it off.

Blood had splattered all over the kitchen floor.

My injured hand had started to swell. Blood oozed from the laceration. At least it wasn't gushing anymore, but it throbbed. I needed to disinfect the wound before wrapping it in gauze.

I probably needed stitches.

Jogging down the hallway to my safe space, I held out my wounded hand in front of me as blood dripped from the gash.

Once I crossed over the salt threshold, I dropped to the floor still clutching the spray bottle with my right hand. My mind had already begun to replay the attack and the images caused my body to tremble. To convulse with a mixture of fear and relief.

If Isabelle hadn't appeared, I would've lost consciousness.

I probably would've died.

My throat ached. I could barely swallow.

I heard the front door open, followed by footsteps. Their pace quickened from the kitchen to my bedroom.

Madeline raced to my side.

No doubt she knew the blood in the kitchen was mine.

"What the hell happened?" she asked.

"I'm, I'm leaving this…this house," I stuttered. "Can you, will you help me pack?"

64

INDIA CLOUD STOOD beside me at my front door.

Leaving Windy Hill Farm three days ago didn't mean I wasn't coming back. My departure simply meant I realized that picking away at the mystery, one puzzle piece at a time, wasn't solving my life threatening paranormal infestation. Not to mention, my sleuthing had reached a dead end once again. And our ghosts had given me no indication they were content and in the mood for moving on.

Options were limited to say the least.

There were no more diaries to read which might disclose who killed Isabelle. Victoria's, Isabelle's, and Vivian's journals all went blank for different reasons. And none had named the murderer. Isabelle's came close, but her ghost ended up refuting the person she had suspected back in 1955. She made a point to communicate that Vincent had *not* been her killer.

As well, no one was left to interview.

I had no more tools to employ either. The Ouija board was out. Too dangerous. And India had no success "passively" trying to identify Isabelle's nemesis. The evil ghost was too advanced, according to the renowned psychic.

The time had arrived to unleash my top gun again. Only this time, I had asked India to reload from passive to high caliber, to give me and my husband our best shot at liberating our home from the supernatural. That's why I had begged her to perform an exorcism.

My hysteria, along with my stitched hand and bruised neck, helped convince India that although she typically shied away from the *e-word*, I couldn't wait any longer for her to secure another expert willing to do the job.

The situation was dire.

As it stood, Windy Hill Farm was unlivable. And unsellable.

Moreover, I was pregnant. Not to mention, neither Dex nor I were bringing in a paycheck.

Sure, there was a market for haunted houses as Madeline had explained. But buyers weren't senseless. They'd ask questions to gauge the severity of the hauntings on the farm. They'd be like the teenagers described by the checkout clerk at Oliver's Grocery Store. They'd know the difference between being scared for fun and being scared to death.

The possibility of being killed (via bone fractures, drowning, fly attacks, strangulation, or stabbing) wasn't exactly a selling point.

Barring burning down the house and abandoning the property—and taking a complete financial loss that would ruin us, an exorcism was the only option left.

This morning, India had met me at the Honesdale Bed and Breakfast where I was staying. We reviewed the plan we had developed to exorcise the hostile ghost, using a Christian format since we were both Christians. We rehearsed our roles. India would take the lead, of course. But since both ghosts had made a connection to me (one good, one bad), she urged me to participate.

Dex and Madeline didn't need to confer.

This was my decision.

The overarching plan was to exorcise the evil ghost. Then, with Isabelle's body exhumed and her nemesis banished, maybe she would voluntarily depart from our Earthly dimension.

Before leaving the B&B for the farm, we glazed our skin with Anointed Oil and sprayed our hair with Holy Water before pulling it back into ponytails. We both wore crosses and carried our Bibles with sticky notes marking the passages India would read. Salt bombs hung from our necklaces. And we carried several small spray bottles of Holy Water in our pockets.

I started to insert the house key into the front door's lock.

"Wait," India said. "Let's spray down again before we enter."

My heart raced. I felt sick to my stomach. I couldn't even swallow to push down my lunch. But I tried to hide my fear as India squirted me with blessed water. The spray beaded on my oily skin.

When she finished, I returned the favor.

India leaned into me and whispered, "We're only focusing on the hostile ghost today. Remember the goals: Identify and expel."

Apparently, exorcisms worked best if the entity was identified and named out loud.

If we were successful, at least *that* aspect of Isabelle's mystery would be clarified. We'd know who killed her.

Unlocking the door, we stepped inside and closed it behind us.

"No matter what happens, don't stop once we've started," she coached. "And project confidence at all times."

Confidence? Easier said than done, especially when I looked at the interior of my forever home.

The house was freezing. Flies buzzed around the closed windows in the great room. How they had gotten in, I had no clue. I glanced into the kitchen. Dried blood was splattered on the countertops and floor, reminding me of my panicked departure. Red pepper strips were still on my cutting board beginning to rot. My sister's apple pie was on the countertop covered in plastic wrap and never touched.

The pile of unused supplies remained stacked in a messy pile on the kitchen island.

More than anything, it was hard to feel confident since the malevolent ghost had affected everyone I loved. Some temporarily. Some permanently.

"We'll stand here," India said, positioning herself in between great room and the kitchen. "Would you mind opening the windows like we discussed?"

We needed to make the ghost's exit as accessible as possible.

I began opening windows in the great room. A strong breeze scattered the insects and sent curtains into a wild, twisting dance.

When I was done, I stood beside India, nodding I was ready.

Goosebumps had erupted on my skin and I shivered.

"We call on Jesus for His divine protections," she started.

"We call on Jesus to be our shield," I added.

FIND THEM

"In the name of our Lord, we are here to confront the hostile spirit haunting this home and property. Haunting this parcel formerly known as lot sixteen."

Glasses in the kitchen crashed and shattered onto the floor.

My fear percolated into terror.

India read two different Bible passages.

The television in the great room turned on. The usual blaring *herrrrr* sound accompanied the grainy screen.

"Jesus," India shouted over the television, with mist billowing from her mouth. "Jesus, we pray You will help us reveal the identity of the spirit possessing this house, this land, so that we might cast that spirit out by name."

"Spirit, reveal yourself to us," I commanded.

Something whizzed toward us from the great room.

Before I could identify the object as our crystal globe paperweight from the coffee table, it struck India in the head and she dropped to the floor.

Unconscious.

Out cold.

The Bible slid away from her fingers, either from the fall or with supernatural help. I couldn't tell.

BANG...

Every window I had opened simultaneously slammed shut.

279

65

Sunday, September 7, 2025
Windy Hill Farm: Boulder, Pennsylvania

OH DEAR GOD. What was I supposed to do now?

India had been knocked out but was thankfully still breathing regularly. Her skin color remained normal, too.

In terms of the exorcism, even if she regained consciousness in the next minute, she'd never be able to pick up where she left off. I mean, she had been struck in the head by a solid projectile traveling at the speed of a well thrown baseball.

Without her lead, I felt my familiar stress response take over.

If I stood completely still, as though my feet were stuck in hardening cement, and I squeezed my eyes shut, maybe the present danger might pass me by. My wishful thinking should be called the ostrich effect: If I acted like I was hiding, maybe I wouldn't be seen.

Then again, "Mr. Hostile" at Union Station didn't play along.

Cabinetry drawers in the kitchen began opening and slamming shut—over and over again. The sound of drawer contents clanking and rattling bounced off the walls.

This ghost knew exactly where I was. There was no hiding.

India's words guided me: *"No matter what happens,"* she had said, *"don't stop once we've started."*

A rush of wind swooshed by me, reentering the great room.

The television blipped off.

A nugget of my research tickled my memory. The subject was about *hiding.* Yes, that was it. Humans weren't the only ones who wanted to hide, to not be seen. I remembered reading that ghosts often found refuge in objects like toys or pieces of furniture.

Or perhaps even…a blasted television.

Come to think of it, more times than not, our television would turn on or off before the havoc started, before V made an "appearance" in our home.

If I was to rid Windy Hill Farm of this ghost, first I'd have to…

Outsmart it.

Tucking my Bible under my left arm, I pulled out one of my spray bottles and walked to the TV. "You can't hide," I said out loud. "Come out and identify yourself."

I sprayed the screen with Holy Water and the television turned on. The static's volume was even louder. The sound assaulted my ears.

A cold breeze exited the television and raced upwards. The light pendants hanging from the timbered beams above me began to sway, as if the ghost was swinging from them.

The temperature in the room plummeted even more.

My exhales formed into streams of icy white mist.

The sliding glass doors instantly frosted over.

But still no manifestation of the entity.

Clearly, this ghost had no intention of revealing its identity, a precursor to being successfully cast out forever.

From everything I had learned, the Williamses had been very protective of each other. I'm sure that was especially true of Virgil and Vivian when it came to their children. Even though Isabelle denied that Vincent was her killer, why not pretend he was?

Goading this ghost might force it to correct the record.

Or…provoke it to hurt me. There was that.

I pulled the electrical plug on the television, shutting it off.

"India wasn't sure," I said. "But I already know who you are. You're Vincent Williams. Poor little Vincent who wanted to get Isabelle's attention. Only, your Daddy got to her first."

The light bulbs burst overhead, sending glass shards raining down.

"I can only imagine how insignificant you felt, Vincent, watching your smart and beautiful stepcousin flirt with your father. *Her* choosing *him* over you. And then when you spied on them while they were making love: How you wished it had been you in her embrace.

Poor pathetic Vincent…having to read in Isabelle's diary that she was pregnant. Pregnant with your Daddy's baby."

I was being cruel, but this was the ghost who had murdered a pregnant teenager in 1955. Who had also tried to kill Dex. Tried to kill me. And had taken over our house and property.

Suddenly, the shelves on either side of the television were wiped clean. It was as if an invisible hand swept across each shelf surface, knocking off trinkets and picture frames. Hurling them through the air until they smashed onto the floor, shattering our mementos.

I had no clue if my strategy would work, but I couldn't stop now.

This ghost was reacting.

My tactics were striking an emotional chord.

"I'm going to set the record straight," I continued. "I'm going to publicize to all the world that you, Vincent, strangled Isabelle with your bare hands and then buried her on Boulder Island. And I'm going to start by telling the Honesdale library. The archives will be added to. Everyone in the Library League will know that Virgil and Vivian's jealous middle child was a cold blooded murderer."

A mist started to materialize in front of me and I backed up until I bumped into the fireplace. My heart thundered in my chest.

"I'll craft your new obituary, Vincent. I'll be sure to identify you as Isabelle's killer. The murderer of your own stepcousin."

Outstretched arms began to take shape. No flies this time. Just swirling particles condensing, moving faster and faster, closer and closer, to resemble solid flesh.

A woman stood before me. One whose features were warped with anger. With hate.

I recognized her, of course: Vivian Williams.

She wore a three-quarter length black dress, probably the one she had been buried in, accessorized with a strand of pearls. Her grayish-blonde hair was pulled into a French bun.

"Leave or die," she sneered, stepping toward me. Her hazel eyes were narrowed. Her forehead creased.

"In the name of Jesus," I said, my voice firm and confident, "I command you to stop."

She did.

"I have been granted authority by our Lord to cast you out from our home," I announced.

Vivian laughed. A devilish heckle.

"I will expel you from this place," I added.

Smiling, she turned away from me and started to fade, as if bored with our encounter.

No, no, no.

I couldn't let this opportunity slip away. I had to read the line exactly how India had rehearsed it, adding the ghost's name.

"In the name of Jesus, I command you, Vivian Hall Williams, to leave Windy Hill Farm."

Vivian turned back and glared at me. An expression of worry washed across her face. It was as if she understood, for the first time, that the authority granted to me carried the weight of a higher power. A power she could not ignore or withstand.

A divine power that could, indeed, permanently evict her.

I padded over to the closest window and opened it.

"In the name of our Lord, I cast you out, Vivian Hall Williams." I pointed at the open window. "I expel you from this house and farm. I banish you from this Earthly dimension forever and ever."

Her image melted like a candle, dripping to the floor.

The energy in the room was also changing. How, I didn't know. But my intuition warned me that I needed to protect myself so I ducked into the corner and stood cowering, protecting my face.

Just in time.

All the windows in the great room, even the sliding glass doors, exploded outward.

I instantly dropped to the floor, placing the Bible on my lap, and covered my ears with my hands.

When the blast was over, I glanced at where the ghost had been.

Vivian Williams was gone.

Our great room was a war zone. Shattered and broken.

But the temperature was returning to normal.

The energy *felt* normal.

India moaned and I raced to her.

"What happened?" she whispered, fingering the large bump on her head.

"Vivian Williams has been expelled."

66

Wednesday, September 17, 2025
Ross Johnson's Residence: Honesdale, Pennsylvania

ROSS JOHNSON WAS livid.

He had called me an hour ago and demanded I return his mother's and grandmother's diaries immediately. As in, *now*. And if I failed to do so, I could expect a lawsuit with teeth.

That's why I was driving on Roosevelt Highway, heading toward his townhouse in Dex's vehicle. Victoria's and Vivian's diaries were stacked on the passenger seat.

A lot had happened in the 10 days since the exorcism, including the televised press conference by the Boulder Police Department about finding the remains of Isabelle Taylor on Boulder Island. The presser aired on Scranton's WSET station two hours ago. Perhaps Ross wouldn't have been so angry with me except Detective Gilbert, from behind the podium, publicly thanked me for my persistent amateur sleuthing which led to finding the missing teenager's 70 year old remains.

I didn't know the shoutout was coming.

If I had, I would've called Ross prior.

Damn it to hell.

Facing him would be unpleasant to say the least. He now knew I had been lying to him ever since we initially spoke on the phone during my first visit to his dying mother.

I still wasn't proud of my deceptions, but at least they helped unearth the truth.

FIND THEM

In my opinion, Ross should be thankful, as in over the moon, that our legal system didn't consider ghosts or communications with ghosts as admissible evidence in criminal cases. If the courts did, his grandmother would probably be found guilty of killing her step niece.

Even still, Ross understood the implications of finding his mother's missing stepcousin in the family's "backyard" instead of anyplace else. And he didn't like it one bit. Boulder was a small town, after all. He had clients who had generational roots in Wayne County, just like him.

Instead of worrying about his practice, though, maybe he should've been ruminating about the horrible crime inflicted on one of his relatives. At the hands of his grandmother.

Maybe he should've extended some empathy toward Dex and me since the brunt of the present day fallout had landed squarely on us.

At least we were all recovering. Dex would be coming home in two days, fully healed. I was ecstatic. Beyond excited.

India Cloud's prognosis was positive, too. She had suffered a concussion during the exorcism and in two weeks, she'd be cleared by her physician to resume work. And my OBGYN affirmed that our baby "orange" was healthy and growing. I'd be 15 weeks on Friday.

As I drove, I glanced at my left hand on the steering wheel. The stitches had already been removed. And the purple bruise around my neck, from where Vivian had strangled me with my apron strap, had faded to tan.

When it came to house repairs, they'd be finished today.

The list had been extensive…

First, I had to hire an industrial cleaner to remove all the broken glass and debris from the bedroom, kitchen, and great room.

Then, our floors in the bedroom had to be sanded and refinished. All the windows and sliding glass doors in the great room had to be replaced. Drywall in the den had to be fixed. Not to mention, we also needed new light bulbs throughout the house, as well as a new flat screen television over the fireplace.

Good news was that today, our forever home would be fully restored to its pre-paranormal glory. At last.

Of course, the price tag was ungodly and insurance covered very little. Which is why I was driving Dex's hybrid SUV. I had to sell my

Tesla to pay the balance of our invoices. Surprisingly, the woman from the general store in Boulder (the one who always called me hon) had purchased it at asking price and paid cash. I don't think she had ever been hugged so hard.

As far as I could tell, Windy Hill Farm was ghost free.

I expected Vivian to be gone, but I wasn't one-hundred percent sure about Isabelle. I knew her aunt killed her, but was that enough? Or did Isabelle expect something more official?

Nevertheless, if she was still "here," her time was running out.

On Saturday, the pastor from White Oak UMC would be blessing our house. Dex and I should have done that from the get-go.

The cabin of Dex's SUV was getting chilly so I turned on the heat.

Fall was no longer teasing about its arrival; the season had already moved in and unpacked, spreading its yellow-orange palette across the mountain range.

SCREECH...

I was about to run a red light.

Slamming on the brakes, I held my breath as my vehicle skidded to a stop, just before entering the intersection. The diaries launched from the passenger seat and thudded onto the floor in front.

Shit de la shit that was close.

Two minutes later, I parked in front of Ross's townhouse. My hands were still shaky. I collected the journals from the floor and took a deep breath.

This encounter would be awkward.

As I walked up the brick pathway, the front door opened.

Ross reached for the diaries but said nothing. No smile. No invitation for tea. The minute the journals transferred, he stepped back and slammed the door shut.

Okay, maybe not awkward. More like...*final.*

And that was fine by me.

Back inside the vehicle, I double blinked in case my eyes were deceiving me. There was a puddle on the passenger seat.

A freaking *puddle.*

Isabelle.

She was still here and had left her calling card for a reason.

What was it *this* time?

Nothing was on the floor in front of the passenger seat.

Stretching my arm over the passenger side to the space between the door and the seat, I felt around. Maybe something had fallen there during my abrupt stop.

My fingers touched something...

Paper.

I clasped it as I glanced up at the townhouse.

Ross was staring at me through his front bay window.

More like scowling.

Slowly, I straightened up, casually looking down at what I had retrieved, keeping the item (an envelope) below Ross's line of sight.

On its front was written...

Open After My Death

67

Wednesday, September 17, 2025
Windy Hill Farm: Boulder, Pennsylvania

NERVOUS ANTICIPATION BUILT during my ride home.

If I had to guess, the handwriting on the envelope looked to be Vivian's. Was it foolish of me to hope that the contents, which were thin enough to suggest a single sheet of paper, included a penned confession? One that could be authenticated and serve as legitimate evidence?

By the time I pulled up to our garage, all the construction vehicles had left the property. They had finished on schedule.

Windy Hill Farm was ready for Dex's return.

Under any other circumstances, I would've paused to admire our farmhouse, but right now, the letter was the only thing on my mind. So I parked and raced inside the house with the envelope.

In the kitchen, I turned on the lights.

With shaky hands, I pulled on a pair of thin plastic gloves in case there were traces of DNA that could still be extracted from the paper and glue. I had no clue if that was possible, but I didn't want to compromise the artifact. In an abundance of caution, I used a letter opener on one of the short sides of the envelope instead of trying to peel and lift the sealed flap.

Sitting on a stool at the kitchen island, I extracted the letter.

As I had suspected, it was authored by Vivian Williams, dated July 26, 1955, four days *after* she had murdered Isabelle. The handwritten letter was two-sided.

FIND THEM

To Whom It May Concern:

Herein is my confession to the murder of my step niece, Isabelle Francis Taylor. Although I admit to experiencing brief spells of madness, I committed this act while predominantly being of sound mind. In other words, there was no fit of rage. No unexpected onset of insanity. Her death was most definitely premeditated.

If I have indeed passed from this life to the next, *before* this confessionary letter is found, then I have succeeded in my mission.

Virgil likened our marriage to a business arrangement. I, however, have always been desperately in love with him, from the first time he turned his mesmerizing smile in my direction. Tragically, his obsessive infidelities repeatedly wounded my heart. And when I learned that Isabelle was pregnant with his child, something changed within me—snapped as quickly as a chicken's neck.

Every entrepreneur protects their business. My husband left me no choice but to protect ours.

Virgil wanted to speak privately over the approaching weekend (alluding it was time to end our business arrangement), and he agreed that having Isabelle return home for a night, claiming to our children that she was homesick, would be helpful during our "deliberations."

Dear lovestruck Virgil, he was so very easy to manipulate.

I developed a plan to make it appear as if Isabelle had returned to Unityville before disappearing. This strategy would yield fewer repercussions for my children and sister. Grief, after all, is far easier to conquer than shame. Besides, Isabelle did not actually share our bloodline.

Wisely, I did not disclose my plan to Virgil until it was underway and could not be altered.

He did not know why I insisted he take Isabelle to purchase a train ticket on Friday, July 22nd. Or why I demanded he make Isabelle wear her hair in a braided ponytail, matching how Victoria wore hers. But with hopes of getting an amicable divorce, he followed my instructions without fail.

Later he learned that my reasons were to establish eyewitnesses who would confuse Victoria with Isabelle. In fact, Isabelle was already dead when Victoria, wearing a similar white dress and braided ponytail, rode the train to Unityville the next day.

Naturally, all of us had iron clad alibis, including our daughter. With persuasion, Victoria agreed, albeit reluctantly, that she and her father drove in his truck to Hughesville. She would never tell that it was *her*, not Isabelle, who rode the train and was seen by witnesses at a distance since passengers were scarce on that Saturday morning.

Planning a murder was easier than I imagined.

Vivian Williams had fooled her entire community. According to Miss Grace, Vivian was described as gracious and altruistic, with a reputation beyond reproach. She even had a shrine in the foyer of the Honesdale Public Library since she had donated the building. But like Isabelle, Dex and I were victims of the woman behind the beloved persona: the side of her willing to maim and kill in order to protect her family's reputation and their financial wellbeing.

FIND THEM

I turned the letter over to read the back.

My plan's execution was quite simple as well...

At dinner on the 22nd of July, I had convinced Isabelle she should go to bed that night already dressed for the next day. Then she could avoid waking Victoria when she rose from bed in the predawn hours. I had also insisted Virgil ask Isabelle to wear her white dress to please her parents.

Virgil did not realize that seeing the outfit the night before would enable Victoria and Vincent to verify what their stepcousin had been wearing on the day she "disappeared." And authorities would never think to ask what Victoria was wearing. They wouldn't realize she wore a similar dress to confuse train passengers.

Later that night, Vincent distracted his father with a late night emergency in the chicken house, the one with the faulty feed bin. My son never fails me. (Virgil had no time to warn Isabelle he would be late for their rendezvous.)

Having stolen Isabelle's flowered sash, I hid behind an elm tree on the hillside. As she waited for her lover by the lake, I strangled her with her own garment.

Virgil arrived to find her dead at my hands. He fell to the ground weeping. I despised his love for her.

When he threatened to go to the authorities, I told him Vincent and I had forged a confession letter, one authored by him. One that described how he seduced his vulnerable step niece, as well as chronicled his burst of violence when he learned of Isabelle's pregnancy. Vincent would affirm that his father eventually strangled his lover to bury her condition. I would state the same.

Naturally, Virgil changed his mind. Complying with the plan was in the best interest of the family business.

I had already placed a long thick rope and two shovels in the rowboat. Crying like a fool, my husband paddled me and the body to Boulder Island.

Near shore, we hoisted and rolled Isabelle's body over the edge of the rowboat and she landed in the water. Virgil wished to carry the body of his drenched beloved to where we would bury her.

Allowed to enact a love stricken knight holding his fallen princess? Absolutely not. That was what the rope was for. I made him loop and tie one end around her ankles. In the old days, whores were dragged through the streets and stoned.

Her body snagged on branches and rocks as we dragged her. Perhaps that precipitated her moaning.

To our surprise, Isabelle had not died when I had initially strangled her. Her resilience was a shock.

If I had not had the pistol on my person, my husband might have overtaken me. I could have shot him and Isabelle, except the children might have investigated the blasts.

So I held him off with several threats and finished the job on Isabelle with my bare hands.

Virgil and I buried her in the center of the island.

FIND THEM

Afterwards, we burned Isabelle's suitcase in our incinerator.

I also planned to burn Isabelle's diary but it could not be found among her possessions. When my husband noticed that a metal box from the barn was missing, we suspected she had placed her diary in the box and had buried it somewhere in the field we identified as number sixteen—the one overlooking the lake. Afterall, Victoria had admitted to her father and me that she had seen Isabelle running past her window carrying a metal box on Friday night.

We agreed, then, that we would search for the box until our final days. And that if the box could not be located, parcel sixteen would never be sold.

In the meantime, Virgil and I would start anew. A true business arrangement.

I was a dutiful business partner.

Without Regrets,

Vivian Hall Williams

A frosty mist marked my exhales and Isabelle's ghost materialized beside the kitchen counter, wearing her soaked white dress.

"I'm so sorry, Isabelle," I said. "It breaks my heart to think about all that happened to you."

She briefly closed her eyes and nodded.

"I'll submit this letter to the police department," I added. "Vivian's confession will correct the record. She murdered you. And Virgil and Vincent were accessories to the crime."

She mouthed, *"Thank you."*

"Would you like the heart locket necklace to be buried with your remains?"

She shook her head no.

I got it.

Even though Victoria had given Isabelle the necklace to signify their close friendship, the jewelry was originally a gift from Virgil to his wife. I'd submit the necklace, along with Isabelle's diary, to the Boulder Police Department. And if they wanted to return the heirloom necklace to Ross, they could. I didn't need to be involved.

"You know you can't stay here, right? And there's no need to. You've accomplished everything you set out to do. It's time to embrace your intended destiny. Your eternal rest."

Isabelle nodded again, only slowly.

"You are a brave woman," I said. "Your tenacity led to the truth. You never gave up."

She blew a kiss at me.

A tear raced down my cheek as I watched her fade and vanish.

I would never see Isabelle Taylor's ghost again.

My emotions were a mix of sadness and elation. I'd miss her for sure, but living without a ghost would be a relief, a burden lifted.

Grabbing my cellphone, I dialed Detective Gilbert's personal number and he picked up on the first ring.

"Why Mrs. Bliss," he answered. "Has your *persistence* yielded something else?"

"I've come across some documentary evidence you need to see."

68

MADELINE INSISTED ON a role reversal.

This time, I sat near the front of my paddle board and my sister stood on the deck pad a few steps back from the middle to balance our weight. She was paddling us to Boulder Island.

My legs were crisscrossed and supported my cotton canvas tote. Inside the bag were two trowels, three dozen tulip bulbs (which would bloom in the spring), a small bag of planting soil, and a watering bucket. In honor of Isabelle, we were going to plant the bulbs by the boulder where her body had been buried for nearly three-quarters of a century. The timing was perfect because Wayne County had already had its first frost and nighttime temperatures were dipping into the 40s.

Today's weather was reminiscent of our first sisterly adventure to the island, with some exceptions. Namely, there weren't any insects buzzing around us. As in, no flies. The mid-morning sun was similarly bright, but it felt farther away—higher in the sky. And mist rose from the lake's placid surface.

Mid-September was the time of year when the air was cooler than the water. Hence, my sister and I were wearing our wind breakers.

I absolutely loved the sound of lake water swooshing with every paddle stroke.

"Do you know what will happen with Isabelle's remains?" Madeline asked.

"When I dropped off her diary and necklace at the police station yesterday, Detective Gilbert told me that Isabelle's relative from Unityville... Remember I told you her name was Francis Nelson? Well, she's going to have Isabelle's remains buried in the family plot beside her birth mother. And I'll be invited to speak at the interment since I *knew* her. (At least better than anyone else currently living.)"

"That's so thoughtful." She cleared her throat like a wave of emotion had gotten stuck there. "I'm glad you didn't give up, Nora. And I'm sorry I didn't always support you."

"Are you kidding me? You researched with me. Did the freaking Ouija board together! Not to mention, you saved me from being drowned in the bathtub. You were by my side when I was scared. When I needed you. I'll never forget all that you did for me."

"Being your big sister means the world to me."

I smiled with my *I love you back* expression.

The peaceful morning quieted our thoughts.

We arrived at the island and trekked to its center.

Planting the tulip bulbs took a little over an hour. I couldn't wait to see the plants bloom in the spring. The white flowers would remind me of Isabelle.

After we paddled back, I left the board propped against a boulder.

Madeline and I climbed the hillside.

When we crested the hill and walked across the backyard and around to the front of the garage, I was surprised to see Roxy's *Breed, Brood, and Biddy* van parked in our driveway.

She rushed out from the driver's side door as we approached. Along with her wild auburn hair, Roxy wore skinny jeans and a white T-shirt that displayed her company logo and the phrase: *Let Us Take You Under Our Wing.*

In typical fashion, her chin jutted in and out as she strutted toward us. Her arms were extended for a hug which I gladly walked into.

"So stoked to see you," she said. "I was just about to leave, thinking you weren't here."

I introduced her to my sister and they exchanged niceties.

"Want to see the flock?" I asked. "They're doing really well."

I tried not to dwell on missing Biddy. Her loss, and Cinnamon's, still felt raw.

"I'd love to see them," Roxy said. "But I'm actually here at your husband's request."

"Dex?"

He wasn't exactly a chicken person so Roxy had my attention. In addition, he was spending his last 24 hours at the rehab facility. What was so important that my chicken liaison and husband couldn't wait until he came home tomorrow? I was beyond curious.

Roxy meandered to the back of her van and unlatched the door.

"Give me a sec," she said, disappearing inside the compartment.

I looked at my sister and shrugged.

Roxy emerged holding a gray hen, its feathers shimmered in the sunlight.

"Biddy can never be replaced," she said. "But Dex thought Biddy would appreciate knowing that another Lavender Pekin was looking out for you on the homestead."

Clearly, my husband was a traveler. He wasn't stuck on Mars.

With extended arms, Roxy held the hen out to me.

"Go ahead," she urged. "Take her."

I was overwhelmed, fighting back tears that welled in my eyes.

"Oh my gosh," I said. "She's beautiful. Does she have a name?"

"I've been calling her Princess Leia." She smiled. "Pronounced *Lay-ah* like with a New York accent. Get it?"

We all laughed and Princess Leia cooed.

As I held my new hen, I realized my heart was full.

The future was promising.

My husband would be home tomorrow. Home, to a place no longer haunted. Vivian Williams had been banished and Isabelle had found her eternal peace.

The Williams' family history would be corrected; their legacy no longer revered. In fact, their photographs had already been taken down in the library's foyer in Honesdale. And that was just the start. Public records would be updated to reflect the truth.

The curses of the Williams Farm were finally over.

New life, the one growing inside me, would be raised amid the tranquil beauty of lot 16.

Our Windy Hill Farm.

69

A STRONG GUST crested the hillside.

"Quick!" I said to Dex. "Lower the umbrella and I'll cover Pippa."

I draped the baby blanket over Pippa who was in her infant bouncer on the ground. I crouched over her chair while snatching up Princess Leia with my free hand.

My husband lowered the umbrella as the gust slammed into us.

Our hair twisted and twirled. The edges of our red and white checkered picnic blanket folded over. And napkins for our lunch somersaulted away. (At least they were biodegradable.)

"Did you hear that?" I asked.

"You mean my cognitive cursing?"

I chuckled. "No, silly. The sound of the wind. There's no wailing."

The gust raced eastward toward the mountains in the distance.

I peeled off the baby blanket, and Pippa squealed as if we were playing a game of peekaboo.

"Because of your bravery, our dream has come true," my Viking said, cranking up the umbrella now that the wind had exited.

He dropped to his knees and leaned over, kissing our baby on the forehead. "Windy Hill Farm has finally evolved into what we hoped it would be: our sanctuary from this crazy world."

I looked around at our acreage, the lake, our house.

I inhaled the peacefulness.

There wasn't another person or home in sight.

298

Our place was rural, all right. A hidden paradise.

"I think I learned that *crazy* can happen anywhere. No locale is insulated. Not even a place like this."

Hard to forget Richard Peter, Vivian Williams's vicious ghost, or the tragedy that happened to Isabelle on this property back in 1955. And everything else in between, including Dex's life threatening injuries and the deaths of Biddy and Cinnamon.

"Is there a positive to that?" He took a bite of watermelon. "Your outlook just sounds gloomy and doomy. Like, there's no place to hide."

"Isn't that what we've learned? Danger has no boundaries. Instead, the *positive* (the hope) is in us—knowing we have the capacity to prepare ourselves. To skillfully react if we need to save ourselves. Save our loved ones. Or anyone who needs help."

"Does this mean you're ready for Union Station?"

Several meetings were in our near future, and we had worked out an itinerary that included me taking the Northeast Regional line from D.C.'s Union Station to Baltimore's Penn Station for my upcoming meeting with Cecelia at D&B's main studio. (My boss and I would be starting negotiations regarding my gradual transition back from a leave of absence to working remotely again, officially beginning in September.)

Pippa Madeline Bliss, who was three months old (born March 14th), would be staying with my sister during Dex's and my road trip.

Initially, we'd drive to our old stomping grounds to visit friends from the Palisades. Then on June 22nd, my husband had a business appointment in D.C. so I'd take the train for my meeting on the same day. After Dex's wrapped up, he'd drive to Baltimore and pick me up before our drive home.

I nodded. "I'm ready."

70

Monday, June 22, 2026
Union Station: Washington, D.C.

BEING PREPARED LOOKED very different from the days of being naively numb to the daily routine of taking the train to and back from work. Of having my mind preoccupied with what I'd be doing when I arrived at D&B. Of processing this, that, and the other thing while I waited for my ride.

First, I wore sneakers, not my fancy red pumps. Meaning, I was on sure footing if I needed to get out of someone's way. Or if I needed to run like hell from a human, a ghost. Whomever.

My heeled shoes were stuffed inside my backpack. And the zipper for my backpack wasn't exposed; it was situated against my back so it couldn't be unknowingly opened by someone skilled who harbored bad intentions.

With the backpack, my hands were free. I was unencumbered.

No more holding a portfolio. Or having my purse strapped over my shoulder. These things complicated a defensive response.

My eyes weren't focused on the tunnel either, waiting impatiently to see my train. I scanned my surroundings. Looking right, left, and behind me. If someone thought I looked on edge, let them. At least they'd stay away from me.

My pepper spray wasn't tucked away where it couldn't be retrieved in time to be useful. I wore my spray canister, a tiny compact bullhorn, and a salt bomb on a lanyard around my neck.

I was all about *think quickly, act quickly.*

300

More than that, I was projecting my readiness to others.

An advancing roar raced along the arched, geometric ceiling.

My eyes were still evaluating my surroundings. Watching.

The grind and rattle of metal on metal grew louder to my left, and I glanced at my ride's headlights. They appeared in the distance—still resembling two yellow, quivering eyes.

I didn't look at my smartwatch for the time. Did it really make a difference? The only thing that mattered was that I arrived at my destination alive, uninjured. In one piece.

The train whistle blared and the shrill reverberated through me.

The sound carried no false promises.

No green light to relax. To feel safe.

So I remained alert.

My baby, my husband, my life: Everything I loved depended on it.

The End

ACKNOWLEDGMENTS

THE POCONO MOUNTAINS are my happy place.

Put me near a lake or on a mountain trail and I'm my best self. In FIND THEM, I've taken an actual locale (Wayne County, Pennsylvania) and embellished it to support my fictitious story. For example, Boulder is not a real town in Wayne County, nor is the wildlife preserve and lake. I've also taken liberties with genuine towns like Honesdale by creating invented histories for places I've imagined (like the public library in my book).

One aspect of Wayne County that is as authentic in my book as it is in real life is the kindness of county residents!

And while growing up in a haunted house has compelled me to create ghost fiction, FIND THEM is not intended to be a "how-to" on ridding a place of paranormal activity. Please consult an expert!

In terms of book production, I have an incredible, dedicated team who helped bring this novel across the finish line, polished and ready for publication. An abundance of gratitude goes to:

Dena Baker (Beta Reader)
Damonza (Cover Designer)
Deb Faroe (Beta Reader)
Jed Faroe (Beta Reader)
Mary Lee (Beta Reader)
Charlene Sharpe (Proofreader)
Diane Stulz (Beta Reader)
Lori Sullivan (Beta Reader)

A special shoutout goes to my husband, Rick, who is my greatest support and cheerleader. Another goes to my daughter, Brooke, who is always open to sharing feedback with me on my writing projects.

To *all* my family, friends, readers, authors, bloggers, reviewers, librarians, bookstore owners/managers, Goodreads community, social media communities, book industry experts, and local news media, please know how very much I appreciate you, too.

Until the next project...

ABOUT THE AUTHOR

JULIA ASH'S FIFTH published book is FIND THEM, her second in ghost fiction. This novel and MYSTIFIED (earned Honorable Mention from Writer's Digest in its 2022 Self-Published E-Book Awards) were inspired by growing up in a haunted house in Pennsylvania.

Julia has also authored a dark fantasy series: *The ELI Chronicles*. This series includes THE ONE AND ONLY (2018), THE TETHER (2019), and THE TURNING POINT (2020). THE TURNING POINT earned Honorable Mention from Writer's Digest in its 2020 Self-Published E-Book Awards and was a Semi-Finalist for the 2020 BookLife Prize competition, sponsored by Publishers Weekly.

She lives with her husband and pups on Maryland's Eastern Shore and also calls the Pocono Mountains "home." A complete biography is on Julia's website. Please join her on social media!

Website:
https://juliaashbooks.wordpress.com

Facebook:
Facebook.com/JuliaAsh.Books

Twitter:
@Author_JuliaAsh

Instagram:
julia.ash.books

Goodreads:
Goodreads.com/julia_ash

Reviews

Please consider providing a star rating
(with or without a written review) of

FIND THEM

JULIA ASH

Vendors make it easy to give ratings and reviews
on a novel's detail page
(the online page where you purchased the book).

Authors appreciate ratings and reviews more than you know.

Thank you!

Made in United States
North Haven, CT
16 June 2024

53686029R10189